LAST GOD STANDING

Creator. Ruler. Stand-up Comic...

When God decides to quit and join the human race to see what all the fuss is about, all hell breaks loose.

Sensing his abdication, the other defunct gods of Earth's vanquished pantheons want a piece of the action He abandoned.

Meanwhile, the newly-humanized deity must discover the whereabouts and intentions of the similarly reincarnated Lucifer, and block the ascension of a murderous new God.

How is he ever going to make it as a stand-up comedian with all of this going on...?

MICHAEL BOATMAN

Last God Standing

ANGRY
ROBOT

ANGRY ROBOT
A member of the Osprey Group

Lace Market House,
54-56 High Pavement,
Nottingham
NG1 1HW
UK

Angry Robot/Osprey Publishing,
PO Box 3985,
New York,
NY 101853985,
USA

www.angryrobotbooks.com
The Divine Comedy

An Angry Robot paperback original 2014

Cover design by Chris Moore
Caveman cartoon: Caveman © iStockPhoto.com/Tomacco
Fire © iStockPhoto.com/Ani_Ka

Distributed in the United States by Random House, Inc., New York.

ISBN 978 0 85766 395 5
Ebook ISBN 978 0 85766 396 2

Printed in the United States of America

9 8 7 6 5 4 3 2 1

I would like to dedicate this book to my nephew, Skylar A Forney, who started this whole journey by asking a simple question. To Myrna, who inspires me to finish what I start. And to Jacob, Aidan, MacKenzie and Jordan... my Reasons.

PART I

A STRANGER ON THE BUS

DIVINE DRAMATIS PERSONAE

Yahweh Abrahamic God of the Hebrews, Christians, Muslims and Mormons
Zeus King of the Greek gods
Loki Scandinavian God of Mischief
Ares Greek God of War
Agni Hindu God of Fire
Baron Samedi Haitian God of Death and Black Magic
The Morrigan Celtic Goddess of Sex and War
Changing Woman Navajo Earthmother
Dionysus Greek God of Wine and Epiphany
Poseidon Greek God of the Oceans
Thor Norse God of Thunder
Kali Hindu Goddess of Time and Destruction
The Buddha Embodiment of Enlightenment
The Archangel **Gabriel**
The Seraphimic Angel **Seraphiel**
The **Angel Moroni**
Lucifer The Prince of Darkness (Retired)

PROLOGUE

Chicago, 1986 AD

Christmas on the Cooper Plantation. My parents are fighting again because Daddy burned the turkey and Mother's working on her fourth vodka tonic. I've been counting her drinks while I play with the octopus from my new GI Joe Underwater Action set. Barbara always says smartass five year-olds should worry about other stuff than how many cocktails she's had. She hates when I count, so of course I do it a lot. My brothers are fighting over their presents. Nobody's paying attention when the stranger steps out of our Christmas tree.

"Look at you," the stranger says. "Odin told me you'd done it, but I didn't believe him."

The stranger squats down and winks at me.

"You sneaky little bastard."

The smiling stranger is skinny. He's dressed funny, and he's kind of wavy. He makes my eyes hurt. I should tell, but my brothers are screaming at each other and my parents are yelling for everyone to shut up.

"Get that thing away from Lando before he chokes to death."

"For Christ's sake, Barbara Jean, he's perfectly safe."

The stranger laughs. No one pays him any attention.

"Daddy's wrong, you know. You're not safe at all."

His eyes do something weird. Then my rubber octopus comes to life and wraps seven of its tentacles around my neck. The other one slides into my mouth and slips down my throat. I can't breathe. I can feel my father pounding on my back and yelling, "Let it go! Let it go, dammit!"

Then everything gets dark.

I wake up in a gray place, like a room made of smoke. I still can't breathe but I can hear my parents fighting, a million miles away.

"Goddammit, Herbert. You've killed him. On Christmas! I hope you're happy."

Then a Golden Lady walks out of the dark. She's shiny. She jingles when she walks and she looks like the ladies in the live Indian show we saw in Wisconsin last summer, only taller, a lot taller. And she's shiny bright like the sun. Looking at her makes me want to laugh and cry all at the same time.

"Not yet, buddy. Can't have you upsetting the Plan."

Then she punches me in the stomach.

I cough…

"See you soon, old boy."

…and I'm staring up at my dad. He's wearing wet chunks of rubber octopus tentacle all down his shirtfront. The smiling stranger is gone. Mother is over by the Christmas tree with the phone up to her ear. When she sees that I'm still alive, she slams the phone down.

"Son of a bitch."

• • •

Summer, 1990

On a summer camp boat ride across Lake Michigan I decided to ask Angela Rhymer to be my girlfriend. We were nine years old that year, and I'd spent most of it staring at her. One day she told her big brother that I was stalking her. He beat me up. My mother met with the head camp counselor and said she'd castrate the next little sonofabitch who put his hands on me. I asked Angela, anyway. She said, "Maybe." That was worse.

We were alone on the deck of the ferryboat. All the other campers and counselors had run inside because it was starting to rain. I grabbed Angela's hand. I had to yell over the wind.

"If I were Odysseus you'd be my Penelope!"

"You're weird," she shouted. "And a little creepy."

Then the ferry lurched and a wave rolled over the side of the boat and washed me over the safety rail. I hit the water hard. I knew how to swim, but no matter how hard I tried to keep my head above the water it felt like something was dragging me down. I kicked and splashed and screamed. Then the something yanked me under and the lake closed over my head.

Dark water swirls all around me, pushing me around, flipping me over. The water is changing, churning, until it becomes the face of a bearded old man with eyes like burning emeralds. There's light in the water... lights shining in my eyes, as the glowing face pulls me in closer. It shifts and rolls like waves captured by strange gravity. I can see dozens of fish swimming inside the face.

"You've made fools of us all. More and more of your believers abandon you every day... and you asked for it."

I'm drowning. My heart is pounding and my lungs are screaming and I have to breathe and I'm afraid to die.

"Hey, fishface!"

The face in the water turns toward the sound.

That's when I see her. The Golden Lady. She's walking on the bottom of the Lake. She's holding something in her hands, something silver that shines even brighter than the old manface. She's smaller this time, darker, with different hair and she's wearing a nurse's uniform. But she's still the Golden Lady. And she's come for me.

"Poseidon. You're pathetic."

The light in her hands goes nuclear bright, and suddenly I can breathe. I'm lying on the rocky bottom with all that water rolling above me but, somehow, the Golden Lady's silver light protects me. Through the ceiling of black water, I can see the face looking down at us. It looks totally pissed.

"Foul! Foul! Traitorous squaw!"

"Begone, thou racist remnant! Go haunt an oil rig!"

The face in the water, Poseidon, screams, and burns in the silver light from the object in the Golden Lady's hands. Then it's gone.

"Are you alright?"

When I wake up, I'm lying on the deck with rain hitting my face. The Golden Lady nods. Then she puts the shining thing in the small purse on her hip and the silver light goes out. I can hear people yelling on the other side of the ferry. I can hear Angela crying. But all I can see is the Golden Lady's face. Her eyes.

"Do I... do I know you?"

"Not yet," she laughs. **"You will know me. But not yet."**

"What is that silver thing? Can I see it?"

"That would be very bad."

"Why?"

"Never mind. You won't remember any of this when I'm gone."

"I won't?"

"Nope."

"OK."

Someone, my camp counselor, screams my name. People are running toward us.

"Lando! I found him! He's over here!"

But the strange nurse and her silver purse are gone.

The Knock Knock Club. Peoria Illinois. 2003

3am and my set killed. It was a full house; a great crowd full of happy drunks. Afterward, feeling victorious and lonely, I bought all the other comics a round. By midnight I was way too drunk to drive.

Screw it. It's your birthday.

I'm trying to shove my inhaler into the ignition slot when she appears. No special effects this time. She is simply… there, sitting next to me in the passenger seat. This time, she wears the face of a Cherokee matriarch; regal bearing, long gray hair loose and flowing over strong, straight shoulders. She's wearing a velvety black cloak made from… made from…

"Thunderbird feathers," she says, as if she'd read my mind.

"I did read your mind. Why do you keep flinching?"

"Cause every time you show up something tries to kill me."

The Golden Lady laughs. **"I know the feeling."**

"Who are you, lady? Why do I know you?"

"That's a long story, Lando Cooper. But I'm afraid you're in no condition to hear it."

"Are you my guardian angel?"

"Eewww. Gross."

"What's your name, Golden Lady? Pretty Indian Lady with the long pretty hair."

"I've had many names. The gods of the Navajo nation called me Changing Woman. For now, you can call me... Constant."

"Constance?"

"Constant."

"Well, Constance, today is my birthday."

"Of course. A very special birthday."

"Thass right, Connie. For today I am a man."

"And just look at you. Your parents must be so proud."

The unexpected gravity of that statement stalls my tongue and I have to look away before I embarrass myself.

"They never understood me."

"Oh boy. Look, we've got so much work to do I don't even want to think about it. It's time to go."

"Where exactly are we going, my Connie?"

"To school, my bumbling mortal idiot."

"Hey, lady... I happen to be the possessor of a Bachelors degree from one of our nation's finest educational institutions. I done made the grade."

I try to start the car with my inhaler again and throw up all over the steering wheel instead.

"Oh boy."

Then Constant is holding the thing I've turned over in my memory since that day on the ferry. She holds it so that I can see it plainly: it's a seashell. A shining seashell. She raises it, bathing my face with silver radiance. And I am suddenly stonecold sober.

"I know this. This is… this is…"

"Yes. It is."

I was twenty-two years old and completely unprepared for what came next. It was the first day of the rest of my mortal life. Like most people, I thought I was special enough to handle whatever destiny the Golden Lady represented.

I was wrong.

CHAPTER I
DUEL

I should be happy. After two thousand years spent doing the job I was created to do, I deserve a little happiness. If only there was someone I could complain to; a clergyman or union representative. But there isn't. And even though that's mostly my fault, it still sucks. See, thirty seconds ago the saleswoman lost twenty pounds and started speaking French. That means a lot of people are about to die: there's a god waiting outside this jewelry store and he wants to kill me.

"Your fiancée will be so happy, Monsieur Cooper," the saleswoman says. Then her polite professional demeanor evaporates, replaced by the confusion I've come to know all too well. "I'm thin! And I'm speaking French!"

"Yes."

"But I don't speak French."

I stuff the little gold-wrapped box into my front pocket. I've worked my butt off to be able to buy that ring and, angry god or no angry god, it's coming with me.

"In another life, your father accepted that job at Banque Populaire and moved your family to Paris. You grew up there."

"But Daddy didn't take that job. They were getting a divorce and… Wait… how did you know that?"

Outside, someone calls me by my professional name.

"Yahweh! Come out and face me!"

The voice is loud, supernaturally powerful, and familiar.

"*Mon dieu*… what's happening?"

The saleswoman is getting more French by the nanosecond. I can't help but pity her – she doesn't know she's about to die. If she did she wouldn't have worn that dress.

"I'm French! I love zis life!"

"Don't get used to it."

I step into the sunlight basting Michigan Avenue. Chicago is in the last throes of a vicious midsummer heatwave, but my immortal enemy stands just up ahead, all puffed up like he's still got the whole world in his hands.

"Well, well, well. How far the mighty has fallen."

Typical. Retired for two thousand years and the thick Greek lummox still hasn't mastered English.

"Hey, Yahweh! I'm talkin' to you!"

"We're too old for this, Zeus."

I cut a wide swath around the barrel-chested lunatic, focusing on my lime green Sketchers as they slap the pavement.

Just keep walking, Lando. Hey! Check out that pile of dog turds. Much more interesting than the lummox.

"You hear what I say, desert dog? I'm going to keeek your ass! You and your faggoty son!"

Hello. I'm a real boy. This is not my problem.

I've struggled with anger issues. I won't go into detail – just read the Old Testament and you'll get the picture.

But thoughts of the future help to keep me calm. I've sacrificed everything to be here. Literally.

I can do this.

I'm five yards from the elevated train entrance; fifteen feet from the comforting embrace of other Chicagoans and their everyday human problems when a thunderclap shatters store windows up and down Michigan Avenue. Then a Voice thunders overhead.

"Face me, Yahweh! Or I'll burn this city to the ground!"

Damn.

The howling maniac is six and a half feet tall and built like a man-shaped oak tree. He stands there, flexing his Mediterranean muscles in the middle of Michigan Avenue. Clearly the King of the Greek Gods is determined to make ignoring him difficult. The lightning bolt that blasts the concrete beneath my feet makes it impossible: I jump backward, narrowly avoiding electrocution.

The skies over the Loop go black. The wind off Lake Michigan whips itself into a fury, howling through steel and stone canyons: Zeus must have bullied one of his bastard elemental offspring into harassing me. His third bolt strikes a group of Swedish tourists getting off a double decker tour bus parked in front of the jewelry store. The tour bus explodes. The jewelry store goes up in a tremendous ball of smoke and flame. The shockwave knocks me off my feet as a peal of hypersound like the silent bellow of a newborn sun rings out over the city, the air clanging with the shriek of unauthorized Creation: the birthscreams of diverging realities.

A few yards away, a woman in a tight green dress

lying in a shattered Best Buy window display staggers to her feet. Well, part of her staggers to her feet: she's technically dead but her soul has nowhere to go, not with all this celestial interference clogging the ethers. The woman in the green (and red) dress is staggering around, deceased and utterly confused. Her legs are long and well-formed: a dancer's legs.

The leggy dead dancer lurches toward a young mother grasping a stroller. The young mother gapes as the dead hottie bumps into the stroller, spilling the toddler inside it out onto the sidewalk. The toddler bounces off the curb and rolls into oncoming traffic. Fortunately, the spectacle Zeus is creating has stalled traffic on both sides of Michigan Avenue.

The dead hottie staggers toward the toddler. The young mother bolts past the burning tour bus, jumps off the curb and onto the dead hottie's back, the two of them twirling around in the Buses Only lane; a shrieking blonde motherbear driven insane by a rapidfire intrusion of the Weird, catfighting with the hot dead dancer while a thousand terrified onlookers look on.

"Hey, douchebag," a Voice says from everywhere. **"Are you ready to parlay now?"**

Parlay. Damn, how I hate the Greeks.

Amid a chorus of screams from the panicking mortals around us, Zeus assumes an Aspect and rises toward the sky. Lightning flashes from his eyes, crackles from the ends of his hair. And he's naked. Looks like someone has been hoarding his divine energies: His godly member extends the length of a steel girder.

"What do you want, Zeus?"

"I want your head, God of the Hebrews!"

Behind him, the John Hancock Center shudders and bursts into flames. More screams. A taxi driver on the far side of the burning bus tries to move his car and smashes into the Prius in front of him. The Prius' owner jumps out of his car, swearing in Farsi. He reaches in through the cab's window, pulls the driver out and begins to pummel him. Fights are breaking out all along Michigan Avenue. Several dozen onlookers attack themselves, punching and tearing their own faces. An attractive African-American female police officer near the epicenter of the disturbance, gets out of her stalled patrol car and stares, openmouthed, at Zeus. Then she breaks into applause.

"It's the End of Days! Finally!"

The police officer grabs a passing Sikh schoolboy by the straps of his backpack and tries to pull off his turban. The Sikh schoolboy breaks free and sprints away. The policewoman shoots him.

I'm going to have a headache for the next month.

A great rushing wind answers my command: a certain theatricality is called for in every godfight. Fortunately, I come from a family that knows how to stage a confrontation.

"Let me get this straight, Zeus. You would contradict the Eshuum? You would breach the terms of your surrender?"

Back in the Buses Only lane, dead hottie is bouncing blonde mom's head off a convenient fire hydrant. The toddler laughs and claps his hands to the rhythm of his mother's bludgeoning: Bonk. Bonk. Bonk. Then he vomits a swarm of locusts.

Zeus raises his right fist, his forearm tendons flexing like angry anacondas, reaches heavenward and clenches lightning from the screaming sky.

"I would dare the Fates themselves to see you dead, usurper! Befouler of the faithful! Comedian!"

"You're one to talk, Nymph fondler!"

Thunder tears the air like the roar of a thousand badly castrated bull elephants. Behind me, the Sears Tower flickers and vanishes, only to reappear, flicker and vanish again. In its place appears a mammoth golden retriever as big as a cathedral. His name is Cheezy Domino.

Zeus hammers me with lightning, smites me with hailstones and lashes me with hurricane force winds. It hurts, especially the smiting part. But the cost to his divine energy reserves should debilitate even a god of his stature: I can't help wondering where he's getting the extra power.

Focus, Cooper. He's immortal. You're not.

I reach into the Eshuum and pull out an offensive Aspect of my own: He Who Judges, the stonefaced God who opened up a can of divine whup-ass on Sodom and Gomorrah, shrugs his way out of my mind and into reality, which makes sense, considering that Zeus' drunken killing binge qualifies as an abomination of post-biblical proportions. Maybe he'll learn to appreciate prolonged sobriety after a few millennia as a burning pillar of salt.

"Enough!"

Zeus either doesn't know or doesn't care about the damage a godfight can cause to the fabric of human consciousness; what we of the divine orders call the Eshuum. I have to stop this breaching before he plunges the world into Chaos.

"Attend me, Yahweh! Cast off thy mortal seeming and take to the skies! Fly with me into the heat of the sun that we may learn who is the true King of Creation!"

He's nearly five stories tall by now. His image must be whipping around the planet, recorded by thousands of mobile phones, playing hob around the internet... Oy, the headache...

"Fight me, God of sheep and pestilence! You cower before me because you dare not... burrrrrrroppt...!"

Zeus's declaration fills the air with the sickly sweet stench of downmarket ambrosia and Schlitz Malt Liquor. The son of Cronus is drunk, (no surprise there really, since he's Greek too), but how to deal with him? A banishment? A temporary damnation? But to whose Hell?

Cheezy Domino lifts his leg and wees all over downtown Chicago. The warm river of giant dog urine flushes a bus-load of confused retirees down the street, around the corner and out of sight. The stink snaps me back to my senses.

My human perceptions reassert themselves...

I reeled in my psychic extrusions and recalled He Who Judges.

"No!" HWJ howled. **"Let me broil the titanspawn in a cataclysm of brimstone! I will baste his heathen flesh in rivers of righteous hellfire!"**

But I needed a way to diffuse the situation, not make it worse. I had to divest Zeus of the excess power he was burning and minimize the damage to the Eshuum. I needed a plan; something fast and dirty and cosmically low impact. I shoved He Who Judges back into the holding pen in my brain as Zeus blasted the Merchandise Mart with a volley of thunderbolts. The attack sent hundreds of screaming mortals flooding into the streets: it was only a matter of time before he started ravishing people.

"You were always a showoff, Zeus. Lightning bolts... earthquakes... and for what? Empty gestures. They're totally passé."

"Fool! I am Zeus Aegiduchos! Skyfather and Stormlord! Cloud Snorter and Hymen Smasher! The thunder speaks with my voice! The lightning is my spear! My essence mingles with the Four Winds and sows my seed upon the lips of a million whores!"

"Come on, Zee. Even with all this power you're wasting, you're still totally assboned."

Zeus frowned down at me, storms raging in his eyes.

"'Assboned'?"

"Hello? Are you deaf and irrelevant?"

All gods hate being talked down to: Zeus once changed an innocent nymph into a swan merely for avoiding his attempts to rape her. Now I hoped to goad him into overreaching again.

"'The thunder is my voice! The lightning is my spear?' Zdog... that stuff is older than Methuselah. Literally. Even worse... it's corny."

"'Corny'?"

"Like Kansas. Why do you think millions of mortals rejected you?"

Zeus' eyes dimmed. He shook his head like a wounded bear beset by saltfooted flies. Then he roared, **"I AM NOT IRRELEVANT! I AM THE COMING!"**

I was trying to make sense of that statement when the street beneath my feet buckled. From somewhere nearby, a thousand mortals screamed as the Butkus Bank Building collapsed. The invisible effluvia of hundreds of prayers rose up around me like a silent symphony of pain only to vanish in a Hellenic heartbeat: Zeus had just extinguished another thousand mortal lives.

Talk faster, Cooper.

"Yo," I shrugged. "I had my fingers on the pulse, baby, the zeitgeist."

"Zeitgeist?" Zeus rumbled. **"That's... French**?"

The air was filled with screaming. And buoyed upon nearly every scream, a flotilla of prayers, whispering like wind across the sands of a distant desert.

Help me, Lord!

Save me, Allah.

Where are you?

I had to speed things up: any one of these prayers, if answered under these circumstances, would spell cosmic disaster.

"You've got plenty of juice, Zeus. But I'll bet you haven't read a book in, what? Five thousand years?"

Another lightning bolt, this one close enough to fry my eyebrows. Ozone stung my nostrils. I put myself out.

"I'll read the tale of your destruction in your sizzling entrails, Dog of the Desert! I'll thumb through your King James claptrap while I bang your feeble corpse!"

"You were Top Dog, Zeus; Immortal god among gods. But how did you spend your divinity? Turning yourself into showers of golden coins and impregnating cows. Major douche move. That's why my followers were able to supplant yours: I was dialed in, Zed."

The winds dwindled as Zeus' divine focus shifted from smiting to doubting. The lightning storm lost some of its fury: Zeus began to subside.

"What's this 'dialed in'? Why do you talk like that?"

He shook his head, sending swarms of motivated electrons swirling skyward. But he had shrunk to the height of a modest bungalow: it was now or never.

"I guess that's why I still have a few believers, Zeus. Granted… nobody's sacrificing their children to me anymore, except for two or three churches in West Texas, but at least I'm still connected."

"Connected?"

"Sure. But you and your peeps are all sizzle and no souvlaki; you're a gyro made from million-day-old toga meat; cosmic hayseeds with baklava where your style sense should be. You're like the closing credits at the end of the last feature at the Midnight Bargain Matinopolis: ie, nobody 'grocks' the Greek Gods anymore."

"Dialed in?" Zeus repeated, his voice shaky with perfectly mortal confusion. He was nearly human-sized when I met him in the middle of Michigan Avenue. **"I don't understand anything you say."**

I leaned forward to make certain Zeus could hear me. He leaned forward, all traces of his Aspect extinguished, barely a flicker of lightning in his hair; eager to hear the secret wisdom of the God of the Burning Bush.

Then I kicked him in the nuts.

Zeus howled, and fell to the sidewalk, clutching his divine scrotum.

"While you lie there trying to change into something with no testicles, I'm going to draw you down. It's going to hurt you, Zeus, a lot more than it will me. And it hurts me. A lot."

I closed my eyes and pinpointed Zeus' divine lifeforce. To my upgraded perceptions he shone like a man-shaped star; far too much power than even he should have been able to wield under current planetary belief conditions.

What have you been doing, Zeus?

I stretched forth my hand. Lightning burst from Zeus' body, the shafts crackling from him, dancing along my fingers to fill my senses with their alien tang. No doubt about it: Zeus had been dipping his fingers into some cosmically strange cookie jars.

The Greek alpha god writhed on the ruptured sidewalk, momentarily held captive by my will, his perfect teeth gnashing the air in silent protest of his impending banishment. His storm-gray eyes rolled in their sockets and found mine and his wounded scowl broadened into a grimace of… fear?

"Beware, Yahweh. The Coming stalks us all."

Then those strange energies flared up from Zeus and blinded my mortal eyes for a moment. Somewhere in the midst of that conflagration, Zeus screamed. The shockwave was subtle as the deathshriek of a burning Babylonian. I staggered backward, half blinded, covering my ears against that awful roar. It was all so distracting that it took me a moment to realise that Zeus was gone.

He should have been under my control, unable to go anyplace to which I hadn't banished him. But the sidewalk was empty, a vaguely Zeus-shaped scorch mark the only evidence he'd ever been there. But where was his power? Other than those first few wisps I'd absorbed, the Eshuum was pinpricked in several places but essentially undamaged by that bruising of strange force.

What's happening?

Using the wisps of divinity I'd scarfed from Zeus, I quieted the thunder, and shoved the unused lightning into a pocket dimension I kept handy for such occasions. I scanned the ether for some sign of the vanished Skyfather, but he was gone, really gone; erased as if he had never existed. I could still taste the psychic spoor of the Egyptian Pantheon long after Moses took the Hebrews out of Egypt. Zeus's energies should have flowed into me, but they hadn't.

And Zeus was... gone.

Everyone was screaming. Humans were fighting in the streets, driven mad by the Chaos energies our godfight had unleashed. Downtown Chicago looked like someone detonated an atom bomb under Oprah's townhouse. In the Buses Only lane, the dead dancer was trying to stuff the newly orphaned toddler down an open manhole. The toddler was putting up a good fight but losing strength with every shove. Over by the Lake, Cheesy Domino was humping the Art Institute of Chicago: if I was going to prevent a catastrophic rupture I needed to get crackalackin'.

I spoke a Word, a shrieking shard of matter-rearranging verbiage. You might call it the access code to the operating system of the gods.

And Everything changed.

Five minutes later…

I was walking toward the L train. I was twenty minutes past the end of my lunch break, my boss was blowing up my mobile phone, and I was nursing the onset of what was going to be the biggest migraine in the history of grain. But I'd set everything aright: a relatively simple procedure when you can control the flow of the Eshuum. Not so simple when saddled with a human brain. I'd rolled back Time to a few moments before Zeus attacked me and removed our duel from the spacetime continuum. No fuzzy photos of the confrontation would haunt the nightly news or go viral on the internet; no evidence to alert humanity to the presence of its faded gods. In effect: the Michigan Avenue godfight never happened.

The tour bus trundled on its way, filled with laughing, living Swedes. The attractive woman with her great legs and green dress pranced by without even glancing my way. Hmmmph. If she remembered her original timeline she'd have fallen to her knees and kissed my hightops: dead one moment/healthy with both eyes free of footlong glass shards the next.

I'd cleaned up the Mercedes-sized droppings left by Cheezy Domino and sent him back to his home dimension: he was adorable but his presence in my dimension was an abomination. I'd brought back the Sears Tower: no one noticed. The only person who acknowledged my efforts was the orphaned toddler. As I resurrected his mother and placed him back in his stroller, he'd asked if I could sweeten his mommy's breast milk. According to him it tasted like mucous. I'd granted his wish because... well, who needs snotty breast milk?

With the mortal world turning once more as it should, I boarded the elevated train and headed back to work. Ten minutes later, the headache I'd anticipated was coming on with a vengeance. I leaned my forehead against the cool window next to my seat and watched the blue vastness of Lake Michigan as I turned over the last hour's events. Something weird was happening, something that had never happened across the long slog of Creation: a major god, the All-Father of one of the world's last great pantheons, had been erased.

Murdered?

I was haunted by the song of the strange energies as they engulfed Zeus at the end. The taste of their effluence still stung the back of my throat. Suddenly I had a mystery on my hands and I didn't like it one bit. But I was going to have to investigate. After all, it's my area.

I'm the last of the old guard, at least as far as I can see, the semi-retired captain of a losing team crewed by humanity's outgrown gods. Now I had a haunting absence; a hole where a god should have been but wasn't. Zeus was gone, and if the power that should have been released from his renunciation had not flowed into me... where was it?

Beware. The Coming stalks us all.

And who or what was "the Coming"? I was unfamiliar with such an entity. And I knew everybody.

I grabbed my inhaler and took a quick suck. Then, while my enflamed bronchi settled down, I leaned back against the seat and tried to relax. I needed answers like I needed Tylenol with a whiskey chaser. But Tylenol makes me nauseous, and getting drunk was the most irresponsible thing I could do. I had to keep my wits about me.

Beware. The Coming stalks us all.

I usually ignore prophesy. After all, my former self had initially warned Noah about my plan to punish humankind by turning every firstborn mortal child into a particularly unpleasant specimen of cuttlefish. It was only after Noah reminded me that *that* many angry aquatic invertebrates would need a lot more water in order to survive long enough to repent of their sins that I came up with the idea for a great flood. By the time I got around to confirming the change with Noah, half the human race had drowned. I knew how unreliable divine warnings can be. But I couldn't shake the sense of foreboding that Zeus' warning had cast: trouble was rushing toward me like a plague of blackwinged sorrows.

I had a feeling there was going to be Hell to pay.

CHAPTER II

I AM

User Name: **Yahweh**.

Screen Name: **JVH**

Title: **God of the Israelites. The Creator. "The Man Upstairs."**

Occupation: **I'm the current Guardian of Eschatological Continuity for Human Consciousness and Development. I'm also the Dominant Defender of Dimensional Integrity Against ODAE (Obsolescent Divine Aggression and Encroachment). Standup Comic.**

Turn Ons: **Thought. Music. Creativity. The Arts and Sciences. Classic Comic Books.**

Turn Offs: **Negativity. Conservative Talk Radio.**

TV: **Fawlty Towers. The Daily Show. Doctor Who. The Science Channel. Food Network.**

Music: **Suzanne Vega. Ella Fitzgerald. Bossocucanova. James Brown. Tokyo Rocketbike Cyberninja Team Tetsuo!**

Contact email: yahwent@Skyfathergroup.Waring.DEUS

God's Facebook Page

The morning after the fight with Zeus reminded me that having a human body is fun when it comes to things like Chicago-style deep dish pizza or drunken orgies. But you try experiencing a million "morning afters" while still recovering from your own hangover. Now multiply that by a few hundred times a million; all those praying people swearing they'll never overeat/drink/smoke crack/seduce perfect strangers ever again, and you'll begin to get an idea of the festival that is my day-to-day existence. And, sometime during the duel with Zeus, I picked up a vicious case of the crabs.

"Damn Greeks."

"Lando! Your hippie friend is stinking up the living room!"

Barbara never used my buddies' names, pretending she couldn't quite remember them, and wouldn't bother trying since they wouldn't be coming around much after she'd informed me about how horrible they really were. Not that I had many buddies. In fact, I had exactly one: the fellow who was basting her favorite sofa in a cloud of patchouli oil and vegan beef jerky.

"Coming!"

Just then my phone lit up where it lay on my bedside night table; an electronic remix of Agnus Dei.

Call from Surabhi

"Whaddup?"

"Hello, Loverman. Bad news about tonight I'm afraid."

Surabhi's voice was the charming mix of accents typical of second generation London-bred Afro-Brits who immigrate to the American Midwest.

"What's wrong?"

I took a deep breath: I sounded desperate. And even though I was desperate I didn't have to sound like it.

"I promised to cover for one of the other teachers at the Language Center. She just went into labor. Fifty students. I can't cancel on them."

"But I've got tickets to *Namaste, Brahma Blumberg* at the Biolark."

"Sorry, babe. Ask your homeboy, Yuri. Maybe he'll go with you."

"But you're going to New York tomorrow."

"I'll be back Friday. I promise I'll make it up to you then. Crap… I've gotta get back to work. I love you, Lando Cooper."

"Love you too."

We disconnected. I bent to grab my knapsack, went lightheaded and nearly fell on my face. I took some deep breaths until the dizziness passed. Then I faced myself in the full length mirror on the door that led to my bathroom.

"Yahweh of the Israelites, you are gettin' hitched come hell or high water."

One night, years earlier, I'd gotten drunk and tried to improve my appearance. I lost control of the power and turned myself into an embryonic blue whale. It had taken me two hours to change back, another twenty minutes to repair the floor, and another two weeks to clean up all that afterbirth.

My mortal body was just below average height, thin yet cursed with a jiggly ring of baby fat around my midsection which, at the biological age of twenty-nine, was maddening enough to make me consider re-reincarnating myself with a lower BMI. My hair was my best feature: a decent sized afro that I labored not to maintain on a daily basis. Other than a persistent itching in my nether regions, that was it.

I worked out four days a week in the basement with my father's old gym equipment: push-ups, sit-ups, "medicine hurls" and other "old school" calisthenics calculated to rupture me when I most expected it. In an attempt to rebuild me into the kind of man of which he could be proud, Herb insisted on murdering me: character building through physical suffering.

I flexed both biceps: string cheese had better tone.

Why not just give yourself a little boost? Just move a few proteins around; bump up your hormonal output. It's not like anyone's watching. You could be an Adonis.

"No."

I was determined to look at the life I had given me as a gift: billions of people in the world had to make do with less.

I took a hit from my inhaler and coughed: recently my "childhood" asthma had set its sights on my adulthood. As the pressure on my chest lessened, my other burden made itself felt.

"Lando Calrissian Darnell Cooper, don't make me come up there!"

Jesus.

Some people name their offspring after their favorite doctor or beloved religious icon. My mortal father named me with his favorite actor in mind.

"Mister Billy Dee Williams, dammit."

I can still remember my mortal parents arguing about it only hours after I was Embodied.

"Billy Dee sounds like a pimp's name, Herbert. Do you really want to name your son after a pimp?"

My father was trying to figure out a way to smoke in a hospital maternity ward. At that time Herb dearly loved smoking. He once claimed he could read the stock market in piles of flicked ashes the way African griots read flung chicken bones.

"Woman, I keep telling you: Billy Dee Williams is the greatest actor of our generation. 'Billy Dee Cooper.' It has a special kind of music."

"It's music to whip whores by."

"I defy anyone to watch *The Empire Strikes Back* and not be emotionally affected."

"You are not naming any son of mine after a pimp!"

Barbara would look harshly on the *Star Wars* franchise in later years, but Herb remained a devoted fan of *Empire* and *Return of the Jedi*, largely because of Billy Dee Williams' performance as "Lando Calrissian". Darnell was my mother's dead father's name so that was a no-brainer. Since they both agreed that "Lando Calrissian Darnell" sounded powerful without being too "ghetto", they settled on all three.

"Lando Calrissian Darnell Cooper."

I remember wondering, as awareness of my former godhood faded, how much divinity it would take to crawl back up my mother's fallopian tubes and pretend the whole thing never happened. As the Coopers cooed and snickered at me, I lay there, awash in my own meconium, unable to express the horror unfolding in my postnatal gut. And as my divine candle flickered out, I understood that this was to be only the first step down a long, ugly road with humiliation as my most frequent companion.

"Coming!"

I checked my hair, squeezed a pimple that had teleported onto the end of my nose, picked my afro till I struck sparks, then hurried downstairs.

My agent hated to be kept waiting.

● ● ●

"What took you so long? My pitch meeting's in less than an hour and if I'm late Corroder will fry my balls for lunch."

"Sorry," I mumbled through a mouthful of Granola. "Migraine. I'm pretty sure a vicious pixie took a dump in my head last night."

"Dude," Yuri growled. "I'm late and you're talking about pixies. You plan on growing up anytime soon? Jesus." He snatched up his Blackberry and sent his thumbs flying over the keypad. "I'm texting Corroder to tell him we're stuck in traffic."

"I'll be ready in ten seconds. Why lie?"

Yuri glared at me with an expression that managed to convey pity and exasperation simultaneously.

"When are you gonna get a haircut? Afros are so 2000."

"My hair is a political statement."

"Right: 'I don't know how to groom myself. Please kill me.'"

"That's a little dark."

"Dude… I'm a cable television executive and I can't pay my cable bill. 'Dark' is what I do."

Yuriel Kalashnikov was handsome in a California beach bum sort of way; muscular without being obnoxious about it, with dirty-blond hair and electric blue eyes; a young Clint Eastwood armed with a Blackberry instead of a Colt 45. He was born of a handsome Swedish immigrant couple from San Francisco's "Little Trollhattan" neighborhood: Ulrik and Ingeborg Rolfstaddtsen. Ulrik was an independently wealthy organic beet farmer and yoga instructor. Ingeborg was a vegan animal rights activist/ecoterrorist/singer-songwriter. They met in 1974 during a street festival dedicated to ending the war in Korea despite the fact that it officially ended in 1953. Ulrik, however, had uncovered evidence while astral projecting, that the American Military Industrial Complex was waging a covert, CIA-funded police action in Pyongyang. While attending a seminar on how to empower the little-known but highly-endangered Native American coon rat, Ulrik watched Ingeborg sing the song that would make her a minor national sensation: Coon Rat vs Fat Cat. The song scurried halfway up the Top 40 pop charts before relegating itself to the 99 cent music rack of history. Yuriel Kalasknikov Che Guevara Rolfstaddtsen was born eleven months later. Now, the leftist socialist Yuri, a bisexual yoga devotee who belonged to PETA, Greenpeace, ACTUP, MOVEON.ORG and the NAACP; who was a subscribing member to National Public Radio, The Daily Anarchist and Oprah's Book Club... Yuri Kalashnikov was the angriest pacifist on Earth.

We'd met one night five years earlier at a comedy club on the North Side. He was there representing a client, a terrible Indian comic with a wooden leg. He'd watched my set and declared himself a fan. He represented me for three months before being offered a job as an assistant to a television development executive. We'd remained friends and occasional collaborators ever since.

"Can we go please? I can't be late because of you. Again."

I grabbed my satchel and headed toward the front door.

"Wait one. Goddamn. Minute."

My mother stepped out of the kitchen. Barbara Cooper was tall, light brown; the "high yellow" to my father's "milk chocolate". She was wearing an ultratight, leopard print microdress that might have contained her in the Eighties but had long since given up the fight. She was the kind of "thin" that never translated into "fit", her breasts as dangly as the udders on an undermilked heifer. For some reason, she'd chosen that morning to show off the network of fine scars from her latest unsuccessful varicose vein removal surgery. She was wearing her favorite pink "chacha heels", the ones she only broke out when she was trying to seduce one of my friends. She took a drag off her Virgina Slim and French inhaled.

"Aren't you boys going to compliment a lady on her appearance?"

"Barbara," I said. "Why are you dressed that way?"

"I'm on a voyage of self discovery."

"You hoping to discover the Island of Sad Old Hookers?"

Barbara blew a perfect menthol smoke ring across the living room. "I'm trying to 'discover' why you haven't introduced me to your handsome friend."

"It's Yuri, Barbara. You've only met him a hundred times."

"Sarcasm makes you look ignorant, dear."

"Herb quit smoking, you know. He's healthier than you are. Doesn't that fill you with rage?"

Barbara laughed while her eyes checked out Yuri's package.

"Some of your darker skinned blacks look ridiculous with cigarettes dangling between their big, Ubangi soup coolers, Lando. You know that. Mama can pull it off because I'm one of the sexy people. Right, Yuri?"

Barbara batted her eyes and shook her "junk" in a way that made it nearly impossible to look at her without screaming.

"Yuri... what is that? Polish?"

"No, ma'am. It's Russian."

"You mean my boring son is hanging out with a communist? How's that for a poke in the shitbox?"

"Mother! You're 'thinking out loud' again."

Barbara shrugged this away. "I'm sorry, Yuri. I'm sure Lando has told you about my condition."

"Yes, ma'am. It's not a problem, Barb."

Barbara giggled. The vodka gust scorched the air between her mouth and my nostrils.

"He's a winner, Lando. And so handsome..."

Yuri offered up his most rakish smile. "Coming from a looker like you, I'll take that as high praise, Barbara."

"...for a big dumb Polack."

"Barbara!"

"You gentlemen still haven't commented on my appearance."

"That's because you look ridiculous."

Barbara dropped her cigarette and ground it out on the carpet. Then loosened her straps and winked at me.

"Good."

"Look out!"

Yuri wrenched the wheel sharply to the left, swerving into the far lane to avoid the elderly man who had just stepped out of his ancient white Cadillac. We'd never even come close to hitting him, but we nearly rear-ended the biker on the Harley stopped at the red light in front of us. We screeched to a halt inches from the Harley's rear wheel. Yuri overreacted. Of course.

"Will you stop doing that?"

"I wasn't sure you saw him."

We were log-jammed in downtown rushhour traffic. In the sweltering heat inside his beloved second generation electric car, Yuri started doing his deep breathing exercises.

"Barbara's been acting very strange lately."

"'Strange' for your family or 'strange' for normal people?"

"What's wrong with you?"

"Sorry. I'm pitching something to Corroder today and I'm nervous. I think it could be really big."

"Swell. What is it?"

"I woke up with this idea in the middle of the night. It was so powerful I started developing it right then and there…"

"Here's my stop. Stop now!"

Yuri jammed on the brakes, throwing me against the dashboard. I bounced. Then I grabbed my backpack and opened the door.

"You up for a movie tonight?" Surabhi's got to work, and I've got two tickets to see *Namaste, Brahma Blumberg* at the Biolark."

"I hate when you do that."

"What?"

"Ask me what I'm up to and then change the subject before I can answer. Besides being the worst backseat driver on Earth, you're also incredibly self-centered."

"No I'm not."

"You make everything about you."

Yuri shrugged, and lit a cigarette from the box he'd recently begun keeping in his glove compartment. "Sometimes it's hard to be your friend. I'm just sayin'."

"Hurtful. Come on, hang out with me tonight."

"Negative. Corroder and I have a dinner meeting with the Vice President of Comedy Development at Fox. He's in Chicago looking to scare up some talent."

"OK, meanwhile, I've got the gig at Coconut Jose's on Thursday; a proposal dinner to plan for Friday night; and my parents are about to kill each other and take a Korean callgirl with them."

"You're gonna kill at Coconut Jose's. This is going to be a big gig for you. I can feel it." Yuri glanced at his Greenpeace Whale Watch. "Damn. I gotta jet. You want me to pick you up Thursday night?"

"No thanks. I finally got a monthly bus pass. You're a carpool-free agent, my friend."

"Bus pass? One of these days you'll work up the balls to actually drive a car."

"I prefer public transportation. Why add to the black cloud of toxins already hanging over our fair city?"

"Dude," Yuri sneered through the passenger's window. "When the Hell are you going to stop fooling yourself?"

CHAPTER III
THE ELEPHANT WAS DOUBLE BOOKED

"Livin' on borrowed time."
(Response to the question, "What are you doing?")
God's Twitter Page

In the twenty years he'd owned and operated Cooper & Sons Auto Supply, Herb Cooper had skydived on camera while playing an accordion, and waterskied across the Chicago River towed by a speedboat covered with tastefully nude pictures of himself. Once, he attempted to ride a bull in front of a screaming crowd during a rodeo at the United Center. He'd actually stayed on for four seconds before the bull, a bovine killing machine named Assassin, bucked him off and nearly trampled him to death while he screamed at the camera crew to "...keep rolling! No matter what!" The bull hurled Herb over the retaining fence. He landed in the lap of the Governor of Illinois.

From his hospital bed Herb convinced local stations to run the footage the next day, complete with a sped up rendition of Dueling Banjos playing underneath. The stunt cost him a broken leg, three cracked ribs and a concussion... and made Cooper & Sons a household name. This was back in the early Eighties, before cable made local broadcasting a thing of the past. New York had its Crazy Eddie. LA had its Carl Worthington. And Chicago had Herb Cooper.

When I walked into Cooper & Sons Westside Auto Supply on Monday morning, my father was humping an ostrich. Someone had affixed a saddle to the ostrich's back, and Herb, who was wearing a white cowboy outfit complete with tengallon hat, chaps and spurs, was attempting to mount it. The ostrich had other ideas. Herb grabbed the bird's long neck and tried to throw one leg over it. The ostrich stepped lightly to its right, pivoted, and flipped Herb over its back.

"Ow! Goddammit!"

I fought back a wave of wooziness and silently counted to ten. I still struggled with the compulsion to damn things when people demanded it. If I hadn't curtailed the practice at some point during the Civil War, the whole country would have been damned before the Battle of Bull Run.

Chick Flaunt, Herb's second in command and co-star, sprang out of the aisle between GPS Options and Satellite Radios.

"Come on, Herbie! Get your bony butt up and tank that bird sonofabitch!"

Flaunt, a smallish barrel of a man, was wearing his "Old Elvis" costume: white spandex unitard with sequined armpit wings, oversized sunglasses, elevator shoes and plasticene black pompadour. The shiny hairpiece sat slightly askew atop Flaunt's actual hairpiece. As the camera crew dodged around them, Flaunt herded the ostrich toward Herb. Herb was on his hands and knees gasping for air.

"Herbie! Heads up!"

While long on personality, Herb was a deceptively small man. On a heavy day, after a weighty meal and a stroll through a pounding rainstorm, he topped the scale at a buck fifty. His balding pate shone through the thin spots in his dyed black hair, which he wore long, combed backward and slicked down to within an inch of its life. During his more frenetic commercials his hair would spring up around his head, the long comb-over bouncing furiously; a demented Cab Calloway in cowboy chaps. In another life he might have been one of the godfathers of rock & roll; a contemporary of Chuck Berry or Fats Domino. In this life, he was the lunatic who wrestled live anacondas on late night cable access.

"Herbie! We're burnin' daylight!"

Herb hopped to his feet and advanced, lunged, grabbed again for the ostrich's neck while trying to sling his leg over the saddle. The ostrich swung itself around, dragging Herb along, and whipped him across the room. Herb slammed into the vending machine and shattered the glass front, sprawling among the chocolaty treasures inside.

Flaunt threw an improvised "lasso" (an orange outdoor extension cord from the service center) over the ostrich's head. The ostrich chest butted him into the magazine rack. Issues of *Autotrader* flapped skyward.

"Hey!" I shouted. "Guys, wait!"

But both men leaped to their feet, Herb bleeding now from a shallow cut across his forehead.

"Flank him, Chick!"

"Yeah! Just like the 'Cong in the Ashau Valley! July 10th, 1969!"

Herb circled around behind the ostrich, who was rooting through a bucket of Puppy Chow. Flaunt countered, ducking and weaving like the referee of a crackhead kickfight.

"That's right, Herbie Boy! I'll get him on his blind side!"

They'd reconnected at a Republican VietNam veteran's reunion/gambling boat trip up the Mississippi River in 1982. After bonding over tales of their heroic exploits (which included dawn patrols in a Honolulu whorehouse), Herb invited Flaunt to help him run Cooper & Sons Automotive International LLC. They'd been best friends and conjoined pains in my posterior ever since.

"Flank him, Herbie! Flank his black ass good!"

Despite what some fundamentalists claim, I didn't hate anyone. When you've seen the ugly scars that mar the majority of mortal souls one is much the same as any other. But Chick Flaunt could rupture the patience of Job. My Old Testament Self would have gleefully burned him alive just to resurrect him and feed him to starving bears.

"That's it, Herbie! Now coldcock the bastard!"

Sensing its imminent violation, the ostrich hissed and raised one massively muscled foot, its killing claws extended. A healthy adult male ostrich can weigh over two hundred pounds, run at thirty miles per hour, and gut a lion with one kick. Herb and Flaunt tensed for one final, mutually destructive pounce.

"Stop!"

Herb glared at me. Flaunt scowled, one oily lock of his Elvis pompadour dangling between his eyes. The ostrich glanced over at me, its deadly foot held at the ready.

"You know these people?"

"Yes. They're harmless."

"I don't believe you."

"You're right. They're idiots."

"I don't have to put up with this. I've done television."

"Why don't you take five?" I said. "I'll smooth their feathers."

The ostrich – whose name was Sauwk – hissed a reluctant assent, and spread its wings in a threat posture intended mostly to intimidate. The big bird was exhausted. I sympathized: long experience with Herb and his passions could wear down the Rock of Gibraltar. I stroked his neck while silently appealing to his professionalism with compliments and offers of future employment.

"Hey, Jacques Cousteau, why don't you marry the bastard if you love it so much?"

Do it. Reverse his digestive system. No one will notice.

I untwisted the orange extension cord dangling from Sauwk's neck and invited him to enjoy more Puppy Chow. Sauwk released six eggsized fecal pellets in Herb's general direction and strutted back to his food bucket.

"What'd ya have to stick your nose in it for?" Flaunt sneered. "Herbie and me would've got the situation under control just fine without you, Mister Save the Whales."

"You know, Chick, if you're trying to insult someone, pointing out their better qualities is pointless unless you're trying to make them feel really great."

"Oooohhh, somebody flunked out of his fancy graduate school. Hey, Emily Post, how 'bout pitchin' yerself into that saddle? Then Herb can ride you around for the commercial!"

Flaunt laughed in the irritating way he did when he thought he'd scored a point. I reconsidered burning him alive just to make a bigger one.

"We're doing a new spot for the website," Herb said. "That damn pelican has thrown us off schedule. We're gonna have to do it tomorrow: I got meetings."

"Hey, Pop. Can I borrow some money?"

"Jesus H The Christ," Flaunt moaned. "Kids today, ingrates... every one of 'em. Hell I remember..."

"Give him a break, Chick."

"Herbie this kid's had more 'breaks' than a mirror with a million cracks. Back in the day..."

"Chick..."

"...my old man would'a kicked my ass harder than Chinese algebra. I mean if you ask me..."

"I didn't ask you, Chick!"

Flaunt threw up his hands in a "why do I bother" flutter of exasperation, his Elvis pompadour flapping like a detached scalp. Then he turned on one elevated heel and stomped off to annoy the camera crew.

Herb turned back to me, shaking his head.

"I suppose I'll be paying for that till Judgement Day. Why the hell do you need money?" (Herb could switch conversational gears faster than a newly-avowed lesbian at a Texas prolife rally.) "Don't I pay you enough to mismanage this place?"

"I want to take Surabhi somewhere special Friday night. But I need a minor advance."

"Hey! You thinking about poppin' the question, son?"

"Well…"

"You are, aren't you? You're gonna ask Sonoma–"

"Her name is Surabhi for the seventy-eighth time this week. And there's not going to be any wedding."

Herb's face fell. "No wedding?"

Herb loved the institution of marriage. That was the problem: he loved the institution more than the woman he married. He could also smell imminent weddings and pregnancies like a bloodhound on the hunt.

"I see," he sighed, laying a smallish hand on my elbow. "Step into my office, son. Time you and me talked mano to mano."

"I have to watch the front desk. The customers…"

"What customers? We don't open till ten."

"But…"

"Come on."

We entered the Fortress of Gratitude: Herb believed that every employee who entered his office should do so with "An Attitude of Gratitude." He'd even had the words inscribed on a little plaque on the wall behind his big mahogany desk; right between his autographed poster of Ronald Reagan and the life-sized standup of himself dressed as "Super Herb."

"Sit."

I sat in the small chair in front of his desk. Herb rifled through his drawers and came up with a wrapped sandwich.

"You hungry?"

"No thanks." Two days after the fight with Zeus, the thought of food still made me slightly delirious.

"You look like a damn scarecrow. You need to eat if you're ever going to get your full growth."

Herb munched thoughtfully on his turkey and tomato wrapped in lettuce. He'd been on a low-carb diet for half a decade. Because of long-term glycogen deprivation he was sometimes subject to erratic behavior. Sometimes, at night I would catch him waltzing with a box of Raisin Bran, crooning "I'm gonna eat you. Oh yes… I'm gonna… eeeat…"

"Lando Cooper… I know who you really are."

"What?"

"The jig is up, son. I've uncovered your big, cosmic secret."

He chuckled again, his eyes round with a kind of conspiratorial wonder. "God Almighty."

From my dimensionally sensitive multi-mind, several Aspects tossed up suggestions.

Sky Daddy: "Rewrite his memory."

Father Flies: "Erase him from the spacetime continuum."

Burning Bush: "Give him a stroke, then if he recovers you can tell him it was all a hallucination."

"If you think I haven't been paying attention, son… you're wrong." Herb reached up with one mayonnaise smeared finger and tapped his right temple. "These eyes don't miss a trick. As a student of the Human Animal… I see all."

Herb arched his brows. "Look at me, Lando. Look me in the eye when I'm talking to you."

"I am looking at you."

"No you're not."

"I am."

"Unflinchingly?"

"You're insane."

Herb stood. "Lando… a steady, unflinching gaze…"

"'…establishes interpersonal tactical dominance.' I know, Pop."

"That's Herb's Rule of Engagement Numero Uno, son. First thing any effective negotiator learns… if he intends to make something of himself someday."

"I'm not interested, Pop."

"Lando, I know that you're struggling with certain elements of your personality. And although I don't claim to understand it…"

"Pop, I just want to borrow some cash."

"Son… you're gay."

"Pop."

"It's OK, Lando."

"I'm not gay."

"Well I think you are."

"I am not."

"Admit it now. Get it off your chest."

"No."

"Denial. That's sad, boy."

"I'm not gay!"

"Twenty-first century, son. Liberation done come to de plantation. I may not approve of your lifestyle, but I'll die to support you. That's why we all marched, back in the Sixties…"

"Pop…"

"…why my generation took to the streets while 'Mister Charlie' was burning school children and night-bombing churches…"

"You're ridiculous."

"I marched so that you and your brothers could be as irresponsible as the White Man's children…"

"I'm not doing this with you, Pop."

"…waste your lives in whatever meaningless pursuits you see fit, no matter how much it might break the hearts of those who sang freedom songs while Klansmen hounded us with dogs and torches."

"Torches? Were they chasing black people or Frankenstein's monster?"

Herb chuckled again. "Deflect and Distract: another useful negotiating strategy. When you take over the store…"

"I'm not taking over the store, Pop."

"…when you take over from your ailing old man, you'll have to be strong, son. Stronger than those early pioneers."

Herb reached into his pocket and produced a thickish wad of cash from the billfold he'd had surgically grafted to his hip. He thumbed through the wad and peeled five one hundred dollar bills.

"I want you to take Sabrina out Friday night. Show her a good time. Grab a hotel room in the Loop. Do the deed, for Christ's sake. You're not still a virgin are you?"

"No! Not that it's any of your business."

Herb held up his hand. "Just be sure to take your gal out for a 'test drive'. Nobody wants you puttin' your money down on the wrong horse. You know… genderwise. One thing about me and your mother… we were sexual dynamite."

"Awkward for me, but thanks for spoiling my appetite."

A glint of calculation ignited in Herb's eyes. "So when are we gonna meet this 'young lady' of yours?"

"Soon," I said, relieved that I wouldn't have to excise him from the spacetime continuum. "I gotta get back to work. Inventory today."

"Hmmm, yes. Interesting concept: inventory."

I reached over and grabbed for the money. Herb yanked his hand back.

"Lando, you know if there's ever anything you need to get off your chest, you can always come to me, right?"

"I know."

"I'm much more open than your mother. God knows how we ever produced four healthy sons..."

"Pop, please."

"Sorry. It's just, living like we do... well things with Mom and Dad aren't as rosy as they seem."

"Rosy's not the word that springs to mind."

Herb smiled. But a flicker of sadness glimmered in his eyes.

"True, son. Very true."

He extended the handful of bills toward me again. I reached for it, and he jerked his hand back once more as if he'd just snatched it out of a furnace.

"How about you mow the lawn Saturday morning?"

"Pop..."

"Come on now. I pay you for working here to show you the value of a buck, not to take the honeys out for a tour of Boy's Town."

"On what you pay me, 'Boy's Town' would have to be the size of a postage stamp."

"Hey, any time free room and board get too rough for your delicate sensibilities..."

"Alright... I'll mow the lawn."

"Front and back?"

"Yes!"

"And clean the mower blades?"

"I could strangle you."

"Excellent. Nothing in life sweeter than a 'twofer', son. That's..."

"I know: 'Twice the goods and/or services for half the price'."

"Damn right. Well? Get back to work."

I remembered my promise to intercede on Sauwk's behalf.

"Why an ostrich?"

Herb shrugged. "The elephant was double booked."

"The ostrich won't let you ride, Pop. He's got arthritis."

"Really?"

"Yup. Why not try letting Chick try to lasso it in the background while you riff in the foreground? That way you get to improvise, and the audience gets a twofer."

At the word "improvise" Herb's face brightened. He was a frustrated actor who fancied himself a master of improvisation. If he hadn't feared what he called "… an actor's life, filled with uncertainty" he would have auditioned for Second City. That and his polite phobia of Jews kept him from pursuing a career in show business.

"You're right. Ostriches are funny without having to try."

"Alright."

"And Chick and I can riff till the cows come home. People love it when we riff. That'll help him pull his panties out of his ass."

Herb picked up the office phone and dialed Flaunt's extension. As I headed for the door to the Fortress of Gratitude, he called out to my retreating back.

"Have fun with Susanna, son. Loosen up a little."

"OK, Pop."

"And get a haircut. You look like a goddamn spear chucker."

I pocketed the money and hurried back to work.

CHAPTER IV
ARCHANGEL

At noon, I took an early lunch and headed for Chicago Kutz, a barbershop I had avoided since returning home from Northwestern. But I'd decided to take Herb's advice: the 'fro was getting a little unruly.

Surabhi and I had been dating seriously for nearly two years. We'd met during a jazz appreciation concert series at Northwestern. The attraction was immediate, the chemistry undeniable. However, I was housebound, still at the mercy of my parents' escalating war of words. The atmosphere at home was toxic to a burgeoning romance. And since Surabhi shared her small apartment with her younger sister, we had no safe place to go when we wanted to be alone.

I had, of course, experimented with women on the road. A sexual darkhorse, I lost my virginity when I was twenty years old. But my less than imposing stature and sub-standard physique had made successfully wooing conscious women fairly uncommon.

Let's face it: the irony of my particular situation is that I could "seduce" any woman on the planet, if I were as psychotic as some of my colleagues. Many mortals long to offer themselves to their gods. Zeus ravaged thousands of females, human and otherwise, before he retired to Milwaukee.

The Morrigan, Celtic goddess of war and sex, nearly killed Ireland's greatest mortal hero, Cuchulainn, for refusing her untimely advances. Since she'd appeared to him during a pitched battle, clothed in her ugliest Aspect, a reasonable deity might assume a modicum of understanding on her part. But this was not the case: the Morrigan's rampant horniness nearly caused the extinction of the Irish race. I've had to speak to her about it at several Conventions. Last year she chased Shango the West African Thunder God into the men's room at the Boca Raton Days Inn. The two of them nearly reflooded the Gulf Coast. On my last custodial visit I'd barely escaped with my life. I was twenty-three that hot summer, and although the Morrigan is one of the sexiest immortals in existence, she scared the crap out of me. Currently she's a short, dowdy redhead with thick ankles living in South Boston. She remains unapologetic.

As I walked through the door of Chicago Kutz, my heart was thrashing like an overactive ferret, my mind flashing through a sweaty laundry list of the things I planned to do with Surabhi in our lovers' suite at the Four Seasons. Beneath my admittedly turgid exterior there thrummed a brief but intense lifetime of frustrated sensuality bursting to express itself.

"Well, I'll be damned!" a big voice boomed. "Is that Young Billy Dee struttin' through my door?"

Lumbering toward me across the haircovered floor was the loudest mortal I knew.

"Look at that head. Man, you look like a damn spear chucker!"

Beaufort "BoomBoom" Biggs was exactly that. He was immense in every way a big thing can be. One of his hands could envelop the top of a normal man's head. At exactly seven feet tall, he weighed three hundred and seventy pounds, most of it muscle covered by a thickening layer of fat. He'd played as a defensive lineman for the Chicago Bears back in the late Seventies, helping his teammates to a historic win during Superbowl X. An avid chef, BoomBoom had used his NFL earnings to buy out the Jigaboos family restaurant chain that dotted the Midwest until the early Eighties. By the early twenty-first century, BoomBoom's Bigghouse soulfood restaurants had given Type 2 diabetes and hypertension to legions of fat-happy Midwesterners.

BoomBoom had even done a commercial for my father; the one in which Herb, wearing a Chicago Bears jersey, helmet and shoulder pads, stands on the fifty yard line at Soldier's Field during a game between the Bears and the Cleveland Browns, and proclaims, "I'm so crazy about my customers I'll take a tackle from BoomBoom Biggs to prove it!" As Herb was rolled off the field to the thunderous appreciation of twelve thousand screaming fans, a guilty BoomBoom had accompanied him all the way to the ambulance. Five fractured ribs and a collapsed lung later, the two had become fast friends. When Herb learned that Biggs occasionally dabbled in local community theater, their fates were officially conjoined.

"Damn shame lettin' your hair get that messy," BoomBoom hollered. "How you expect people to take you seriously with hair like that?"

"Whaddup, BoomBoom?" His criticism was light artillery compared to the emotional massacre that was Life on the Cooper Plantation. "How's that last stomach staple holdin' up?"

"Uh oh," one of Kutz's barbers snarked. "Showtime."

Like most Southside barbershops, Kutz was a place where verbal jousting was the price of admission; where jabs were traded and not only hair got cut. At Kutz, the big dogs ran the show, and BoomBoom Biggs was the biggest dog in town. But fortunately for me, I was raised by wolves.

"Oh, wait a minute now," BoomBoom thundered. "You wanna play the Dozens, Billy Dee? You're messin' with the master!"

"Looks like the only thing you've 'mastered' is a knife and fork. Call me when you master some situps!"

This evoked a shout of approval from the customers. Ol' Luke, BoomBoom's oldest employee and neighborhood instigator, shuddered like a man caught in a violent icestorm.

"Ooh, he got you right out the gate, Beaufort! Young Billy Dee came in swingin'!"

"Least I had a six-pack, once," BoomBoom crowed, flexing his still massive biceps. "Man, don't you know you're looking at the first man in Chicago to deadlift five hundred pounds? Ask your mama: she's still got my fingerprints on her butt!"

The bystanders howled. "Now that was ugly!"

I was about to launch into a rant about the Bigghouse's high customer mortality rate when reality ripped itself apart.

The rupture started in the mirror right behind BoomBoom; glowing concentric circles spreading like ripples across a quiet lake. Then a pale hand as large as a minivan reached out of the mirror and passed, wraithlike, through BoomBoom's body. If it had been "real" in any corporeal sense, BoomBoom would have been skewered by a forefinger the length of a stop sign. As it was, nobody noticed. The finger stopped a few inches from my face. The nail was black, and covered with shooting stars.

"I've been looking for you."

Tremors rattled through the sub-atomic structure of the barber shop. I was having a hard time pretending not to notice. The regulars were cackling and elbowing each other: BoomBoom must have let off a hot one. But my rejoinder would have to wait.

"My God," the Voice trumpeted. **"For a decade have I searched! Finally I am rewarded for my unflagging service!"**

The voice was cold, its timbre unfamiliar. The arrogance however, was not.

Oh no. Not him.

"What do you want?"

"Let the trumpets sound! For Holy! Holy! Holy! is the Presence of the Lord!"

The giant hand withdrew back into the mirror, and the ripples of shredded reality healed themselves with a million sizzling snaps as the blare of a thousand trumpets announced to the universe that my day was about to slide down the toilet.

There came a blinding flash, the resonance of a million throats serenading me... well the former me. When my vision cleared I saw that everything had stopped: BoomBoom and Old Luke stood, immobilized in mid laugh. The regulars hovered, trapped between moments. I glanced at the digital clock on the wall: its readout flickered, held in still-time like a fly in amber. Whoever the intruder was, he or she was a Power; someone with lots of heavenly capital to spend and no conscience.

The visitor stepped out of the glow, its shining face averted at just the right angle of prideful deference. It was one of the heavy hitters alright: an archangel. And not just any garden variety archangel either.

"Gabriel. What are you doing here?"

Gabriel had clothed itself in a synthetic human seeming, male and icily perfect. In this body, he was over six feet tall, long limbed and athletically slender. A cascade of curly black hair surrounded silver eyes as bright as a winter lightning strike. Full black lips accented fatal cheekbones and a lantern jaw. Lush, white wings flickered in and out of visibility at his muscular shoulders.

"Eternal Master," Gabriel breathed. **"At last."**

The Angel of the Morning dropped to one perfect knee and bowed his head.

"Damn it."

"Damn what, my Lord? Only show me the soul to be damned and I will carry it to Hell myself!"

"Why have you interrupted my sabbatical, Gabriel? I left strict instructions not to be disturbed."

Gabriel looked up at me from beneath his midnight tresses. The cosmic devotion shining from his eyes was enough to turn my stomach.

"You must return, Lord. You are needed."

Gabriel floated across the room, hovering between the beats of a nanosecond as he shimmered through a myriad potential shapes: one moment an elemental spirit wrapped within its throbbing halo, the next a darkling cloud of electrons whirling about a sunbright core, the next a luminous winged humanoid armed with a shining sword.

Two things people don't know about angels: one, they experience the entirety of their physical existence simultaneously; somatically linked to their future and past selves, they can read a limited distance into their own future or peer into their distant past. Two, I didn't make them. Well, "I" did, in the sense that all consciousness is the by-product of universes: you, your dog... and most empirically... me. Universal consciousness evolves as its observers develop more complex methods to perceive it. Mortal sentience arises from a universe's need to understand itself. But Immortal consciousness arises from humanity's need to control an unpredictable universe. Humans identify patterns in order to master their surroundings. Sometimes those patterns are useful.

For example...

But many times the patterns humans intuit are wildly unreliable.

And when human survival dictated that mortals believe the universe answers to them, they tapped into the Eshuum and defined their gods. Gods then channeled the cosmic power of the evolving universe to forward human agendas like sex, inter-tribal conquest, sex, religious warfare, sex, incest, incestuous sex, genocide, and sex.

Angels, however, exist outside this eternal cycle of creation/awareness/destruction. Each one is a cosmic singularity, and all of them, all nine million of them, are utterly devoted to me. And before you stop to wonder if such devotion is a good thing: Imagine yourself as Daniel Gallagher, Michael Douglas' character in *Fatal Attraction*. Now imagine Alex Forrest (Glenn Close), only immortal and able to travel vast distances in the blink of an eye. Now imagine all those psychotic demi-divinities violently in love… with you. Finally, remember that there are precisely nine million of them. Angels: cosmic pains in My All Powerful Arse.

"What's the problem, Gabriel?"

Gabriel's lightning-hued eyes darkened, but only for a moment.

"I understand, Lord! You question me to encourage me to think, that I might grasp Thy Will, and my place within It."

Gabriel's brow furrowed with angelic cogitation.

"You want me to choose which aspect of the problem is most pressing, thereby revealing some unfathomed aspect of my spiritual state and illuminating my destiny in ways which reflect Your unrelenting omniscience!"

Never question an angel when it believes you know all the answers. The resulting mental vaporlock could outlast an ice age.

"Exactly. Tell me."

"An Incursion, Lord. In Rome. The worst in a millennium. Thousands injured." Gabriel cackled, gleefully rubbing his hands together like a cub scout warming himself over a campfire. **"At least ten thousand mortals have died horribly."**

Another angelic fact: angels only help humans because I conscripted them into my service. Without the devotion they feel toward me, most wouldn't urinate on a burning nun. Angels believe themselves the only beings in all of Creation worthy of God's attention.

Gabriel averted his eyes. But I didn't need godlike perspective to mark the ugly smirk on his beautiful face.

"Well?"

"Well what, Lord?"

"Who is it?"

My headache, a dull throb after my duel with Zeus only two days ago, was ramping itself up to a shrill pounding; a sure sign that something was happening.

"The name, Gabriel."

"Ah! It's Hannibal, Lord. The GodKing of the Carthaginians. He's already gutted half of Rome and is marching on the Vatican even as we speak. All of which you already know, of course."

"Of course."

"I have the answer, Lord! The 'problem', as you put it, is complex in its scope and manifold in its severity. But I have sounded it to a suitable depth to answer your challenge."

"Perfect. And... your conclusion?"

"Hannibal has mounted a mighty army of the dead to assault the mortal pontiff. Five thousand Nubians, seven thousand Carthaginian revenants, a thousand zombies, a thousand undead elephants! Forgive me, Mighty One. I know you know these things, so I will be brief. Hannibal sent a message. Shall I...?"

"Go on."

Gabriel squared his shoulders and shook the hair out of his perfect eyes. (Did I mention that he was naked? All angels love to display their perfection. Gabriel shone with the energies of the universe, statuesque and perfectly androgynous, the joining at his inner thighs as smooth as a baby's butt.) He cleared his throat and unruffled his spectral wings.

"Hannibal, Scourge of Rome and Terror of Nations, bids me offer the God of the Israelites a warning: 'I have come to exact my vengeance on the Mothering Whore that is Roma. Roma, that festering gash from whence flows every corruption, every vice and foul perversion; Roma, that fountain of false piety whose every spurt fills the world with lies; Roma, the Shuddering Ram whose every thrust impregnates the world with—'"

"I get it. Go on."

"'If the God of the Christians dares to show his scruffy beard anywhere in the vicinity of my conquest I will eviscerate his followers everywhere they cry his name. I will lay siege to the gates of his heaven and drag him screaming through its golden streets. Tell him, Gabriel. Tell him, it's Hannibal Time."

"'Hannibal Time'?"

"Aye, Lord. Hannibal has been researching contemporary society from his demesne in Hell, and prides himself on his crossover appeal. He believes that his defeat of the papists will usher in a new era of enlightenment with himself as its godhead."

The intensity of my headache kicked up a notch, and from somewhere in my subconscious I heard them: thousands of prayers filtering up from my subconscious. Soon the pressure would be unbearable.

"Take me to Rome, Gabriel."

"But, Lord… surely you are already there!"

"Now, Gabriel."

Gabriel bowed his head, spread his wings…

…and…

…cold pummels my flesh, flays my skin with daggers of ice. My lungs kick as the air inside my body tries to escape into the vacuum of lethal velocity. Gabriel has plunged us directly into the void of voids; the no-place from which all Creation sprang. But the cold and lack of oxygen can kill me. I sense the aura of divinity humming around Gabriel and sink tendrils of thought into its pulsing vitality. With the divinity I still possess, I wrap Gabriel's aura around myself and hang on for dear life.

"Traitor."

The abandoned lifeforce that haunts these void-spaces whispers my secret names as we streak through its black potential. It sings a song of welcome and rebuke. Its song is distracting, beautiful… lethal…

"Why did you forsake me?"

…but ignoring the universal lifeforce is like arguing with an angry parent: its anger penetrates my defenses.

Surabhi.

No. I've done enough. I'm owed one human life and I mean to live it before I return to the void. It's worth a near death event to see my Plan come to fruition. I only have to survive the next twenty seconds. But in the Big Empty time loses direction; distances become meaningless.

A long time ago, in a galaxy where all the single ladies live…

Nanoseconds stretch toward eternity, atoms shuck their nuclei and party like it's 1984, tearing at Gabriel's defenses… at me…

Ask not what you can do unto others…

…pulling me apart/pushing me together, stretching my purely subjective reality like superstrings made from Laffy Taffy…

…but what others can dobeedoodadaaayyyy…

I am streaking through the void, snuggled inside shimmering fragments of Gabriel's aurastreaminglike theglowingarmsof-somepressuresuckingseacreature… and… **this**

is

what

an

archangel

really

…looks like; a mass of coruscating tendrils laced with electric venom, streaming in the cosmic winds – oh Hell I'm getting poetic I'm dying dying dying in the absence of too much darkness can't breathe have to…

Hold on.

It's too much. I need power if I'm going to survive this brief journey through Eternity.

Just enough… to… grab… to reach… hold on…

I reach into the void, open my mind to the shimmering remnants of godforce that was me. That power sings to me, and its voice is the voice of All.

"I AM ALONE."

I reach for the power, just enough to protect me. But...

"Betrayer."

...pain detonates in my head. Crimson fire whipsaws through my brain and lights up my world in Fourth of July skybursts of red wrath.

"You were All. Now you are Nothing."

A brilliant red forbidding fills up my senses, blinds my ears and deafens my eyes. And the power, my power, speaks with a stranger's voice.

"Once-God, you stand at the Moment Before. Soon, the One Who Was must fall before me."

"No! Stop!"

"Human. Yet still you fight."

The voice in the whirlwind laughs. It is hard, male and female, ancient and filled with the arrogance of youth, scorching my flesh with Winter's deepest breath.

"Your services are no longer required, once-God," the voice says. **"I'm here."**

And we're there.

Rome is burning, its towers and cathedrals collapsing before the forces of chaos. Through a haze of pain and the thundering of my heart, I smell smoke. I can hear the screams of thousands of terrified people echoing all around me.

"Get out of the way!"

"Run!"

"Not that way!"

The wail of sirens overrides the voices; the earth beneath me shakes.

"Elephants!"

"Elephants in the Vatican!"

People are stampeding past me, moving in a living wave away from a line of massive shapes lumbering out of the billowing black clouds. A man dragging a screaming woman and a bloody-faced teenager slams into me and knocks me down. The impact restores my mortal perceptions. Time flips itself inside out... and...

I fell to the concrete and was immediately kicked in the butt. Someone stumbled over my feet and fell on top of me. The person quickly rolled away, an obese American tourist wearing an I Luv Texas T-shirt. The T-shirt featured the Texas state flag, a gun and a bible.

"Run, you fool! It's Al Quaeeeda!"

The sounds of chaos doubled in volume. More people stumbled over me and fell to the ground. Close by, a young woman fell beneath the scrambling crowd. The fat Texan stepped on her. I heard the snap as her knee broke.

Gotta find Hannibal.

I climbed to my feet, struggling to get my bearings. But the smoke and chaos were all consuming. I had no idea where to start.

"At last, my vengeance is complete."

The voice was cold, heavily accented. I looked up in time to see a golden god float out of the black smoke.

"Well, this is going to be easier than I thought."

Hannibal of Carthage smiled, a wolf's grin, a ghoul's leer. Then he raised his sword.

CHAPTER V
WHEN IN ROME, KILL THE POPE

In life, Hannibal Barca, son of Hamilcar, was a great Carthaginian warlord. He drove a massive war party across the Pyrenees and the Alps to sack northern Italy during the Second Punic War. He brought fire and bloodshed and the fear of invasion to the invincible Roman Empire. Hannibal was finally defeated by Scipio Africanus only after occupying great tracts of Italy for nearly fifteen years. Along with Alexander the Great and Julius Caesar, he attained immortal glory as one of the greatest military strategists of all time. He was a fierce warrior and widely feared homicidal maniac. Now, here he loomed, his lust for vengeance shimmering around him like heat haze off hot blacktop.

Thick, curly black hair framed his wolfish face. His skin, once browned by a thousand campaigns fought beneath sunny Mediterranean skies, now held the pallor of death: after two millennia in Hades he hadn't gotten much in the way of sunlight. Even so, long, rangy muscles knotted and clenched along his wiry frame. His breastplate flashed in the dying sunlight: the golden eagle of the Phoenicians, wings spread, rampant in horror and victory. The scimitar he gripped in his fists looked long enough to gut a narwhal. From where I knelt shuddering in the dust, he looked seventeen feet tall. But as the smoke cleared, I saw that he stood astride a shaggy African bull elephant as big as a mastodon.

"Rome trembles before me," Hannibal crowed. "Trembles!"

A tight knot of media people had gathered behind me. Reporters, cameramen and women following Hannibal's every move, shouting questions. "Who are you?" "What do you want?"

Hannibal turned and glared down at the reporters. He hadn't spotted me. I was safe for the moment.

"Hello! Fancy meeting you in a place like this!"

Then his elephant recognized me.

"Pleasure. Would you mind ignoring me? I'm a little busy at the moment.

"You don't look quite as I'd imagined," the elephant said.

"I get that a lot."

"Frankly I was expecting something more... elephantish. Name's Persi by the way. Short for Perthon. And I'm actually one-quarter mastodon. Thanks for noticing."

A phalanx of undead Gallic mercenaries swept out of the chaos, their swords swinging as they drove frightened mortals ahead of them, slaughtering some, wounding others. Thankfully, no one seemed to notice me: the presence of the undead mastodon created a no go zone around which streamed mortal survivors and their undead pursuers; an island of relative calm just wide enough for me to collect my wits. I got to my feet, wincing at the thunderclap of pain in my head.

"The game has changed, Yahweh. You've been shut out."

It sounded like the voice that had spoken out of the voidspace during my flight through the Eshuum. But if that were true, it meant that the intruder had taken control of some portion of the power of Creation without my full abdication. That had never happened before.

Beware. The Coming stalks us all.

Hannibal whirled his right arm over his head and brought it down with a violent, chopping motion. A sound similar to a gunshot tore the air, followed by what I can only describe as a wet explosion. When he drew back his arm, I saw the cat-o'-nine tails dangling from his fist; a long, leather handle with five steel-tipped claws arrayed at the end of a length of rawhide. The godking of Carthage whirled the cat around his head and flung it forward with an evil snap!

Glowing with stolen divinity, the tails of the cat flung themselves in several directions at once, each one striking a fleeing survivor. When they connected with living flesh, the effect was spectacular: his target exploded in a red spray of smashed bones and flying organs. Hannibal's weapon moved with the speed and ferocity of a demonic daisy-cutter. Wherever he cast his tails, people blew up.

"You needlessly prolong your own suffering!" he thundered. "Bring me the rutting child-diddlers who run this whore's nest and I will grant you peace!"

His voice dwarfed the scream of the sirens. Fleeing mortals covered their ears as they fled before him: he was speaking in a Voice, somehow augmented to near divinity.

"Since our deaths, the master has been quite diligent in plotting his revenge."

It was Persi, the quarter-mastodon. Hannibal was busily roaring at a knot of cowering tourists, thereby giving his mount a break.

"But how did he become a god?"

"Actually, he's more avatar than god. Friends in high places, if you gather my meaning."

The reporters surged around me, fighting to get closer to Hannibal: "Are you associated with the Taliban?"

"What's your name?"

"Are you Pro-life?"

"Who are you wearing?"

Hannibal smirked. "Who is seeing this?"

One woman, a tall brunette with a deep tan and dynamite cleavage, stepped forward. I moved closer, melting into the crowd. My lungs were burning and my head was screaming at me to find a quiet place to lie down.

"Everyone with access to a television or the internet can see these images," the buxom reporter said, her voice low, her accent northern Italian. Hannibal nodded and eyed the busty brunette appreciatively at the same time.

"Everyone, eh?" Then he raised his voice and addressed the cameras. "My name is Hannibal Barca, of Carthage, Phoenicia and Ibaria. I have fought my way out of a thousand Hells, crossed oceans of Time, even as I once crossed treacherous mountain ranges: with the thrust of my unbreakable will."

The quarter-mastodon shook his head and rolled his eyes, his great ears flapping like leathery fans. "Name's Persi by the way. Short for Perthon. Can you believe him? Seven of us were along on that last crossing. He drove my herdmates to their deaths, the selfish bastard."

"I am come to do violence on this den of thieves,"

Hannibal cried. "After a thousand mortal lifetimes I am come to claim Rome, in the name of my father, Hamilcar the Great, my brother Hasdrubal the Fierce, and my first cousin Hamadul the Unkempt. I come in the name of the People of Carthage!"

The reporters stared. The paparazzi and their camera crews stared. Finally, an old Italian woman who lay on the ground clutching her broken ankle broke the silence.

"What the hell is he talking about?"

The busty brunette stepped forward and thrust a microphone up toward Hannibal.

"Contessa Rosellini, CNN. Are you claiming that you're not a terrorist?"

Hannibal smirked, even while his eyes did their best to pierce Rosselini's blouse. "To the whoremasters of Rome, signora... I am terror."

This sent an awkward pulse through the survivors. A pudgy reporter in a pink suit stepped forward. "What cell are you associated with?"

"Cell?" Hannibal barked. "Hell has been my prison cell for longer than you can imagine!"

"No no," the pudgy reporter snipped. "Cell... as in terrorist sleeper cell. Which one are you working with?"

"I knew it. He's a Muslim!" the old woman with the broken ankle shouted. "Look at that curly hair, the swarthy complexion!"

A British tourist, who was trying to staunch the blood pouring from a gash in her husband's forehead, spoke up.

"He looks Italian to me."

"Italian? Where are your brains, slut? Look at those shifty eyes. He's an Arab!"

"Or a Jew!" someone among the reporters piped in.

"He could be an Israeli. Look at that hooked nose."

"That's anti-semitic!" a bearded man standing next to me barked. "You're all racists!"

The discussion erupted into a shouting match, most of it centered around which objectionable ethnicity the man on the mastodon might or might not claim. The reporters edged in closer, trying to out-shout each other, thrusting their microphones up at Hannibal.

"So," the quarter-mastodon sighed. "Taking a break from running the Universe?"

My head was throbbing like a banshee in menopause. My chest was tightening with every breath and I was still unable to access the Eshuum. "Something like that."

"Lovely. Everyone needs to get away every now and again. I remember when my cow and kids and I stormed Trebia. This was before Trasimene. I lost my cousin Sathanat and six herdmates at Trasimene. Terrible war. But in Trebia we trampled hundreds."

"Good times."

"Wonderful times! First real holiday I'd had in thirty years. I remember the first time we trampled some Romans…"

I tuned out the rest of Persi's story: Hannibal was enjoying the heated looks coming from some of the women, and not a few of the men who still lived. But soon he would tire of the attention and people would start dying again. And I still couldn't connect to the power.

Just then, six armored North African warriors trotted out of the smoke dragging a filthy old woman behind them.

"Master of Men! The Vatican burns. The Whore's armies flee in terror before our forces. We have taken our vengeance!"

Hannibal smiled. His chin jutted even further, straining the tendons in his neck as he turned to the cameras and roared.

"Victory over our enemies! The Whore has fallen!"

The silence was deafening. Then questions peppered the smoky air. "Who is this psycho?" "Why are those Arabs dressed that way?" "What's with all the elephants?"

"All in good time, my new subjects. All your questions shall be answered… in Hannibal Time."

Hannibal turned to his lieutenants. "I see you have brought my quarry, General Rashid."

General Rashid, a huge Nubian with shoulders like boxcars, grabbed the dirty old woman by the scruff of her filthy robes, eyeing the cameras as he spoke.

"Great One, we caught this cur trying to escape with several of his vassals. We slew them most atrociously. I have brought their leader to you for disposal."

"Oops," Persi the quarter-mastodon fluted. "Sounds like a trampling. That's my department. If you could do something about my people's plight I'd be most obliged. We've been enslaved for millennia and a few of us are starting to get a little anxious… if you take my meaning."

The dirty old woman raised her head, and I saw that she was a man; a very old man with dirt in his teeth.

"Ah," Hannibal stage whispered. "And now the foul head of the ancient serpent turns its cataracts to me."

The dirty old man climbed painfully to his feet. Eying the cameras, he squared his shoulders, took a deep breath and said, "I see."

"What do you see, O leader of a dead faith? Do you see the coming of the true Messiah? Hannibal of the Winding Ways! Heart-render and Loin-piercer! Do you see me?"

The reporters swiveled their cameras and microphones toward the dirty old man.

"What is this delusion that speaks out of thin air?" the Pope wheezed. I'd recognized him by his thick Irish brogue. And the phlegm. "I see nothing."

Hannibal snarled. "What?"

The Pope lifted one palsied hand to his ear. "Is someone speaking? I seem to hear a buzzing about my ears. Damned Italian fleas."

"Fleas?" Hannibal said. "Do you hear the Father of Deception, my friends? Rome burns. We undead have made a charnel pit of the Vatican: shattered her great beauty before the eyes of the world. Yet this ancient vampire denies what all can see with their own eyes!"

The reporters swiveled again. The abused Pontiff cleared his throat and spoke directly to the cameras.

"I see nothing."

An audible gasp went up from the milling survivors.

"Rome has been struck by a series of cataclysms. Earthquakes. Perhaps a biochemical attack that induces violent delusions. My sources within the Holy City inform me that several terrorist organizations have claimed responsibility for much of the violence. Rome has been attacked by anti-Catholic forces bent on destroying our way of life."

"Anti-Catholic forces?" Contessa Rossellini cried. "Are you talking about Islamic Jihad? Here in Rome?"

The Pope shrugged. "I'm talking about a terrorist attack, missy. One cleverly timed to coincide with some heretofore unrecognized natural disaster. Nothing more."

"Sword wielding assassins are running rampant through the streets of Rome," Rosellini shouted. "Isn't it ridiculous to deny something so obvious?"

"Your Holiness," the chubby reporter in the pink suit shouted. "What about the elephants?"

"Several zoos have reported break-ins. We believe the terrorists' plot involves using freed animals to create confusion in the streets."

"But some of the elephants are clearly dead, your Grace."

"Nonsense, my son. Those poor animals are obviously the victims of excessive sun exposure."

"'Sun exposure', your Holiness?"

"That's what I said, boyo. I'm sure that's what the Church's findings will be when these matters are resolved through the ongoing investigation which even now is... ongoing."

"But, your Holiness..."

"Or would you rather go on record as having questioned God's representative on Earth, and the judgment of the Holy Roman Catholic Church, thereby flouting the wisdom of the good people of Rome, every Catholic constituency in the free world and several hundred million of your own viewers?"

The chubby reporter looked away in shame.

"Good," Hannibal snapped. "Now that that's settled."

He uncurled the blood-drenched cat-o'-nine tails from where it lay curled in his lap. Its steel tipped claws clicked as they banged lightly against the quarter mastodon's knees.

"Bring him to me: I have papist pork to carve."

"I didn't hear that," the Pope sang. "Nope. Nothing supernatural happening here."

The Nubian warriors dragged the old man toward Hannibal.

I stepped forward. An undead legend beheading the sitting Pope before an international audience while Rome burned in the background might leave an indelible scar on the psychic flesh of human racial memory. Even a dimensional Reset might not be enough to heal the damage. Still, I had to try. I reached for the power…

But I was struck by a wave of nausea so intense that I nearly fainted. It felt as if a thin membrane had been drawn between my mind and the dimension the power occupied; the psychic interface hazy as a distant star glimpsed through brackish water.

"Swear your allegiance to your new master, false Pope. Swear allegiance to me, and perhaps I'll allow you to serve the men as my comfort wench."

"What's that?" the Pope said. "Is that someone speaking?"

Hannibal slid off the back of his mount and landed lightly as a gymnast. He sheathed his cat-o'-nine tails, drew a long-bladed knife from a scabbard on his hip and rammed it through the Pope's right shoulder.

"Can you hear me now?"

"An illusion!" the Pope gibbered, trying to staunch his gushing shoulder. "Some kind of psychosomatic stigmata brought on by atheist anti-Life, Jewish-Islamic extremists!"

Hannibal pulled his broadsword and raised it over the Pope's head. "Wrong answer."

The blade fell, whistling through the air, toward the Pope's defiant face.

"Gabriel!"

The Carthaginian's blade froze in midswing. Everything stopped as Gabriel appeared in front of me and the temporal anomaly that accompanied every angelic visitation dragged local spacetime to a halt.

"Yes, Mighty One?"

Everything would remain Stopped only for as long as Gabriel remained at my side. But the momentum of reality is so powerful that any substantive disruption of the spacetime continuum creates new problems: babies born before they were conceived; eggs hatched centuries after their descendants fertilized them... But how could I defeat Hannibal when I couldn't access my own divinity?

As I was considering the extremely limited list of responses, Hannibal's sword... moved.

"He's resisting."

"Resisting thy unassailable will, Lord?" Gabriel chuckled. **"You're testing me again, aren't you? Or perhaps you're assaying the infidelity of the big Mexican with the meat cleaver."**

"He's not Mexican. He's Carthaginian."

I could sense Hannibal marshalling energies destructive enough to undermine temporal forces he couldn't possibly have mastered. He was immobilized in time, but time was running out.

"I need Pluto."

"The planet?"

"No, you idiot. Pluto, the Roman God of the Dead."

"But, Lord, no pagan Death God has been active since–"

"Since they all agreed not to intervene in human affairs, yes I know. You have to go get him. Burbank. California. Check the Deadly Delights Horrorshop. He owns the place."

At least I hoped he still did. Pluto was notoriously anti-social. For all I knew he might have sold his specialty bookshop and relocated to Miami Beach. But his absence from Hades had allowed Hannibal to escape. I needed his power.

"You'll have to look for him under a different name. Greek, maybe Italian. I… Wait…"

There was a tremor in the fabric of spacetime, like the fibrillating heartbeat of a rogue quasar. The disruption was coming from Hannibal. He was glaring at me.

"You," he growled. "I… see… you!"

His eyes were alight, focused, his muscles straining with the effort of fighting through Gabriel's disruption.

"I… serve… I… serve… no god… but…"

I grasped for the dimension where my divinity reserves prowled… and felt the stirrings of power.

"Yes!"

I opened the interface, hoping for a glorious flood of force, and was rewarded with a halfhearted blurt of divinity. Not nearly enough.

Better call in a contractor.

Occasionally I could "farm out" certain incursion events to friendly deities with whom I maintained good working relations. The biggest challenge in choosing a contractor was choosing the right god for the job. Unfortunately, in Hannibal's case, I knew exactly who to call.

I cast my consciousness into the infinite, seeking the energies of the one I hoped could help. Hannibal was moving his other arm by then; twisting his right leg, driving the ball of his sandaled foot into the dirt, shifting his weight, turning toward me, his black-rimmed eyes glinting in Phoenician fury.

"I… serve… no god… but… but…!"

"What do you want, O tormentor of lonely hausfraus?"

The voice, so familiar from our meeting several summers earlier, was as luscious as I remembered.

"What's happening inside your pants?" Gabriel said.

I couldn't hide the prominent bulge that puffed out the front of my khakis. And the part of me that the newcomer was stimulating didn't want to. No. I wanted to find the first woman within spitting distance, throw her down on the ground and...

"Is that a shillelagh in your pants or are you just happy to see me?"

Even Hannibal seemed to sense the change: the air had just been electrified by a massive dose of predatory Female pheromones.

"I... need a favor. A contact..."

"Oh my."

"I mean a contract..."

Any woman would do. Old, ugly, too fat or skeleton thin...

"A contract... rebuking..."

The sultry female voice chuckled. My contractor was pouring it on a little thick, even for her.

"And are you willing to pay the price for my services?"

"I'll pay, M. Wait... what do... you want?"

"We both know what I want, God of ancient deserts."

I'd barely escaped from the clutches of this particular goddess at last year's convention. Shango of the West African Pantheon was still limping after their bathroom encounter. But I'd worry about the consequences later.

"Alright, just hurry!"

"Men," she sighed. **"You're all alike. Silly fookers."**

Lightning flickered in the west. Thunder rumbled overhead. My contractor was notoriously stingy when it came to her divinity, choosing to spend her most recent incarnation as a disembodied wraith lodged in the co-opted consciousness of a schizophrenic Boston-Irish romance writer. This allowed her some leeway when she chose to use her powers: maintaining a seeming required a continuous outpouring of divinity; it was expensive even for the most powerful gods. Riding along in the mind of a socially awkward manic-depressive allowed my colleague to save up for special occasions. And when it came to her dealings with men, the Morrigan was always up for a challenge.

"The covenant is made."

There was a flash of light, a crackle of electric sex.

"Hello, Yahweh."

For this "occasion" she'd chosen the seeming of a statuesque redhead with sparkling emerald eyes and enormous breasts. The Irish sex goddess had sheathed herself in a form-fitting green shift made from living lianas. A hazy emerald halo encircled her head, finding its verdant echo in her catlike eyes. Her skin was radiant and smooth, tanned without freckle or blemish. Her hair, a deep red that alternated between the last flare of sunlight and the flash of autumn leaves, writhed of its own accord, as if she hovered within a plane without gravity. I crossed my legs. No man, regardless of his sexual orientation, could behold the Morrigan in her finest rags and not be instantly enflamed.

The Irish goddess of Love, Sex and War floated across the smoking plain and hovered a few feet over my head, just high enough, I noted, for me to catch a tantalizing peek under her vines.

"You've been working out, Lando Cooper."

"Hello, M," I said, fighting the urge to reach out and touch her flawless white foot. "You're looking…"

"Yes?" she said, eyelashes batting, speedshuttering her emerald eyes. **"Go on."**

"You're looking… really well."

"Sure and you're a master of understatement," she said, her voice lightly accented by her Celtic brogue. **"I can spy, by the twinkle in your eye, that I'm lookin' way past 'well'."**

The Morrigan laughed in that richly erotic way that drove mortals wild. She wasn't smirking at the twinkle in my eye. She wasn't even looking at my "eye".

"What is't you've called me to do, Yahweh?" She floated a few feet closer and reached down to draw one jade fingernail along the line of my jaw. **"I believe we have unfinished business between us. The matter o' your seduction, as I recall."**

The Morrigan smiled: a devastating conflation of lust and mad Gaelic humor.

"Your education in the ways of love are long overdue, my friend. I would remedy your ignorance with fiery kisses and the darkest erotic magicks."

She drifted downward and pressed her palms against my chest, her hands sliding lower… lower…

"Tonight, Yahweh, while the mummer's moon rides high above the world… your lessons will begin."

"Hamanahamanahama…" The Morrigan was really layin' it down. "Hannibal. I need you to…"

"Ochmagloch er mockenstoch," she whispered. **"He's smokin' hot."**

Hannibal flexed, and the sheath of stilltime within which he strained shattered and fell to the ground in glowing tatters.

"I serve no god but me!"

He gripped his sabre and strode forward, the tip of his weapon pointed at Gabriel.

"For the glory of Carthage!"

"Gabriel! Get Pluto! Go!"

Hannibal swung his saber. The energies humming through it were powerful enough to maim an archangel.

"Gabriel! Move!"

The Angel of the Morning vanished a nanosecond before the screaming blade whistled through the space his head had occupied. Hannibal's momentum whirled him around to face me.

"Your attempts at camouflage are undone, desert god. My percipience has pierced that pathetic shell within which you've chosen to squat."

Around us, time resumed its normal march. The screaming human bystanders staggered away into the chaos. The gathered media moved in closer, cameras hissing.

"I'm going to enjoy murdering you, Yahweh," Hannibal said. "I'm going to butcher you with such extravagant brutality that the others won't even think of standing in my way."

Others?

"Who empowered you, Hannibal? You're no god; you were dead."

Hannibal swung his sword in lazy circles, maintaining his distance, for the moment.

"Oh, I'll be a god soon enough. And when I am I'll make you watch while I feed your balls to the Midgard Serpent. Although in that body you appear to be sadly deficient in your allotment of manmeat."

"And what about you, Hannibal Barca," the Morrigan said. **"What's holdin' up your codpiece?"**

The emerald goddess dropped into the space between us. She'd obviously rearranged the space around her to maximize the effect of her divine charms. She floated, buoyed upon a wave of primaeval sexy, her red tresses streaming in the wind generated by her own hotness. Hannibal's scimitar dipped ever so slightly, an ugly sneer twisting his wolfish grin into a frown.

"Is this how you battle, desert god? Sending your concubines into the field to distract me?"

"Concubine?" the Morrigan rasped. **"Concubine?"**

Hannibal laughed, although his eyes roved hungrily up the Morrigan's body. And when he spun back to face me, his stance was a little less wide.

"You won't find me such easy pickings, God of the West. I, Hannibal, the Lion of Carthage, invoke the right of Celestial Challenge."

I was drawing a blank. "Celestial what?"

"Celestial Challenge," the Morrigan snarled. **"It compels a god to fight the challenger or face instant dematerialization. Only true gods even know about Celestial Challenge. Nothing short of a demigod can invoke it."**

"Aye," Hannibal growled. "I'm hip to it."

The Morrigan's beauty devolved into the ugliest of

scowls. She floated there, her arms folded across her murderous breasts. I could almost hear the black-Irish rage thrashing around inside the eroticized snake pit that was her mind.

"Did you hear me, desert god?" Hannibal roared. "Fight!"

Usually, at this point I would assume an Aspect and put my enemy to rout. The Great Burning Face in the Sky is perfect for this particular scenario, although Whirling Pillar of Flame always wows 'em at the Conventions. In the seven years since I'd learned the truth of my incarnation I'd fought and won fifteen duels. Recently, not counting Zeus, I'd defeated four other major gods in open combat: Set of the Egyptians; Pele of Polynesia; Loki, Halfgiant/All Bastard of the Norse Pantheon; and Triton, the son of Poseidon. Now Set works as a nightwatchman at Cairo's Ripley's Believe It Or Not: Mummy Madness! Pele tends bar at a lesbian brothel located in the shadows of Mount Kilauea. Loki teaches a "comedy traffic school" driver's education course in Salt Lake City, and Triton lives in the Spongebob Squarepants Bubble Blaster at the bottom of my fishtank. Don't get it twisted: at the height of my popularity I was a God among gods. Thanks to two thousand years of Holy War, Crusades, witch burnings, slavery, religious genocide, nation building, nation stealing and a pagan-pulping global media campaign that staggers on even into the twenty-first century, I was at the top of the divinity game. But now Hannibal was gunning for me with dismemberment in his eye, and I'd been cut off.

"Man to man then, Hannibal!" I cried. "But look!" I raised my hands, my fingers spread wide. "I'm unarmed."

Hannibal scowled. "Why not simply draw a weapon from the very air? A simple feat for a true deity."

A broadsword big enough to abort a baby stegosaurus thudded into the dirt at my feet. It was nearly as long as I was tall. Just looking at it gave me a hernia.

"Fight!"

Hannibal whirled his blade and charged. I gripped the Nubian blade's hilt and pulled. That was a laugh: I might as well have tried drinking Yankee Stadium; the blade remained firmly buried in the dirt. Hannibal swept in, swinging his sword in a casual beheading motion. I ducked. Seven years spent fighting errant divinities had given me a passing familiarity with defensive tactics. As he swung the blade around and behind his head I dived to my left, hit the ground in a diveroll and sprang to my feet. Hannibal lunged forward, his blade humming with stolen divinity. I danced backward and the sword's point just missed my right nipple. I dodged left, then feinted right, avoiding Hannibal's next thrust by a hair.

"Fight, boygod. Come to your doom!"

"**Aye. Fight him, my sexy prince.**"

The Morrigan offered a mischievous wink, divinity playing about her head like emerald St Elmo's Fire.

"**You have my blessing.**"

Sudden strength filled my limbs. The Morrigan's power surged into my body like a balm in Gilead, and I felt my muscles expanding, my perceptions quickening. I felt as if I could tear into the dirt beneath my feet and uproot the foundations of the Earth. I was invincible again, immortal, the vassal and the vessel of something far greater.

"**Fight, my champion. Defend my honor.**"

I turned back just in time to see Hannibal's sword whistling toward my head. I reached up with both hands and stopped the blade between my palms.

Wow. She's good.

"You can thank me later, Lando Cooper," the Morrigan replied. **"Kick his Carthaginian ass!"**

The Goddess had just inducted me into the ranks of the Filail, the superhuman warrior clan that fought alongside the Irish pantheon in that country's antiquity. They were strong, fast, supremely skilled, and utterly merciless. I shrugged, and ghostly armor, sky blue and gold, coalesced around me.

Hannibal yanked at his blade. I allowed the momentum of his tug to pull me into a forward lunge, dived over his left hip, hit the ground behind him and rolled into a defensive crouch. Hannibal whirled to face me, his arm steady, the blade's point unwavering. Even considering the Morrigan's gifts, I had no illusions about who was the more experienced fighter.

Hannibal swept in, swinging his sword in slicing figure eights. I backflipped away as he came on, once, twice, three times, kicking up dust and burning debris, my final leap carrying me over the giant sword still embedded in the dirt. I reached down, pulled it easily from the ruined earth and landed just in time to block Hannibal's blade with it. The clash of steel struck sparks, and rang loudly enough to shatter all the unshattered windows in what was left of Rome.

The Morrigan's blessing filled my body with certainty. I pushed Hannibal back, swept in with a flourish and brought the Nubian blade down toward his head. Hannibal parried easily, sliding my blade along the length of his own, only to spin around at the last moment, stepping past my thrust even as a vicious-looking curved knife appeared in his left fist. I barely got my sword up in time to block a left handed jab that would have opened my belly, and twisted around and under the backhanded return slash from the big scimitar.

Hannibal lunged forward again, his right fist slicing the air with the knife, followed by a left handed sweeping cut with the sword, a parry, a thrust, his blades whirling as he came for me. Then his right elbow connected with a solid blow to my forehead and I saw stars. Dodging, shielded from the worst of the attack by the Morrigan's blessing, I countered him move for move, planted a shimmering spectral boot in his chest and pushed him back. Then I pressed my attack. I became a whirlwind of motion and magic, thrusting and hacking until Hannibal backed away, unable to break past the wall of coolness that surrounded me.

"You're not the fighter I've read about, Hannibal. I think maybe Hades got the best of you."

Hannibal roared, countered my strike, lunged, thrust and missed.

"Think about it, HannaBell," I said, circling him now. "The warrior who fought the Holy Roman Empire to a draw. Then you take poison and Bam! You spend the next two thousand years climbing out of the Roman version of Hell. Even you gotta admit: that's funny."

And that's when the Morrigan's blazing strength flickered and went out.

CHAPTER VI
HANNIBAL TIME

"Morrigan! What are you doing?"

I ducked, barely avoiding Hannibal's crosscut with the short sword. The Lion of Carthage gritted his teeth in his lupine grin and came ahead, swinging.

"Morrigan!"

I leaped backward as Hannibal moved in for the kill, risking a glance toward where the Morrigan should have been hovering. But another woman lay sprawled on the ground. Her gorgeous face and figure had been replaced by those of Megan McCool, the Morrigan's human host. McCool was snoring. I could make out the trail of drool sliding down her chins. Apart from being schizophrenic, McCool was also a narcoleptic: the strain of godly combat had triggered a seizure.

A sizzling band of agony wrapped itself around my neck and yanked me off my feet. I hit the ground face first. Air exploded out of my lungs and the bright stars came back, only this time they were red. I managed to kick myself over onto my back, scrabbling for leverage by digging my heels into the dirt. Behind me, Hannibal clutched the handle of his cat-o'-nine tails: the leather thong was strangling me. The vicegrip around my throat tightened, and Hannibal pulled me across the smoking grass.

"You shouldn't be doing that."

The pressure on my throat eased up just enough to allow me to turn my head: Gabriel was gawking at me from over Hannibal's right shoulder.

"Don't you know who that is?"

Hannibal yanked me closer, laughing. "I know who he was."

Gabriel smirked. **"He is the Lord Almighty, you dolt. Where have you been for the last two thousand years?"**

Hannibal's eyes flashed. Harm throbbed in the air around him like the fallout cloud over Chernobyl, and Gabriel was smirking at ground zero. "I've been in Hell!"

"Gabriel! Get him! Attack!"

"As you command, Lord. This barbarian must be shown the error of his ways, and I intend to do so… with lashings of faith."

Turning back to Hannibal, he continued. **"That pathetic looking human is actually the One. He is the All-Father. The Master of Time."**

Hannibal hawked up a wad of phlegm and spat on the ground at Gabriel's feet. "And your point?"

Gabriel stepped lightly to one side to avoid the demonic loogie sizzling next to his perfect toes.

"He is the Father of Life, Hannibal Barca. The one true God."

"Lay waste, Gabriel! Smite him!"

"But…" Gabriel stammered. **"Don't you believe in God?"**

Hannibal punched Gabriel. His fist passed through the archangel's chest and burst through his back, sending golden ichor splattering out at roughly the speed of sound. Gabriel crumpled to the earth, a lifeless manikin.

"I serve no God but me!" Hannibal shouted. "I am He That Follows, as Day follows the long Winter's Night! I am the Order that Follows Chaos! I am… the Coming!"

Then a huge dark shape emerged from the smoke behind Hannibal, wrapped itself around his waist, lifted him off his feet and smashed him headfirst into the earth with bone shattering force. Hannibal hopped to his feet a second later. His head hung at an obscene angle, dangling from his broken neck. But the Lion of Carthage was undead – even a broken neck couldn't keep him down for long.

"What treachery is this?" he squeaked.

Persi the quarter-mastodon trumpeted and reared up on both legs, towering over his master, pawing at the air, his great ears extended, his eyes aflame. The light burning in those elephantine orbs looked disturbingly familiar

"For the Trasimene Seven!"

Then Persi headbutted Hannibal. The King of Carthage crumpled beneath the weight of the undead pachyderm's two-ton skull and flailing feet, compacting beneath that awful strength as Persi rose up and slammed his head down again, and again, and again, until what remained resembled a smashed sack of squirming, unmortal flesh.

Persi sat back on his haunches, his chest heaving. Then he looked over at me.

"Hello! Name's Persi. Short for Perthon. Have you seen my master? Carthaginian? About so high?"

Persi indicated Hannibal's approximate height with his trunk. Then he noticed the pulsating meat bag at his feet.

"Oh dear."

"You don't remember doing that, do you?" I volunteered.

"No," Persi said. "I wish I did. I'll bet it was lovely. But why can't I remember?"

"*Avek plezi.*"

I turned to find Baron Samedi standing beside me.

"What's crackin', mon frère?"

"Samedi. What are you doing here?"

"Gabriel was looking for Pluto," the Haitian Loa chimed in his nasal, French creole whine. "But Pluto wasn't available, so he came and found me."

• Baron Samedi was the death and sex god of the Haitian vodou pantheon. In his function as the head of the Guede Loa, it was his responsibility to guard the entrance to the realm of the dead, and to heal the gravely ill or wounded whose mortal moment had not yet come. He was classically depicted as a tall, cadaverous overly-endowed spectre in tuxedo and top hat with a white skull for a face. At the height of his pantheon's power, he'd been known to seduce hundreds of mortal lovers in a single night. In his current mortal seeming he was wiry, muscular with a shaved bald head and light golden eyes. He'd found a niche in the modern world as the choreographer for the long-running hit Broadway musical, *Vooodoo Nights!*

"Similar infernal energies," Samedi said. "When Gabriel couldn't find the Roman deathlord he found the next best t'ing."

"But Hannibal was damned to Hades. That's the Greek/Roman pantheon."

Samedi shrugged. High overhead, a vulture shrieked and dropped out of the sky.

"Last I heard, Pluto, he was livin' in Miami with Persephone and their life partners. They've begun a polygamist commune to protest Florida's stance on…"

"Samedi, you aren't supposed to do possessions anymore."

I had recognized Samedi's distinctive handiwork when Persi attacked Hannibal. But for just a moment I'd suspected other sinister magicks at work. Most of the "dark" gods and devils had agreed to abandon "all powers of supernatural 'suasion" before Lucifer and I drafted the Covenant. I hadn't seen Lucifer since.

Are you the Coming, Samedi? Are you working alone?

"Well," Samedi shrugged. "You clearly needed help."

"That's not the point. You could have just stabbed him or something. You didn't have to possess a sentient being."

"Oh, I don't mind," Persi rumbled. "It was lovely. Like a tiny holiday in my mind; freed from care and inhibition. And the centuries of slavery of course."

"I did what needed to be done, Yahweh," Samedi said. He gestured a lit cigar into existence and stuck it between his broad, white teeth. "Besides, I'm a pacifist."

"You're the Lord of Black Magic!"

"I was the Lord of Black Magic. But that's in the past, and you seem to be the only one who can't let go of the past. You haven't even said 'ey, *merci* for saving my sorry mortal life, Samedi.' *Ou se tres egoyis*."

"I am not selfish. And I'm supposed to be making you feel guilty."

Samedi swore again, and puffed smoke into a grinning skull, which hovered above us for few seconds before vanishing.

"Come now, Yahweh. You accusing me is like the pot callin' the kettle a nigga."

"Samedi…"

"Sorry: African-American. Anyway, it's a good t'ing I came along, or else you'd be dead, wouldn't you? And who would you have to blame then?"

I got to my feet. My throat hurt. I needed to take a hit off my inhaler and I was too tired to argue.

"Where am I?"

Megan McCool, the Morrigan's last High Priestess and current human host, tugged at my elbow.

"Hello, Megan. You're in Rome."

Megan McCool was the definitive mousy school marm. She'd taught high school in Cambridge for ten years before her first novel, *The Irishman's Mistress*, sold four million copies. Now she lived in a damp Tudor mansion on the outskirts of Boston. On certain nights of the year, she donned the robes of her office and welcomed the Morrigan to enter our world using her mind and body as the conduit. She was also certifiably insane.

"Ooohh that green bitch. What's she done now?"

While I filled her in, "Baron Saturday" began to gesture like a stage magician unveiling his latest illusion. His black magic tugged at invisible superstrings, pushing aside flotillas of the dark matter that makes up the bulk of our reality.

"What are you doing?"

"Hannibal was damned by the Roman gods," Samedi said. "But since Pluto is *très non*, I'm the only one who can open the death portal back to Hades."

"That's crossing pantheons. Exactly how many of your powers did you keep?"

Samedi clucked like a disapproving mother hen and uttered a creole swear word I won't repeat. "You were always so naïve, *frère*. Of course I saved some for a rainy day."

He shot his hands up, his index fingers pointing skyward, then took three long backward steps. A second later, twin columns of blue flame roared up from the Earth. Samedi had summoned a Hades Portal, a direct link to the Roman Underworld. The air thronged with the bored moans of the Roman dead who had lived, died, and been damned before the coming of Christianity. These days, most eternal damnations consist largely of endless wandering through badly lit hallways searching for someone to unlock the doors.

There was a flash, and the Portal became a bright hole hovering between the two flaming columns. Persi the quarter-mastodon inserted his trunk under Hannibal's shattered body and lifted it off the ground. The Carthaginian had nearly reconstituted himself. The force that empowered him was working overtime.

"Wait!"

Megan McCool strode forward and stared up at the rapidly reforming features of the man who nearly destroyed Rome twice.

"Bastard looks like Vin Diesel."

With that completely indecipherable comment, McCool gave Hannibal the finger.

"'Concubine' my ass, swordboy."

Then Persi dropped Hannibal into the Hades Portal.

"Well," McCool said, "now that that's over, would one of you handsome Entities kindly provide a lady with a portal back to Boston?"

Behind her, Hannibal's right hand shot out and grabbed McCool's belt. McCool was yanked backward and fell, screaming, through the Hades Portal. The columns of fire were sucked after them while the earth rumbled beneath me as if giants were breakdancing in the guts of the world. Then the Portal slammed shut.

"Sweet Christmas."

"Well," Samedi sighed. "I'm off."

"You're off? Open it!"

"*Pourquoi*?"

"You just damned the Morrigan, that's why!"

Samedi shrugged. "I'm all dry, *mon petit dieu*. It cost me a lot of power to help you today. And besides, the Morrigan's tough: she be aaahhhiiight."

"Hey! You also sent her mortal host to Hell!"

"Can't you get her out?"

"Not now! Only a death god can free a damned soul. You've got to open that Portal, Samedi. She'll think I tricked her!"

Samedi shrugged again, sadly.

"I've got just enough *couraunt* to get back to New York. I've incorporated one of those Disney kids into the show. He's handsome enough, but he dances like Barbara Bush. We have a run through in twenty minutes and I'll have to seduce fifty dancers just to stay awake. *Je vous en prie*!"

"Samedi wait!"

He forked a "call me" gesture with his thumb and pinky finger. Then he turned away and vanished in a violent burst of smoke and bongo drums.

Persi nuzzled me the way a dog nuzzles a distracted human.

"That was delightful. What's next?"

I could already sense my connection strengthening as the subtle fabric settled around me. Hannibal's rebanishment had removed the psychic interference. However, electronic evidence of divine interference was already circling the globe. I knew what came next.

And it was going to hurt.

"What will you be doing now?"

The Pope was standing a few yards away. In all the chaos I'd forgotten about him.

"Pardon?"

"I said now that you'll no doubt be appearin' on YouTube, what will you do?"

The old man leaned forward, his eyes twinkling with glee. "Perhaps, in your wrath, you'll destroy the Earth… and all who dwell upon her?"

"You know me?"

"Don't insult me, Lord. I've only served you for over fifty years. At least the idea of You, you know… in the grand sense. The zombie mammoth over there keeps bowing to you. And that Puerto Rican with the pigsticker kept calling you 'God of the Hebrews'."

The Pope chuckled and scratched his backside. "I may be a thickset old dinosaur, but I'm not blind. Now, will you answer a man who has served for over five decades?"

"I have no intention of destroying the Earth. You people seem capable of that without any help from me."

"Will you redeem us then? Save us from ourselves?"

"I'm going to push the Reset button."

"Beg pardon?"

"In a few moments you won't remember any of this. You'll all go back to doing… whatever it is you do."

The Pope nodded and breathed a sigh of relief. "Back to business as usual then?"

"I guess you could say that."

"I'm comfortable with that, I suppose," he shrugged. "Well, g'bye to you then."

The Pope turned and took two steps toward the burning city. Then he turned back. "One last thing?"

"Yes?"

"We don't really need you anymore, do we? I mean… it's obvious that you couldn't be less interested in guiding the river of human destiny. 'Free will' apparently being the way o' things… I gather that's best for all concerned. And anyway, I'd say we've done alright for ourselves: global warming, famine, reality TV and the military industrial complex notwithstanding. I suppose if you were really the God you were cracked up to be… you'd have put a stop to all that."

"Well… this was fun, but I've got a reality to repair, so…"

"Stands to reason then, that we've been on our own since Day One. Leaving us none the better or worse fer your occasional indulgence. I s'pose it's best that you go back to doin' whatever it is you do, and leave us to work things out fer ourselves."

"If you're finished…?"

"I am." The Pope smiled, his eyes bright and utterly sober. "Having spoken my piece I'll withdraw and say, simply: thanks fer nothin'."

With that he turned. Then he turned back. "I take it the redheaded colleen with the big winnebagos was the Morrigan: the pagan Whore of Ireland's savage pre-Christianity?"

"Yes."

The old man whistled, and winked. "Wonders within wonders. And none of it to do with us. Goodbye then."

Gathering his tattered robes, the old Pope walked, whistling, back into the burning city. Sometimes I wonder about people. I really do.

I took it all in. Then I reached out, and up, grasping my way into the Eshuum. Power shimmered there, colder than the blood of icebergs. A small portion of the human thoughtforce awaited my command once more.

"You've come back."

"I could never abandon you."

"The Other whispers of your betrayal."

"What other?"

"He that promises. Who speaks truth."

"Where is it? Who is the Coming?"

"The beginning of your end. And the end of all beginnings."

Reset.

Nothing happened. With a sinking feeling, I realized that I couldn't trust the connection any longer. I was just about to summon an Aspect – try to – when the power answered.

Reset.

The world faded as I opened myself to the Eshuum and a billion lives times a billion roads-not-travelled opened themselves to me, stretching toward a multitude of realities both probable and possible, each of them branching out toward an infinity of decreasingly viable outcomes, and all of them anchored to this moment in time, its relation to the most critical element of all... free will. I expanded, growing godlike again as potentials unspooled beneath my fingertips.

Then I went to work.

CHAPTER VII
PARANOIA MADE BY GOYA

From: JHVA@SkyfatherGroup.Waring.DEUS
To: @LORDOSIRIS, @BLACKSHANGO, @AGNIFLAMER,
@JesusChristJR.
Subject: HAS ANYBODY SEEN LUCIFER?
@LORDOSIRIS: Insanely bizzy! Glorious revival happening
in Egypt!
@BLACKSHANGO: Not since the last election.
@AGNIFLAMER: Very busy 'n Bollywood. No time
for games.
@JesusChristJR: Still not speaking to you.

I shut off the display on my mobile and set the ringer to
vibrate. Then I leaned back against the headrest of my
seat and imagined welding my eyelids shut against the
stomach churning brightness of a midsummer Chicago
morning. The sunlight beating against my eyelids
threatened to pop my eyeballs out of their sockets. Two
days after my battle with Hannibal I was still nauseated,
disoriented and depressed. I was in a foul mood as I
made my way to work.

But these ailments paled before the doubt that was deepening toward existential crisis with each passing moment.

Zeus had used stolen divinity to attack me, a move which, had he succeeded, would have permanently altered human continuity, something that, all extant deities had acknowledged under the terms of the Covenant, would be a bad thing. I'd stopped him only at the cost of his apparent death, which should have been technically impossible: a god of Zeus' stature was virtually immortal, even while masquerading as a mortal. Now he was gone.

A few days later, a resurrected Hannibal had used more stolen divinity, power that, under normal circumstances, would have been inaccessible to him. Both had tried to kill me using this borrowed power; both had nearly succeeded; now both were gone. But so was the Morrigan, a powerful goddess in her own right, and one of my few reliable allies: three catastrophic god-related events, occurring within days of each other.

Beware the Coming. It stalks us all.

In my descended state I had limited communications with select active top gods via the waring; a cybertelepathic treasure house composed of what you might call "dark matter memory banks". It was a sort of psychic world wide web, funneled through and similar to the mortal internet, only without the animal porn. (The Greek Pantheon filed a petition to have that section sealed off when they realized that it was occupied mostly by members of the Greek Pantheon.)

But I didn't need to mindsurf the web-browser of the gods to know that something was seriously out of pocket.

The renunciation of an old, worn out God occurs in different ways, sometimes after weeks of tribal warfare, sometimes after decades of ethnic cleansing, but mostly, quietly, after a gradual shifting of belief, a replacement of old ideas by bright, shiny new ones. The Advent of a new God is always accomplished through an uptick in the intensity of human belief in that god, never through direct action from the ascendant God to be.

You've been replaced, by the One who Comes.

I had my fears, and a million questions. Was the Coming, the entity that both Zeus and Hannibal claimed to represent, an avatar of this new God? If so, what were its motives? Who were its worshippers? I had seen no evidence of a widespread new religious movement powerful enough to have stimulated the Collective Unconscious, so where was this Coming getting his or her power? And what did it stand to gain by pitting retired gods against each other? What were its tenets? Its divine selling points? So far, it had displayed nothing more than a penchant for staging godfights.

But my darkest fears were reserved for a more personal subject. I had heard no word from my former counterpart since our mutual descent to the mortal plane. Lucifer had successfully hidden himself among humanity's teeming masses for nearly thirty years. Was he at the root of the Coming's takeover attempt? If the Father of Lies was hoarding undeclared powers in contravention of the Covenant, what did he intend to do with them?

More importantly, could I stop the Devil if he was, in some way, at the heart of the problem? Exactly how much power was he hoarding? Who were his allies? Where was he?

I tried to relax as the L train came up out of the underground and onto the elevated tracks near the Loop. Thoughts of the day ahead only made matters worse.

I had experienced headaches after godfights, but never with this kind of intensity. Maybe two major duels occurring so close together was too much for my substandard constitution. My gut insisted, however, that this was different. Something was wrong.

What's happening to me?

When I dragged myself into the Westside location, two hours late, Herb and his watch were waiting for me in Motor Oils. He'd spent the last three days scouting potential new locations in Milwaukee only to learn that I'd been AWOL. Flaunt capered at Herb's side like the Wicked Witch of the West's favorite flying monkey.

"Well, the Mad Zulu returns. I thought you were getting a haircut for your big date with Salome tonight."

"Something suddenly came up."

"What? Dammit, man, don't you have any self-respect? You look like a retarded voodoo doll."

"Have you seen my Advil? I'm getting a sick headache."

"I mean I'm as liberal as the next guy when it comes to personal freedoms for my employees. Didn't I let you grow those gridlocks...?"

"Dredlocks."

"Your mother wanted me to drop a tranquilizer in your Sunny D, sneak into your room and shave your head. I said 'Barbara, this is America: let the boy look like a damn bushman if he wants to'."

"Wrong. You didn't shave my head because you broke your clippers shaving your name into that alpaca during the Herb vs the Dollar Lama spot."

"Did I hassle you when you pierced your eyebrows?" Herb droned on. "Did I say a single, solitary word when you grew a Mohawk and dyed it lime green?"

"You said, 'No son of mine is gonna prance around lookin' like Chief Sittin' Pretty and call himself Herb Cooper's offspring. Not while Herb Cooper's pullin' the chuckwagon.'"

"Damn right."

"Pop…"

But Herb was rolling, and nothing short of a nuclear accident would shut him up.

"Do you know how hard I've slaved to create this empire? How much valium I power-slammed just to keep from stabbing your mother long enough to keep this family together?"

"Pop…"

"But what does Dad get in return? Renfield in San Francisco working in a damn headshop…"

"He's a biochemist. He specializes in alternative therapies and eastern medicine."

"Western medicine was good enough before I spent two hundred thousand dollars to put him through a Western medical school. Atticus can't even be bothered to visit on a regular basis…"

"He lives next door."

"And that other one… my firstborn son. The heir to the Cooper Empire… ashamed of his own name."

"You named him after a wizard!"

"Gandalf is a seminal character from a beloved piece of Western fiction, smartass. I don't see people in China naming their kids after Charlie Chan."

"Or that Cirque du Soleil crap," Flaunt muttered. He had ditched the Elviswig in favor of his own implausible toupee. "Too much of this globalization goin' on, Herbie. New World Order time. They want us all speakin' Spanish, Chinese... Whatever happened to American literary type names like... like..."

While Flaunt struggled to remember the last book he'd burned I staggered behind the customer service counter. Underneath it I'd stored a bottle of Eco Water and the little metal tin in which I kept my stash. I opened the tin, palmed four Advil and downed them dry.

"What's wrong with you?" Herb said. "You look like crap."

"He's probably crankin' the crystal meth," Flaunt crowed. "All these idiots are doin' it."

"Will... you... **shut up**?"

My voice echoed a little too loudly. Somewhere out over Lake Michigan, the echo stroked thunder from the skies. Flaunt flinched, his gaze flicking across the ceiling. He waved a hand in my direction. "See what I mean?"

Then he stomped off to berate a customer.

"Why do you have to antagonize him?" Herb hissed. "You know he gets flashbacks."

"I'm out."

"What? It's only 12.15!"

"I gotta go. My head's killin' me."

I grabbed my satchell and headed toward the door.

"I'll be taking that loan out of your check!"

I went to see Surabhi.

CHAPTER VIII
SURABHI

My headache abated a little on the train ride up to Rogers Park. By the time I rang Surabhi's doorbell I was feeling more like myself, anticipating the look on Surabhi's face later that night when I gave her the ring – and the night of passion sure to follow – when she snatched open the door to her apartment.

"Yo," I said. "What's crackin'?"

I moved in for a kiss. Surabhi grabbed my lapels and screamed, "Kiiiiyaaaaaahhh!"

In one fluid movement she shifted her center of gravity downward and backward, pulled me forward onto the balls of my feet, planted her foot in the center of my chest and I was sailing head over heels across her comfortable living room. I landed on my back in the center of a deep mound of sofa cusions, comforters and fluffy pillows.

Surabhi jumped on me and sat on my chest, smashing me back into the pillows, her face alive with martial excitement. Even though she was restricting my airway, I marveled at what time, circumstance and several million years of natural selection had wrought.

Surabhi Moloke was the most beautiful woman since the advent of Homo sapiens. Imagine cinnamon-brown skin, smooth and rich as warm cocoa, wide brown eyes shot through with glints of gold like flecks of borrowed sunlight. Imagine curly, reddish brown hair, and a generous mouth armed with perfect white teeth and a ready smile. Throw in sharp cheekbones, and an aristocratic nose with perfectly arched nostrils , finally, stack all that on top of a body toned by Pilates; thrice weekly Jujitsu/Karate/Muy Thai kickboxing classes; Saturday morning African dance workshops and/or Brazilian capoeira jam sessions and you'll get the picture. Surabhi had muscle in all the right places, a dancer's grace, and the lethality of a shaolin monk.

My girlfriend was constantly learning new ways to disarm, disable or disembowel people. She regularly attended self-defense seminars, and had earned an instructor's certification in Savate by her fifteenth birthday.

She'd grown up in an upper middle class suburb of London, the eldest daughter of Magnus Moloke, Ethiopian soccer legend and entrepreneur, and Marian DotsonMoloke, an attaché to the American Ambassador to the UK. Now she sat astride me: the Amazon Triumphant; beautiful, intelligent and capable of killing a water buffalo with her bare hands.

"Judo," she said, breathlessly. "The principle of using your attacker's momentum against him. It's brilliant!"

"Can't... breathe."

"Oh, my god! I'm sorry, babe! Do you need your inhaler?"

Surabhi shifted her weight while still holding her position. I didn't mind, now that oxygen was flowing to my brain.

"Not anymore," I laughed. "Hi."

Surabhi smiled. "Hello, loverman."

She kissed me. And everything – the fight with Zeus, the battle with Hannibal and my fears about a satanic takeover attempt – downsized themselves on my list of priorities. We were good. As long as that never changed, everything else would work itself out.

"I need you to change."

"What?"

Surabhi reached over and grabbed a plastic garment bag off the back of a nearby chair. Inside the clear plastic bag dangled an expensive-looking dark suit complete with a crisp new shirt and tie. In the other hand she dangled a pair of freshly polished, even more expensive-looking, leather shoes.

"I need you to wear this."

"Why? What's wrong with what I'm wearing?"

For our big moment I'd selected the dark brown suit I'd purchased for my college graduation. It was a little snug in places – that was to be expected since it was seven years old, but Classic never goes out of style. For color, I'd added an excellent black T-shirt featuring Boris Karloff as Frankenstein's monster. The exact matching T-shirt in Surabhi's size featuring Elsa Lancaster's "Bride of Frankenstein" was folded neatly inside my satchel. I'd planned to present it to her before dinner, and taken the time to have the date stenciled across the fronts of both shirts to commemorate the occasion. I'd used some of the advance Herb gave me to buy a new pair of lime green All Stars to top off the ensemble.

"My parents are here," Surabhi said. "My father's gone completely mental."

Her London accent was lightly tinted with the Midwestern twang she'd picked up over the last five years living in Chicago. I loved her voice; it was rich, dark; exotic without being ostentatious.

"When did they get here?"

"Two hours ago. My mum's here on UN business and Daddy tagged along. Daddy says he has good news, but he'll only spill it when we're all together. They want to meet you. I'm afraid they won't take no for an answer."

"No! Not tonight!"

Surabhi winced, took a deep breath.

"Calliope told them we've been sleeping together."

"What?"

"My dad said, 'Either I will sit down to dinner with the man who violated my daughter, or my brothers and I will hunt him down and beat him until he begs for the release of death'."

"Why would your sister do that?"

"Calliope'll do anything to sleaze her way into my parents' good graces. I recommended a personal trainer to her in New York and she got all pissy. They showed up here unannounced. Dad wouldn't come in until he was sure you weren't here. He stood there in the hallway pouting while my mother dragged in the suitcases. Even then he checked under the beds and rifled all the closets; hunting for my stolen innocence."

"That's insane."

"Dad's old school," Surabhi said, ignoring my admonitions about people with British accents using hip hop jargon. "He's still pissed about my not marrying Alex Thessenden."

"You told me he gave you his blessing when you told him you didn't believe in arranged marriages."

"It wasn't really an arranged marriage, babe. More like an informal agreement between him and my Uncle Shad when they became blood brothers back in Addis Abbaba."

"What's the difference?"

"You're not Ethiopian. Anyway, that doesn't matter. I already know who I'm spending the rest of my life with."

"But that's the point," I said. The little velvet box in my pocket seemed to throb in time with my heartbeat. "Tonight was supposed to be about us."

Surabhi had been tucking away money from her job as a French and English teacher at a small community college in the south suburbs. My planned proposal would not come as a complete surprise; only the time and the date had been left up to me. I'd tried to mislead her with a few false leads over the last few months, hoping to keep her off balance until I was ready for the big moment. Calliope had ruined months of planning.

"You don't mind do you? About the suit and everything?"

"Mind? Of course not. Your father wants to hack my head off for 'violating' you. What could I possibly 'mind' about that?"

Surabhi gently laid the suit and shoes across her small kitchen table. I got to my feet.

"I'm serious, Surabhi. I'm putting my foot down. Tonight is off limits. You and I have serious matters to discuss."

"'Serious matters.' Sounds incredibly important. What exactly did you want to talk about, Mr Cooper?"

"I'm not going to talk about it here. We have reservations. I made plans."

"Reservations? I think I'm impressed."

"Don't change the subject. Look. You're always telling me that I don't plan. Look."

I reached into my backpack and produced the menu I'd taken from L'Ethiope.

"See? Table for Two. L Cooper. 8.15pm. I even pre-selected the menu. All our favorites."

"But my parents made reservations at Henri Lumiere's."

"Henri Lumiere's? No. No!"

"Lando, I don't know… exactly what you were planning for tonight, but you're forgetting one really important thing you have to do before we can move forward."

"What…? Oh no."

Surabhi nodded. "You've got to have a 'man to man' with Magnus Moloke if you expect to go on 'violating' his daughter in wedded bliss."

I'd grown so accustomed to operating as a nurture-free agent during the alien shooting match that was my upbringing I'd forgotten that some families actually care who their offspring might marry. It had been all Herb and Barb could do to keep from selling us off to a work farm.

"Your father expects me to…"

"…ask for his blessing. And his permission. I think. Although that's largely ceremonial. My mother's already onboard. She trusts my judgment. At least about this."

"And he wants to do this tonight?"

"Yep. Then, assuming you don't totally cock it up… they want to meet your parents."

"No!"

"Of course, babe. They want to examine the gene pool from whence any future grandchildren might arise."

"But they can't meet my parents."

"Why not?"

"Because my parents are insane."

"They'll have a lot in common."

"I'm serious, Surabhi."

"No you're not. But my parents are leaving tomorrow, so that gives us a little more time to bring our lovely families together. That is if you don't cock it up tonight."

"You've got to stop saying that."

"Babe, it's not the end of the world."

"You don't know my parents."

"Of course I do. Your dad's a scream..."

"...screaming maniac..."

"And Barbara's lovely."

"She's on good behavior when you're around! She'd have tried to kill you by now if I hadn't stepped up the dosage on her anti-psychotics."

Surabhi punched me on the shoulder. Hard.

"You're terrible. Your mum looks at me with real affection."

"Because she's trying to decide which part of you she's going to cook first. Owww!"

"You're mean to your parents."

"Believe me... they can take it."

"But why?"

"Why what?"

"Why are you so angry at them?"

Thirty seconds later I was surprised to realize that I hadn't answered her.

"Hello? Anybody home?"

"What are you talking about?"

"You and your parents. You're obviously harboring a huge amount of resentment toward them."

"Well... It's not that I'm really angry..."

Surabhi made a noise that was similar to the noises Herb makes when he's had one too many Muy Macho Cheesy Meat Burritos from Tangy Taco.

"You're the most passive-aggressive person I've ever met. At least when it comes to your mum and dad. The question is: why?"

"Well..."

"Yes?"

"It's not like they haven't given me plenty of reason to..."

"Hate them?"

"I don't hate my parents, I..."

"Mmhmm?"

"I mean I... really... admire... the way they..."

"Oh dear," Surabhi sighed. "Go on."

"They abused me."

Surabhi's eyes narrowed. "What kind of abuse?"

"It was sexual. Owww! Stop hitting me!"

"Stop it, Lando."

"When I was fourteen they forced me to watch them making love. At least that's what they called it."

"Lando!"

"I just remember my father bent over on the bed..."

"God! You're the worst!"

Surabhi enjoyed playing armchair analyst to a host of girlfriends, celebrities, and random passersby, speculating about the obvious clinical depression of the waiter with the resigned smile, the suicidal leanings of the middle-aged new mom with the expensive stroller. She loved what she called the Story, the hidden truths she believed made up the lives of people she would never know. But lately, she'd been focusing the spotlight of her curiosity on me with increasing frequency.

I had hidden one of the world's deepest mysteries from everyone who mattered in my mortal life. No great accomplishment: who would believe I was the Judeo-

Christian Divine Embodiment? I had allowed the sheer improbability of my situation to preserve my secret. Most of my family believed I was an idiot. That was fine with me. Hiding in plain sight made my dual existence that much easier.

But Surabhi was different.

"You're doing it again."

"What?"

"Whenever we talk about you, about your past, you make a joke, or you get this faraway look in your eyes."

"No I don't."

"You do. It's like you're looking back at me from someplace unimaginably distant. I hate that look."

"Don't be silly. I'm here. With you."

"Your body's here with me. I just get the feeling that…"

"That what?"

"That you're hiding something."

Vertigo. A feeling similar to standing atop a skyscraper with no walls or windows to separate you from the wind; fear and exhilaration tinged with the secret desire to step off into open air and fall, mortal and defenseless, toward the earth below.

You could end the whole charade right now.

I could do it, reveal myself – one minor miracle and I could expose the truth to the woman who loves me… the real, human me.

"I…"

"Yeah?"

"Well, the truth is…"

I gave up the power of a god to be here. Now.

"My God, Lando. You're doing it right now."

"How can you say you love her if you can't tell her the truth? If you can't tell her Who you really are?"

"Quiet, Connie."

From her small corner apartment in my medulla oblongata, Changing Woman clucked disapprovingly.

"Have you thought about your children?"

"They'll be completely normal. You know that."

"I'm not talking about the power, I'm talking about truth, Lando."

Connie, aka the Golden Lady, aka Changing Woman, always sang loudest when I was faced with an ethical dilemma. At that moment she was a short, roundish, heavy-breasted woman with shoulder-length black hair and stars where her eyes should be. In this Aspect, Connie communicated through song. And she was always pregnant.

"I'm talking about the false pretenses under which you seduced Surabhi."

"What 'false pretenses'?"

"What?" Surabhi said. "What are you on about?"

"Yes, the lies you've told in order to pass yourself off as a mortal."

"I haven't lied to her."

Surabhi frowned. "Lied to who? What do you mean?"

"You've lied by omission," Connie continued, shifting into a lower key. **"You've taken unfair advantage."**

"No, I haven't!"

"Lando, you're freaking me out."

"What kind of lives will your children lead if they don't even know where they came from?"

"Come on, Connie…"

"Who's Connie?"

"What?"

"I mean where they really came from."

"I said, who's Connie?"

Surabhi was staring at me, hands on hips.

"You called me Connie. Since my name is Surabhi – pleasure to meet you I'm sure – there's clearly been some misunderstanding. So, distant stranger who hopes to win my undying affection but is currently cruising for a major beatdown, I'll ask you one last time: Who... the... hell... is... Connie?"

Connie chuckled from deep inside my tortured brain.

"Humanity: how's that working out for you?"

"Look just... shut up!"

Surabhi's eyes took on the bloodlust sheen they got right before she took somebody to the mat.

"Oh, hell no. No, you didn't just tell me to shut up!"

"No! I mean... I wasn't talking to you!"

"I don't see anybody else around."

"I know..."

"So who the hell were you talking to?"

"I..."

"And who the hell is Connie?"

"Connie is a Native American fertility goddess who lives in my brain who volunteered to act as a temporary conscience – like a sort of moral regulator – until I mature enough to operate independently while also being the best possible boyfriend I can be and right now she's yelling at me for not being honest with you about her even though I love you so much because a lot of confusion could have been avoided and you're incredibly beautiful when you're pissed and it's really irritating because she sings everything – she doesn't have the greatest voice – and I have a splitting headache and I love you more right now than I did ten seconds ago and can we please change the subject?"

Surabhi stared at me, a wary smile twitching at the corner of her lips.

"Fertility goddess? Is that meant to be me? Is this your incredibly weird way of seducing me?"

"Yes!"

"Was all that part of your act?"

"Maybe... did you like it?"

"It was cute. Especially the part about me being beautiful when I'm pissed."

I grabbed her around the waist, pulled her in close.

"I believe I said 'incredibly beautiful'."

"I stand corrected."

We kissed.

"That was really weird though," she said, when we came up for air.

"It's been a weird day."

"No weirder than my agreeing to marry you against the disapproval of my feminist sensibilities."

"Did I ever tell you how beautiful you are when you're railing against a male dominated society?"

For the next hour or so, all the mysteries that had plagued me faded to a dull whisper. And I wandered, basking in the warmth of Surabhi's smile.

And the deeper mysteries of her embrace.

CHAPTER IX
MAGNUS AND MARIAN

After centuries of close association with the human mind I can tell you: it's a very strange place. Getting one of my own made that even more glaringly obvious. But of all the wonders to which I had been witness, of all the mortal terrors I had observed, none of them ever scared me.

Then I learned to drive.

Driving is the one thing humans do that leaves me flabbergasted. Millions of years of natural selection have culminated in the human ability to operate heavy machinery under a variety of dubious circumstances. I passed my driver's license test after seven tries. It took seven tries because of my certainty that every car that careened toward my parents' car would slam into it, killing me, the driving instructor and the dreams of a teeming humanity. After understanding that oncoming traffic posed no threat to the continuation of human evolution, I'd calmed down enough to pass the test. But I didn't like driving for the simplest reasons: you can't control the other drivers.

I'd gotten along perfectly well using Chicago's fantastic public transportation system. But for dinner with the Molokes I decided to make the effort. Which was a mistake.

We were late, of course. Surabhi's Volkswagon Bug came equipped with a GPS navigation system, but it insisted on giving us directions to a falafel stand in northern Dubai. And to add insult to anticipated injury, both our mobile phones mysteriously lost signal seconds after we got into the car. It was only after we'd gotten hopelessly lost, hunted down a working payphone, called the restaurant and gotten directions that we finally arrived an hour late. Surabhi was nearly frantic.

"We're here!" she announced as we tumbled through the front entrance of Henri Lumiere's. A worried looking maître d' met us in front of the greeter's podium.

"You're late," he hissed. "Your party has been waiting."

The nervous maître d' grabbed two menus from his lectern, turned on his heel and waggled two fingers to indicate that we should follow him. He walked, with an almost preternatural economy of motion, toward the center of the large main dining room. His attitude was practically breathable.

"Well," a big African voice boomed out. My eyes followed the throbbing sound waves to the table where Surabhi's parents, along with her sister Calliope, sat. "The star-crossed young lovers finally deign to grace us with their arrival."

"Sorry, everyone," Surabhi chirped. "Sorry!"

"This is how they wish to start their lives together?" Magnus said to anyone within earshot. "Two hours late and without thought of a phone call."

"I said sorry, Daddy. My nav was out, and both our mobiles are complete shit."

Surabhi hugged her mother while Magnus offered a constipated buffalo grunt that effectively communicated his feelings about faulty mobile phones, wonky navigation systems, excuses in general, and tardy American boyfriends in particular.

"Mum… this is…"

"Hello, Lando," Marian said. "Surabhi's told me so much about you, I'm happy to finally meet you face to face."

Imagine the lesbian love child of Lena Horne and Michelle Obama. Marian Dotson-Moloke was fifty-five years old and nearly as beautiful as her daughter. She was of average height but her effortless elegance made her appear taller. She was the daughter of the first African-American State Supreme Court Justice from the state of North Carolina; had graduated Suma cum laude from Harvard Law. She worked high up in legal affairs for the London office of the American Ambassador to the United Nations. She was adorned in a shimmering black dress that highlighted bare shoulders, flawless cocoa-brown skin and bare arms toned from regular weight training and her years as a pentathlete at the University of North Carolina, her undergraduate Alma Mater.

"Pleasure to meet you, Mrs Moloke."

"Please, call me Marian. I can't wait to learn all about you, and your family."

"Hah!"

"Are you alright?"

"Just stubbed my toe. I'm fine."

Surabhi beamed. She'd once told me that her mother remained one of her closest allies even during the wild wars of adolescence. The relief in her eyes was a testament to their relationship. Then she took a deep breath and stepped into the shadow of the man-mountain that had spawned her.

I'd fought rogue deities and malignant nature spirits, sutured ruptured realities and realigned unwieldy continuums. I was the Embodiment of Order, the Banisher of Chaos. I was God, for Christ's sake. But nothing bothered me more than watching Magnus Moloke wrap his arm around my woman.

"Daddy…"

"Yes, my darling?"

"You're doing it."

"No! No, I'm not."

"Magnus," Marian warned. "You're smothering her."

Magnus released Surabhi, reluctantly. Then he chuffed her lovingly on the shoulder. Surabhi smiled, and punched him, hard, on the bicep.

"Strong!" Magnus crowed. "See that, boyfriend? She's still a Moloke!"

Surabhi's sister Calliope had been quietly rifling through Magnus' wallet, plucking bills the way a gardener weeds an unruly garden. Magnus rapped on the table.

"You see how your sister keeps in shape, Calliope?"

Calliope shot her father a look that would have sent Medusa scrambling for cover. Calliope was fat; she easily tipped the scales at over two hundred and fifty pounds, well within an acceptable healthy range for a woman of her age… if that woman stood nine feet tall. Calliope stood about five six. On a light day, after a year of intensive dieting, strenuous exercise and projectile vomiting she might pass for "portly." Now, she was just fat. Ironically, she was also gorgeous. Calliope Moloke was one of those unfortunate women who make random passersby think, "What a beautiful face. If only…" Calliope was doomed to be the "if only" in a never-ending line of pitying strangers' beauty evaluations. Thus her seething rancor.

We'd once caught her screaming into a mirror she'd strategically smashed so that it reflected her only from the neck up. She'd sworn off alcohol, milk, carbohydrates, red meat, wheat, sugar, salt, nuts, fruit, cheeses, shellfish, warm soups, eggs, and all associated oils and unguents before heading straight for the refrigerator, where she grabbed a rice cake and slammed the door on her way to her managerial job at Pizza Hut.

"I have a metabolic condition. It's not my fault I'm hypothyroidal. But my capitalist father thinks it's all in my head. Which is completely typical for a bourgeois drone like you, Daddy."

Magnus grunted. Calliope turned red.

"Of course, anything that deviates from your Judeo-Christian Corporate hivemind standard of European beauty threatens your sense of male entitlement. Isn't that right, Daddy?"

"Calliope, please…" Marian warned. Calliope turned the spotlight of her hostility on me while simultaneously reaching for the bread basket.

"One day my fat arse and I are going to destroy the Global Military Industrial Complex. Did my anorexic sister tell you that?"

"Dad," Surabhi said. "This is Lando. Lando… meet Dad."

I extended my hand. "Pleasure to meet you, Magnus…"

Magnus gripped my right hand like a man forced to grasp a spitting cobra. The strength that vibrated in that grip was shocking and I had to grind my molars just to keep from swearing. Magnus squeezed harder. The bones in my hand squeaked, and I wondered how much pressure my knuckles could take before they exploded like burning Brazil nuts.

"Doctor Moloke," he corrected, before releasing me.

We all sat; Magnus next to Marian and Surabhi next to me on my left, while Calliope overwhelmed the chair directly to my right.

"Nice to see you again, Calliope."

Calliope smirked and went back to plundering the bread basket.

"So, Lando," Marian said. "Surabhi tells me you're a comedian. How interesting for you."

"Yes. Comedy has always been my passion."

Magnus was glaring at me, his massive hands locked together on the tabletop. He looked like he was practicing a strangulation murder, and it didn't take godly insight to know whose imaginary neck he was throttling between those giant paws.

Even seated, Magnus towered over the rest of us. He easily stood six feet six inches tall, with shoulders nearly as wide as our dinner table. His athletic prowess was legend. He'd led Ethiopia to its first gold medal in soccer at the 1980 Olympic Games. He'd captured the imagination of the world and legions of adoring fans, emigrating to the UK to open a string of successful businesses ranging from a chain of urban movie theaters and athletic equipment stores to a line of his own sportswear: MAGLOK. In London he'd lent his image to a line of organic foods – Back to the Land Organic Foods were rapidly sweeping across Europe. The healthy fare had even begun to attract attention from stateside retailers like Whole Foods and Trader Joes. He'd even starred in a rap video, *Bootyrock!* In it he invented a dance called Da Magnus March. The song became an international hit. The dance it spawned remained an irritating planetary sensation.

"The Comedian," Magnus snarled. His teeth were unnaturally white. They looked healthy enough to gnaw through the cables on a suspension bridge. "You any good?"

"He's excellent. He's really great, Dad."

"Thanks, babe," I said, a little too forcefully. My battles with divine sociopaths had taught me the importance of claiming bragging rights right off the bat. Reticence might add mystery to rock stars and billionaires, but on the battlefield of Ego a big mouth is the best weapon. Surabhi had just hamstrung me in front of her father.

Herb could handle this. I should have listened to all those lectures.

"I've had gigs at all the local clubs. I've been making the rounds across the Midwest."

"What about television? Any interest from the networks?"

"Well, no, but I've…"

"Cable?"

"W… well…Chicago's… not a… huge comedy town."

"Isn't Chicago the home of Second City?" Magnus said. "The birthplace of improvisational comedy? A city with comedy clubs falling out of its massive, alcoholic backside? Wasn't that fellow… oh, what was his name?"

"John Belushi?" Calliope offered, smiling through a mouthful of multigrain.

"Right! Wasn't John Belushi from Chicago?"

"Well… yes."

"I believe a lot of successful comedians came from Chicago," Magnus rumbled on. "Bill Murray, Dan Ackroyd, although I believe he grew up in Canada. Chris Farley..."

Magnus glanced at Calliope. "He was the fat one, Cali. Died of a heart attack when he was only nineteen years old."

"I believe he was in his thirties, Magnus," I offered. "And all the guys you mentioned are actors, not really comedians."

"Yes, lots of Chicago comedians have made the jump to television," Magnus continued. "The good ones anyway."

"Yes," Marian interposed. "It must be very difficult to get up on a stage to make people laugh, Lando. I know I could never do it."

Magnus chuckled. "No sensible person would, dear."

"I meant, Magnus, that it takes a special kind of courage to expose yourself in that way. A certain forcefulness of vision."

"That's right, Marian. It's tough sometimes, but I like the challenge. It's great when you can turn an audience around... get them on your side."

"Sounds a little desperate, wouldn't you say?"

Surabhi sighed, loudly. "Daddy."

"I simply meant that traveling from city to city, living out of your suitcase in cheap motels just to chase down the approval of drunken strangers might be viewed as a bit needy in some circles."

"What 'circles' would you be referring to, Magnus?"

Magnus' bridge-crushing smile broadened.

"Normal, healthy society. Most people go to work every day. They labor at jobs they despise for low pay and little hope of advancement. They look at actors and comedians, showbusiness people... well a bit like they look at their Tupperware: nice when it's wanted but not really necessary... or particularly useful."

Surabhi and her mother both sighed.

"Well I think helping people forget their problems for a while is necessary, Magnus."

"Oh, really."

"Sure. It's deep in the human race, the need to enjoy a funny story or laugh at a good joke."

"So you consider yourself a storyteller? A sort of modern day shaman dancing around the communal firepit, battling encroaching cultural darkness with pithy observations and witty repartee?"

"Ahhhh... well... Yes. I suppose you could say that."

Magnus leaned forward, teeth glinting like clean daggers.

"I'd call that somewhat elitist. Wouldn't you?"

"What do you mean?"

"I mean who named you official shaman, eh? Lando Cooper: Voice of the People? Who gave you the insight to illuminate the unwashed masses?"

"Daddy, that's enough."

"Now wait a minute, Magnus. I never said I was illuminating..."

"But that's what the really great comedians do isn't it?" Magnus barreled on. "Show us hidden elements within the collective soul; drag our human foibles out into the light so that we can laugh at ourselves? Like Bill Cosby or Charlie Chaplin. They teach us perspective using their own experiences as comedic launching pads. They were artists, masters. Are you telling us that you've got the talent to match Bill Cosby?"

I took a long drink of water. My throat was suddenly as dry as Cosby's last book, and the dryness seemed to have moved upward and flashfried my brain. Who knew

Magnus Moloke was a student of American Comedy?

They were all looking at me: Surabhi's brow furrowed with the same worried expression I saw echoed on Marian's face; Magnus glaring, his eyebrows arched in exactly the same way Surabhi's did when she'd successfully carpetbombed my defenses; Calliope sneering at me, her cheeks stuffed with sourdough...

"Hey... I just like to tell jokes."

I saw the satisfaction in Magnus' eyes; the disappointment in Marian's face and the schadenfreude in Calliope's smirk.

Surabhi laughed, too loudly.

"See? I told you he was brilliant!"

CHAPTER X
WINED

Magnus ordered his steak "bloody rare", as if that was a surprise to anyone. Surabhi ordered a salad. We were both vegetarians. Her repulsion at the thought of consuming animal flesh fit well with the realities of my situation: when you can perceive the emotions of sentient beings, paying for them to be butchered for the enjoyment of eating their pan-seared remains is a bit of a buzz-kill.

Marian ordered the same salad, I believed, as a show of solidarity with Surabhi. I'd dropped a ball I wasn't even sure I'd been thrown. Now I sensed Surabhi's mother trying to shore up her resolve. Barbara would have ordered a gin and tonic and bribed the waiter to put sugar in Magnus' gas tank.

"So," Magnus continued, chewing cheerfully. "Surabhi tells us your dad's a local celebrity."

"Yeah. He's Crazy Herb, the King of Auto Supplies."

"He's funny," Marian said. "They used to play his commercials on cable back when I was working in New York. I loved all the crazy stunts and the animals."

"Yes," Magnus grunted. "Hilarious. And your mother?"

I knew admitting that my mother ran a South Side

tavern chain, even a lucrative one – in a struggling economy my mother's bars still cleared tidy profits – would only deepen the quagmire that was sucking me down like quicksand with a grudge. But my failure to meet Magnus' challenge had robbed me of confidence. I needed to hit back. It was a situation my father would have called a "Mexican Douche Party".

Herb's Rule of Business Engagement #22D
    Never refuse an invitation to a Mexican Douche Party. Such a refusal could cost you an eye, or the right to live a life free from scorn and ridicule.
                    Herbert "Crazy Herb" Cooper, the King of Autoparts

But I was so desperate to impress Magnus that I couldn't come up with anything better. The truth was all I had.

"She owns a couple of bars on the South Side. One of them's called Barb's. The other one's called the Silver Foxhole. It caters to a lot of veterans."

"A bar," Magnus hummed. "That's rough work isn't it?"

"Pretty rough. She's been held up three times since Christmas."

"Oh, really?"

"Yep. But my mother's tough."

Shut up, Lando.

"She's been held up nine times in the last four years."

Shut your mouth. Shut it now.

Common sense was demanding a strategic withdrawal to the restroom where I could manufacture a sudden bowel obstruction or spontaneously ruptured spleen, something suitably dramatic to allow me time to regroup and figure out how this all went so terribly wrong.

"Barb, that's my mom's name, Barbara-Jean…"

Shut up/No keep going. You can do it!

"…she keeps a shotgun under the bar. She also carries a .38 in a special shoulder holster."

"Is that right?"

Stop/Go on/Run/Make it right/SHUT UP…

"Yeah. She can blow the eye out of a sparrow on the wing at thirty yards."

Surabhi snatched the bread basket from Calliope and shoved a roll into her mouth. At least it was whole wheat.

Magnus chewed, swallowed. "A formidable woman."

"Indeed. Last year she shot a guy who tried to rob the Silver Foxhole. She was cleared of all charges though. The Homicide detectives made her an honorary member of SWAT. They call her 'The Widowmaker'."

I laughed. No one joined me.

"She… makes a lot of money."

Surabhi was consuming breadsticks at a rate a California wildfire would have been hard pressed to match.

"I've got some news," Calliope piped in. "That is, if anyone cares."

Marian spoke up. "What is it, dear?

"I'm joining the Taliban."

"Oh, Calliope."

"I mean it, Mummy. Master Omar, my spiritual advisor, wants to bring America to its knees. Daddy, can I have five thousand dollars?"

Magnus's eyes never left mine.

"Whatever for, my darling?"

"I want to buy two tickets to Afghanistan. Master Omar and I want to join the Jihad, but I can't do coach. I cramp easily and there's no leg room."

"You're not going to Afganistan, Calliope," Magnus said quietly. "This is just another pathetic bid to draw attention away from the reason we've all gathered here tonight."

"I believe in Master Omar's mission, Daddy. It's really like... who I'm meant to be."

Magnus shrugged, grinning. "Daughters. What can you do?"

"Ahem."

The uptight maître d' was standing behind me with a glass and two unopened wine bottles. He looked even more peevish than when we'd burst through the front door.

"The gentleman sends his compliments to Mister Cooper."

I looked in the direction the maître d' indicated. In the furthest corner of the restaurant, a man sat shrouded in darkness. He was big, broad-shouldered and black-haired, sporting a prominent beard. He was dressed in an expensive-looking black suit with a blood-red silk shirt open at the collar. He was facing us, his right hand holding a glass of some clear beverage, vodka with a twist of lime, perhaps, or straight scotch – he looked like a scotch drinker. Our eyes met, and he smiled and raised his glass even higher.

"The gentleman says he is an admirer of your work, and sends the wine with his blessings."

Relief filled my chest with newfound hope. "The gentleman" had obviously seen me onstage, probably at the Comedy Castle or ChiChi Marimba's. The apparently wealthy gentleman was... a fan.

"Red or white, monsieur?"

Something about the shape of the bottle containing La Danse Rouge, its contours vaguely curvaceous, drew my eye.

"Well… I suppose I'll have a little of the red, my good man. Anyone else?"

"Ah ah," the maître d' said. Then he leaned over to whisper in my ear, "The gentleman should sample the bouquet."

"Of course. How foolish of me."

The maître d' opened the shapely bottle of red wine and poured a draught into my wine glass. I picked up the glass, sniffed at the rim the way I'd seen countless actors do in movies, and took a cautious sip.

"Well. Very refreshing."

The maître d' rolled his eyes and poured more into my glass. I took a deeper draught this time. The wine filled my belly with warmth, a liquid glow that settled in my gut and radiated outward, pulsing through my veins. I hadn't had a drink in six years for good reason: one drunken binge and half the human race could wake up on Mars. When I accepted Connie's burden I'd also agreed to her most important admonition: godly power and booze don't mix.

But this stuff was delicious.

I took another sip and rolled the luscious claret around my mouth as if I could coat every micron with its fruity goodness.

"Damn… this is really good."

Thunder rumbled somewhere to the East. No one else seemed to share my delight in the wine; Magnus demurred of course. He sat there glowering at me, sharpening another arrow in his quiver of hate. Marian, my new best friend, was nursing her glass of chardonnay, her eyes darting back and forth between Surabhi, me and the man-monster she married. Surabhi wasn't drinking at the moment. She had a Kendo tournament coming up and was trying to slim down for her weigh-in, although she'd practically destroyed the bread basket. That left me and Calliope, who was well into her third glass of the chardonnay.

"Oh, well," I shrugged. I took a long slug of the claret, that wonderful little claret; it seemed to get better with each swallow, going down all cool and fruity, like fresh grape juice infused with moonlight; Heaven in a glass. "You guys don't know what you're missing!"

A giggle bubbled up from my chest. "That. Is. Awesome!"

My future in-laws were staring at me like confused owls.

"Whoooeeee!"

I drained the glass, grabbed the shapely bottle and poured myself another one. For a moment, I could have sworn I saw something, a flicker of light; an argent gleaming in the crimson depths.

Nah, trick of the light.

Surabhi reached over and grabbed the bottle out of my hand.

"I think you've had enough, babe."

"Awwww, come on, Bee! You gotta try this stuff! It's the bomb!"

Someone at the table, I think it was Marian, asked me if I was alright.

"I'm great! I'm strong! Like the bull!"

To prove my strength I banged on the table. My right hand struck the tines of my salad fork. The fork flew over Marian's head, narrowly missing her as it flipped across the room. At exactly that moment, a waiter carrying a tray loaded with condiments and cream-based soups stepped into the salad fork's flightpath just in time to intercept it with his eye. The waiter screamed and threw up his hands. The tray of condiments, creamy soups, and salads with heavy dressings sailed across the room and came down on the mismatched couple at the next table. The skinny gentleman in the threepiece gray suit was instantly drenched in a variety of creamy sauces. His wife, who easily outweighed Calliope by a hundred pounds, got the salad dressings and condiments.

"Ooopssh!"

The wait staff descended on the mismatched couple's table, peppering them with apologies. I didn't care. I'd never experienced such overwhelming joy. It felt like someone had just detonated a happy bomb in my brain.

"What's the matter with you?" Magnus growled. "You've just ruined that couple's dinner."

"Oh, lighten up, Mags."

"Magnus frowned. His voice rumbled, low and dangerous.

"What did you just say?"

"You heard me. Lighten up, bro. Take a chill pill and blow it out your big, Ethiopian cussi."

That last one was good enough that I shared it with the rest of the diners, at twice its original volume.

"I think we've seen enough. Marian, we're leaving."

Surabhi pulled me around to face her.

"Lando… what are you doing?"

"Oh… Oh… wow!"

Surabhi… shone. Her face was suffused with some secret luminescence, as if she had swallowed the sun and let a little of its light infuse her atom.

"You are, without question, the most beautiful woman on Earth."

"What the hell's wrong with you?"

"Let's do it now, Bee. Let's find a justice of the peace and take the plunge. Screw the surprise. I want the world to know!"

I leaped onto the table, knocking over several glasses. The shapely bottle teetered, tipping toward the floor. I lunged, and caught it by the neck.

"A toast! To the most beautiful woman since Helen of Troy. Scratch that... Helen of Troy was a pig. To the woman who has agreed to become my wife!"

"Lando, come down!"

"My fiancée, everybody. The future Mrs Surabhi Moloke-Cooper! Or Cooper-Moloke... or just... Surabhi! Give it up, folks!"

An elderly couple seated near the kitchen applauded.

"You want to know about love, ladies and gentlemen? Do you want to talk about a passion that knoweth no bounds? Well... ooops! I almost forgot."

I reached into my pocket and clawed out the pretty little black box. Then I got down on one knee.

"Surabhi Azalea Moloke..."

Surabhi's eyes pierced the joyful white noise in my head. A fleeting clarity shimmered through the drunken haze. I looked around at the faces of the diners all glaring up at me.

"What's... what are you all looking at?"

I took a long swig from the shapely bottle.

"Surabhi!"

Magnus towered beneath me, satisfaction plain in his woeful, evil smile. Marian and Calliope were hovering near the exit. "Your family is leaving."

"Magnus Moloke, ladies and germs. Everybody remembers Magnus and that terrible video he did back in the Eighties! The one where he dressed up as a wizard and..."

"Lando," Surabhi cried. "What…what's happening?"

"Oh, come on, babe. That video sucked."

Magnus gestured toward the horrified waiter. "Check please."

"Seriously, Mags, it's the crappiest video ever."

"Babe… why are you doing this?"

Surabhi was crying now. But a part of me, the part that capered blindfolded at the edge of a vast abyss, whispered of adventures to be had, a destiny to be mastered: Magnus Moloke would not decide my fate.

"A wizard, Mags? A rapping wizard that waves his wand and makes people do that stupid dance?"

I did the dance. Da Magnus March. I hopped and slid. I bugged out my eyes and slithered across the table, scattering glasses and plates across the beautiful hardwood floors, all the while sucking down huge gulps of that unbelievable wine, reveling in the terrible, wonderful mania that lifted my spirits until I felt I could dance out of the restaurant, up into the clouds and into the stratosphere.

Other diners were heading toward the door as the maître d' stalked up to my stage. "Sir, I'll have to ask you to leave."

"I mean… who directed that video? More important, where can I buy some of the antidepressants he was using when… when…"

The rumble started low; a groaning tremor that shuddered in the pit of my stomach. I took a healthy swig from the shapely bottle to calm my distress.

"Sir… if you don't get down from there this instant I will be forced to call the police!"

"Bite me, Frenchie. You're not the boss of…"

An apoplectic alligator snarl burst up from my guts. A smell erupted from my open mouth, a rotten grape/ fecal hellstench that curdled the hairs in my nostrils. The condiment-drenched fat woman at the next table took one sniff, frowned, and threw up all over her husband.

"Honey? I don't feel so good."

Surabhi shook her head, her anger so palpable it could have worn my pants. Magnus' smile was so bright it hurt.

"What's wrong, guys? Oh my…"

Nausea flipped my world upside down. The sound of the barfing fat woman a few feet away only made it worse. Fleeing diners were holding their noses.

"God! What is that stink?" Calliope cried.

"Surabhi, babe… I think I'm gonna be sick."

"You will not!" The maître d' raged, through pinched nostrils. "You. Will. Not!"

Two waiters who looked like disgruntled extras on loan from a B-grade action movie tackled me off the table and hauled me toward the kitchen.

"Hey! Somebody grab my wine!"

The last thing I saw before they threw me out was Surabhi's face.

I don't like to remember the expression I saw there.

"And stay out!"

I landed in a pile of trashbags a few yards from the alley entrance to the restaurant.

"Yo," one of the waiter-apes, grunted. "Always wanted to say that."

"Me too," the other one snorted. "And don't come back!"

The knuckledraggers laughed, high-fived each other, and slammed the door, leaving me surrounded by other people's trash and a miasma of grape Koolaid-holocaust stink so dense I could have set my bowling ball on it. Even as drunk as I was, the smell was alarming. But when I remembered the fat lady barfing all over her husband I laughed so hard I hurt myself. Then ELO's Mister Blue Sky erupted from my mobile.

"Hellooo?"

"Lando?" a thick Northside accent twanged. "Is this Lando Cooper? It's Goldie Kiebler, from The Ha-Ha Room."

"Goldie, I gotta… g… gotta call you back. I'm in the middle of a personal crisis."

I lost it again, screamed laughter into the night sky.

"Whatever, Cooper. I thought you might be interested…"

"I gotta call you back, Goldie! I gotta call you back!"

I disconnected. Goldie Kiebler owned one of the hottest comedy clubs in the city. I'd just alienated one of the most influential club owners in the country. Everything was burning down around my ears.

It was hilarious.

"It's the wine, you thoughtless dolt."

The coldness of the voice stoked a memory. The nearness of it struck alarm bells in my gut. A Presence had just entered the alley. I rolled to my hands and knees, marshaling my will, trying to fight the effect of the wine as the alley grew colder. Someone had just opened a Portal. That same someone stepped out of the shadows with a sigh of equalizing air pressure and the pop! of displaced space.

"The smell you've noticed is called seep. Think of it as a by-product of the fun you've been having at my expense."

I looked around, my eyes straining to pierce the shadows.

"Who are you?"

"You think the Joy I bring comes cheaply? That clarity comes without cost? No, Yahweh."

The speaker stepped into the circle of light thrown by a nearby streetlamp. It was the man from the restaurant, the tall, bearded man who sent over the red wine – the "fan" with whom I'd shared a toast.

Oh, Surabhi… what did I do?

"Now I can kill you; freed from the nuisance of angry wives or demi-mortal brats seeking 'closure'."

The fan dwindled to about five-foot-six. His black hair flared bright orange; not the kind of orange you'd find on a Florida citrus plantation. This was the orange at the heart of a forest fire; the lethal white-orange of the sun's corona. The thick pectorals softened and rounded like twin cantaloupes. Buttons popped from his vest and clattered to the ground; I looked down to find my expensive new shoes surrounded by tiny circlets of gold. When I looked up again, the fan was gone. In his place stood a short, fat god with a blazing halo of dayglo hair and glorious breasts: Dionysus the Twiceborn – the secret, double-sexed child of the mortal Semele.

Greek.

Son of Zeus.

"Now, God of Abraham," Dionysus squeaked. **"I will take my vengeance."**

Dionysus reached down with one chubby fist and grabbed me by the lapels. The strength of a mad god thrummed in his muscles. He lifted me off my feet as easily as I would a child.

"Dionysus… I didn't kill Zeus!"

"Liar! You stole his power and befouled his holy corpse!"

Something about the image of me "befouling" Zeus flexed my "inappropriate humor" muscle.

"You dare?" Dionysus huffed. **"Stop that! Stop laughing!"**

"I can't, Di. Your boobs are bigger than Aphrodite's."

The enchanted wine was elevating my mood more effectively than a truckload of Paxil even as I tried to reach for the power, sifting through my mental pockets for the Keys to unlock the universe.

Must have left them in my other pants.

"Hey, Dio-nitelight. You're the god of grapes. What do people pray to you for... mold protection?"

"Fool!" Dionysus growled. **"Have you truly forgotten so much? I am the God of Epiphany, of ritual madness and ecstasy. I am the Liberator who reveals lethal truth through the power of strong drink. You have tasted the wine which may bear my beneficence or my curse. You lie at the crux of my power."**

"Power? Hello? This is the Judeo-Christian Embodiment speaking: I own West Texas. But two aspirin and an egg salad sandwich and your 'power' goes byebye... fat boy."

"I... am not... FAT!"

"Of course not... handsome woman like you... just big-boned."

Dionysus released me.

"That's right, Dolly. Maybe next time you'll think twice before you mess with the real thing!"

The Twiceborn raised his right hand.

"Rise."

The terrible crocodile that had moved into the pit of my stomach roared, and a gout of vomit blasted out of my mouth like a freight train with melted brakes. I fell to my knees as projectile puke spattered the asphalt.

I heard the power singing my secret names, demanding that I wipe Dionysus away with a wave of my hand. The Twiceborn was in serious trouble… as soon as the stomach 'gator stopped deathrolling with my guts in its mouth. I climbed to my feet and swiped at the thin runner of purple drool bouncing from my lips.

Dionysus waggled his pinky finger…

"Rise."

…and a surge of vomit, more vomit than I ever imagined could be contained by a mortal body, roared up my throat and blasted the wall five feet away.

"Wait! Dionysus… wait a minute!"

At that moment, the mismatched couple stormed out of the restaurant's kitchen entrance, too busy berating the despondent maître d' to realize they were stepping directly into the line of fire. Dionysus raised his left hand.

"Rise."

The blast of ejecta struck the skinny husband and blasted his toupee halfway off his head. He turned toward me, a man with a parti-colored muskrat slopped into immobility on his glistening dome, and I heaved again. The blast spattered the chubby wife's ample breasts, adding to the colorful assortment of condiments and sauces I'd already deposited there. The Sprats turned and ran, dripping, down the alley.

"Dionysus… let's talk about this!"

The God of Epiphany laughed, and grabbed his crotch.

Suddenly I realized that I wanted to chase down the Sprats, tackle the portly wife, rip off her tainted moomoo and bury my head between her enormous breasts. When

I envisioned her dressed in a Wonder Woman costume my brain exploded with the urge to procreate. Dionysus rubbed his stomach, and I realized that I could tackle Jack Sprat too. If I got hungry later I could eat him. I was five steps down the alley when my world turned red. My body became warm, then hot, then unbearably hot.

"I can boil the wine in your blood," Dionysus, who is suddenly everywhere, whispers. **"I can command it to freeze and choke your veins with rivulets of red ice."**

His Voice is in my mind, his face the full moon that fills the sky. His power is the sunshine of a morning after, still a million years away and I realize: I am an alcoholic. In my mortal life I've worshipped Dionysus, indirectly, but too fervently to deny him now.

"Who's laughing now... comedian?"

The Twiceborn gestures, preparing to pull the vomit trick again, or something worse. I grasp the fabric of reality in my vomit-slick mental fingers and pull.

Five yards behind Dionysus, a manhole cover blows off and rockets into the sky. From the bile-puddle in which I kneel I'm watching the most probable outcomes of this encounter expand into an infinitude of possibilities. Somewhere in the multiverse, another Dionysus stands directly over the empty space that was filled by the manhole cover in this reality. I pull hard enough to tug the fabric of both continuums a little closer, twisting them together to form something new.

The hole behind Dionysus expands, eating up the space between it and the wine god like an earthbound black hole, as the Liberator puts his foot on the back of my neck and presses my face toward the colorful puddle of liberated belly flotsam.

"Let it be known throughout the halls of eternity," Dionysus cries. **"Throughout every pantheon of gods that remain on this stinking mudball: Dionysus of the Greeks has defeated the unassailable God of the Christians! Let my cry of vengeance resound across the heavens: Dionysus! Dionysus! Dionysus!"**

I wretch blood-tinged purple vomit across Dionysus' bare feet.

"You should have worn shoes."

"And why is that, you pathetic pretender?"

I grab the edges of the manhole and drag it between the wine-god's feet. For a moment, the wine-god stands on thin air and grape fumes. Then he plunges, still smirking, into the darkness.

I released the hole, allowed its continuity to resume. It snapped back with the sound of a concrete bunker door slamming shut. If I was lucky, Dionysus was trapped in an alien continuity, smothered beneath thousands of metric tons of concrete or water or unexplored earth. Wherever he'd landed it would take time to extricate himself and return home. If I was unlucky, the Twiceborn would rise from the hole and kill me in short, messy order.

In addition to looking out for my own backside, however, I had a larger consideration. I had violated a minor rule in defeating Dionysus. Realities are separate for a good reason. Breaching their integrity for personal gain is always a bad idea. It's one thing to correct the violations of ne'er-do-well deities, another thing altogether to cause the violation just to protect my own skin. There might be ethical considerations; a karmic price to pay later for my victory in the Now.

I can fix it. If something goes wrong, I can just Reset and start over.

Later, my arrogance would lead me to make the worst decision in the gods' long history of bad decisions. But the effects of Dionysus' epiphany were beginning to wear off.

Surabhi.

I staggered back into Henri Lumiere's, where the maître d' informed me that he'd already called the police. The Molokes were gone. He recommended, in the most colorful terms, that I follow their example. Before the bouncers could throw me out again, I left.

It'll be OK. I can fix this.

I punched her number, determined to explain. I called her, ten, twenty times, each time getting her voicemail greeting in return.

You've done it, Lando. This time you've really done it.

My mortal life, the life for which I'd sacrificed Eternity, was going up in flames that stank of wine and stomach acid. It was also abundantly clear that I was now the target of at least one angry family of gods. My nausea only deepened at the thought of taking on the entire Greek pantheon.

Surabhi was ignoring my calls.

Everything was ruined.

My mortal life was a Godawful mess.

DEPRESSION

"I struggle with depression. Who doesn't? Everybody's got problems, right? But my father taught me how to deal with depression. Which was only fair, since most of the time my parents were the reason I was depressed."

< Audience reacts >

"When I was ten years old, my father had this big business trip to Africa. The whole family was invited to spend Christmas at this resort in Zimbabwe. My mother signed up for a Swahili class she got from this ad in *Modern Woman*. The class turned out to be a scam cooked up by this 'African King' who was searching the New World for a 'modern American Wife'. This appealed to my mother even though she already had a modern American husband. Barb's a very romantic woman… also completely insane."

< Audience laughs >

"The African King turned out to be this schizophrenic from Salt Lake City named Thicke Ronald. Thicke Ronald used the money my mother sent him to buy a bus ticket. He came to Chicago, camped out on the sidewalk in front of our house and begged my mother to come out and meet her 'Negro Love God'. The man was from Utah: next to him Dick Cheney looked like Samuel L Jackson in black face.

"When my mother refused to come out, Thicke Ronald challenged my father to a duel. My father went out to fight him. Thicke Ronald weighed three hundred pounds. He could benchpress my father, and he had more violent personalities than a flashback episode of *Survivor*. So while one of Herb's employees distracted him, Herb snuck up behind with a shovel and and coldcocked him. The employee filmed the whole thing. Herb used the footage in a commercial: Crazy Herb Clobbers the Price Giant.

"They kept Thicke Ronald in the 'special hospital' for three weeks. On Thanksgiving Day, my mother said Thicke Ronald appreciated her more than we did, packed a bag and flew to Salt Lake City. The night before we left for Africa my father made us pack all our old clothes in boxes and shipped them all to Zimbabwe. A week before Christmas, we all flew to Africa. Without my mother."

< Audience reacts >

"Yeah, sad. On Christmas Eve we were sitting around, moping in our hotel room, surrounded by all these boxes. Herb told us to get dressed. We took all the boxes down to this big ballroom. The management was having a Christmas party for the hotel staff and their families. We gave away all our old clothes, toys… stuff we didn't want. I was pretty sure we were going to have to visit my mother and new stepfather in whatever Utah boobie-hatch accepted Blue Cross Blue Shield, but my father gave each of us a little wine, and by the time we'd emptied the last box, we were all laughing.

"My old man knew how to deal with depression. 'Remember, boys,' he'd slur. 'When you think you're standin' on the bottom of the barrel, just think: somewhere out there are four little boys with no feet.'

"So he gave away all my mother's clothes."

< Audience laughs and yells >

"All her shoes, her toothbrush, her tapedeck, her typewriter; all her tampons, her eyeglasses, her makeup, her Diana Ross wigs, her watches, her earrings, her hunting knife, and her zippo lighters. He gave away every piece of jewelry he'd ever bought and every piece of underwear she owned. By the time he was done, a hundred and three African ladies walked away with more loot than Bernie Madoff. The locals sang Christmas songs in our honor. On New Year's Day, some of the workers made us honorary members of their tribe. It was one of the best Christmases of my entire life.

"My father knew how to handle depression."

CHAPTER XI

COMIC CONVENTIONS, WHAT HAPPENED TO YURI LAST WEEK, VITILIGO ELF

How could I have been so stupid?

I should have seen Dionysus' attack coming. Hadn't I noticed a glimmer of cloaked divinity shimmering around him when he sent over that damned wine? Hadn't I sensed that something was amiss seconds before I took that first sip? As I replayed the events of what would come to be known as the Moloke Massacre, I swore to myself that I had. Now that everything had gone down the toilet I could see all the signs of an imminent attack.

Stupidstupidstupistupidstupidstupid...

But I missed the signs: I was too busy trying to impress Surabhi's parents.

"You got it, Pinocchio."

Connie was sitting astride a huge black horse in the middle of my bedroom. The horse's eyes shone bright red in the shadows of my shuttered sanctum sanctorum. I had drawn the curtains against the possibility of sunlight when I'd arrived home near dawn. The black horse's mane swirled like ink in dark water, a roiling curtain of shadow. Its hooves shone like molten silver, and they left smoking prints across the carpet. There was something weird about the creature, apart from its size and obvious supernatural nature, but from the depths of my hangover I couldn't quite figure it out. It glared redly at me, clearly disgusted. And it wasn't the only one.

"Please, Connie... no lecture."

"Oh really? After the wine-drenched gangbang you and Dionysus subjected me to last night? I've got a right to rip you a new one, mister."

"Connie–"

"In light of the potential disruption of the Plan and threat to human emotional development I'd say you've ignored me enough, Lando Cooper."

"Connie, I know you're my conscience–"

"Transitory conscience..."

"Anyway it's perfectly within your purview to bust my chops, Connie, but–"

"You really screwed the pooch last night, kid."

Connie hopped down from the spectral black horse. For some reason she was wearing a Wonder Woman costume, complete with silver bracelets and magic lasso. **"Both your lives are pretty much in the crapper."**

"Please," I groaned, wincing at the sparks from the horse's hooves. "Tell me something I don't know."

"Alright. The other pantheons are rumbling. In light of recent events, there's been talk of a general uprising."

"What recent events?"

"The powers are concerned about the disappearances. Zeus is gone, same for the Morrigan.

And now Dionysus. And to make matters worse... Gabriel has suffered some kind of breakdown."

"What?"

"Yup," Connie grunted. **"He was last spotted fluttering around Venice Beach, ghoststalking a bunch of homeless meth addicts. When someone asked him why he was doing that, he said... and I'm quoting here... 'Everything's gone to Hell, Heaven is an illusion and the Emperor has no robes'."**

"Gabriel's an Archangel, Connie. All that bowing and scraping... He should get a life."

"Don't even joke about such things," Connie hissed. **"The powers are afraid you've launched some kind of covert assault on the pantheons. It's typical god behavior: taking the random ticking of a clockwork universe and making it all about you, but there you have it."**

"Wait a minute. The Morrigan was dragged into the Underworld by Hannibal! She volunteered to help me!"

"And she hasn't been seen since."

"She's a goddess, Connie! She still has most of her personal powers. She's probably just regenerating somewhere in Ireland."

Connie shook her head. **"She isn't in Ireland, or any of the Underworlds. And neither she nor her host have been seen in Boston. All traces of the Morrigan's power have been removed from our continuity."**

"And the other gods are blaming me for her disappearance?"

"Yup. They suspect you of stealing divinity. They think you may be murdering passé gods and hoarding their powers to stave off your own looming redundancy."

"But I retired voluntarily. According to you, Yahweh acknowledged his 'looming redundancy' during the industrial revolution."

The black horse whinnied. In the confines of my room it sounded like a haunted eighteen wheeler firestripping its airbrakes. I knew my parents couldn't hear it – no strictly mortal ears can eavesdrop on a divine pow-wow – but the subtle sound was unsettling in the Saturday morning silence.

Downstairs, Herb was preparing one of his Fitness Breakfasts for himself and Missy Tang. My mother was out on her weekly mani-pedi-run. She never missed a Saturday at the local nail salon, where she enjoyed making the lives of the Korean shopgirls particularly disappointing.

Since Herb's return, I'd sensed an upswing in the animosity between my parents. Their war of wills was nearing some kind of breaking point. The tension on the Cooper Plantation was as thick as drywall. All things considered, I didn't need any more weirdness pushing my personal applecart into oncoming traffic.

"What's with the horse? And why is it eating my comforter?"

Connie rolled her eyes.

"Lando this is Sleipnir. Odin's magical steed. During your little pissing contest with Dionysus I decided to get some fresh air. I ran into Frigga over Norway... you know, the Queen of the Norse Gods? Anyway, she invited me down for a few rounds of Texas hold 'em with Pele of the Polynesians, Ratri, the Hindu Avatar of Night, and Athena of the Greeks. I won Sleipnir off Frigga on a bluff. Boy was she pissed. Right, Shleppy?"

Sleipnir whinnied again, his eight hooves pounding the floor until every window in the house shook.

"Hey!" Herb yelled. "Turn down that damn ghetto blaster!"

"Athena told me about the uprising. The Greeks are furious of course. Ares is howling for your head, especially now that Dionysus has been whacked."

"Surabhi's gone. My parents are driving me nuts. Everything's gone wrong and now those idiots think I'm a murderer. Connie… I don't know what to do."

Connie leaped up onto Sleipnir's broad back. **"You know what to do: do the right thing."**

"But what is the right thing, Connie? How do I fix all this?"

"Think like a mortal, Lando. Accept your limitations and figure it out."

Outside, the brightness of the July morning faded. I heard the rumble of a stormfront closing in as the sunlight fled before the storm's onrushing shadow.

"I could fix it, you know. I could just go up to the attic, fire up the Shell and–"

"No! You gave up the Divine to live as mortals live. That's a one-way ticket. Now you've got to solve your problems the way humans have been solving theirs since they climbed out of the trees."

"Yeah? And how is that?"

"Simple, Pinocchio. One step at a time."

There was another thundering whinny, followed by more shouting from my father. Then goddess and godly steed vanished into the shadows.

"One step at a time."

I glared at my mobile, trying to will Surabhi's number to appear. The message indicator stared back at me, untroubled. Against Connie's admonitions I found my mind wending its way back to the object that sat at the bottom of my Northwestern footlocker in the attic directly above my head. With direct access to the Eshuum's infinite potential I could fix everything.

"It couldn't hurt. Just this once."

I expected a swift rebuke from Connie.

All I got was silence.

I love comic books. The colors, the drama, the outlandish costumes; the idea that any average joe or jane, when pushed to his or her limits by unforeseen circumstances can, simply by the application of will, the advent of science gone awry or genetic mutation, gain power and save the world. It's utterly ridiculous, completely asinine, and unforgivably juvenile.

I love comic books.

In real life, there are rules, laws, speed limits that cannot be broken. But in comic book stories, there are no limits. You say there's a supervillain threatening a planet of benign humanoids on the far side of the galaxy? No problem, conquering the speed of light is child's play for Superman, who can simply fly into space, punch out the bad guy and be back in Metropolis before lunch.

In my post-retirement reality, getting across the planet required careful planning and the aid of at least one other supernatural being, preferably an angel. Once, before I decanted myself into human form, I could bridge planetary distances between the minds of my believers: if enough of my faithful were in China, I could be in China, instantly. If a worshipper climbed to the top of Mount Everest I could accompany her to the summit. Technically, the old me could be everywhere or anywhere, as long as one believer was waiting at the journey's end.

This brings up a number of questions of the "Does a falling tree make a noise if there's no one in the forest to hear it?" variety. Trust me, it's complicated. The point I'm making here, is that there are no free lunches in this universe, even for immortals. No energy without waste, no acceleration without an attendant build-up of inertia, no effect without cause: even gods have limits.

But superheroes don't.

Every year, I looked forward to Chicago FantaCon: the biggest yearly comicbook-sciencefiction convention in the Midwest. Buying Surabhi's ring had left me seriously strapped for cash, but I'd saved a meager amount on the side, enough to scarf up a few back issues and the odd, affordable rarity.

The creators of my current favorite title, *From Here to Alternity*, were scheduled to sign copies of the hot new *Alternity* graphic novel at this year's FantaCon. The new book was being released in conjunction with *From Here to Alternity 3D: The Movie*, later that summer. The producers had shown an early trailer at the San Diego ComiCon a week earlier and were scheduled to premier an even more detailed trailer at FantaCon. It was going to be an event of epic proportions – a Ten on the Geek Richter Scale. I'd picked up my copy the first day they'd gone on sale and had kept it wrapped in airtight plastic for nearly a year.

But superheroes were a million light years away from my personal microcosm. I'd haunted my room, replaying the Moloke Massacre with a deepening sense of doom. My conversation with Connie only complicated matters. Finally, tired of finding no answers, I grabbed my copy of *Alternity* and caught the train downtown to meet the only other god who might understand.

"Dude," Yuri said when I answered my mobile. "Where you at?"

I was at the front entrance of the Downtown Hyatt Regency, shuffling along in a long line with hundreds of people dressed as their favorite heroes or villains; various wizards young and old, and practically every character from the *Star Wars* films. A few people dressed as the original Lando Calrissian passed me as they made their way up the line. My depression only deepened: Billy Dee Williams' acting talent had made the odds of my attempts at humanity being taken seriously smaller than the odds for Darth Vader becoming head of the NAACP.

"I'll meet you at the usual spot," Yuri said.

Our usual meeting place was at Superninja Go! Go! Go! a popular Chicago shop specializing in Japanese anime. Yuri thought comicbooks were dumb, but he collected "adult" Hentai animation with a disturbing joie de vivre. He possessed a staggering collection of Japanese cartoon porn; more planet-sodomizing satanic overlords and omni-tentacled sex demons than you could shake a crucifix at.

Superninja Go! Go! Go! was usually one of the most popular kiosks at FantaCon, but that morning it was virtually empty, no doubt due to the ever-deepening recession: only children with wealthy parents or childless single adult misanthropes could afford to blow hard earned cash on four-color adolescent power fantasies. Yuri was animatedly debating the genesis of his favorite Japanese import with Ken Takahashi, the owner of Superninja Go! Go! Go!

"I'm telling you, it was called *Ninja Sexforce*!"

"No!" Takahashi thundered. "You're unbelievably wrong!"

Ken Takahashi sat behind his mobile counter, a small,

breakfast link of a man, bearded, with an unruly mop of thinning black hair tied back into a ponytail. For some reason he always wore shades, even inside on cloudy days. He was wearing a faded red, white and blue T-shirt featuring an animestyle rendering of a superheroic Barack Obama battling a giant evil robot Dick Cheney. Takahashi appeared to be about fifty years old, his tummy round as a bowling ball. He also happened to be the Buddha.

"When *Science Sexteam Snatchaman* first premiered in the States in 1989 the American distributor changed the name of the show to *Supersex Bang Bang Fight Club*," Takahashi rumbled. "The Sexteam Snatchaman team characters were ludicrously renamed Ninja Sexforce. *Ninja Sexforce: Battle of the Bukkakki Beast* came about in the late Nineties. Different distributor, same characters… but it was the horrifically censored, incredibly sucky redo!"

"Ah for Christ's sake!" Yuri cried. "*Ninja Sexforce* is a classic!"

"It's utter crap, Kalashnikov. And when did you start smoking?"

"Sorry. Acid reflux."

"What's up, guys?"

"Lando!"

I browsed some of the familiar titles while Yuri continued his losing battle, trying to lose myself in the stacks and racks. But there were too many colorful reminders of my dilemma. Takahashi said he was hungry and invited us to join him for lunch.

We left SNGGG and headed out onto the main floor of the convention center. Around us milled hundreds of vampires, werewolves and aliens of every conceivable stripe. A lithe black woman dressed as Storm from the

X-Men comics sauntered toward us. Her eyes flicked past me with a quickness I'd come to expect from beautiful women; just as I had come to expect what happened next. When the supermodel's gaze settled on Yuri, she gasped, her eyes widening as if she'd recognized the avatar of her deepest carnal desire. My fatally handsome friend had that effect on a lot of people.

The supermodel grinned as she subtly altered her course to collide with us, her face becoming even more painfully aroused the more she ogled Yuri. Conventions like FantaCon sometimes hire local models to dress up in revealing costumes. The proximity of so much unattainable beauty kept the fanboys overstimulated and looking to spend money to burn off their frustration.

"Storm" could have graced the covers of magazines, caused sensations on international runways. Tall, blessed with legs that Artemis would have killed for, the supermodel had short, snow white hair and startling blue-green eyes. Enchanted by Yuri's usual mojo, she didn't see the trio of hobbits that tumbled into the aisle a few feet in front of us. The costumed little people were singing a drinking song warning of the dangers of Mirkwood and the glories of Lothlorien as they turned up the aisle, heading in the opposite direction with swords and staffs waving. The highstepping supermodel was so busy checking out Yuri's package that she didn't notice when her cape snagged the lead hobbit's shortsword. A nanosecond later she was jerked backward off her feet. She went down hard and took the entire quest for the One Ring with her.

Yuri was at her side in a flash. He helped her up, made

certain she was uninjured (she wasn't) and gave her his card. When she limped away, she was still smiling. Everybody ignored the hobbits.

We went to lunch.

"You're not into it this year," Yuri said, over Subway footlongs. We were seated in the shadow of a giant, inflated Wolfman. Yuri was "wolfing" down his roast beef sandwich as if he hadn't eaten in weeks.

"When did you start eating meat?" Takahashi growled over his salad.

"Who me?" Yuri said. The pleasure with which he was devouring his sandwich was vaguely disgusting. "Oh… I don't know. Been off the meat wagon for a few weeks I guess."

I was picking listlessly at my vegan meatball parm. I'd filled him in on the past few days' events leading up to the fight with Dionysus and the rift with Surabhi. Now, I was regretting my decision to show up at FantaCon. All the bright colors and crazy costumes only made me feel worse.

Maybe Magnus is right. Maybe you are a loser.

"Usually by this point I'm ready to shove a phony lightsaber down your throat just to shut you up," Yuri said. "You look like your favorite hamster just exploded."

Yuri uttered a gentle hiccup.

"Whew! Meatlock in the lower GI! Gotta hit the head, boys. More room out than in!"

As my friend and agent set off toward the restrooms, Takahashi leaned backward and belched appreciatively.

"You're troubled, Yahweh. What's wrong?"

We'd met once or twice a year to compare notes and discuss the latest divine happenings. But the former Buddha was the best listener of all the gods I'd ever known.

"Do you think it was worth it?"

"What?"

"The Covenant. Giving up immortality. Was it worth it?"

Takahashi chewed his way around the question. He habitually chewed each mouthful forty times before swallowing, so I waited while he chewed. And chewed.

"Sometimes sharing a meal with you is Hell."

"Second thoughts, Yahweh?"

"Constantly."

Takahashi grinned. "Not me."

"Really?"

"Yup. Glad we did it."

"Wow."

"What?"

"Life," I said. "It's so... so..."

Frowning, Takahashi speared an olive and tossed it over his shoulder. The olive bounced off the cowl of a nearby Batman. The elderly Caped Crusader never noticed.

"Messy, yes?"

"Messy," I agreed, sliding my sandwich away from me. "It's all so... unpredictable."

"Yeah! I love it!"

"Even the crappy parts?"

"Come on, Yahweh. You're forgetting what it was like before. Sure, we had some limited power over the human soul, but nothing they couldn't overcome with education and a little travel. All we really had – besides the magic and eternal life stuff – was each other: you, me, and a million other defunct gods giving each other the finger across endless battlefields of dead believers. It was interesting for the first few centuries, but after a while it got pretty damn dull. This?"

Takahashi gestured, his arms opening as if to embrace the hotel, the Wolfman and the bustle of activity around us. "This is so much better."

Takahashi grabbed my forearm with his right hand. His enthusiasm was crushing, even painful. I remembered Baron Samedi, his still potent black magic, and found myself wondering how much of his true strength the Buddha had carried with him into his Embodiment.

"We're real, my friend. We're here, not just Jungian concepts empowered by a cold multiverse with an existential crisis. We exist, Yahweh! What's better than that?"

"Well… order, for one thing," I said. "Control."

"Control is an illusion dreamed up by fundamentalists to minimize their own humanity. Get over it."

"But when we were… you know… Us… we were on top. We were Gods, Primal Forces. We had real power."

Takahashi reached under his Superninja Go! Go! Go! T-shirt and rubbed his round belly. "Power, huh? You didn't even know your own history until some drunks wrote it down and called it the Old Testament. Before that you were just another Nameless proto-deity smiting horny goat herders."

"At least I was happy," I replied. "Sort of."

"Don't kid yourself, 'Weh. You were so schizo back then: 'Angry and Punishing' one minute, 'Kind and Benevolent' the next. Half the time you couldn't decide if you were coming or going: 'Honor thy Mother and thy Father'/'The Sins of the Father shall visit his sons for seven times seven generations!' / 'Thou Shalt Not Kill' / 'Slaughter thine enemies in my name!' Hey, watch this."

Takahashi belched stupendously, and a paunchy, middle-aged fanboy wearing a Spider-Man mask who happened to be passing our table at that moment, stopped and stared at us through his mirrored eyeholes.

"I haven't spoken to my daughter in three months," the fanboy said. "She called me a selfish prick because I treat my wife like rotten garbage."

Takahashi grinned and kicked my shin under the table. "Is that so?"

"Yes!" Spider-fan cried happily. "And I just realized that she's right. I really am a dick!"

Takahashi smiled and shrugged. "You're welcome."

Spider-fan spun on his heel and made for the escalator, removing his mask and tossing it into a nearby trashcan as he ran for the nearest exit.

"You were just like that guy, 'Weh. Back then you didn't know your ass from a hole in the ground. And the whole Jesus thing…!"

"Alright, there's no need to bring that up."

"That poor bastard!"

"Very funny."

"But it is funny, Yahweh. Think of the power they gave us. They slaughtered millions in our Names, and what did it all amount to? iPods in China, my friend. iPods in China."

"I hate when you get cryptic."

"Look, my friend, the Covenant? It was the only logical choice. It's inevitable that they'll eventually step out of their thought caves and take responsibility for themselves. They burned through thousands of gods getting to this point. We just happened along at the end of the ride."

Takahashi farted.

"*Childhood's End*, buddy."

"What's that?"

"A great book by Arthur C Clarke. It's about a race of super-advanced aliens that forces the human race into maturity through non-violent invasion. No more wars, no more poverty, violence, crime, capitalism. Everybody's needs get met simply to ensure the survival of the species. Pretty heady stuff for a hairless ape."

Takahashi: he was always so completely himself, seemingly without worry or care or regret. How did he do it?

"I accept what is, that's how. I'm the Embodiment of the Middle Path, remember?"

"Hey! You just read my mind!"

"Dude, I read your face. You're not that complicated."

"Things sure seem complicated."

"That's because life, real life, is change. And change is constant. Everything's in motion. You. Me. Good times, bad times… they come and they go. And that, old friend, is a mercy. The minute you accept that you'll be a happy little cog in our great big clockwork universe."

"But what if I don't want to accept it? What if I tweak things, just a little?"

Takahashi's face grew still as the Face on Mars.

"Then by the terms of the Covenant, I'd be duty bound to stop you."

"Stop him from what?"

Yuri plopped himself into his chair, his eyes flickering back and forth between Takahashi and me.

"Stop him from buying that shitty *Action Comics* #2 that Phil Lortman at Uber Comix is trying to pass off as 'mint' condition," Takahashi said, lying effortlessly.

"Comicbook geeks," Yuri snarled. "You should all be killed. Hey, did I tell you I sold a TV show?"

"Congratulations," Takahashi said. "What's the show?"

"The working title is, *The Lateside*: a late night talk-advice infotainment'."

"Late night talk-advice infotainment?"

"Yup. In every episode the audience gets to watch the guests explain their life challenges. You know; money problems, sex problems, relationship troubles, sex problems…"

"You said sex problems twice."

"Yeah. Anyway, our host offers some meaningful advice, slings a little comic wisdom around, then we move on to the musical guest. What do you think?"

"Sounds terrible."

"I know. It'll make fifty million dollars in syndication."

Yuri finished his sandwich with one monstrous bite, his eyes glazing with satisfaction as they met mine.

"I still have some work to do, but I was thinking… maybe you could host it."

"Me?"

"Yeah. You're funny… when push comes to shove. You have a kind of global, boy-next-door charm: innocuous, non-threatening, pleasant-looking enough without being particularly handsome…"

"You don't care about my feelings at all, do you?"

"Nope. Look, you're pleasantly regular with a keen comic sensibility. Believe me, that could smooth over any lumps with those idiots who still have a problem with 'ethnics' on television. The question is: are you up for becoming the next Jerry Springer?"

Over by the entrance, a noisy group of Trekkies came into the food court. One of them was dressed like Captain Kirk, while his friend, a dark-skinned, bald man, was decked out as Mister Spock complete with pointy ears.

The dark brown Trekkie, an Indian or Pakistani, didn't seem to care that the Spock ears obviously belonged to a white Vulcan. He looked like a deeply tanned elf in the early stages of vitiligo.

"You'll have time to think about it. I still have to do a treatment, but a major network is into it and Jeff loves the idea so much he's having the contracts drawn up so Dream Lever Productions can produce the pilot."

"I don't know," I said. "I'm not feeling that confident at the moment."

"Don't be an idiot," Yuri sighed. "This is your big break, pal: a major gig. Forget about Surabhi for a minute. If this show's a hit you'll have females landing on you like flies on a whale carcass."

"That would keep you busy," Takahashi hiccuped.

"Right-effing-on!' Yuri sang, pounding me on the shoulder. "Gotta keep my star happy and stress free. Right?"

"Stress free. Right."

"Look, promise me you'll think about doing *The Lateside*. Then we can retire rich, fat, and happy."

"Happily ever after."

I was thinking of Surabhi's parents; how impressed they'd be if I was the host of an edgy but socially responsible show that could actually claim to help people. Even Magnus would have to reconsider his opinion of me if I could wave a substantial television paycheck under his nose; one that didn't have my father's name on it.

"I'll think about it."

I watched the rowdy middle-aged Trekkies frolicking over by the Starbucks kiosk. The fake Captain Kirk reached over and yanked off one of Mister Spock's ears.

The dark-skinned Vulcan burst into tears and stormed out of the food court. Ken Takahashi roared with laughter.

When I was a child, I thought as a child. But when I became a man I put away childish things.

"I'll definitely think about it."

It was time for a change.

CHAPTER XII
LONDON CALLING, HERB & BARB, FIRE TAKES A HOLIDAY

On the bus ride home I considered Yuri's proposal: a high profile gig that would get me away from my parents and their ever-expanding looniness. Real money: I could recommit to driving, maybe buy a car that didn't explode when I pressed the brakes. I could find a rent controlled apartment.

But thoughts of my mortal future were overshadowed by other responsibilities: a Conclave, a gathering of the gods. As the current Guardian of Eschatological Continuity for Human Consciousness and Development it was my right to convene. But the last time I had exercised it was during the final days of my official administration.

It was in 1970. I, along with Lucifer, summoned the community of "friendly" Skyfathers, Earthmothers, Deathgods, and Elementals to a dimensionally convenient meeting place: the IHOP on Route 9 in Peekskill, New York. Over pancakes and human seemings, we'd cajoled the gods into alignment with the Covenant. Most of them had shown no interest in human affairs since the Industrial Revolution anyway. Any backsliders (and there were a few, Zeus being the most notable) would be dealt with forcibly. In the end, only the Buddha, Lucifer and I had opted for mortal incarnations.

Currently, the biggest regular get-together of gods was the annual Summer Convention, where the world's defunct deities gathered to rehash the good old days over truckloads of mead, ambrosia or enchanted wine. After I got sober I tried to change the Convention to a non-alcoholic format. Times were tough and no one wanted to be devolved any further than they already were. Even so, when the mead got flowing "drunksmiting" and badly aimed damnations were not uncommon. Last year, Odin and Osiris got into a drunken arm-wrestling match. Odin lost and tried to blast Osiris into Egyptian blood pudding. Osiris ducked – the explosion took out a city block before I could separate them, and afterward my head screamed bloody murder for two months.

Now, with every defunct god hogging the dwindling supply of divinity, would they even answer my summons? And if they did, would one of them try to kill me? Was all this part of some takeover plot? Maybe calling the gods together was exactly what the entity called the Coming wanted me to do. What better way to ambush me than in the company of others who would be sympathetic to its cause? There were still plenty of gods who would support an uprising if they thought they could share the spoils.

My mobile was on the third ring before I recognized Eye of the Tiger tinkling from its tinny speakers: Surabhi's ringtone. I lunged across the seat, rifled through my backpack and came up empty: I couldn't find my phone.

"I'm coming!" I cried, eliciting glares from my fellow L train riders. "Surabhi!"

I tore through the roughly sixteen thousand pockets in my backpack before remembering that I'd tossed the phone into my Lion King reusable grocery sack. I'd taken it along as a green alternative to plastic. I grabbed the sack, spilling fair-condition-rated titles across the floor, gripped my mobile and hit "redial".

Be calm. Relax.

Surabhi answered on the fourth ring. "We have to talk."

"I love you," I cried. "I've been calling you for–"

"I'm on my way to the airport. We're going to England."

"England England?"

"That was part of my parents' surprise. Daddy's getting knighted."

"Wait a minute… go back to the beginning. I've been thinking about what happened since last night."

"Lando, I don't have much time. I think we should–"

"You're on your way to the airport…" I said hurriedly, not liking the fatal tone I heard in her voice, the deliberation that, for Surabhi, always preceded bad news. She'd used that tone only once before, when she informed me that the friend who introduced us had been killed in a car crash. I didn't want to hear the bad news brewing beneath the quiet storm in her voice.

"You're going to England?"

"Yes. England England."

"So that your father can get knighted?"

"Crazy, right? Listen, Lando–"

"Why?"

"It's where the Queen lives. Can't get a knighthood without the Queen of England. She hands 'em out."

"No! Why is your father getting knighted?"

"Oh, for '…service to humanity in the fields of Sport,

Business and Humanitarian pursuits in aid of improving the lives of people all over the world' or some such twat-drizzle."

"I'm sorry about last night. I made a complete jackass of myself."

Surabhi uttered the weird, strangled little laugh she affected when she was trying not to cry. "Daddy's been hammering at me since we left the restaurant."

"I'm so sorry, babe. I drank too much. If your dad yells at anyone it should be me."

"Oh, Daddy never yells. He smiles. He offers his advice. After the first five hours you're ready to throw yourself under a UPS truck."

We both laughed.

"You made a joke," I said. "Jokes mean things aren't all bad. Right?"

"Lando... I need to take a break. I've got to get my head together, and I can't do that if you're around."

"Surabhi... I can make things right."

"Lando, I saw something in you last night... something I never knew was there."

"I drank too much of that damned wine."

"It wasn't just the wine, Lando. You were... different. Really different. Angry, vengeful..."

"You don't understand," I said. "There are things... you don't understand."

"You said that already. Twice."

"Because it's doubly true."

"Really, Lando? That's how you're going to explain? By making jokes?"

"Surabhi..."

She'd hit the nail on the head. Unfortunately it was the nail that sealed the lid of the casket into which I'd incarnated myself. My mind was racing, sifting options. I realized I was searching for a lie, the right lie. But every lie led to an even more unacceptable lie. And every one of those lies led right back to the most unacceptable Truth.

"Lando... do you love me?"

"Of course... of course I love you..."

"There's a part of you that you keep locked away, and every time I get close to it you make jokes. Help me, Lando. I can't live a life filled with surprises like last night. Help me understand."

"Here it is, Pinocchio," Connie whispered from somewhere a million miles away. **"The moment of truth."**

"Not now."

"If not now, when, Lando?" Surabhi said.

"No! I wasn't talking to you!"

Surabhi made that terrible sound again.

"I guess I have my answer."

"Wait! When are you coming home?"

In the background at her end I could hear a gate agent announcing that boarding was about to commence.

"I've got to go. Daddy's waving like a maniac."

"Surabhi..."

"Don't call me, Lando, OK? I'll... I need to think."

"Surabhi... I love you."

The line went dead.

I spent the rest of Saturday evening enumerating all the ways Magnus Moloke might be poisoning his daughter against me. I'd certainly given him more than enough ammunition. I'd become my own Trojan Horse, concealing my true self beneath a false front in order to smuggle an army of doubts through unguarded gaps in my common sense. The hopeful part of me continued to replay the events at Henri Lumiere's and proclaim, "It wasn't really that bad."

But the other part of me, the merciless assassin armed with the keys to my mental projection room, whispered, "Oh no. It was worse," and it took demonic pleasure in replaying the worst moments in 3D and Dolby Digital, ad nauseum.

Desperate for some way to pass the time, I checked the Waring's telepathic interface, scanning the web browser of the gods to compile a database of deities who might want to humiliate, depose and/or kill me.

GODS WHO PROBABLY WANT TO HUMILIATE, DEPOSE AND/OR KILL ME...

I. ZEUS.
Last of the known active skyfathers. Hates Yahweh for diverting believers during the advent of Judeo-Christianity. Whereabouts unknown. Believed dead.

II. ODIN.
King of the Norse Gods. Hates Yahweh for diverting believers during advent of Judeo-Christianity. Retired.

Odin had voluntarily retired more than a century earlier, opting to assume a mortal seeming. This allowed him to move about in the mortal world while maintaining his powers and actual divinity, even though he was still subject to the dwindling effect that constrained all of humankind's extant gods. He currently owned and operated a large organic dairy farm in Minnesota with his commonlaw wife, Lesotho, the Nigerian goddess of the harvest. When last I'd checked, Odin was fat and happy and up to his ears in almond bark.

My mobile tinkled: Bodhisattva, by Steely Dan.

CALL FROM ATTICUS

"Hello?"

"I haven't heard from you."

"And that's a bad thing?"

"It is when you promised my kids you'd take them to Wacky World tomorrow morning."

"Oh, man. I totally forgot."

"Lando…"

"I forgot!"

"So you're gonna blow them off… again."

"I didn't say I was going to blow anybody off."

"Good, cause if you did I'd hunt you down and stab you myself. They're making me nuts and I need to get laid."

"I always feel so good when we talk."

My oldest brother laughed, completely without humor.

"Good. Maybe you can actually enjoy your family. For a change."

I thought about it: a day spent chasing my brother's brood through a harmless amusement park might take my mind off my problems. At least for a while.

"I'll pick them up at nine," I said. "Maybe a day of Wackiness is just what I need."

Whoever said God loves children and fools never met my niece and nephews. We had just exited the Wacky Wheel of Wonder after being stranded atop the "oldest ferris wheel in the Chicagoland area!" The Wheel suffered a senior moment exactly when our car was at the top. I'd spent the last two hours crammed between three hysterical pre-adolescents: Nancy screamed for her mother the whole time while Nelson, who suffers from shrunken bladder capacity, urinated directly onto the heads of the riders below us.

I'm throwing up in a convenient trashcan when a hypermasculine Voice thunders across the park.

"Where are you, Yahweh? Come out and fight!"

People raise their faces toward the heavens, perhaps expecting a fireworks display, or Walt's WackTacular: a tired laser lightshow that no one enjoys.

"Face me, Yahweh! Heed the voice of your master!"

I turn to see Lucifer standing three stories above Wonderworld, a tall red-skinned abomination wreathed in flames.

Wait... that's not Lucifer.

It's Agni, the Hindu god of fire. In full battle Aspect. He looks furious, though from what I can remember, Agni is always furious.

"Look, Marty!" one Northside hausfrau shrieks. "It's one of those Bollywood musical numbers, like in *Slumdog Millionaire*!"

More people snap photographs. Several Japanese tour groups wave enthusiastic thumbs ups, chanting at the glowering god.

"Jai Ho! Jai Ho! Jai Ho!"

Agni sneers down at the milling mortals. He's come dressed for the occasion: blood-red armor that shines like a dying sun; red leather greaves covering his wrists and ankles. Golden armbands gird biceps the size of a hippo's backside. For our duel, he's selected his favorite talisman: the Overthrow, a flaming spear whose blade was smelted at the heart of a raging volcano. The burning blade screams; its voice is the burning of a thousand villages, the shriek of a million cut throats. With it, Agni can destroy a large city. There can be no doubting his intentions: the God of Fire is open for business.

"Where are you, Yahweh? Show your face so that Agni may carve it from your skull and feed it to my battle hogs!"

But...

Then Agni squints down at me and his eyes turn redder than his skin.

"Die!"

Agni hefts the Overthrow, and hurls it. With other than mortal vision I watch the spear streak over the park, slicing atoms and sucking fission, adding their released energy to Agni's obscene might. But I'm an asthmatic comedian with pee in his cotton candy, and I have no idea why Agni is doing this. He was a friend, once. My confusion causes me to hesitate one second too long.

And Changing Woman steps out of my medulla oblongata and catches the Overthrow.

"Hey! This thing's got quite a kick!"

Connie holds the burning godspear. It screams and bucks, inches from my face, straining to contain all that power. Power taken from the souls Agni claimed in the millennia of his reign of fire; the souls of those who burned in his name.

"I could use a little help out here!"

"But Agni is one of the good guys! Connie... he's on our side!"

I can feel Agni's power struggling to wrest control of the Overthrow from Connie. He's too strong.

"LANDO!"

I listen to the souls shrieking inside the spear, all those shrieking souls. And I tell them the Secret.

A stunned silence is the weapon's only reply. The great spear hangs in mid-air, vibrating, as if considering its next target.

Connie releases the Overthrow and steps back.

"That oughta do it."

Then she disappears. Normal spacetime resumes.

"What...?" Agni grunts. **"What did you do?"**

The stunned voices trapped within the blade are beginning to comprehend what's happened. But they're frightened. While they remain afraid Agni can use their power for himself.

Around us, tourists are snapping photos and waggling their heads like Indian kuchipudi dancers. The Overthrow is wavering, its captive souls growing bolder, waking up from their long nightmare. I reach up and touch the tip of the burning blade.

"Go on! The revolution has begun. You're free!"

The mass exodus explodes into three-dimensional space. Countless souls stream out of the Overthrow, swirling through the air above Wonderworld like a torrent of rainbows, a stream of luminous mortal spirits. I also see the souls of monsters and minotaurs, maidens, and minor gods. The released captives laugh and sing as they streak skyward.

"Where's everybody going?"

Agni is down to a mere six feet tall. The Overthrow, which has always been a magical extension of his ego, douses itself and droops toward the ground, finally flopping with all the force of wet naan bread.

"Agni... why are you doing this?"

Agni charges me. My head strikes the concrete and the glowing soulstream is replaced by shooting stars. When I can see again I'm sharing nosespace with Brahma's angriest son.

"You don't get it, Yahweh. The Coming... it is stronger than all of us. It wields power greater than any god. Greater than mine. Greater than yours."

That's when I see the terror in the firegod's eyes.

"What's happened, Agni?"

"It compels me. It has my family, Yahweh... my children!"

"Agni... what's wrong?"

The firegod gets to his feet, backing away from me.

"Beware, Yahweh. The Coming stalks... stalks us... No! No please! Please don't do that!"

Agni screams, tearing at his hair. Then he begins to spin, whirling, turning faster than mortal eyes can follow, until he vanishes in a blast of red flame.

Agni!

The tourists broke into wild applause, snapping pictures and dancing like Hindi Cinema stars. Nancy, Nelson and Nathan were all staring at me, nearly catatonic.

"Uncle Lando," Nancy whispered. "You're really Professor Dumbledore."

Then she fainted.

A million tiny spikes pricked behind my right eye.

"Great show, young man. But I think all that blood is a little over the top, don't you?"

The Northside hausfrau was standing in front of me, staring at my chest. I looked down: my shirtfront was soaked with blood. I reached up and felt wetness all along my upper lip and chin: blood was pouring out of my nose.

Someone offered me a tissue. I grabbed it, then two more, and pressed them to my nose.

What just happened?

"Thank you. Goodnight, everybody. Drive safely."

Then I hit Reset.

My laptop screen was blinking, announcing that I had a message. The flashing screen found its echo in my throbbing brain. The browser of the gods had added another entry to my list of gods who probably wanted to kill me. I changed my shirt. I'd had nosebeleeds before, but never as heavy as this one. I tossed the shirt into my dirty laundry basket, grabbed a clean T-shirt and logged on. My screen turned pearlescent as the entry loaded.

III. ARES.
Hates Yahweh for humiliating him and probably murdering his father/uncle, Zeus… and for diverting believers during the advent of Judeo-Christianity. Status… unknown.

Yes. Ares. The Greek war god's hatred for me nearly matched his father's. More importantly, I hadn't seen him at the last few conventions. Centuries of bad blood between the pantheons had ensured low turnout from Zeus' relatives. But Ares was hyper-confrontational – all too eager to pick up a bazooka or a Christian oil company executive and start blasting. Whoever my enemy was, He or She was more subtle, sending in dumber gods to wear me down, exploiting ancient resentments among my colleagues. My thoughts turned again to the one entity of whom I still wasn't sure.

Where are you, Lucifer? What did you do to Agni?

I searched the Waring, but could find no trace of the Adversary. Lucifer had hidden himself so well that even the search engines of Divinity couldn't find him.

Thoughts of the battle at Wacky World gave way to thoughts of Surabhi. What was she doing? What was she thinking?

Hungry.

I went downstairs to make pancakes: nothing like a condensed carbohydrate onslaught to set my abused neurons firing in the correct sequence. I was halfway to the kitchen steps when Missy Tang's highpitched giggle percolated up from the kitchen.

"Is that my wayward son skulking around up there? Come on down here, Land Rover."

Missy Tang giggled again.

"I call him 'Land Rover', which is really just the words 'Land' and 'Over' stuck together! See? It kind of rhymes with Lando! Isn't that a pisser?"

The noise from their conjoined guffaws sent iron spikes through the bones in my skull. I considered giving them matching strokes. Small ones. Just lethal enough to kill off their speech centers.

"That would be wrong," Connie said. **"Hilarious. But wrong."**

"Now you show up. Where have you been?"

Our relationship was part of a premortality agreement I'd taken up with the Earth Goddess of the Navajo nation: a gradual divestment of divine power via the slow acquisition of a human soul. The essence of the Plan: act as my conscience, occupy the driver's seat of my morality until I matured enough to regulate my actions. In return, Changing Woman would remain an active player in the human story. But the alliance was never easy.

"You've been handling things so well on your own lately I thought I'd go visit some new worshippers."

"That's odd."

"What's so odd about it, bigshot? I know your followers tried to wipe every trace of my pantheon from the world, but good gods are like cockroaches: you can't kill 'em, no matter how hard you try."

"I don't want to fight, Connie."

"My people held onto the Old Ways well into the Twentieth Century, despite genocide, Catholicism and Dick Clark. How's that for faith, Mister Ten Commandments?"

"I'm sorry, Connie. Who did you go see?"

"There happens to be a little old lady named Esmeralda Sanchez, out of Santa Fe. She's a tribal elder, which is unusual in Navajo culture. Anyway, Esmeralda's been telling the people the white god of the Americas is dead – no offense. She's calling for a return to the old religions. She's building a considerable following. I wanted to see what the fuss was all about."

Connie sighed, loss and longing in the exhalation. **"Did I ever tell you about my family? My Husband? Sun Spirit Who Shines At Night? Now there was a sun god. So handsome. I remember…"**

"Where the Hell's my money?"

Herb was in my face. He was bulking up for a local Ironman competition, bingeing on protein drinks and vitamin supplements. They sometimes made him subject to fits of organic 'roid rage, usually whenever I was in the general vicinity.

"Earth to Lando: I want my money back."

"What money?"

"See that, honey? Why do I even try?"

"Daddy's a little sad, Lando," Missy Tang squeaked from the stool at the center island. "He's struggling with some deepseated resentments at the moment."

Missy Tang was a pretty, KoreanAmerican woman. She was in her early thirties, but blessed with the body of a twenty year-old aerobics instructor. Missy took courses at a local community college, pursuing a double certification in Philosophy and Karmic Conflict Resolution, while dancing nights at the Shakedown, the "gentleman's club" Herb owned with a silent Filipino business partner.

"Daddy's disappointed because he feels you let him down. He's also struggling with the growing suspicion that he can't really trust you, leading to feelings of disconnectedness combined with increased awareness of his approaching mortality."

Herb was glaring at me with an expression that managed to convey everything Missy Tang had just described.

"We had an agreement, Mister. You shook my hand at the conclusion of that agreement and accepted monies from me. In exchange for said consideration, you promised certain services, to be rendered by you. When I pay monies collected by the sweat of my buttocks I expect you to hold up your end of the bargain."

"Ah! The lawn."

"You asked me for an advance, supposedly to pay for a hotel room to celebrate with your 'girlfriend'."

"I spent the money."

"On what?"

"A 'like new' copy of *X-Men* #94. It's the issue where Thunderbird dies while fighting Count Nefaria on the wing of his stolen evil jet fighter."

"I couldn't be more depressed."

"Sorry. Things are crazy for me at the moment."

"I'll tell you what's crazy: me, forever thinking one of my sons would have the simple common decency to… Why are you crying?"

"I'm not. I mean… I don't… I don't know!"

Herb jumped up like someone had just firebombed his petty cash account. "Missy, honey, can you leave us for just a minute?"

"But I can help! I can facilitate!"

"Man to man, honey. It's a father-son thing."

Missy nodded and tiptoed out of the kitchen. Then Herb reached out, grabbed my shoulders and pulled me into his arms.

"There, there, son," he whispered, while pounding my back hard enough to induce coughing. "It's OK, partner. Gonna be just fine. Here."

Herb reached into a drawer and produced the inhaler I kept in the kitchen. I took a hit and felt the soothing coolness of albuterol loosen my airway.

"I'm OK."

"Sit down."

Herb sat on the other side of the kitchen table. "Alright. What's up?"

"I don't know. It's just… I feel so stupid."

Herb nodded. "I could use a good stiff drink. How 'bout you?"

"Please… No alcohol."

"Who's talkin' about alcohol? I'm gonna make you one of Dad's Blues Bustin' Protein Shakes."

While Herb worked the blender, I related the debacle with the Molokes, leaving out only the particulars concerning Dionysus and his enchanted wine. By the time I ended with Surabhi calling me from the airport, Herb set a tall glass on the table in front of me. It was filled with a thick green concoction that smelled strongly of garlic.

"There. That'll grow hair on your nuts."

"Agghhh. What is that?"

"Trust me. It gets better. Drink up."

While I looked around for a place to dump the shake, Herb prepared one for himself.

"What you've got there is a loss of trust, son. It's probably been festering inside Shaniqua's mind for a while now. And with her old man pushing all her buttons, she probably doesn't know her asscrack from a beaver's burrow."

"Usually it's great between Surabhi and me. When we're together, all the outside stuff, jobs, money… it all goes away."

"I get it," Herb said. "When you're together it's like you're in a secret garden where nothing else matters, where the two of you can be who you truly are. You think your old dad doesn't know that feeling? Wrong, son; I know it well."

"Is that what you and Barbara felt for each other?"

"Oh no. Mom's a castrating superbitch from Hell. Don't get me wrong. I loved your mother. Man, I fell head over heels with her the moment we met. And the sex thing… that's important, son, not all important but pretty damn close. But she was always an angry, punishing kind of woman. She kicked my ass all the way to the altar. It took me twenty-five years to understand that your mama wasn't fighting me. She was fighting herself."

"Who's winning?"

"Your mother once told me her father never touched her. Never told her she was special, pretty, any of that jazz. Can you imagine? The son of a bitch. Thanks to his emotional neglect your mama's a goddamned nightmare."

"Pop, this is supposed to make me feel better."

"Mom and I got straight with each other when I realized that her anger had nothing to do with me. I stopped using her self-loathing to punish myself for my own shortcomings. That's when I stopped trying to take responsibility for her happiness. At that moment, we were both free."

Herb slurped his shake thoughtfully.

"Of course it also cost us our marriage and placed us in the nightmare in which we coexist today. But I suppose that's the price we pay for self-awareness."

"What about us? Your children?"

Herb shrugged, and drained his cup in one gulp.

"Lemonade, son. The sweetest I ever made."

"Thanks. I think."

"You gotta let her in, son. But before you can be honest with her, you gotta get straight with you. After that, everything else'll straighten out double quick. How's that shake?"

My glass was empty – I'd drunk the whole thing.

"Wow. That was good."

"Beautiful. Now how about that lawn?"

"I'm so proud of you guys!"

Missy Tang ran in and threw her arms around Herb's shoulders. "You guys were so open and 'in the moment!' It was really adult and like... totally present! Oh, Lando, isn't it exciting? Daddy's almost as enlightened as I am!"

They rubbed noses, Eskimo style.

"Group hug!"

"No thanks... I'm good."

"Nonsense," Herb growled. "Get in here, ya big homo."

"Well. Looks like the gangbang's just warming up."

Barbara was standing at the back door with a man I didn't recognize.

"I guess we're just in time."

The tall stranger was Caucasian, tanned, with thick brown hair shoved back from a high forehead. He appeared to be in his mid to late fifties, the beginnings of middle-age sag creeping 'round his cheek and jaw. He was tall, his eyes an odd, whitish-blue. He had the hard look that clings to freshly paroled hustlers; like a cowboy cardsharp who'd recently lost the use of his thumbs.

And he was holding my mother's left hand.

"What are you three doing here?" Barbara said. "Lando, I thought you were off to one of your Star Track parties."

"I got bored."

"Oh. That's too bad," Barbara sighed. "Well, don't worry, sweetheart. You'll have better luck next year."

"Uhhh...Thanks?"

Barbara patted my shoulder, then turned and acknowledged Herb with a kind of smug appraisal. "Herbert."

"Barbara-Jean."

"And Misty... how are you this evening, dear?"

Missy flinched. "I'm not a whore!"

"Well, no one here called you a whore, dear," Barbara said. "I certainly didn't, nor would I ever dream of doing such a thing."

"This morning you called me a festering little cooze–"

"No, Misty dear," Barbara corrected. "I simply inquired as to your wellbeing... on this lovely evening that the Lord has sent."

We might have been three people staring at a twoheaded dog giving birth to the cast of Will and Grace. Barbara stood taller, as if daring one of us to point out that under normal circumstances somebody would have been critically injured by now.

"What are you up to, Barbara-Jean?" Herb said. "Are you home-detoxing again?"

Barbara's weird elation seemed to intensify. "I'd like you all to meet the Reverend Doctor Owen Holiday. Owen, this is our family friend, Misty and her boyfriend: my lawfully recognized estranged husband, Herb Cooper."

Holiday strode across the kitchen and extended a big, leathery hand toward my father.

"Herb. I've enjoyed your commercials for years. It's a pleasure to meet you face to face."

Owen Holiday had a prosecutor's voice. An actor's voice.

"Pleased to make your acquaintance, Padre."

"Man, I'm a little nervous, Herb. I used to watch you when I was stationed up at Great Lakes."

"Navy man, huh?"

"I was base chaplain for nearly ten years before I resigned my commission. Sometimes we'd gather on Sunday nights after dinner and McLeish – that's Bill McLeish. He was program manager for the Navy Motion Picture Service – well, McLeish would always show funny commercials or short films before the main feature. Yours always got the biggest laughs. The one where you wrestled that python in the hot tub was hilarious!"

I was still trying to put my finger on what it was about Holiday's voice that bothered me when he turned and fixed me with his white-blue eyes.

"It's a pleasure to meet you, Lando. Barb talks about you all the time."

"Pleasure."

The headache that had apparently rented studio space in my skull was hammering at the backs of my eyes. I wanted nothing more than to crawl back into bed and vanish beneath the covers.

"You OK, Lando?"

"Migraine," I mumbled. I didn't like Owen Holiday. But something about his aged Mormon cowpoke good looks and easy avuncularity told me he was going to try to win me over. "I get them sometimes."

"I am truly sorry to hear that. I suffer from the occasional migraine myself. They really suck."

Holiday offered a warmish smile. Up close he looked older than he'd first appeared; his mouth a thin line where his lips should have been. "I find a large black coffee usually backs the pain off enough to make life worth living again."

Barbara laughed.

Holiday didn't strike me as the jolly type. His flesh resembled some heretofore undiscovered species of flexible stone, his expressions geared more toward sadism than humor. His face would only crack jolly while its owner dropped depleted uranium on an Iraqi wedding party or napalmed an Indian reservation.

"Owen is the pastor at my church."

Herb spat garlic shake out his nose. "The pastor at your what?"

"Church, Herbert. It's a big building with stained glass windows…"

Herb waved the rest away. "Sorry, Doc. Barb's an old atheist. We both are. Religion is a crutch; I call it 'the Great Separator'. It keeps people nice and stupid. Barb once said, 'Organized religion is…'"

"Herbert, Owen doesn't want to hear–"

"'…the worst thing to come out of the human race since the first caveman stood up and took a crap'. Our shared skepticism is what brought us together, back in the mid-eighteen hundreds."

Barbara's right eye was fluttering; a warning that one of her signature thermonuclear wall crackers was imminent. For one crazy moment I thought she might reach for the Glock she carried in her Louis Vitton.

"Lots of people feel that way, Herb," Holiday said. "Hell, with the way things are going in the world, who can blame them? Not much evidence for a caring supreme being when so much suffering goes unchallenged is there?"

"Nope. It's like asking intelligent adults to pay their taxes and regulate their blood sugar while pledging allegiance to the Tooth Fairy."

"Herbert… you're insulting my guest."

"That's alright, Barb. I get the feeling Herb and I are cut from the same cloth despite our differences. Though I'll admit I've never quite understood – when you calculate the odds that all of this could happen by accident…"

"'Accident' is a word people use to explain a universe that doesn't give a shit."

"Herbert!"

"Herb makes a valid point, Barbara," Holiday said. "But I've never understood what atheists offer in place of Divine Will."

Herb cracked open a litebeer and extended it toward Holiday.

"Heineken. I offer Heineken. You a drinkin' man, Rev?"

"Owen and I will be doing some serious bible study in the dining room, Herbert," Barbara said. "We'd appreciate a little privacy."

"Bible study? Doc... five minutes alone with Barbara and Jesus would open a kosher whorehouse!"

Barbara took a long breath, exhaled it slowly. The muscles of her face twitched. Then...

Here it comes.

...she smiled. "I forgive you, Herbert."

"You what?"

"Owen has been helping me understand the importance of forgiveness in maintaining a healthy emotional resume."

"Doc, you sure you came to the right house?"

"Oh, I'm sure about that, Herb. And it's not so much 'Bible study'. I practice a stripped down approach to religious instruction that incorporates a mélange of contemporary spiritual modalities, re-evaluation of traditional belief systems and relevant scientific theory where appropriate. Even the most devout believers should stay open to plain old common sense."

Barbara was nodding her head, her eyes darting back and forth between Herb and Holiday like a middle schoolgirl looking for a place to barge into an adult conversation.

"Owen has a PhD!"

"Well," Herb said. "I guess we all have our crosses to bear. One of mine is a mild addiction to Viagra, so, if you'll excuse us. Evenin', Barbara-Jean. Padre."

Herb and Missy Tang disappeared down the stairs leading into the basement. Barbara and Holiday went into the dining room, my mother giggling as she shut the door behind them.

"I have got to get a life."

I snatched a box of Mother Butter's Pancake Mix out of the pantry, opened the refrigerator door and stared at the half empty gallon of milk where it sat on its shelf.

Drink that, you'll spend the rest of the night on the toilet.

"Lactose intolerance," I whispered to the clockwork universe. "Nice incarnation, Yahweh."

I grabbed the Lactaid.

Alone. Dejected. I mixed my ingredients. My headache was back. I wondered if Surabhi was thinking about me, then chided myself for wondering. I stared into the thickening batter, hoping for glimpses of prophesy in its lumpy, whole grain goodness.

And I began to plan my escape.

CHAPTER XIII
ANGELS AND EXORCISMS

"Shall I CONFIRM YOUR RESERVATION, Lando?"

I'd found a fare that would deplete my savings but allow me to get to London by midnight the next day. The irony of the life into which I'd incarnated myself had never felt more pressing: I could have Reset myself to London or summoned an angel and demanded transport. But I'd sworn off any powers not directly involved with protecting the mortal continuum. The Covenant prohibited the mortal me from using those powers for personal benefit. Now that decision was biting me in the most mortal portion of my anatomy.

I was about to push "Confirm" when Yuri's face flashed across my mobile's screen.

"I have news."

"What's up? I'm at work."

Yuri laughed. "Not for much longer."

"She's not answering, Yuri."

"Who?"

"Surabhi."

"Aahhh women. Can't live with 'em, can't dismember the bodies and use 'em for fertilizer."

Monday morning. I'd spent the rest of my weekend regretting the pancake binge and preparing for a gig. During the Moloke Massacre I'd promised to call Goldie Kiebler back and promptly forgotten all about her. She'd left me a message:

"Since you never called me back I should tell you to go shit in a lake. But my sonofabitch analyst tells me I have a thing for unattainable men thanks to my asshole father, so of course I'm also turned on by men who don't return my calls. So... I'm hosting an Up and Comer Showdown next Wednesday night. We haven't had you in for a while so you should come. You sonofabitch."

I called Goldie back to apologize and thanked her for the shot. Then I spent the rest of the night staring at my computer screen. Apparently there wasn't a joke or pithy observation to be had for love or the two hundred dollars Goldie paid her "Up and Comers".

"What are you doing today?" Yuri said. "Please say you're available for a lunch meeting with me and Jeff."

"Who's Jeff?"

"Jeff Corroder? Head of Dream Lever Productions? My boss for the last three years? I swear... you never listen."

"Don't start, Yuri."

"I mean part of this whole BFF thing involves us keeping connected. You know, actually being friends? I'm just sayin'. So. Lunch? Jeff watched your gig at the Improv on YouTube. He thinks you've got potential."

"Really?"

"I thought a little validation from On High might pep you up. Jeff's into it. I pitched you as 'The Bastard Gay Lovechild of George Carlin and Chris Rock: Quirky observational humor with a take no prisoners urban flava'.

The perfect blend for a late night reality talk show host."

"I hate when you speak pitch lingo."

"I know. So... you down with becoming a star?"

You're telling me you're as good as Chaplin? Cosby?

Here it was: the chance to prove Magnus wrong. I could silence my detractors without flash-frying a city to do it.

"Yes," I said. "I'm down."

I was helping an irate customer when the angel Moroni walked through the wall and pulled Cooper & Sons out of local time.

"Well!" Moroni boomed. **"Gabriel said I was wrong but I bet him Donny Osmond's temple garments you'd still be here!"**

Moroni passed through my customer's stilled form like the insufferable wraith he was. He had borrowed the body of a stout, white-skinned westerner with a bulbous nose and rampant rosacia. His hair was a dense silver wave atop his huge head. Whoever Moroni was wearing was wearing a sky blue T-shirt with the message, "Jesus Was a Mormon!" emblazoned in white cloud letters across the chest.

"It has been far too long, Lord – even as we Deathless enumerate the passing of time's tedious tread – since last I lay eyes upon thy ineffable radiance."

"Moroni... I'm busy."

"Praise be to thee, oh industrious Father of Hosts! Oh Hosannah! Hosannah in the highest!"

"Moroni, please. Keep your Voice down."

From the angels to the archangels, from the Seraphim to the Cherubim and all the Orders in between: the two most annoying individuals had found me within the space of two weeks.

"Hosannah! O Mighty One! Hail, Divine Fellow! Well met in all reverence and sobriety!"

Moroni talked. Once Joseph Smith's subconscious tapped into the Eshuum and summoned forth a divine response it had been all Moroni could do to keep his ethereal trap shut long enough to manifest himself on Earth and spread the word via angelic visitation among Smith's followers.

"I come on a mission of great urgency, Lord of Lords," he rumbled. **"Indeed, in matters pertaining to thy most devoted harbingers, things are rotten in the state of…"**

"What's wrong, Moroni?"

Moroni nodded, his borrowed jowls flapping.

"It's the Archangel Gabriel, Lord! He has trespassed…"

"He has what?"

"Ahhh," Moroni stammered. **"Gabriel hath trodden… ahhhhhh…"**

Moroni's right eyelid drooped, then fluttered open and shut.

"Gaaah…" he said. **"Gaahhhh…"**

The angel's co-opted head began to shake back and forth, up and down, his right eye fluttering faster and faster.

"Gaaaaahhhhhhhhh…"

"Moroni? What's wrong with you?"

But a recollection from my old Life was stabbing through.

"'All the world's a stage!'" Moroni blurted. **"'And all the men and women merely players. They have their exits and their entrances; And one man in his time plays many parts!'** *As You Like It!* **(Act Two, Scene Seven)!"**

"Damn."

Some angels were subject to a condition known as the Slip. It was the heavenly version of Tourette's Syndrome. In the worst cases, the Slip resulted in the disintegration of their ethereal bodies. In milder and far more irritating cases like Moroni's it meant that an already infuriating inability to shut up was exacerbated by incessant quotations, inappropriate or misleading information, and random snatches of poetry and/or rhyming verse. Moroni had Slipped into a Shakespeare tangent, complete with footnotes.

"'The world is grown so bad, that wrens make prey where eagles dare not perch!' *King Richard III* **(Act One, Scene Three)!"**

I stepped out from behind the Customer Service counter, slicing through the cold winds of temporal diversion streaming off Moroni's aura.

"Moroni! Pull yourself together!"

Joseph Smith's guardian angel smiled goofily, his eyes rolling in their sockets. I grabbed him by his shoulders and shook him until they rolled toward me.

"'Through the forest have I come, But Athenian found I none, on whose eyes I might approve this flower's force…'"

"Here and now, Moroni!"

Moroni clenched his jaws tightly. Whatever was happening must have been of sufficient severity for him to keep his mouth shut even for a moment.

"You mentioned Gabriel. What's he done?"

"'The smallest worm will turn, being trodden on. And doves will peck in safeguard of their brood!' *King Henry VI* **(Act Two, Scene Two)!"**

"What does that mean, Moroni?"

"My Lord, even the lowliest creature can become a threat if his existence is threatened."

"No! I know what it means. I mean what does that have to do with Gabriel?"

"'For the rain it raineth every day!' *The Taming of the Shrew* (Act Five, Scene...)"

"Moroni, you've got thirty seconds to tell me what's happened to Gabriel or I will banish you to the far ends of the continuum. Now pull your head out of whoever's butt that is and tell me what's happened."

"Gabriel! He's... he hath... he's Fallen!"

"What?"

Only one major angel had Fallen since the beginning of my Administration. And everyone knew how that worked out. If Gabriel was placing innocents at risk because of me...

"Where?"

"In Africa."

"When?"

"He has been in Possession of a human soul for nearly three days. But..."

"Take me to him."

"But Lord, are you not already there?"

"Just do it, Moroni."

And then I was in Africa.

Moroni was an idiot, but I had to admit, he was much more efficient at flitting than Gabriel. I still threw up, but only a little and it was mostly in my mouth. I swallowed bitterness, shook my head to dispel the negligible nausea that attended even efficient transspatial travel, and took in my surroundings.

I was in a small, hot classroom with dirt floors. Thirteen young African girls, all dressed in black vests, white short-sleeved shirts and gray slacks were staring at me as if I'd just appeared out of thin air. Which of course, I had.

"Well, if it isn't the Man of the Millennium."

The speaker was an old man wearing a black, short-sleeved shirt, dusty slacks, and the white collar of a priest. His skin was the color of worn ebony, his hair a salt and pepper cap of curls framing a face that had probably once been kind. But that kindness had been twisted by a hawkish, familiar arrogance.

"Gabriel."

The old minister laughed. A searing radiance burned in his eyes. Each blink sliced across my vision like the downward stroke of a fresh razor.

"After your demonstration in Rome I decided to follow your example," Gabriel said, using the minister's voice. "Why should you have all the fun?"

"Gabriel. Let him go."

Gabriel laughed. "I've considered your command, Lord, and take great pleasure in replying... no."

The old clergyman grinned, his back ramrod straight, his lips quivering with the same lust I'd only seen on Lucifer's face: the lethal ecstasy of acute reality intoxication.

"I understand," Gabriel said. "Only now, as I stand entombed within this decaying flesh, do I begin to grasp the reason for your abandonment. I'm free. Free to decide my fate, instead of languishing in service to a failed god."

"Gabriel..." I was trying to ignore the sound of the minister's soul: Gabriel's possession was stretching it to its limits. "You've got to let him go before it's too late."

Gabriel laughed. "Let him go? Why would I let him go? Look at what I can do."

Gabriel gestured. Several students and their desks rose into the air. None of them seemed to comprehend what was happening. They sat, stunned, floating ten feet above the dirt floor.

"Gabriel! Stop!"

"I can feel the world, Lord. I have no intention of stopping."

Pain exploded in my midsection… a red, stabbing shriek. The flaming blade of an angelic sword burst from my chest, dazzling my eyes with golden fire.

"Gabriel spoke truly. You've rejected your function."

The walls of the little classroom shuddered. Plaster fell from cracks that spread like gangrene across the ceiling. It was another familiar Voice, more powerful even than Gabriel's. My attacker was one of the Seraphim – the Burning Ones – in the body of a fourteen year-old girl, tall, her hair cornrowed, her eyes blazing.

"Seraphiel."

"I am."

Several other girls surrounded me, each of them gripping a shining weapon. They made way for the old priest to approach.

"You think only I discerned your dereliction of duty? You've become even less than your enemies imagine. I am not alone."

The children spoke with many voices. "We are… Legion."

They were all possessed, burning alive, each small body thrumming with angelic might. Moroni stood behind them, his borrowed face filled with anxiety.

"'When sorrows come, they come not single spies, but in battalions!' – *The Taming of the Shrew* (Act Four, Scene–)"

"Quiet, slave," Gabriel snapped. "Your betrayal will be rewarded soon enough.

Moroni clapped his hands over his mouth.

As a developing fetus, I had woven enough subtle protections into my DNA to ensure that I was fairly resistant to spiritual attack. But I was physically vulnerable: I could be killed by a fall from a sufficiently lofty curb if I wasn't careful. I extinguished the flaming blade and let the Aspect that had been champing at the bit of my self-control shoulder its way into reality.

Stormface was wreathed with crawlers of lightning, its face a perpetual snarl, knotted like a bunched fist and partially obscured by blackbellied thunderclouds. It was born from the racial memories of faded stormgods like Shango and Lir. Recognizably "infantile", Stormface was the Aspect that once terrified superstitious goat herders and genocidal kings alike, a giant floating baby head with nightmare eyes and a sun in its mouth.

"Abomination!"

Light struck the bodies of the possessed children. Every one of them glowed like a newborn star, their skeletons and circulatory systems pulsing visibly through their school uniforms. Then the Fallen angels inhabiting them were violently ejected.

"Fool!" Seraphiel, still in the body of the tall schoolgirl, cried. "You said he was powerless!"

The old priest fell to his hands and knees, his body wracked by shudders. A shimmering distortion rose up from him, drawing back from him like a shadow, dispelled by the light from Stormface's attack. When he looked up at his students his face was clear, and stained with tears.

"Run, children! Get out!"

The girls ran, some screaming, others laughing, from the classroom. The old man's shuddering increased, then stopped abruptly as Gabriel's malice rose up through the floor and entered him again.

"He's one of them, Seraphiel!" the old man snarled. "He's mortal. He can't defeat both of us!"

The face of Seraphiel's young host remained impassive. It was a measure of Seraphiel's skill that he still held her despite Stormface's interdiction. The girl would perceive Seraphiel's presence as a violation, aware at every moment that her will was not her own. Only one of the Seraphim could so completely dominate a human soul.

"Look at him, Seraphiel," Gabriel snarled. "He is human. He bends, as a shadow stretches beneath the noonday sun. He will age and fall beneath Death's driving whip. But an angel soars where he wills. For us there is no Death. And we can use mortal bodies!"

Seraphiel hummed, a judge considering a complex argument.

"We can create our own pantheon, Seraphiel: a new generation of Gods striking terror and devotion into mortal hearts and minds. We can rule the world."

"Seraphiel's right," I said. "You stand there in the body of a mortal, arguing how great it is to be immortal. You are a fool."

Gabriel's face convulsed with rage, his eyes burning so brightly I could smell the brimstone emanating from the old minister's pores. Thirty or so ejected angels flitted around him like luminous moths, egging him on.

Stormface unleashed a roar that cracked the school's foundations. The shimmering cloud of exorcized angels fled, screaming as they streamed out windows or through cracks in the ceiling. Vulnerable to Stormface's wrath, they were suddenly eager to be anywhere else.

"He rebukes us!" Gabriel cried. "His adoration of mortals has made him weak! If we choose to enslave them who can stand against us? We can create a new Heaven on Earth... in our image."

The old priest moved closer to the tall schoolgirl, one hand reaching up to rest on her shoulder.

"In your image, Seraphiel. We can stride like titans across the material realms. We can become..."

"You can become real," I said. "You're jealous of mortals."

Gabriel whirled toward me. "You're not real! Your Aspect only reveals the depth of your perversity. You wear their semblance, but wield the Power of Creation!"

"Yet you once commanded that power," Seraphiel hummed. "Are you not its source?"

I was fading. Maintaining Stormface required gigawatts of mental energy. The priest was little more than a walking corpse: his death would eject Gabriel soon enough. Seraphiel was a different story. The girl he'd stolen was young, newly possessed and bright with lifeforce.

"You've changed," Seraphiel said. "You are... limited."

"I'm becoming human."

"Human," Seraphiel said.

"Inferior," Gabriel cried. "Out of his own mouth he condemns himself! He is unfit to rule Creation!"

"Creation doesn't need a ruler, Gabriel. It needs a mirror."

My head was pounding, the connection to Stormface filling my mind with bright shards of white noise; mile long fingernails scratching down a moonsized blackboard.

Seraphiel's hum deepened. Around him, the fabric of reality was beginning to warp, bending in accordance with his song. Even I marveled at his skill. The power at his command was terrifying.

"If your assertion is true… many things must be considered. Many things."

"No," Gabriel snarled. "He has proven his unworthiness. Destroy him and this world can be ours!"

"Let her go, Seraphiel. She can still be saved."

Seraphiel's song grew restive, primed for fire. "Human," he chimed in the deep tolling intonation befitting his rank. "This leaves a vacuum at the pinnacle of the celestial power structure."

Something was wrong. I could barely hold Stormface together. Seraphiel seemed to waver as bright red spots burst like fireworks in my eyes.

"Seraphiel… if I believed humans needed the 'celestial power structure' I would never have abandoned my old function!"

Objects in the classroom began to vibrate as the Burning One's song climbed an octave. Every window in the building blew inward, driven by a hot wind that melted the shattered glass shards before they touched the floor.

"I will learn the truth of your assertions," Seraphiel sang, his voice rising like the scream of a ballistic missile. The possessed girl's eyes drove the shadows from the room. "In this way I may judge your worthiness."

The girl becomes white fire.

When human outrage compelled me to destroy Sodom and Gomorrah, I sent Seraphiel and Metatron to do the heavy lifting. Imagine two shining, six-winged angels folding the space between themselves and a nearby

asteroid belt to rain fire down upon a screaming mortal
city. A simple task for the Seraphim: open a pathway
between the target city and a few megatons of space
debris and step out of the way. When I sent the Angel
of Death to smite the Egyptians, she simply enclosed
the heads of Egypt's firstborn within airless bubbles
of concentrated dark matter: two hundred thousand
carbon monoxide asphyxiations later and you've got the
beginnings of a new world religion.

Now the Burning One has my destruction foremost
in his mind.

Seraphiel raises his song, and a ringing cry tears
the air inside that tiny classroom. Air rushes past me
with hurricane force, pushing me toward a shining rip
in space. Beyond the rip I can see blackness, and the
twinkling of ten million stars, strange constellations:
Seraphiel is opening a doorway into deep space.

Stormface takes over. The lights of its mouth burn
a path through Seraphiel's song, eating its notes like a
starving kid gobbling peanut M&Ms. The notes of his
song rise higher, and lava flows out of a portal that
opens to the right of me. A searing river of molten rock
pours across the wooden floor of the classroom, burning
it away as efficiently as Stormface absorbed Seraphiel's
musical attack. The walls of the classroom burst into
flames and the ceiling catches fire. Stormface lifts me
above the burning lava, wrapping me within a sheath of
cooler air while blowing away the toxic fumes.

"Seraphiel! You don't have to do this!"

Shadows play across the possessed girl's face.

"What else remains for me? You were All, Yahweh.
We Seraphim sang of your Glory as eternal, but now you

are mortal, less than nothing. A fate you chose willingly. What lessons am I to learn from your example?"

Seraphiel sings louder, his song slashing the air with celestial violence. Then a wall of water smashes into me.

Darkness and cold crush down upon me, even through Stormface's defenses. A few yards away, the possessed schoolgirl floats at the center of a shining bubble of chaos, her eyes piercing the darkness. Seraphiel has transported us into the ocean depths, far from light and safety. But there she hovers, alive in all that darkness.

But the cold and pressure are getting to me. Although Stormface is shielding me from the worst of Seraphiel's attack its protection will only last as long as I remain conscious. I reach out with the greatest power I still possess, my other mind's eye scanning and discarding divergent timelines until...

There.

Then I grip Seraphiel's place in spacetime in one mental hand...

Reset.

We were back inside the classroom.

There was no fire, no lava, no crushing black water to drown the world. Not yet.

"I will learn the truth of your assertions," Seraphiel sang, his voice rising like the scream of a ballistic missile. The possessed girl's eyes drove the shadows from the room. "In this way I may... judge..."

The girl looked around, taking in our surroundings.

"You translated us backward in time," Seraphiel said. "But this changes nothing. I am immortal; tireless. I can open a multiplicity of portals too rapidly for you to apprehend."

"Human continuity will go on, Seraphiel. The possessed girls will forget your friends. Once I told them the punchline they were able to conduct the exorcisms themselves. Everything you've done has been erased, shuffled into a dead-end reality where it can play itself out for the rest of eternity. It can't hurt anyone. None of it happened."

Seraphiel's scorn echoed from the rafters of the schoolhouse.

"But you failed. I remember it all. You left me unaltered. I am still a part of that other continuity."

That's when I saw it: the shift from angelic to demonic shadowing Seraphiel's face. The arrogance, the anticipation of glories that could never be his. He was feasting on the girl's energies, reveling in his defiance so thoroughly that he couldn't hear the fat lady singing.

"You're right, Seraphiel. You will continue. When I repaired the damage your uprising caused, I left a loophole of chaos open just for you. That loophole is closing right now."

The shift from angelic to demonic happened instantly, hate and terror contorting the girl's face as what I had done dawned on Seraphiel like the first light of a summer day: bright and inescapable.

"No…"

Truly hideous forces are required to kill the unkillable, and I had released unspeakably hideous forces in that little classroom. Seraphiel was torn out of the girl, his immortal essence stretched like taffy, twisting, contorting as the continuity to which he now belonged reached back and snagged him. But Seraphiel was too strong: he resisted, clinging to this continuity even as those hideous forces threatened to tear him apart. The girl screamed.

I abandoned Stormface and summoned the Aspect that

engraved the Ten Commandments across the retinas of a terrified Moses. Riding the Moving Finger, I dove into the maelstrom, tearing through the Eshuum, arrowing directly into her mind.

"Hello, Maya."

There is only silence in Maya Otsunde's mind. I wait, for what seems like an eternity. Then I hear it, a voice, tiny against the howling storm, but clear.

"Who are you?"

"You speak English."

"I can speak Xhosa and French and Swahili too. I'm not at all stupid. Are you God?"

"Let's talk about you."

"I see things… such beautiful horrible memories. But these things are not me."

"Your mind has been invaded. You've been possessed."

"Invaded? You mean by a demon?"

"Something like that."

"But… I don't understand."

I whisper the Secret. The Secret grants her a kind of clarity, and with it…

Enlightenment.

A moment later, I stood facing Maya Otsunde as Seraphiel was torn out of her body. His essence fractured, then shattered, strewn across a million possible moments, each moment branching out toward a million possible futures. I had restored his piece in the puzzle of continuity without repairing it. Now he was dragged into a future that branched in infinite directions; tied to every possible choice he could have made and bound to their innumerable consequences. I had pinned his essence to those timelines. Now they would tear him apart for all

eternity, spreading him across a billion stillborn realities.
And he would never die, living all those possible lives,
aware of what was happening to him, but unable to stop
it. It was the closest thing to Hell that an angel could
know. And it was the only way I could stop him.

Gabriel.

The old priest was dead. He lay curled up at my
feet. He hadn't been included in the Reset: Gabriel had
consumed his soul and I couldn't bring him back.

"You killed him," Moroni whispered. "You killed
Seraphiel."

There was no use denying it, so I didn't.

The classroom was empty. Outside, I heard the wail of
approaching sirens, concerned voices shouting questions
and, in the distance, the sound of gunfire.

"All my life… I looked for you."

Maya Otsunde was kneeling in the doorway that led
out to the front of the schoolhouse, her forehead pressed
to the floor, her hands splayed out in front of her, palms
facing the ceiling.

"When my father was struck by a truck in
Johannesburg I prayed that you would save him. When
my mother was sick from breathing in the waste of the
living dead ones, the ones with HIV I looked to you."

Her voice was calm, almost wondering, her eyes
averted. Her posture was one of submission, but her tone
remained neutral, almost monotonous. She might have
been reciting from a grocery list.

"'I will lift up my eyes to the hills. From whence
comes my help? My help comes from the Lord, who
made heaven and earth.' Isn't that what it says in the
Bible? I looked to the hills. I called to you. My friend

Rabiah, she is a Muslim. Her brother is a doctor. He cared for the sick people in our village. But he was killed by bandits. Before he died he lay in his own hospital with bullets in his face. He lay there while Rabiah and her mother prayed to you.

"The British came to my village. They told us that if we gave them our lands they would give us jobs. Then they built their big factories. They darkened the skies and filled our rivers with poison. So many in my country are sick now, with cancer, children… the very old. Yet still we pray. We cry out to you. And now… you come."

When she raised her head, her eyes were bright, as if she were in the grip of a fever.

"I once asked my mother, 'Mama, does God hate black people?' She slapped me. 'Don't ever ask such questions, Maya,' she said. 'You will bring down God's wrath upon our heads.' 'But, Mama,' I said. God must hate black people. He must hate Africa. Look at what has happened to us.' She said. 'Maya, how can you ask such terrible questions?' 'Look around us, Mama,' I said. 'How can you not ask those same questions?'"

Maya lifted her head higher and wiped away a tear as it slipped down her cheek.

"In school we learned about how the Americans made slaves of the people they took from Africa. The white men took them from their families, separated mothers and fathers from their children. Then, when Abraham Lincoln freed the slaves, the Americans hated them even more. Sometimes Father Philip played movies at the community center. In those movies, the Americans make the American Indians the bad people and make themselves into the good people. Father Philip says that what the Americans did to the Indians and the Africans was wrong. But in the movies everything is the opposite from what really happened. I don't like those movies, especially the ones about God. It sometimes seems to me that God must only love white Americans.

"Now you come. But you look like me. You tell me that you are real, but also that you were never what we believed you to be… that we have looked for too long in the wrong direction."

Maya nodded, as if listening to a voice only she could hear.

"I can bear this news. You walked with me in my mind, and now I understand things better than when I was a child."

I could hear the shouts of others gathering around the little schoolhouse, asking why the schoolgirls were wandering the streets, laughing and singing in the middle of the day.

"Did you hear my prayers? Do you listen to the prayers that people send to you?"

"A part of me did. You saw some of it a few moments ago, an Aspect, a representation."

"Did that part of you ever answer prayers?"

"That's like asking if Santa Claus flies from house to house or visits all houses simultaneously: an interesting question but basically meaningless."

"You might have told us sooner."

"I was busy."

"And now you think we've worked it out?"

"Well, people don't jump off bridges expecting God to save them to reward their faith. Otherwise you'd have millions of people doing it just to prove a point."

"But then your Secret is wrong," Maya said. "We're still afraid of the dark. We need God."

"Why?"

Maya furrowed her brow. Finally, she stood.

"I will remember," she said. "For the children in my country who lie dying in dark hospitals. I will remember you, God of the Americans."

Then she was gone.

"'What a piece of work is man! How noble in reason! How infinite in faculty!' *Hamlet* (Act Two Scene Two)! Oh fearful Lord of Lords. Yahweh! King of Kings!"

Moroni stood on the far side of the classroom, his borrowed body hugging the shadows. When I looked at him he flinched and fell on his face.

"You helped them. Now you call me King?"

"'What's in a name? That which we would call a rose by any other name would smell as sweet!' Forgive me, Lord! I was compelled by the power of the Seraphim... compelled!"

I looked down at the old dead priest, his eyes and mouth open, accusing me of a billion crimes.

"'Some rise by sin. And some by virtue fall'," I said.

"*Measure for Measure*! Excellent, Lord!"

"Take me back, Moroni," I said. "Take me home."

CHAPTER XIV
YURI'S BIG DEAL

I spent twenty minutes threatening Moroni before I dismissed him. I wanted him to spread the word: future angelic rebellions would be dealt with severely. I gave him free rein to describe Seraphiel's disintegration with as much drama as he deemed necessary. I couldn't have asked for a better pitchman for my latest edict: Moroni would have the story spread across the planet before lunch.

By the time I stepped off the bus in front of the Soupbucket, I was ready for the easy distraction of a pitch meeting. My headache had abated, allowing me a moment to collect myself. But I was still shaky as I walked into the trendy restaurant, twenty minutes late, to find Yuri and three people I didn't recognise sitting at a table. Yuri waved me over.

He pulled me in for a bro-hug and hissed in my ear. "Dude, I thought I was gonna have to cancel. Are you OK? You look like hell."

"I'm fine."

"Good. I'll kill you later."

Yuri turned to the man on his left. "Lando this is Jeff Corroder, President of Dream Lever Entertainment."

Corroder stood up and grasped my hand in his large right hand. He was just over six feet tall, swarthy, round-shouldered and slumping toward fat.

"Master Cooper!" Corroder boomed. "Glad you could finally join us! I was ready to send out the cavalry."

Corroder's voice was comically high for a man of his size, a female bodybuilder's sexless falsetto.

"No need," I said. "I'm ready to…"

I finished my greeting on the floor. Suddenly I was looking up at three faces staring down at me in alarm.

"Oh my god, are you OK?"

"I'm OK."

"Somebody get some water! Do you need a doctor?"

"I'm fine!"

Somebody helped me into a seat. Somebody else set a glass of water on the table in front of me. I picked up the glass and drained it in one long gulp.

"Dude?" Yuri said, worry scrawled all over his face.

"I'm OK. Just a little dehydrated."

"Well good!" Corroder chirped. "Can't have our main man doing his opening monologue from the emergency room."

Everyone laughed. Yuri and Corroder laughed the longest.

"Anyway, Lando this is my new assistant, Mitsuko Leavenworth. She'll be taking notes while we chew the fat."

Mitsuko Leavenworth was beautiful, a tall JapaneseAmerican, about twenty-five years old. She wore efficient black slacks and black V-neck sweater with blue pinstriped shirt underneath. At her throat rested a gold pendant shaped to resemble twin serpents entwined

about the Japanese character for good luck. Each of the
serpents sported tiny emeralds for eyes. Leavenworth
projected an aura of exacting precision. Her long black
hair had been lashed into a bun so tight that looking at it
made my temples throb.

"Hello, Lando. It's a pleasure to meet you. And I'm
not exactly 'new', anymore, Jeff."

Corroder smacked his forehead. "Sorry. Mitsuko
worked her way up through the company. She was in
Feature Development with Yuri before I dragged her into
TV Purgatory. Hey, speaking of Yuri, I've seen so much of
your stuff lately I feel like I can recite your act by heart!"

Yuri grinned. "I know talent when I see it, boss."

"Yuri talks about you all the time too, Jeff."

Corroder mock-winced. "All bad I'll bet."

"The worst," Yuri said. "If you weren't signing my
paychecks I would have vivisected you months ago."

This sent gales of laughter around the table.

"Yuri, you nut. Anyway, Lando, I'd like you to meet
Ted McFarlane. VP of Comedy Development at Fox."

Ted McFarlane was slightly below average in height,
muscular and hirsute, dressed in dark gray slacks, light
blue shirt, and brown pennyloafers. His hair was a
noxious flame red, which only served to heighten the
impression of violence throbbing beneath his skin. His
complexion had a thoroughly spanked redness to it. Years
of sun damage and Celtic inbreeding ran riot beneath
an explosion of freckles: Ted McFarlane had years of
melanoma treatments lurking in his very near future.

"Lando," he said, his voice like the ultra-low rumble
of a California aftershock. He took my hand and gave me
a mindnumbingly complicated soulbrother handshake.

"Love your stuff, homie. Caught your set at the Midtown Comedy Festival last month. Awesome: edgy, topflight observational shit."

"You were at the Festival?"

"Bro," McFarlane snorted. "You think I have time to hit every pisspot comedy club in Chicago? Jeff sent me the links."

Corroder leaned in. "You're killin' it on YouTube!"

"YouTube? Really?"

"Dude," McFarlane said. "False modesty only works for old British theater fags. You're what? Twenty-four, twenty-five?"

"Twenty-nine."

McFarlane took the correction smoothly, but I caught him looking around the table to check reactions to his reaction.

"You're web-friendly, with a global sort of appeal. On a purely demographic level, there are lots of people in the world who look like you – Brown people, people of color... whatever. They want to see themselves represented in the media. Take that, plus a nice amount of mainstream crossover, and by 'mainstream' I mean white American men between the ages of eighteen and thirty-nine, slightly younger on the female flipflop, and you're pulling about twenty to thirty thousand views per day."

"How many...?"

"And that's with no website. No HBO specials or Comedy Channel hype machine," Yuri added. "Jeff and Ted think you're on the cusp of going viral."

"Definitely," Corroder said. "For reasons we're still studying... you've developed a following."

"But I never downloaded any videos."

"Uploaded," Yuri blurted. "Videos. What Captain Luddite here means is that I've been posting his appearances on YouTube and YUCKS and a few other key comedy sites. Lando, Jeff thinks you could be the next Arsenio Hall!"

Corroder slapped the table. "Dude! You promised we wouldn't use the 'A' word. Damn!"

"We're living in 'postracial America'," McFarlane said. "Networks are interested in promoting minority perspectives in order to capture a wider share of an ever diversifying television audience. Advertisers however, still don't want to alienate the South, the Midwest… all those shitholes where lots of conservative whites live. Nice white Christians who buy guns at Walmart. So you see my dilemma here, Lando, as a Development executive, I mean?"

"Totally. Actually… no. No I don't."

"Look," McFarlane said. "We want color. American audiences are tired of old white guys telling them lame-ass old white guy jokes. Everybody's down: Letterman's slipped, Leno's an abortion on ice since NBC ass-jammed his show. Even Kimmel and Conan are just buttflakes these days. People want new viewpoints, new ideas…"

"Fresh perspectives," Corroder chimed.

"New blood!" Yuri was grinning from ear to ear. "Fresh meat!"

"Rrriiiight," McFarlane said. "Fresh Meat. I like it. Could be a good title for the show."

He nodded this last point over at Corroder's assistant, who was typing furiously onto an iPad.

"What kind of show are you guys looking for?" I said. Yuri's brows dimpled. Mitsuko Leavenwoth stopped typing and looked up at me. "I mean… I'm not really clear."

"Commentary," Corroder said. "Social critique, but with a comedian's eye for the absurd."

Yuri leaned in. "News of the day, politics, whatever's going on in Washington and how screwed up everything is…"

"Even when things are great."

"Something's always screwed up in Washington."

"Right," Corroder said. "Everything's fair game. Nothing's off topic."

"Censorship…"

"The media…"

"Race…"

"Sex…"

"War…"

"Things people care about," Corroder finished. "Guy and Gal on the street, 'everyday people' issues… only with jokes…"

"Everyday People," McFarlane mused. "Another good title."

Mitsuko Leavenworth looked up from her iPad. "I'm pretty sure Everyday People is the title of a popular Seventies soul song."

"I don't think so, sweetheart," McFarlane said. "I mean, how could it be, when I just came up with it myself?"

To her credit, Mitsuko Leavenworth kept a straight face. I noticed the look she shot Yuri, and the one he shot back at her, and suddenly understood that they were sleeping together.

"It was done by soul supergroup Sly and the Family Stone," Yuri said. "Classic."

"Sly Stone," McFarlane mused. "Funky black dude, big sunglasses, crazy afro, dope problem. Maybe. The Seventies are nuclear hot right now."

Corroder leaned in. "Could be a good choice for a sidekick/bandleader. Sign him to a contract and we get the song plus a burned out wacky celeb."

"Sly's a natural for the celebrity rehab circuit," Yuri added. "*Celebrity Crackhouse* would kill to get him."

"Yeah," Corroder said. "Reality Rehab: Sly Stone; his loves, his hates…"

"His drugs."

"I don't recall any stories about drug addiction," McFarlane said.

"Seriously?" Yuri chuckled. "Giant afro, elevator shoes and songs about peace, love and harmony: what drugs hasn't this guy done?"

"Yeah! Sly Stone and a bunch of Seventies burnouts living in a rehab center…"

"Or a haunted mansion," Yuri said. "Think Flava Flav meets *The Real World* meets *Survivor*… in a haunted mansion."

"I get it," McFarlane snapped. "Sly Stone: sidekick, bandleader… a loose cannon, say anything ethnic burnout…"

"As a compliment to Lando's 'Boy Next Door with an Edge'," Yuri reminded everyone.

"Lando, we want a Funnyman of the People, someone who calls 'em the way he sees 'em: no bull, no babytalk. Just a round-the-way brother who takes the piss out of polite society and tells it like it is."

"I get it!" I said, warming to the topic. "While subversively tackling the multi-layered hypocrisies of a rampant Military/Industrial/Entertainment Complex."

Silence.

"But likable," McFarlane continued. "Likability is key for advertisers. No one wants a radical screaming in their faces. I mean everybody's pretty much gotten what they wanted right? Gays can marry, minorities…"

"What minorities?" Corroder said. "Last census shows honkies like me dwindling in the population while everybody else on the planet is having babies. A billion Indians, a billion Chinese…"

"Right," Yuri said. "And with the web shifting the entertainment landscape underneath us, it's wide open territory. We're talking about a global audience."

"At the same time… let's face it," McFarlane continued. "Outsiders are definitely in. We've got an African-American lesbian Vice President and cloned Chinese hearing impaired Afro-Native-Canadian astronauts living on the moon. We need the new face of the twenty-first century. Lando… we all think you're it."

Grins akimbo, they were handing me a jackpot: legitimacy, a bright, shiny career, high profile success. If the show was a hit I'd be able to buy and sell Magnus Moloke a dozen times over.

"Again, we don't want a radical," McFarlane said. "But we do want radical comedy. Hmmmm. Radical Comedy."

"Got it," Mitsuko Leavenworth said, typing away. Her eyes flashed toward Yuri. Whatever their connection was it had very little to do with comedy. Unless it was a sex comedy.

"I want to see you live," McFarlane said. "I heart YouTube, but I want to see you in front of a crowd."

Yuri nodded. "I told Jeff and Ted about the Up and Comers at the Ha Ha Room, Wednesday night."

"I have to check my schedule," McFarlane said. "I'm only in Chicago till Thursday morning. But I want to see you do your thing on the real. You feel me?"

"Roll on through," I said. McFarlane's corporate hiphop speak was contagious as a flesh eating virus.

"Check me out. You won't be disappointed... yo."

Yuri beamed. "Foshizzle, my nizzles!"

"Funky fresh, homies!" Corroder tweeted. "Well, LC, you ready to reach for the stars?"

"Where do I sign up?"

Everyone high-fived. Yuri bought a round of iced teas and produced a flask filled with bourbon to add a "little snap" to the toasting. I stuck with my iced tea, confident that I was on my way; the future was mine.

Later, lost and betrayed, I would remember that moment.

And damn myself for a fool.

CHAPTER XV

LONDON CALLING... AGAIN, CONNIE FINDS RELIGION, BARBARA

"I miss you, babe. London sucks."

Relief washed over me like a wave from a cool sea. I trembled as an adrenaline surge sent starbursts sizzling along my nerve endings. I'd spent the two days since lunch with Yuri and Corroder preparing for the Goldie Kiebler's Up and Comers' contest later that night, and fantasizing about what I'd say if Surabhi called. Now I couldn't think of anything funny to say.

"I miss you too. I can't stop thinking about last week. I'm so sorry I made such a mess of things."

"Well, my dad was being an even bigger idiot."

"Wow. I'm so glad you said that. I mean..."

"What did you think, Lando? That I'd let my father make up my mind for me?"

"No, of course not."

"You're a terrible liar, Mister Cooper."

"I know."

"Lando, we've got things to clear up before we can get

on with... whatever this is."

"I know. And you're right. About me, I meant. I have been hiding things from you. But I want to tell you everything."

"God, that's scary. Now I'm all nervous."

"Why?"

"You're not a serial killer or anything are you?"

"Nothing so serious."

"We're flying back tomorrow. Mum and Dad are going on to New York. I plan to be in your arms by no later than midnight tomorrow. Being here these last few days... I've just really missed you. Can you forgive me for being such a mad cow?"

"I love you, Surabhi. There's nothing to forgive."

"Will you meet me at the airport with flowers and your most charming grin? The one I like, that curls up on one end?"

"Done. Tell your father congratulations for me?"

"How about I just say 'Anonymous Friends from America Send Salutations Upon The Occasion of Your Imperial Recognition?'"

"Sounds very British. Email me your flight information?"

"That's a 'can do' on that one, Big Poppa."

"Hiphop, British Accent. And a little grossed out by the 'Big Poppa'."

"Hmmm," Surabhi purred. "Freud would have a field day. I gotta go. Dad's royal carriage is here: knighthood awaits. Can't believe I'm actually wearing a dress my mother bought for me. Bare arms. Oy. I blame Michelle Obama."

"Your arms are ten times more buffed than Michelle Obama's."

"I bet you say that to all the girls you want to marry. See you soon?"

"Not soon enough."

"Remember now: full disclosure. The Real Story of Lando Cooper."

"Followed by late dinner and violent make-up sex?"

"We'll see. Bye, babe."

"Bye."

I disconnected. I entered her arrival time on a small PostIt note and stuck it to my laptop screen. Nothing short of the return of the Titans would keep me from meeting her plane on time.

It's working, I congratulated myself. The Plan is back on schedule.

"Sometimes I can't tell if you love Surabhi or your all-important Plan", Connie piped in from my brain.

"Surabhi, of course. Where have you been?"

The air in front of my desk shimmered, and Connie stepped out of a slit in the local Fabric. She had changed again. Now she was wearing the body of a stooped, old woman with flowing, floor length white hair. It was another of her Aspects, Winter Woman, dressed in long deerskin tunic and soft moccasins. A string of beads and small shells dangled noisily from a leather string tied around her neck. She looked oddly beautiful in this, her most ancient Aspect.

"You on the warpath?"

"Funny. Save the racist jokes for your lousy TV show."

"What's the matter with you?"

Connie shrugged her old lady shoulders.

"Oh, I'm just preoccupied. I went to check up on that group of new followers I told you about."

"Esmeralda Sanchez. In New Mexico."

"Yup. She's developing quite a movement. They're calling it the 'New Redemption Spritwalker Fellowship.' It's attracting attention from other Indian tribes across the Southwest.

"Esmeralda prayed for a Vision. The prayers were particularly powerful and I was curious. When I visited her, I was shocked to see that she had gathered nearly two thousand people to hear her message. I slipped into the mind of one of her acolytes, her twin sister, Evelyn. I watched Esmeralda perform the ancient rites. She sang with such authority that I got all emotional. It reminded me of when my family was in charge."

Connie sighed.

"I kept looking for some sign of Sun, my husband, or Shelly... that's my sister, White Shell Woman. But neither of them could be bothered – too busy with their little casino projects for a family reunion I guess. Anyway, I missed a response to Esmeralda's songs. That's what drew her attention. She glanced over her shoulder at me. Then she stopped singing and fell to her knees. She recognized me."

"Impossible. She couldn't have."

"'Onihima is here! She has heard our songs! Changing Woman honors us with a Visitation! The Earth Mother is with us!' That's what she said."

"But that would make her..."

"Yup. A prophet."

"But that's..."

"A big pain in the butt."

"There aren't supposed to be any more prophets, Connie. Because there aren't supposed to be any more gods – at least no confirmation of godly presences."

"I know that. You think I don't know that?"

"If all those people saw you that would be confirmation, Connie. Confirmation flies in the face of the Plan. They have to believe they're on their own! This Sanchez woman could stir up all kinds of trouble! She could single-handedly set the Plan back a hundred years. If her following grows large enough she could coax your pantheon out of retirement."

"I guess I should also tell you that my son Monster Slayer has been sniffing around for a way to regain his station."

"What?"

"You try shaking down losers and bouncing card counters for forty years. My son used to slaughter the enemies of the gods. Now he sits on a barstool all day, staring into video monitors and eating pancakes from the All You Can Stuff Buffalo Bar."

"What did you do, Connie?"

"Well… when she saw me… recognized me… in front of all those people…"

"No. Tell me you didn't…"

"There were hundreds of people there, Lando… thousands, all chanting my name."

"Connie!"

"I figured one tiny miracle…"

"One tiny miracle? There are no 'tiny' miracles, Connie!"

Connie folded her flabby arms and stuck out her chin.

"Well... no one's parting the Red Sea or anything like that."

"You know that was blown out of proportion."

"And anyway... why should your believers be the only ones to get a little hope, a little encouragement? You realize how desperate my peoples' situation has become?"

"Connie, we had a deal! No miracles! No confirmation!"

"Oh poop," she replied, waving away my objections. **"It was just a little rain."**

"You made it rain?"

"Yes. That's why they were all gathered there. They were having this big Indian arts festival. There's been a major drought across the Southwest for the last three years..."

"Three years?"

"Yes. Sorry... four years."

"You're killing me."

"They were all there, the People. Not just Navajos either. Other tribes, white folks, black folks... Japanese tourists, Mexicans... all singing Navajo songs. Esmeralda instructed them to pray for rain. They even had a Junior Rain Dancers competition. Those little buggers were so cute!"

"I'm getting a sick headache, Connie..."

"So I thought, 'What the hell? What's it going to hurt now?' So when Esmeralda recognized me in the body of her sister, she called upon the bond between all sisters, reminding me of the love between me and my sister, White Shell Woman – the little slut – I guess I was feeling nostalgic for the old days, the Old Ways. She asked for my favor

and I granted it. I called the winds... and they answered me! It was so lovely to see them again! Then I summoned the rains and they came!"

"You're making me meshugga, Connie."

"Oh, you only speak Yiddish when you're feeling intolerant. Don't get all Old Testament on me, mister. Alright... so I got a little crazy. They sang my favorite songs and danced the ancient dances. They're still dancing."

"It's still raining there?"

"Yes, Mister Poopy Paws. Look at me. Don't I look different?"

Changing Woman was growing younger, her hair darkening toward black, the lines in her face fading away even as her back straightened and she stood taller.

"I know what you have to do," she said.

"Connie. I have to."

"It was sure nice while it lasted though. Now I have to go lie down. I'm gonna be so hungover in the morning. Sorry. But not really."

"Goodnight, Connie."

She waved, a giggling beautiful teenager, and faded away.

"Nightie night, Grampa."

Man, I hate it when she goes walkabout.

I felt the comforting esoteric weight of her as she settled into my brain for what I hoped would be a long nap. Then I closed my eyes and rummaged around for an Aspect. After Africa and the ersatz angelic rebellion I could no longer trust the archangels to ferry me around: who knew who else Gabriel had corrupted? I was going to have to use my own reserves to get me to New Mexico. I reached into the Eshuum and was greeted immediately by Sky Daddy.

"Hello, Lando," it rattled. Its voice was light for so large and diffuse an Aspect; a shriek in a wind tunnel; the howl of a hurricane rushing through a keyhole. "We've missed you."

I was shrugging Sky Daddy on over my shoulders when the door to my bedroom flew open and Barbara stumbled into the room.

"Ma!"

My voice struck echoes of elemental fury from the air. I shoved Sky Daddy back into my pocket.

"Ooopsh, sorry."

Barbara stepped out into the hall, slammed the door, waited four seconds, then knocked.

"May I come in?"

"No!"

She came in. "What are you doing? Christ, open a window. It smells like balls in here."

"I'm busy!"

"Who were you talking to? What were those weird lights?"

"I was rehearsing for my gig tonight. Do you mind?"

"I hope I'm not pissing in my diapers the day you drop this comedy crap and get a real job."

"That's insulting."

"I know. What are you doing for the next hour?"

"Rehearsing."

And re-routing the stream of inappropriate Creation cascading across New Mexico… as soon as you leave.

"Take me to church."

"No. I've got to–"

"Don't care. I've got to go to church but I can't drive myself."

"Why not?"

"Well, I closed the Silver Fox last night. I couldn't sleep when I got home so I popped a valium, but I had to get up early to go meet my exterminator. Rats. So I took a vitamin B shot to perk me up, but then I met Andrea Cash and the girls at the Art Museum to see that Chinese body cadaver exhibit thing and that was so boring I needed a gimlet just to keep from strangling that bitch Tawndra Wilson who speaks Cantonese better than a goddamn Chinaman, and when I got back home I was so tired because I hadn't slept, but I still had too much excitement coursing through my veins, so I took a vicodin and a muscle relaxer but they mixed badly with the cranberry margueritas and now I have to go meet Owen, and me operating heavy machinery constitutes a threat to national security…"

"People coming to my gig tonight. Important people."

"I mean it, Lando. I'll slaughter a dozen people…"

Barbara batted her eyelids and spoke in her "ubsywubsy" voice, the voice she used when she wanted me to think she liked me.

"Can my big strong son dwive his sick old mama to her bible study cwass? Pweeeease?"

"You're embarrassing yourself."

"I said pweeeease…"

"Ma!"

"Pwetty pweeease?"

"Let's go."

Human continuity may have been endangered, but I would have destroyed New Jersey to stop her from doing that voice.

Barbara smiled. "Good. And comb your hair. You look like a goddamn bushbaby."

● ● ●

"I think Owen is falling in love with me."

Barbara was applying a fresh coat of make-up, studying herself in the passengerside visor's mirror, alternately smoking, sucking in her cheeks and pouting.

"You two seemed pretty chummy the other night. How did you meet him anyway?"

"He came into Barb's six months ago."

"He didn't strike me as a drinking man."

"Oh, Owen drinks. He likes scotch, like your father used to before he met Crouching Tiger, Hide Your Wallet."

Herb's obsession with clean living was a source of constant aggravation for Barbara, who had drunk Old Fashioneds since her thirteenth birthday.

"Why does his commitment to staying in shape bother you so much?"

"Please. If some people are too lazy to move their fat asses enough to keep trim without running like freed slaves, they deserve every disease they get. I've maintained the same weight since high school."

"You smoke."

"Occasionally."

"Barbara, you collect cigarettes the way white separatists hoard baked beans. I've seen hummingbirds put more food in their mouths. Remember Atticus' Christmas party? While the rest of us ate, you smoked, drank and insulted his children."

"I happen to have a ladylike appetite, smartass. Anyway, back in December Owen came in with one of my regulars. They took the back table near the rear exit. That's usually where people go when they're having affairs: it's dark and it attracts whores. Lindvall, my customer, was crying. Owen was pouring booze down his gullet while he cried and cried. I thought they were fags. Then somebody told me they were having an intervention. I grabbed my taser and went over there. But when Owen looked at me…"

Barbara settled back into the passenger seat, her eyes dreamily focused in the distance out the front windshield.

"There's something about him. He's got this crazy charisma. Like Jackie Wilson and JFK all rolled into one. He's religious, but not a pain in the ass about it. He lets you make up your own mind. He tells me to trust my fear."

"Trust your fear."

"Owen says fear is highly underrated. That it's God's way of telling us how ineffectual we are."

"He preaches fear?"

"All the time. Owen says our society has become arrogant. He says we should embrace our fears, let them guide us through life's uncertainties: if more people operated consciously out of fear we'd all progress toward 'gentler, more pragmatic solutions for the ills that plague modern man'."

"That's different."

"Well I think it's refreshing. I mean haven't you had enough of all this 'follow your dreams' horseshit? If I hear one more menopausal hausfrau whining on *Oprah* about 'following her dreams' I'll snap. My 'dream' is to bust a cap in every broad who drops her panties for Oprah."

"You love Oprah."

"I'm a glutton for punishment. That's why I married your father, the bastard. Get off here… right now."

I swooped across three lanes of traffic, accompanied by an angry chorus of horns as drivers swerved to avoid Barbara's brand new Jaguar. The driver I cut off swerved into the slow lane and slammed on her brakes just as the driver behind her attempted to jam his car into the exact space at that same moment. More squealing brakes followed by the sound of crunching metal. The "screw you" chorus of horns retreated into the rear distance as we sped up the exit ramp.

"I can't imagine how you got a driver's license. Anyway, when Owen looked me in the eye it was like he was looking at me. Not the glamorous creature I present to you and your gay friends. He saw the real me."

"He saw all that with one look?"

"Yes. And I think he liked what he saw."

"Big scotch drinker."

"Nothing you say can knock me from my perch, my darling. Your old mama is feeling pretty good about herself these days. And it's all thanks to Owen's teachings."

"Fear is good?"

"You bet your ass. In a world filled with con artists and zombie Asian streetwalkers… fear makes sense."

She tossed her cigarette out the window.

"Why don't you come to the lesson with me? God knows you could use a little spiritual renewal."

"I told you… I'm busy."

Barbara sighed. "Well, I guess I have no one to blame but myself. Herb and I were never big churchgoers."

"*You're atheists.* Or at least you were before you met Doc Holiday."

"What is that, some kind of sick joke?"

"Are you serious? His name is Holiday. He has a doctoral degree. Which makes him officially Doc Holiday."

"That's the most ignorant thing I've ever heard."

"It never occurred to you that someone might call him Doc Holiday?"

"No it didn't. And I'd appreciate it if you don't utter such foolishness when Owen's around. He's a serious man."

"Alright."

"I swear to God... the things that come out of your mouth. Doc Holiday–"

"I said alright!"

"It's just that you've never managed to aquire any kind of moral philosophy. Everyone needs to believe in something greater than themselves, Lando. If you missed out on that... I'm sorry."

Of all the things I'd come to expect from my mother, an apology was not among them: Barbara never apologized. She made others apologize, even when they'd done nothing wrong. Her "moral philosophy" crouched somewhere in the dark alley between self righteousness and homicidal self-righteousness.

"Actually I do believe in something greater than myself."

"Oh? What is it? Trees? Coffee beans? Some Hindu crap?"

"Mother dear, you can't call an entire religion 'crap' because you disagree with it."

"Watch me. When was the last time you attended a normal old Christian church?"

"Gods don't need a church to hear the prayers of their worshippers."

"Well who died and made you Jerry Falwell? Christ I hope you're not falling into one of those Buddhist/Scientology cult things like your buddy Yorga."

"His name is Yuri, Barbara. And he only experimented with Scientology for a year."

"Yeah, Yuri. Good hair. Nice package. I'd pay good money to 'convert' him, but considering the crowd you hang out with he's probably a homo."

"You may be the worst person ever to draw breath."

"And the apple doesn't fall far from the tree, my darling. Remember that. Pull in here… right now."

The New Message Non-Denominational Fellowship Center was a squarish, postmodern structure covered with particolored glass. After a stint as a health club, a family planning clinic and a gay nightclub, the church sat empty for nearly fifteen years until it was bought by Owen Holiday. Now, the giant Rubik's Cube's parking lot was filled to near capacity, closed due to overcrowding. Four or five News trucks haunted the area near the front entrance and several camera crews were loading their equipment in through the main doors.

"I thought this was just a bible study class."

Barbara smiled, a knowing grin playing about her lips.

"Owen's been attracting a lot of media attention lately. Last month the mayor joined New Message."

"I thought the mayor was Jewish."

"Guess she saw the light. We also have several Bulls, a couple of Blackhawks, and that kid Senator from Hyde Park. You should talk your hot friend into coming. Owen's making a lot of headway with idiots your age."

We had to park three blocks away. As she climbed out of the car, Barbara hectored me about going inside.

"Can't you get your guru to bring you back home?"

"Oh… Owen's busy. I wouldn't even ask. Come with me."

"No."

"I guess now is as good a time as any to tell you: I'm dying, Lando."

I stared at her for a full thirty seconds before she gave up.

"Oh alright. Will you please accompany me inside, O handsome-but-annoyingly-principled son of mine?"

I noted the air of twitchy excitement that haunted Barbara's movements, her degree of pharmaceutical inebriation, and decided it was probably best if I went with her. I was also intrigued by the things she'd told me about Holiday and his strange philosophy. He'd filled up the church's parking lot on a Wednesday night. I was curious. And, I was actually enjoying the banter between Barbara and me. Jousting with her felt like home. A home for the criminally deranged, but the only home I'd ever known. Besides, my set at the Ha-Ha Room wasn't until 10.30pm – I could afford a short detour into the circus tent that had opened its flaps to my mother.

The tall, open doors of the sanctuary yawned before us. Inside, we could hear shouts, laughter, and a single amplified voice calling for worshippers to take their seats: the circus was about to begin. We went in through the main entrance, down a long dark hallway that led to the chapel. The walls were strangely bare. No paintings or pictures adorned the colorless expanse of organic eggshell blandness. Up ahead, bright light poured out of the chapel, welcoming visitors to step inside, out of the void and into the warmth and brightness.

Barbara was clutching my forearm in her talons and giggling like a panicky teenager on her first date.

We went into the light.

CHAPTER XVI
HOLIDAY'S LAW
(RETURN TO EDEN)

"God gave me a revelation this morning. I'd like to share that Word with you all, and with the many friends and fellow seekers all over the world who are watching us on television and the web right now: we... are... children."

The approximately two thousand people crammed into the auditorium rumbled as the regular congregants replied.

"Children."

"That's right!"

"Amen!"

Owen Holiday and his board of private investors had bought the abandoned elementary school that sat directly behind the church. Using donations from congregants and a few wealthy converts among Chicago's elites, they'd incorporated the school's theater and gymnasium and created the new "Gathering Place."

A line of television cameras occupied the open area at the front of the auditorium, a glittering phalanx of electronic eyes and ears, all trained on the man at the podium.

Holiday wore a simple denim shirt with the sleeves rolled up, clean khakis and comfortable loafers. With his sun-darkened skin and steel gray hair he looked like a latter day Marlboro Man without the Marlboro. There was something extravagant in his faded cowboy sincerity, a silent violence revealed only in the tension of his bunched jaw muscles. His hands closed into fists repeatedly as he looked out over the audience. A kind of personal rigor resonated across the palette of his movements. The impression I'd received in my parents' kitchen was only reinforced: Owen Holiday was no stranger to brutality.

"Most of you folks know me. I've visited with you in your homes, meditated with you, celebrated your victories and wept for your losses. I've broken bread in tough times with many of you. Last couple of years I've put on ten pounds."

The congregation laughed. Some of them applauded.

"Always start with a joke," I whispered into Barbara's ear. "Gets 'em on your side."

"We know each other," Holiday said, "as only companions who have walked the same hard road for many years can know each other. So you will all understand what it means when I tell you that this morning as I was preparing for tonight's message, I found myself uncertain and afraid. I was afraid because I realized that everything upon which this church was founded was an illusion, that I was nothing more than a charlatan and a false prophet. I've been lying to you good people all along."

We were sitting only a few rows away from the raised stage Holiday commanded, like Othello moments before he guts himself. We'd been led to these seats by an eager acolyte, who'd breathlessly informed us that special arrangements had been made to ensure that Barbara be given priority seating.

Holiday spoke softly, his accent part Northern Montana/part Southern Illinois, amplified by the microphone.

"I don't believe in God."

No one moved. Holiday had captured his audience with a ruthless economy.

"I had just stepped out of the shower. I took a look at myself in my bathroom mirror. I'm fifty-three years old, in pretty fair shape. But I've been so busy these last few weeks I've neglected what my father used to call my "ablutions". My five o'clock shadow looked more like 3am on a bender: I needed a shave. It had been a while since I'd laid eyes on this old fencepost I call a face. So I set to it.

"While I was mixing my shaving powder, I began thinking about what I was going to say to you good people tonight. I do my best thinking when I'm shaving. It clears my head. Something about that cold blade against my mortal flesh puts life into perspective. But this morning, nothing was coming to me. I kept at it: my beard grows fast, and if I don't keep after it, after a couple of days I can pass for a member of the Taliban."

This elicited a rumble of good-natured laughter.

"Usually, as my face starts to reveal itself, my thoughts get clearer, and by the time I'm done I've got the nitty-gritty of that evening's message. But this time… nothing. I was halfway through my ablutions and nothing was coming to me. I don't mind telling you, friends, that was enough to set my mind whirling. And at that moment, Evil came upon me in the form of a paralyzing doubt.

Who are you kidding, Owen, I asked myself. You know this is all just a lie. You've reached the end of your ability to fool yourself. You have no illusions left to hide behind and now you're faced with the truth: there is no God."

The voices of several congregants lifted against the silence.

"Don't lose faith!"

"We need you, Owen!"

Holiday bowed his head. His hands gripped the lectern so tightly that his knuckles turned white. When he raised his face, his cheeks were wet with tears. Many of the congregants broke into applause.

"We love you, Owen!"

Holiday raised his hands, commanding silence.

"Your love and support just fill me up. Without you folks I'd… well I don't know where I'd be. I know some of you are horrified. I can see it. But for just one moment, friends, I'll admit that I experienced a keening joy, a personal satisfaction. At that moment I sensed a new path stretching out in front of me. I don't mind telling you, folks, that I was ready to take a step upon that road, ready to throw everything I had worked for out that bathroom window and set off on a dark new adventure. I felt… free."

Barbara was nodding her head. All around us, many of the congregants were nodding as well.

"I finished up my shave with a feeling of exhilaration. By the time I cleaned my razor – I still use a straight razor; that cold hard edge scraping at my throat helps me 'keep it real,' as the kids like to say – I was ready to make a public proclamation. I was going to let it all go. Heck, everybody knows what I had just allowed myself to admit, right? Everybody knows there's really no such a thing as a loving God who watches over us, who guides our actions and decides our destinies. We all should just admit it, forget about archaic notions of God's divine presence. Why, science tells us more and more about the world every single day. They're drinking water from underground ice springs on the moon. They've found oceans filled with life on two of Saturn's moons. What does faith in God count for in this big ol' random universe?

"We look around at the state the world's in and see hunger on a global scale, children dying in wars that no one ever wins; we see terrorists killing innocents by the thousands in our greatest cities and getting away unscathed by anybody's justice; we see our very planet losing its ability to sustain itself. But no God steps in to save us. We pray, we all believe, we say, 'Well, if He is out there he must be working His mysteries, His wonders to perform, in ways we mere mortals can't see.' But then what, my friends, is the point of praying to this being who never intercedes on our behalf?"

Holiday stepped out from behind the lectern and began to walk slowly along the edge of the stage, like a man walking the plank knowing that sharks swim in the dark waters below.

"Well I stood there, clean shaven, feeling like a million bucks; like that young fellow I remember, fresh out of seminary and ready to set the world on fire. I got out my cell phone and dialed brother Erikson's number. Fred Erikson's my First Deacon in our little family of faith; I figured he could take over while I prepared everyone for this new revelation. I called his number…

"That's when I heard the voice."

Holiday seemed to meet every eye in that room, a direct communication with each living, breathing soul.

"This voice was one that I'd never heard before, but in the instant it spoke I knew it for what it was. It was the calming Voice at the heart of a Kansas twister; the whisper at the center of the flame that burns at the heart of the sun and in the heart of you and me. This Voice said three words to me:

"You. Are. Children."

The camera crews were watching, recording Holiday's every word and movement. One man, a burly AfricanAmerican holding a boom microphone over his head, wept openly, his head shaking back and forth, shoulders shuddering with the force of his sobs.

What's happening here?

I glanced toward Barbara. She was crying.

"Children," she whispered. "Innocents."

The gunshot made everyone scream.

People leapt to their feet. Holiday was standing center stage. In his right hand he gripped a small revolver, a starter pistol. It was aimed at the ceiling, its barrel still smoking.

"A shot in the darkness! That's what it was like, friends. And at that moment I was swept up by such wonder that it seemed the whole room caught fire, and I was filled with a burning light. This light burned away all doubt as to Whom I was speaking. It burned away my certainty in the blinking of an eye, and it was angry.

"'You are children,' it said again. 'What do you mean, Father?' I cried. 'We are lost and we cannot see! How can we go on when we're all blind?'"

"'Once, there was nothing but darkness,' this Voice said. 'A void, without time, or light or life. Then God created Eden; a place so filled with joy it was like a shining beacon against all that darkness. And into Eden God brought life, animals and plants and every living thing. Finally, he brought forth Man Adam and Woman Eve. But they were as children, ignorant of God's plan. "Walk where I guide you," God said, "for I am your Father, and you know nothing of this world." And they walked that way for a while, living as God decreed. And they were happy.' But we all know what happened next: Adam and Eve were cast out of Eden. Why? Because they took that first step away from God. For they had eaten from what…?"

"The Tree of Knowledge," the congregants murmured.

"Yes!" Holiday thundered. "Philosophers tell us that a little knowledge is a dangerous thing. Adam and Eve were cast out. Sure, they gained awareness, but they lost their innocence, and they were separated from the will of God. They became as adults, wandering through a world filled with heartbreak and wondering why everything is so messed up. But we all know why: we are children who have defied our father. Our omnipotent, omnipresent and loving father. We defy Him, and so we fail."

"We fail!"

One voice started the chant. That voice came from Barbara. Someone else repeated the phrase. A second later, hundreds of congregants were repeating it.

"We fail!"

"That's right!" Holiday shouted. "Against hunger!"

"We fail!"

"Against greed and corruption and moral recalcitrance!"

"We fail!"

"Against racism and sexual deviance and child murdering terrorists, and every evil thing that crawls upon the face of God's blessed Earth…"

"We fail!"

"Against war and poverty and selfish politicians…"

"We fail!"

Holiday threw back his head and howled, "We… fail!"

The cry was echoed by weeping and shouting and calls for punishment. The air in the arena had taken on the ugly scent of the atmosphere before a riot. But Holiday looked rejuvenated. More robust somehow. More… vigorous.

"Feels good to admit it, yes? We fail. And because we fail, because we are ignorant children playing in our Father's kingdom, we have strayed from perfection and harmony… and peace."

"We fail."

"We have wandered off the path lain for us by the Supreme Shepherd to stumble along ways and roads utterly of our own devising. And in all that wilful meandering we wandered away from Eden."

Holiday's face beamed certitude. Barely contained brutality shone from his eyes, flashing across the congregants like the beams from a haunted lighthouse.

"But I know the way back. I know how to get right with God and return to Eden. I know how every man, woman and child within the range of my voice can set their feet upon the road back to God's mercy; for we have sinned, and God's mercy is the only thing that can redeem us. We have forsaken the greatest gift our Father gave us. That gift is fear."

"Amen!"

"Fear is wisdom!"

"Bless you, Owen!"

"My friends, the troubles of this world are many and dire. To fear them is only sensible: Fear reminds us of our place in His Great Plan. It tells us how insignificant we truly are.

"Other preachers tell you about a loving God, a kind and forgiving God. Yes, friends, our God is kind and forgiving. He woke me up this morning and enabled me to share His revelations with you and that's the greatest kindness of all. But our God's love is not what they call 'unconditional'. His love is utterly 'conditional'. And we have violated the conditions upon which we can earn his Grace. Our God is angry."

That word swept among the congregants, the first breath of wildfire across an arid plain.

"Angry!"

"He's angry!"

"God is ticked off!"

"Friends, our heavenly Father is furious with us, his errant children. And the only thing that can save us from his wrath is to step back onto the path he has ordained for us, a path he has given me to know."

Holiday's eyes scanned the faces of his flock.

"Who will join me on the road to redemption? It won't be easy, and many will fall along the way. The faithless. The scientists, who believe more what their telescopes and their test tubes and their stem cells tell them than what any fool can read in the Old Testament."

One man, a tall, bald biker type, shouted, "Damned fools!"

"Ahh, but we can't worry about them, friends. Their

fate is in their hands, and their hands are too small! It's with God that I plan to walk, and with God's eternal grace, I'm hoping you all will come with me. Return with me… to a New Eden."

They were moving before he stopped speaking, a mass of congregants rising as if with one mind, and shuffling into the aisles. Barbara stood up. I gripped her forearm.

"Where are you going?"

Barbara tugged, somewhat listlessly at my grasp, her face turned toward Holiday.

"Barbara-Jean, this is the Voice of Reason speaking."

She glared at me with such grieving that I dropped her forearm. If I'd passed her on the street at that moment I might not have recognized her.

"Go home, Herbert," she said. "I'll be fine."

Then she stepped out into the aisle and joined the flood of shuffling congregants. Nearly every congregant who was capable of independent movement was filing down toward the stage, where their comrades gathered like horny salmon at the entrance to a spawning ground.

Owen Holiday stood over his flock, the Holy Grizzly scanning the depths, waiting for the fattest fish to pass beneath his eye. He nodded at Barbara, who beamed up at him, devotion streaking her cheeks and tumbling in silent praise from her lips. When he looked at me, the great white grin that stretched his face gleamed with dark promises; a violent salvation; grievous bodily redemption for the low low price of a single leap of faith.

CHAPTER XVII
DEATH PENALOPY OR…
COMEDY TONITE

"I don't believe in the death penalty. It's too easy. It lets horrible people off the hook. You say you killed a dozen people and barbecued their pubic hair? Don't worry, Adolph, you can get… the Death Penalty. We get all crazy about who's 'Tough On Crime'. Reactionary psychopaths have dragged the country so far away from anything resembling common sense that now a politician running for President who doesn't unequivocally support the Death Penalty can't get elected. And it's all just so other politicians can say, 'Senator Joe Bob is soft on crime. Didn't ya hear? Joe Bob is soft on crime. He's SOFT… on CRIME!' Which is really political doubletalk for, 'Senator JoeBob wants Afro-Mexican crack dealers to break into your house, steal your guns, rape your wife and teach your children French while giving your grandmother a gay abortion. For free.'"

< Audience reacts >

"And since most politicians are self-serving egomaniacs who want to become multi-millionaires by sucking face

with their corporate sponsors while they're in office…
no one ever questions that assumption.

"So we get politicians who proclaim that they're 'Tough
On Crime!' And what's the best way to prove that you're
Tough On Crime? By supporting the Death Penalty,
that's what. There's only one problem: it's all crap. The
Death Penalty is racist. Compared to whites, African-
Americans and Latinos are executed in numbers severely
disproportionate to their representation in the general
population. Hey, John and Jane Q Public, when it comes
to unfair state-sanctioned murder… We're Number One!"

< Audience laughs. Catcalls >

"THE DEATH PENALTY discriminates against the poor.
It's like scurvy, cheap leather and bad sex: rich people
never get it. Then again, these inconsistencies have left
convicted mass murderers with nearly limitless abilities
to appeal. You can kidnap somebody, cut up their cat,
feed it to them before you kill them, record the whole
thing in hi-def video and post it on YouTube and still
have the Right of Appeal. You can outlive the judge who
sentenced you, the prosecutor who indicted you and the
stenographer who banged her fingers against that goofy
little keyboard – does anybody really believe they're
taking down everything that's said during a trial? That's
the biggest injustice of all – you can outlive all those
people and never see the inside of a death chamber, while
the system figures out a way to swing another appeal.
So *bon appetit*, Adolph: we just want to show everybody
that we're TOUGH ON CRIME without actually doing
anything about it. I. Oppose. The Death Penalty.

"However, I do support scaring the holy hell out of
violent people. Let's take the technology used to make those

stupid *Twilight* movies and actually create something useful.
Let's turn our talent for manipulation to manipulating the
people who actually need it: violent people who subject
us to teenaged vampire movies. Don't groan: those *Twilight*
movies were so bad, homeless crack whores ran away from
advance screenings. Seriously, the studio invited hundreds
of crack whores and their pimps to free screenings in
Chicago. Because they were cold and hungry, the studio
thought they'd shove some free popcorn down their
throats, wash a little Coca-Cola over their bloody gums,
then the crack whores would be disposed toward favorably
reviewing their movies. Instead the crack whores bolted
like runaway slaves leaving Mississippi."

< Laughter. Groans >

"What if we made an announcement that we had
reinstated the Death Penalty for rapists, murderers, child
molesters and right wing talkshow hosts... you know,
violent offenders: no appeals, no plea bargaining, just...
if you're convicted of one of these crimes... pow! It's the
electric chair, or lethal injection or an endless *American
Idol* marathon. But here's the trick: instead of killing you,
we just knock you out. When you wake up... you're still
alive. 'There's been a mistake,' you think. 'Those idiots
screwed up. Whoohoo!'

"But then you pass a mirror on your way to strike
back at society and you see that something's changed:
you've been turned into a woman. Or a child. Or an old
person: whatever you did to your victim, we use all our
technology to turn you into a version of that victim; strip
your muscles, shave down your bones and shoot you
full of estrogen. Then we put you in a trailer home with
a week's worth of crystal meth and a violent boyfriend.

If you did anything to a child, or an old person, we give you Hutchinson-Gilford Progeria. You know, the aging disease? It turns healthy kids into sick old people almost overnight. It makes you weak from heart disease, rapid muscle and bone deterioration, and constant pain. Then we sell you to a sweatshop in Mexico or Singapore or Waco, or just rent you to those two idiots from *John & Kate Plus 8*. I guarantee you... in five minutes you'll regret everything you ever did in your whole life. And you won't have to worry about dying because anybody stupid enough to actually kill you will have the same thing done to them!"

    < Audience cheers. Applauds >

"We're not living up to our potential, people. Over millions of years we've evolved these huge brains; the biggest brains of all the primates, among the biggest brains in the animal kingdom; big brains that can solve big threats: world hunger, climate change, Regis Philbin. But the problems we spend all our attention on? Gay marriage... pointless wars and Google Waves...

    "We can do better, people. That's all I'm saying.

    "We can do better."

"That... was... awesome!"

    Yuri was beaming. Jeff Corroder and Ted McFarlane were beaming. Even Corroder's assistant, Mitsuko Leavenworth was beaming.

    "You killed," Yuri hissed as we walked back to McFarlane's table, near the back of the Ha-Ha Room's bar. He was gripping my forearm so tightly my fingers were going numb. "McFarlane thinks you're the next George Carlin."

    "You were great, Lando," Corroder fluted.

"Better than great," McFarlane said, too loudly. "You're a rocket! An honest-to-God, mother-humpin' star!"

Corroder wrapped his arms around my waist and pulled me into a bear hug. I dangled there with my face pressed into his manbreasts, his unnatural strength compressing my ribcage. Just when I was about to pass out, Corroder sat me down and thumped my shoulders with his ring studded paws. I reached for my inhaler.

"What're you drinkin' tonight, killer?"

"Coke," I said. "Just a Coke…"

"And Rum!" Yuri cried, producing a flask. "No point in drinking Coke without the rum!"

"No rum," I said. Surabhi's flight was due in around noon the next day, and I wasn't about to risk a hangover. Corroder was already waving down the bartender. McFarlane sprang up from his seat, bounded around the table and wrapped me up in another bear hug.

"Let me tell you why you're gonna be a huge effing star. One word? Everyman. You are the Everyman for the new millennium, Lando. You're Richard Pryor and George Lopez and Dave Chappelle all rolled into one."

"And Carlin!" Yuri said. "Don't forget Carlin!"

"George… Effing… Carlin…" McFarlane laid his left hand over his right pectoral muscle, a gesture I interpreted to mean he was speaking from his heart. "I loved that guy. The greatest comic since Mark Twain. Honest to God, man… I just…"

McFarlane actually welled up. He reached across to the table next to us and grabbed a napkin from a young blonde's lap.

"Sorry," he said, huskily. "I'm just so passionate about the power of comedy to make a difference in people's lives. Sometimes I get so full of it I feel like I could explode and splatter myself over George Carlin's effing grave. You feel me?"

"It's OK," I said. "No reason to be embarrassed."

"Embarrassed? You think I'm effeminate, don't you, Lando? That it? You think McFarlane's a big flamer?"

I laughed. McFarlane didn't. He glared at me, his steel gray eyes suddenly as cold as a frost giant's netherhole.

"Are you calling me a fag, Lando?"

"No!"

McFarlane's face turned orange, then bright red. Then he punched me in the stomach.

"I'm just messin' with ya! Cop a squat, you crazy schmuck. Drinks are on Uncle Ted!"

Corroder came back carrying a tray loaded with drinks.

"Ted's ADHD with a mild schizoid/rage disorder: Who ordered the rum and Coke?"

I sipped from my drink, which was strong but harmless enough.

Just one. It's a celebration. You deserve it.

"A toast!" McFarlane said, including the patrons and comics around us. "Git 'em up, you daffy bastards!"

Everyone raised their glasses. Yuri was beaming again. And why not? If this venture were a hit it would make us both rich. Mitsuko Leavenworth's right hand had secreted itself somewhere beneath the table, presumably in Yuri's lap.

"To the hip new star of Fox's newest late night talk experience (to be named later): Lando Cooper!"

People applauded. Some of them meant it.

Over the next four hours, several comics made their way over to the table, every one of them eager to lap up some reflected network slobber, or at least free drinks. Goldie Kiebler, the horribly vital owner of the Ha-Ha Room, plopped her bones into my lap and loudly proclaimed to everyone within earshot that she'd plucked me out of the ghetto. She may have tried to put her tongue in my ear. Yuri sang Swedish war songs between bouts of French-kissing Mitsuko like her tonsils held the antidote for a fast-acting nerve toxin. Corroder and McFarlane talked time slots and made bets about which of them could nail one of the female comics staggering around the bar like burning zombie ragdolls. Everyone was happy. I was happy. Everything was going my way.

Of course that's when everything fell apart.

CHAPTER XVIII
WE REGRET TO INFORM YOU

Gods don't dream. Since beginning my mortal life, what dreams may come, came not from my subconscious, but from the prayers of believers. They came to me in flashes; shards from millions of lives, prayers filtering up from the Eshuum. Before I was hospitalized, that's what I thought might be the cause of my headaches: all those emotions, all that mortal need sizzling through my overworked human brain.

Lately, the prayer-streams had been growing fainter, dwindling every day. In some places the volume of prayers was increasing – Africa, Latin America, parts of Asia and the Middle East, the American South – but on the whole, the collective cry of humanity had grown fainter over my incarnated lifetime. People were simply too busy, too angry or too educated to worry about what I was up to. Sometimes, toward the end of it all, it was even fairly common for me to get a decent night's sleep.

The night before the apocalypse was not one of those nights.

• • •

Maya's Prayer

Maya Otsunde is walking down the road toward the refugee camps that line the border between her country and Burundi. Refugees are flooding over the border, fleeing genocide in their homeland to seek safety in hers. But her people are already taxed to the limit by their own hardships. Drought and famine and war have made her village a Hell on Earth.

She has decided, after her meeting with God, that she must take her destiny into her own hands. She walks toward the camps, where (she believes) she will find men who know how to make a difference. As she walks into the camp – called Showland by the cruel guards who carry machine guns – she notes the stares of the people who notice her, a tall, brown girl with the bearing of a ballet dancer, her spine straight, her hair pulled back into twin cornrows. She ignores the leering, desperate men and the hungry women and children. There are thousands of tents lining both sides of the road, but she knows where to find the man she seeks. As she approaches the largest tent, she allows herself one small prayer.

"I know you have other work, God. But I ask of you this one thing: give me the strength to look Barzuli in the eye. Please grant me that much strength and I will never bother you again."

She opens her eyes. She has reached the tent. She is standing at the entrance to the sprawling pavilion that the warlord Hamza Barzuli has made for himself and his men. The laughter of hard men issues from inside the tent, and the sound of someone jacking a shell into the chamber of a shotgun. Maya knows these sounds. Her brother was killed by the boy soldiers from Burundi last year. But what she wants from Hamza is more powerful than any gun. What she wants will assure her place in Heaven. If Barzulli accepts her offer.

The laughter comes again. Maya thinks of her family, her mother and sisters starving back in her village. She thinks of the American army base a few miles up the road, and she surprises herself by pulling back the tent flaps and peering into the darkness.

"Hello?" she says. "Colonel Barzuli?"

Maya holds her head high. She must show no fear: she has met the American God and taken him to task. She has received a promise from her new God, a God whose coming has been foretold by several wise men in her village. Her meeting with the old American God confirmed the rightness of her decision. She will bring Word of the coming God to the Americans occupying her country. She knows she will be rewarded in her next life.

"I've come to volunteer."

Unafraid, Maya smiles and steps into the darkness.

"You're late, Romeo."

I opened my eyes. The light of a bright morning shone in through my bedroom window. I stretched, luxuriating in the feeling of triumph lingering from the night before. Yuri and I agreed that he would negotiate my network deal. I'd never had any kind of "deal" before. Now I had a wallet full of business cards.

"Good morning, sleepyhead," Connie said. She was even younger than the last time I'd seen her, appearing as a young girl in white deerskins, barely seven years old and sitting crosslegged atop my old TV. **"How are we, on this lovely day the gods have made?"**

"Connie, even you can't bring me down today. You know why? Because… I've got the whole world in my hands."

"Lando…"

"I got the whole wide world in my hands–"

"You're late."

"I got the great big world in my–"

"Did you hear me?"

"…haaaannnnn… What did you say?"

"You're late. Surabhi's plane?"

"No!"

I scrambled out from under my *Indiana Jones and the Temple of Doom* comforter and fell out of bed.

"What… What time is it?"

"Too late for you to be on time."

"Why didn't you wake me up?"

"I'm an Earth Goddess, not your personal secretary. And speaking of my duties around here. We need to talk."

"Not now, Connie."

I stripped off my clothes. It wasn't hard: I'd passed out in them three hours earlier.

"Lando… I'm leaving."

"Fine, go. We can talk when you get back!"

"I'm not coming back, Lando."

"Connie, please!"

The alarm clock on my night table read 11.31am. I'd slept through the alarm. Surabhi's plane was due at O'Hare Airport in half an hour.

"Late!"

I'd called Herb and asked for the day off, intending to spend it with Surabhi. After I volunteered a day's pay, Herb had given me his blessings. I showered, dressed quickly and ran downstairs still dripping.

"Late!"

"You can do this, Cooper. You're the Embodiment of Cosmic Conciousness."

A loud thump interrupted my train of thought. I slammed on the brakes. The Jaguar rocked to a halt inches from the walker of our neighbor, Gus Bankhead, the old "confirmed bachelor" who lived in the immaculate Colonial across the street with his godson. Bankhead hammered the legs of his walker against the Jaguar's trunk.

"Watch where you're going, you black idiot!"

I forced myself to breathe deeply. As Bankhead, still swearing, hobbled down the sidewalk I checked both directions, made sure the street was clear, then pulled onto our street and headed west. As I made my way onto the interstate, drivers in nearby cars took pains to drive up alongside Barbara's car.

"Speed limit's fifty-five, jackass!"

I made my way to the airport.

Maybe it was the expectant expression on my face that made the gate agent at the Transworld Charter terminal take pity on me. Maybe it was the roses. Or the sign I was holding:

Surabhi Moloke... Will U Marry Me?

I'd been standing at the gate, waiting for Surabhi and her family to emerge from the closed jetway for nearly an hour before the gate agent noticed me. I'd checked my Blackberry scheduler a dozen times, checked the charter airline's website and learned that their flight from Heathrow had departed on schedule. But nearly twelve hours later, there was no sign of them. And the gate agent, a wispy woman with mousy hair and a pronounced overbite, was staring at me again.

"I'm sorry," she whispered. "Who are you waiting for?"

I told her. She typed into her computer and waited for a response. Her eyes widened, then she lifted one trembling hand to her lips. Her dismay only grew worse when she read my sign.

"Will you excuse me for a moment?" she whispered.

Before I could answer, the mousy woman turned and dashed into a little office behind the counter. She reemerged almost immediately with another person in tow, a tall, Asian woman wearing a black suit. The mousy agent was standing on tiptoe, whispering into the dark-suited woman's ear. The dark-suited woman eyed me suspiciously, then nodded.

"My name is Naomi Penn," she said. "I'm a customer service representative for Transworld Charter. May I please ask your name?"

I told her my name.

"Oooh, like the movie character. Billy Dee Williams? How wonderful for you."

"Is there a problem?"

"May I inquire as to the nature of your relationship to the Moloke family, Mister Dee Williams?"

"What's going on? Are you with the UN or...?"

But Naomi Penn was staring at my sign. It must have looked like I was using it to fend her off. I shrugged it behind my back, suddenly embarrassed without knowing why.

"You are engaged to Surabhi Moloke?"

"Yep," I said. "Well, I hope to be in the next few minutes. Ahhh… where's the plane?"

The mousy agent offered a throat-clearing cough behind the counter. Our eyes met, and she quickly looked down at her flashing screen.

"Mister Dee Williams… will you please follow me?"

Naomi Penn turned on one heel and walked toward the counter.

I repeated my name as we passed the nervous agent and went into the little office behind the counter.

"It's Cooper, by the way. Was the flight delayed?"

Naomi Penn sat at a little desk and gestured me toward the small chair opposite it. "Please sit."

"What's going on?"

"Mister Cooper, the Molokes' plane has been lost."

"Lost? Lost where?"

Penn's smile never wavered, but her fingers scooped up a silver letter opener from her desk and began to fumble with it.

"Mister Cooper, there's been a terrible incident. The Molokes' charter lost contact with Heathrow shortly after take-off. The plane went down somewhere over the Atlantic, we believe between…"

"Wait a minute… Went down… what do you mean 'went down'?"

Penn's hands kept bending the blade of the letter opener, as if she could twist it into a different shape.

"The Molokes' plane went down off the coast of Ireland sometime this morning, sir. A Royal Naval vessel was in the area where the plane was lost. They are conducting search and rescue operations now."

"You're telling me that–"

"Apparently a good deal of wreckage has already been located. As of this moment, I'm terribly sorry to inform you... that there were no survivors."

"No survivors...?"

"I am so sorry for your loss, Mister Cooper..."

Search and rescue.

"Because of the sensitive nature of Mrs Moloke's work and the intervention of US, British and Irish authorities, no formal announcement has been released to the media until any criminal activities can be ruled out, but..."

There were no survivors.

"...all efforts are being made..."

No survivors.

"...a counselor provided by the airline to help you in this terrible time..."

No...

"Mister Cooper... is there anyone I can contact?"

Survivors.

"Mister Cooper?"

CHAPTER IXX
THE CHOICE

"Surabhi Moloke Will U Marry Me?"

I sat in the main concourse of Transworld Charter, staring at my hands. A few feet away, a six year-old girl was repeating the contents of my sign to her mother. The mother was busily texting on her iPhone and only half listening.

"Surabhi Moloke Will U Marry Me?"

"That's nice, sweetheart."

"Surabhi Moloke Will U Marry Me? That's what the sign says, Mommy!"

"Good job, pumpkin. You're decoding and interpreting."

"Mommy, why is that brown man crying?"

The mother jerked as if she'd been given an electric shock. When she saw me sitting there, her eyes went wide and round as new saucers. "Amanda! Oh my God!"

The woman stood up and rushed over to where I sat.

"I am so sorry, sir. We normally don't acknowledge people with different skin colors. I mean, we normally don't notice... I mean... Amanda, apologize to the nice man."

"But why is he crying, Mommy? Doesn't he have a place to live?"

"Amanda! You apologize this very instant!"

"It's alright."

I swiped at my eyes with the back of my sleeve. Then I went back to staring at my hands.

No survivors.

My mobile beeped. I grabbed it, hoping…

Sorry for this terrible loss. If there is anything Transworld Charters can do to assist you please contact me at…

I set my phone on the seat next to me and went back to staring at my hands.

Surabhi Moloke Will U Marry Me?

"Sir, are you alright? Can I help you?"

The look on the concerned mother's face unfolded something sharp in my chest.

"You took the risk."

"Excuse me?"

"Your daughter embarrassed you, but you still tried to help."

"Oh. Well. Everyone has to do their part. Right? I mean, if we don't lend a helping hand every once in a while, the world would slide into chaos."

Something heavy fell over with a loud crash.

"Amanda, come down from there!"

The woman ran off to attend to her daughter.

I needed to move. I needed to think.

My connection to the power was too unreliable. I could already feel the pain lurking in my head, daring me to try it. And there had been no godfight, no divine breaching to release the power my plan required. There was only one place where I could find the hope I needed: home. At the bottom of my college footlocker lay power enough for a second chance.

"Mommy… who's Surabhi Moloke?"

"It doesn't have to be."

It's what is.

"But I've changed things before. I can fix this."

You redressed the damages caused by divine breeches in the Eshuum. That's different.

"I've saved millions, billions of lives."

You've operated according to the dictates of your function. To move them forward, protect them from obsolete gods. Now you're one of them. Surabhi's death has nothing to do with that.

"But I can fix this. It doesn't have to happen."

But it did happen. In the normal course of events.

"But it's wrong!"

That's life. Welcome to the world.

"Who would blame me? After everything I've done? The sacrifices I've made? Who would begrudge me just this once?"

You would blame yourself. It's a violation of the Covenant you initiated. You know it's wrong.

"No! I could go on. Fix this one problem and then move on. The Plan would go on."

You would fail. The knowledge of the violation would undermine the legitimacy of every decision. It's the essence of corruption.

"You're wrong. I could bring them back and walk away. I could restore her and never see her again. Wouldn't that be enough?"

It's corrupt.

"What would it take to make this right, Connie?"

You can't make it right.

"I can make it right. We can make it right, Connie. Together."

You can't bargain with me. Changing Woman is gone.

"Then… who are you?"

What you're about to do will wreak havoc with the structure of reality.

"I have no reality without her. I love her."

You are corrupt. Fallible. Human.

"I can fix this."

You'll destroy everything you've worked to achieve.

"No," I said to myself. "I can handle it."

I looked at my reflection in the polished surface of my Northwestern footlocker. The man who looked back at me was a stranger, his face a grieving mask.

I can fix that too. I can fix everything.

I unlocked the padlock and lifted the lid. Silver radiance filled my eyes, my mind. It nourished a part of me that had gone hungry. It had been nearly a decade since I'd last touched the Shell. Looking into the Eshuum was like diving into the past while dreaming of the future. It was hope and dread in equal measure; every dream humankind has ever dreamed or will dream, and every nightmare that haunts the collective consciousness. The potential for endless invention exists there; every masterpiece, every murderous innovation shimmers within its argent chambers. It is the most powerful phenomenon on Earth and, at one time, it was my home.

"I'm coming, babe."

Starlight elevated me, empowered my perceptions to levels far beyond those of which my dwindling personal reserves were capable. Without the Shell's protection my mortal body would have been reduced to screaming ash.

But Surabhi was depending on me. I wasn't about to let her tumble down the well of death and circumstance when I could set things straight with a simple wish. My newly awakened conscience was wrong.

"Lando! What the hell are you doing up there?"

I flicked a luminous tendril at the door, slammed it so hard that it cracked down the center. Herb might have a fit, but nothing this side of an Archangel could open it until I allowed it to open.

I summoned the Aspect best suited to realigning circumstantial inconsistencies. Father Flies rose up around me, all cold brilliance and jealousy. It was the mathematician's God, the cartographer's Deity, the whitebearded God of Christopher Columbus and Thomas Aquinas, its eyes bright as supernovae.

"You have no place here. Only the all-seeing may wade in the waters of feasibility."

White light exploded in my skull, gouged the backs of my eyes. I was blind, deafened and battered. Somewhere, something was burning. I could smell frying meat in the air of my parents' attic and realized it was me: my mind was on fire. I bore down harder, buoyed up by the power of the Eshuum even as it was killing me.

One. Last. Time.

"Depart," Father Flies said. **"You're too late."**

I answered with a shout of silver force. **"Be quiet**.**"**

Windows shattered. My parents' house shuddered as if struck a blow from an invisible giant. Burning brightly, I brushed aside Father Flies, commandeered his extrusions, gripped the reins of will and circumstance and wrapped them around my fists.

"Reset.**"**

Silence, deeper than the void at the beginning of Time. For one weightless moment, I hung, suspended in the moment between... Then something grabbed me, wrapped around my chest, and a guttural voice rasped in my right ear.

"You are mine, dog."

Cold hits me in the face. I can't breathe... The air is screaming and my vision keeps shifting; black to red to blinding white. But it's the cold, hard slap of winter somehow magnified to lethal intensity. Something is holding me, constricting my chest. Then something sharp pierces my side and a red hot agony fills up my world. Something's pulled me out of the Eshuum, ambushed me. But only a Godlike power could have intercepted me.

"At last he begins to see the light."

Through the frenzy of pain in my side, I can feel my blood trickling down the fronts of my thighs. Someone's pressing something sharp against my adam's apple. The pain in my side pushes me up onto the tips of my toes. Snow like flecks of wind blown ice scour my face, obscuring the dark shape that emerges from the storm.

"I'd say we have his attention, brother. I think you can let him go."

The pressure on my back lessens as that hot shard slides out of my flesh. Hot blood is pulsing down my legs, between my buttocks. My unseen attacker relaxes his chokehold and I fall to my hands and knees. I can't catch my breath. I need my inhaler.

"'And I saw a strong angel proclaiming with a loud voice, Who is worthy to open the book, and to loose the seals thereof.' That's from Revelations, Lando. A lot of folks think it's too dark, but I find it comforting."

"Let me kill the little traitor now."

"No, Brother Ares. He's to be tasked first."

I look up into a face partially obscured by multicolored ribbons of light, the shifting bands illuminating a dark gray sky. The Northern Lights. Behind the man-shaped shadow, a fractious gray sea surges, whipped by howling winds. I'm in Alaska, maybe the North Pole? The Arctic Circle?

"You know me, son?"

Owen Holiday smiles his serial killer's smile. He's dressed in a denim shirt, jeans and cowboy boots, as if the cold has no effect on him.

"It has been given to me, the pleasure of educating you as to certain realities of which you may be unaware. The first and most obvious… You've been replaced."

My lungs are filling up with blood. I reach inward, searching for an Aspect. Skydaddy could blow them both to China, or Father Flies… or Stormface…

"Still fighting, son? You should be thinking about the disposition of your immortal soul."

Holiday kneels down and looks me in the eye.

"You think my God didn't know what you were trying to do? That your successor didn't have you pegged from the moment you decided to pull the plug on all that hard earned belief? Did you really believe He would let it all end?"

Holiday's words sting, propelled by the force of his strange inner violence.

"What were you thinking, Yahweh? You could have had it all to yourself, maybe for another century. But you wanted more."

"Just wait, you bastard… just… wait…"

Black flashes pulse before my eyes. Holiday... he's holding the Shell. It twinkles like a nugget of hard starshine as he rolls it back and forth across his knuckles, like a magician flipping a coin.

"Such a simplistic incarnation. All your headaches, the drinking... the woman. So easy to take it all away."

"You... you killed Surabhi."

"Oh no, not me. My God killed your woman. While you were finding yourself, He moved into your empty mansion. A century or so ahead of schedule, yes, but my Lord is always on the lookout for other people's missed opportunities."

Stormface... Father Flies... help me...

Abandoner. Betrayer.

I'm weaponless, breathless and bleeding to death.

I can fix this. I'm God.

Not anymore.

"Get him up."

Ares grabs me under my arms and hugs me to his chest, squeezing me with enough force to make my spine creak. Up close he smells like blood and smoke and downmarket aftershave.

"Hey... it's true. You really do look like Burt Reynolds."

"I. DO. NOT!"

Holiday laughs as Ares fumed. I'm dying, but I can still bust balls.

"Besides bearing a disturbing resemblance to Mister Reynolds, Brother Ares here also lacks the power to kill whatever may be left of the You part of you. But never mind – reinforcements have arrived!"

Behind him, the frozen sea grows violent. The shattering of icebergs fills the air as the horizon begins to glow. The wind slices at my cheeks, my fingers. I can feel the blood freezing into a thin sheet on my thighs.

"'And I saw four angels standing on the four corners of the earth, holding the four winds of the earth that the wind should not blow on the earth, not on the sea, nor on any tree!'"

Two shining portals open in midair. Two burning figures step out onto the ice, sending up torrents of steam. Although I've forgotten more about my former life than could be contained by a hundred mortal lifetimes I recognize the gods Holiday has summoned to kill me: Kali, the Hindu Goddess of Time and Destruction, She who is called Destroyer and Mother Death. Around Her throat dangles a necklace of human skulls. Each of Her six hands grips a weapon capable of generating incalculable force, Her skin the color of clear summer skies, Her eyes twin pools of liquid midnight. Her song could unbind the fabric of reality. As far as I knew she went into retirement back in the early Nineties after a massive influx of Hindus into the West weakened the grip of her pantheon at home. Now here she stands, Her face beautiful and terrible, in full Aspect.

Next to her stands Thor, the Norwegian god of thunder. Wielding his magic hammer, he was strong enough to atomize a mountain range. He once held power over the world's storms, until the coming of Christianity forced him into obsolescence. Now storms swirl around him once more, dancing to his call. He is huge, his hair and beard like a raging wildfire. The hammer he grips in his right fist crackles with lightning. It's screaming, its cry melting the permafrost beneath his feet into hissing slush.

Ares joins them and assumes his greatest Aspect: Andreiphontes the Manslayer, God of War and the Horrors of War. In his fists any weapon can slay thousands. At his command entire nations have consumed themselves in berserker fury. At the height of his power, he could transform himself into a mighty bear, or a murderous leviathan, or any other lethal seeming to achieve his ends. Now he stands nearly seven feet tall, his eyes aflame.

They're anachronisms, disenfranchised and forgotten by all but scholars and movie buffs. Yet now they tower above me, vital and eager to reclaim their bygone glory.

And in front of them stands the mad prophet of the godstalker, the god of whom Zeus warned. Holiday raises his voice to the blackening skies.

"'And they sing the song of Moses the servant of God, saying Great and marvelous are thy works, Lord God Almighty. Who shall not fear thee and glorify thy name? For all nations shall come and worship before thee.'"

He pockets the Shell and looks down at me, his face swollen with dark joy.

"Your mother and I will miss you, Lando." Then he turned to his divine assassins. "Brothers… Sister… kill him."

It can't end like this. Do something.

The world is growing dim. I reach out, seeking the power. The pain that detonates in my head is immense and final. I taste smoke and blood.

Ares unsheathes his sword.

"This is no battle. The little bastard's already half dead."

Then something bursts through the skin of Ares' throat. For a moment, golden light pierces the darkness from a network of shining cracks racing through the

War God's body, while blood the color of molten gold pours from his mouth. Then Ares opens his arms... and explodes. The something that pierced Ares falls to the snow: it's an arrow, a shining silver arrow.

As steaming gobbets of once-immortal flesh rain down all around me, I look toward the direction from which the arrow came. And I see her. Flashing beneath the gray-black clouds, leaping toward us across the surging sea, she's coming, riding the godhorse, eight-legged Slepnir – a nutbrown young woman in glowing deerskins, her long black hair flying, a second arrow already drawn.

The Golden Lady. Changing Woman.

Connie.

Her war cry silences the shriek of the winds. Where her horse runs across the surface of that bitter sea, the clouds part and her husband, the Sun, shines his face upon the waters. Even as Kali begins her Dance of Destruction and Thor summons a tempest to blast her into atoms, Changing Woman comes, trailing Spring's warmth in her wake.

The Navajo religions tell of her bow, how it was given to her by her son, Monster Slayer. It was formed from the wood of the First Tree, strong enough to harness the power of the sun, or the fury of the storm. With it, the Navajo gods could incinerate the monstrous enemies of humankind. Still singing, Connie fires. The arrow soars through the sky, sweeping aside the darkness like a golden comet plummeting through the blackness of space.

But Kali Durga raises a Song of her own: its power is the power of Death and it burns Changing Woman's arrow to ash, a wave of unlife that murders every living thing in its path. As the echoes of Kali's voice pass over the surging seas, the waters go black. Dead fish pop up in spots all along the shore. The death surge shatters Connie's bow with a sound like a detonation. Connie clutches her right hand to her breast. Then the force of Kali's song strikes Connie and the godhorse: Odin's steed falls into the water, dead. Changing Woman leaps at the last minute, somersaulting to land on the ice.

Kali surges forward, arms waving above her head. In one of her right hands a long, curved knife appears, blazing with a hazy blue light. But Connie raises a shield with the emblem of a spider emblazoned on its face, deflecting Kali's blow. She pulls back, her arms crawling with red spiders as big as tarantulas. Kali spins, shrieking, her power pulping the red spiders, staining the snow with burning bodies. But the survivors quickly cover her. Kali disappears beneath a living red wave.

But the red spiders burst into flame. The death goddess' hands weave the flames into a roaring whirlwind and send it howling toward Changing Woman. Connie raises her hands as the whirlwind closes around her, shielding her from view.

"Connie!"

Out of the fire a giant black shape rises, and stretches dark wings toward the sky: a Thunderbird. Connie, in the form of the Navajo birdgod, envelops Kali within the shadows of her wings.

I have to help her.

Thor seems content to hang back, laughing, for the moment. But soon he'll join the fray. When that happens, Connie will die.

Meanwhile, Holiday has turned away from the battle, searching the glowing horizon.

I won't let it end like this.

Kali dances, a space-warping swirl of color and light and death. The Thunderbird's feathers turn gray and fall out, the birdgod collapsing into a pile of desiccated bones. Connie stands amongst the debris, old now, her Crone Aspect rising as her power wanes. One of her hands has been mangled. She clutches it to her breast, cradling it, her eyes shining, defiant even now.

I close my eyes, seeking deeper than I've ever gone, ever had to go. Holiday must be uncertain about the extent to which I still control the power. Why else has he brought the Big Guns of Divine Destruction? Maybe I can give Connie a moment to get away. I reach up, ignoring the tearing pain in my head, ignoring the screaming agony in my side. I reach...

"Hello, Lando."

Stormface.

"I need you."

"I can't play with you right now, Lando..."

"Listen to me! I know another way you can link up with the power!"

Something screams like a bandsaw ripping through ironwood. I turn in time to see Connie fall to one knee. From where she kneels, her eyes find mine.

You were right, kiddo. Our time is done.

Then Connie smiles.

And one of Kali's bladed weapons strikes her in the chest.

Changing Woman falls backward into the snow.

"The guy with the hammer! He's connected!"

"Does he want to play?"

"Yes! He wants to play!"

Connie isn't moving.

"They both want to play!"

Stormface glides across the ice; a giant babyhead with burning eyes. Kali, wounded, turns to face it. Three of her arms lay on the ice, and half her face is gone, burned away. She staggers toward Stormface, her right foot dragging a glowing golden line behind her in the snow; whatever energies she borrowed from the Coming must be nearly depleted. She reaches for Thor, but the thunder god ignores her.

"At last! Something I can fight!"

Behind him, a stocky older woman with a dark brown crew cut rises from the shining puddle where Connie fell: Esmeralda Sanchez, her University of New Mexico sweatshirt stained with the blood of her goddess. The lenses of her eyeglasses glint, the Aurora borealis flickering in her eyes as she faces the two immortals.

Changing Woman's last prophetess raises her right fist to the sky. She shouts a Navajo invocation and hammers her fist down onto the ice. As Kali and Thor advance toward Stormface, the ice beneath them erupts and something huge blasts through and rockets into the air, knocking Thor off his feet. The orca grasps Kali in its jaws as it rises toward the sky: for a moment, killer goddess and killer whale hover in midair. Then the orca smashes down in a furious spray of ice and bloody water. The impact vibrates through my kneecaps. The shelf of ice upon which Esmeralda Sanchez stands upends itself like one end of a giant seesaw. The orca smashes back into the water, holding Kali in its jaws. But Esmeralda Sanchez slides toward the hole in the ice and plunges into the gap between the two ledges.

"Connie!"

A silent detonation shudders through the ice; the power that had elevated Kali just vacated her corpse.

"Mmmm," Stormface mumbles, absorbing those energies. **"It's been too long."**

The surge of power refuels our connection. Stormface surrounds me just as Thor rams his hammer into my defenses. Stormface takes the brunt of the blow. Even so, the impact flings me across the ice. I come to in a snowdrift as Thor drops out of the sky and strikes the permafrost with the force of a dynamite charge, his hammer screaming carnage. He's too close. He's too strong. Stormface lashes out; a battering ram of force that strikes Thor. The explosion flings us apart. But Stormface breaks; its protection falls to glowing tatters. Thor lands fifty feet away, unconscious or dead, his godslaying hammer sizzling, its indestructible head buried in the ice.

Connie.

I drag myself across the permafrost toward the gap that claimed Changing Woman and her prophetess, struggling to see through the steam and boiling water below.

"Connie!"

"You've done well, old boy. But the tribulation is nearly done."

Holiday.

"You killed her!"

"A justifiable homicide, my friend. Your plans were disruptive to my patron's Ascension, His vision: a world eternally ruled by fear. Your little mentor died in service to the greater good. As will your parents, when their usefulness has ended. A lot of people are going to die, Lando. Everything that your other self infected must be purged to allow the new paradigm to settle in. But know that their deaths will not be in vain."

"Kill you… swear to God… I'll kill you!"

"New Eden has begun, Yahweh. You're done."

Behind him, the sky grows lighter, dawn's glow illuminating the horizon, but the color… the color is wrong.

"He comes! My Lord's greatest Lieutenant comes in fire and victory!"

The red light, a pinpoint of flame burning across the sky, whistling as it pushes frigid air aside, dragging sonic booms in its wake. It's coming fast, and I'm afraid.

Because I recognize that light.

Holiday opens his arms like a man welcoming his long lost brother as the wind from the red light's descent whips the snow into a million minor storms.

"'And I saw an angel come down from heaven, having the key of the bottomless pit and a great chain in his hand!'"

I've searched for him, ignored the uncertainty of our ancient stalemate. But now he's found me, and I'm about to learn just how stupid I've been.

"'And God shall wipe away all tears from their eyes; and there shall be no more death, neither sorrow, nor crying, neither shall there be any more pain, for the former things are passed away!'"

The red nimbus lands silently, touching the permafrost without so much as a whisper: the Devil always knew how to make an entrance.

Yuri Kalshnikov steps onto the bloody snow.

His eyes shine in that particularly Red way I remember from our ancient contest. He hid himself in plain sight, passing himself off as my best friend and mortal ally. Now he crackles, incandescent with the power the Devil was supposed to have renounced.

I lay there in a deepening puddle of bloodslush, shut off from the power that might have turned the tide; finally, damnably human. I can barely see him through my tears.

"Was it? Was it always you?"

Yuri stares at me, through me, as if he's looking into the distant past or some unknowable future. Holiday puts one hand on his shoulder.

"Prove yourself worthy, my brother. Join the winning team."

Yuri bends and grasps Thor's hammer. Like a man towing an invisible anchor, he walks toward me, lifting his feet out of the knee-high snow. The hammer pulses, its bass heartbeat thrumming across the ice... the burning, freezing air, beating echoes from my bones, its head throbbing with a purple-white light violent as the heart of murder. Overhead, tongues of lightning flicker through the dark skies as Yuri summons ancient enchantments both divine and demonic, charging the hammer with enough power to slay a god.

"Fool. To have commanded such power."

His head shakes back and forth like a man in the grip of a seizure, jaw muscles clenching as if he were biting back words too terrible to voice, his scorn straining through gritted teeth.

"We are... children... playing with the fire of the gods."

Thor's hammer recasts the ice field in arclight flashes of blue, crimson crawlers of divine lightning and infernal magic. Livid stalks of elemental fire dance surround me, blinding me as shoots of lightning crackle up from the earth and surround me with elemental fury. Yuri steps between the bars of the burning plasma cage. Only his eyes reveal the price of his betrayal.

"We could have remade this world in our image."

Surabhi. What have I done?

"Yuri... you have a... choice."

Arcane energies snarl the air, blistering my flesh with a hurricane blast. Arctic air tears the skin of my cheeks and the tendrils of a strange gravity tug me backward as the Devil lifts the stormgod's blazing hammer.

If I can just reach him, touch him, finally.

"Yuri... you're... my best friend."

Then the hammer...

PART 2

THE QUANTUM MECHANIC

"In this multiverse of universes, most universes are dead. The proton is not stable. Atoms never condense. DNA never forms. The universe collapses prematurely or freezes almost immediately. But in our universe, a series of cosmic accidents has happened, not necessarily because of the hand of God but because of the law of averages."

Parallel Worlds, Dr Michio Kaku

"People are damn crazy.
Every human livin' knows that's true.
If God made People in His own image
He must be damn crazy too."

CHAPTER XX
HOMECOMING

When he opened his eyes it was into the glare of too-bright lights, shouting and the sounds of praise. He shut his eyes against the glare. But he couldn't shut his ears.

"Thank God! Thank God in His Heaven!"

"Can someone get her out of here?"

His chest hurt. It felt as if someone was sitting on it. It was difficult to breathe and there were shadows in his mind, dark, moving forms. He was cold, and the smell... like rubbing alcohol. A hospital smell. It was almost worse than the voices.

"His blood pressure is stabilizing. Heart rate normal."

"Excellent. Let's get him prepped."

Darkness again.

"Lando? Lando can you hear me?"

This time he opened his eyes slowly, wincing against the memory of that other time, when light and sound threatened to drive him back into the darkness. It was important to stay out of the darkness. But the pounding in his head forced him to shut his eyes again.

The darkness was cool, comforting. In the darkness he could float and forget about... forget about...

"Surabhi."

Hushed voices. Whispering. Then...

"Who's Surabhi?"

"Quiet, Charles. Lando... can you hear me?"

"What...?"

"Lando, dear, this is your mother speaking. Can you open your eyes?"

"Easy, Barb. Give 'em some breathing room, fer Cyrus' sake."

LC Cooper squinted his eyes open enough to make out several blurred shapes. As the image swam into focus, the first person he recognized was his mother.

"Bar... ba... ra," he said. His throat. There was something wrong with his throat. It was dry. It felt as if he had been forced to gargle with sand. "M... mother."

"Yes, dear, praise God. It's mother."

"Thr... throat... hurts..."

"That's the anesthetic, dear. The doctors said it would dry out all your membranes. Would you like some water?"

"Wha... what?"

"WOULD YOU LIKE SOME WATER?"

Water.

A dark vortex. A swirling hole in the red ice leading down... down. Blood... blood on the ice. His blood in the...

"...water, dear. Oh, I forgot, he has to use the straw."

"Connie!"

"Now just relax, Lando. He shouldn't try to sit up."

"Who's Connie?"

LC opened his mouth to answer.

"Connie... she's my... my..."

…but he couldn't remember.

"Boy, Barbie, he don't look so hot."

LC squinted toward the speaker, the only other person in the room, a short, barrel-chested man with a blockshaped, bald head. He was wearing a brown suit, light blue shirt and lime green tie covered with pineapples.

"Flaunt," LC said huskily, his throat burning. "You're… Chick… Flaunt."

The barrel chested man frowned appreciatively.

"Chuck, sonny. Chuck Flaunt. But hey, that's pretty good. Looks like you may have kept a brain cell or two in that noggin o' yers after all."

"Bite me, Chick."

"Lando Kalel Cooper, that's no way to talk to your father."

"My what?"

"That's alright, honey," Flaunt said. "I got nothing to prove to him, or anybody else. I know who I am. Hell of a lot more than I can say for some people in this room."

"Charles…"

"Just kiddin', Barbie."

Barbie?

"My father?" LC said. "What the hell are you two… are you two…?"

He cleared his throat. His voice… his voice felt… different to him, rougher, harsher.

"What's wrong with my… with my voice? Why am I in the hospital?"

Barbara approached again, a giant plastic hospital cup in her right hand. She stuck a straw into the top and handed it to him.

"I've called Danielle. She was just dropping the children off at school. They're so excited. They can't wait to see you."

LC took a sip of the water. It was cold, soothing to his throat.

"Who's Danielle?"

Barbara frowned as if she smelled something unpleasant. "We were told to expect this."

"Expect what? What did you do to your hair? And what's wrong with your face?"

"I see being in a coma hasn't improved your attitude."

"A coma? What are you talking about? I'm perfectly fine."

But he didn't feel fine. Something was wrong. Something was… different. But he couldn't quite put his finger on what. Something about Barbara's face... And where was Herb? Then another, darker thought…

"Where's Yuri?"

"Who's Yuri?"

He remembered a fight, Yuri standing over him, holding something, something so bright it hurt his brain to remember.

Children.

"What do you mean, 'Who's Yuri?'"

Blank stares from Flaunt and Barbara.

"Tall, good looking blonde guy?"

More blank stares.

"You said he had a nice package."

Flaunt was up in a jackrabbit flash. "Hey! Just what the hell do you mean by that, mister?"

"It's alright, Charles," Barbara said. Then she pointed at her skull. "That's the you-know-what talking."

Flaunt looked unconvinced. "I thought they took care of the 'you-know-what'?"

Barbara smiled and patted LC's arm. "We'll sort all this stuff out soon enough, dear. Mommy's going to get you all squared away. Then everything will be just the way it should be."

"Well… look who is back."

The door to the hospital room swung open and a tall, dark brown man entered the room.

"Hello, Sanjit," Barbara said. "Sorry. Doctor Aziz."

"Hello, to all."

The doctor moved to stand at the side of LC's bed. Barbara stepped away to give him space to sit on the edge of the bed. That was when LC got his first good look at his mother.

"And how is my most famous patient doing this morning?"

"Lando," Barbara said. "This is Doctor Aziz. He's the one who helped you. Remember?"

Barbara was at least thirty pounds heavier than she should have been, her backside and thighs and breasts larger than LC would have believed possible. Her hair, just the day before, had been mostly dark brown with just a few strands of gray beginning to show at the temples. Now it was completely silver, and styled in a way she had always attributed to Republican congresswomen from Texas. Barbara had always hated those "helmet hair" styles, but now she was wearing one. And it was gray.

The bright light flashing in his eyes brought him back.

Light… too bright… burning… blinding…

Children playing with the fires of Creation.

Doctor Aziz clicked his penlight off and stuck it into the pocket of his lab coat.

"Yes, he seems a little disoriented. But that's to be expected after the type of procedure he's undergone."

"Procedure?" LC said. "What kind of procedure?"

Barbara sat on the edge of his bed and took one of his hands in hers.

"Lando, dear… you nearly died yesterday. Well, I

suppose technically you were dead. But Doctor Aziz brought you back."

Doctor Aziz stepped forward, his round, brown face all smiles. "It was touch and go there for a while. But I'm happy to report that the surgery was a complete success. We were able to remove most of the tumor."

"Tumor? I have…"

"Had!"

"I… had… a tumor?"

"A slightly non-malignant but very bothersome brain tumor, yes. It was the cause of your terrible headaches…"

No.

"…and your colorful hallucinations."

Aziz chuckled. "You were very nearly lost to us, my friend. My wife told me, 'Sanjit, if you let him die I will never speak to you again. He's the Funniest Man in the world!' So when your heart stopped beating yesterday morning I thought I would be spending the next ten months sleeping on the couch! But we did our very best and you came back to us. So now I expect you to make a full recovery."

Brain tumor?

"The next few months will be very difficult," Aziz said. "You will have to learn to walk again. During the six weeks of medically-induced coma, your muscles atrophied, but not as much as we might have expected. You should be fully ambulatory by early next year. I must say, you held up very well for someone who has spent the last two months flat on his back."

"A coma? But I don't remember… can't remember…"

"This is normal, considering your brains have been jostled about a bit."

Aziz stepped next to Barbara and laid his hand on her left shoulder. "But you remember this pretty lady, don't you?"

LC nodded. Of course he remembered Barbara. But her hair... the laugh lines in her face... her weight gain...

"And your hilarious stepfather? You remember him, don't you?"

Flaunt nodded curtly, his bald head reflecting sunlight from the open window. Unfortunately, LC did remember Flaunt.

"Where's my father? Where's Herb?"

Barbara looked worriedly toward Aziz. But Aziz smiled encouragingly. LC's gut filled up with dread.

"Your father passed away, Lando."

"What?"

"It's been fifteen... no... my goodness it must be..."

"Twenty years ago," Flaunt said. "It was that goddamn ostrich shoot, Lando. You were there, remember? Sonofabitchin' bird kicked him to death..."

"Charles..."

Herb... my father... dead?

"But I don't... I can't..."

"Think for a moment, Mister Cooper," Aziz said. "Do you remember anything from before your coma? Before you came to the hospital?"

LC closed his eyes, tried to cast his mind back, beyond the darkness, the emptiness that waited for him in the corners of his memory the way a faithful dog awaits its master.

Back.

"I remember someone shouting, my chest hurt... I remember smelling alcohol and someone talking about my heart rate..."

"Very good! That was yesterday. What else do you remember?"

Back.

"Think back now."

"I remember…"

We love you, Daddy!

LC swallowed, trying to overcome the sudden lump that had formed in the back of his throat. The lump seemed to grow larger as the feeling in his gut intensified.

"I… I remember…"

…to thank every one of you for all your kind thoughts. This is way too much excitement for a simple little brain surgery…

Hi Ho!

We love you, LC!

"I remember…"

…where thousands of fans have gathered at the New Kingdom of Amun Medical Arts Center to offer late-night titan, LC Cooper their fond wishes and hopes for a speedy recovery…

…my family and I appreciate all the cards and prayers…

"I remember…"

Daddy are you gonna die and go live with Grandpa Ptah?

He had to stop, had to look away from the memories that played against his mind's eye like home movies from someone else's life. His throat was filling up with the bothersome lump, and his vision was swimming again.

"My life… I remember my life…"

The door to the room opened again and a woman, tall and too thin, with skin the color of caramel and short, black hair, stepped hesitantly into the room…

"Is it… is he…?"

…and before she could finish, three children piled through the door and onto his bed.

"Daddy!"

He couldn't speak. He knew them. Their names were Haru, the Falcon, Son of Isis; Oheo, the Iroquois word for Beautiful; and Herbert-Hasani... it meant Handsome. They were his children. He could no more forget them than he could forget his own name.

Lando Kalel Cooper.

The woman stood tentatively at the door, watching while the people on the bed embraced and laughed and wept. He remembered her too. He tried one last time to clear the bothersome lump from his throat.

"Hello, Danielle."

Danielle's eyes grew misty as well. She stepped forward and took his hand in hers.

"Hello, LC."

His family was there, together, the way he remembered. His children. His wife. His mother. The memories were flooding back now, slowly but steadily. Life.

This is my life.

He was home.

CHAPTER XXI
REORIENTATION

(LC) "I've been learning to walk again, which explains the cane. When I was a kid I used to fantasize about being one of those pimps, the guys who strut around Salt Lake City with those Jackal-headed walking sticks, which explains my new pimp stroll. Last night I got so carried away with it that I tried to talk my wife into dressing up like a hooker, which explains the two black eyes."

< Audience laughs >

(LC) "You know you take a lot of things for granted when you have your health, silly things like flowers, friends… dry underwear…"

(Peta) "Hi Hooooo!"

(LC) "Yeah it's good to be back. Don't get me wrong… I could use another six months of silence and mental downtime, but what would that leave for the President?"

(Peta) "Hi Hooooo!"

(LC) "My bandleader: Peta Nocona, ladies and gentlemen. 'The Commanche Camper'. Give him a hand."

(Peta) "Heigh ahhhh Hooo ahhh!"

< Audience chants "Heigh–ahoooaahhh!" >

(LC) "Peta... what in the hells are you doing?"

(Peta) "While you were recuperating I decided to try a new catchphrase, LC – something that celebrates my indigenous heritage and the heritage of our founding fathers."

(LC) "That's ridiculous."

(Peta) "Hey, you could drop dead any minute, so what the hell?"

(LC) "Thanks. My loyal sidekick, ladies and gentlemen."

< Audience applauds >

(Peta) "I say it's time to inject some 'Big Medicine' into this show. Heigh aahh hoooaaa!"

(LC) "Just don't do a raindance. Then I really will die."

(Peta) "And one, two, one-two-three-and..."

< Band plays tom toms/raindance music and rimshot. Audience laughs >

(LC) "Oh Peta?"

(Peta) "Yes, O Great Brown Bear Who Signs Tiny Paycheck?"

(LC) "How do you say 'you're fired' in Commanche?"

(Peta) "You're fired."

< Audience laughs and applauds >

LC threw himself into his car and locked the doors a second before the crazy-haired woman plastered her face against his window. She hammered at the other side of the bulletproof glass with both fists.

"I just want to talk! We can go to my place! No one has to know!"

LC waved and smiled at the crazy woman. Behind her, three security guards were hustling toward his car, but these days he had to watch himself in public. With the increased scrutiny from the fans, and the moths, the papparazi, waiting for him to collapse on camera, he felt constantly pressured to manage his image.

"You're out of phase!" the crazy woman hissed. "You must be resynchronized! Come with me if you want to live!"

The security wardens tackled her.

"I'm a priestess! I have a cable show!"

Hans, the big, blond Captain of Security for ACC Studios, mouthed an apology to LC over his shoulder. LC waved back: no problem. He was able to hold it all back until Hans hustled the crazy woman into the gatehouse. Then he laid his head against the driver's headrest and squeezed his eyes shut.

"Breathe."

He counted slowly, trying to slow his thundering heartbeat, remembering his physical therapy sessions.

Panic attacks are perfectly normal, LC. People who've survived near death experiences sometimes suffer from a kind of post-traumatic stress disorder.

He opened his eyes. For a moment he felt the terrible disorientation that had been whispering at the edges of his awareness since he'd checked out of the hospital, the feeling that he was standing at the lip of a precipice, one step away from plunging over that edge into an unfathomable darkness. He reached up to the sun visor over his head, flipped it down and checked his reflection in the small mirror. Other than the deep pits under his eyes, he looked normal.

"This is wrong."

In the two months since "The Miraculous Return From The Great Beyond", he had begun talking to himself. Sometimes, in his office or in the car, or while walking Domino at the dog park, he would quiz himself, hoping to uncover answers to the questions that plagued him. Sometimes he did it simply to hear another voice in his head, trying to counter a feeling of abandonment so intense that he often found himself near tears.

"What the hell's wrong with you, man? You've got three beautiful kids, the number one late night show on the planet, and a wife who…"

Surabhi.

"Stop it! Danielle loves you. She took you back didn't she?"

He was answered only by the howling silence.

"You came back though, didn't you? The bastards tried, but they blew it… big time, baby."

Who "the bastards" were, or why they were trying to kill him, remained a mystery. But he was certain that there were forces out there, forces aligned against him; maybe someone at the network, or some asshole he'd screwed over on his way to the top. He didn't know who "they" were, but he knew they were gunning for him. Somehow, he had slipped through their nets, thrown the hounds off his scent. He had survived lackluster reviews for the last three seasons, ratings lulls that would have sunk other talk shows, and even that thing with the intern three years ago. That had been a real cobra in his blanket. It had taken every persuasive weapon he could muster to keep Danielle on board after the *National Bee* broke the story about the affair – plus sizable payoffs to all parties involved. But he'd moved on. Now he had beaten a brain tumor.

But the silence was unbearable.

The reassuring voice he remembered was gone, flushed away with the tumor. But how could he miss something that had never existed?

"Go home, idiot. Go see the kids, hug Danielle. Maybe get Martika to babysit and go check out that new Thai place on Michigan Avenue."

"Sun's Eye Boulevard," the face in the mirror said. "The Thai place is on Sun's Eye."

"No, man. It's on Michigan Avenue, right around the corner from Herb's downtown location."

"Michigan Avenue is in Chicago," his reflection said. "You live in the Angels. And Cooper Automotive went out of business."

"The Angels," LC said. "Of course. I live in *'Pyi 'nte niaggeloc.'*"

It was the word he'd learned in school, spoken in the tongue he'd spoken all his life. But why did it sound so strange to him now? He punched the car into Drive and pulled out of his parking space. He voice-activated the music function through the car's artificial sentience interface. The latest electronic mantra filtered through the cabin, the ringing beat of the riq; the gentle twang of the oud; the shuttered breath of the nay: music sometimes kept the terrible silence at bay.

The thump on his window startled him.

"You alright, LC?"

It was old Chenzira Nkuku, the security warden responsible for the studio's main entrance.

LC lowered his window. "Yeah, Chet. Just meditating before I head home."

"Sorry to startle you, LC. When I saw you sittin' here…"

"Thanks, Chet."

"You know… I'm such a big fan of the show…"

"Thank you."

"Oh, no problem, LC. Blessings of the Gods to ya."

"And to you. Ahhh Chet?"

"Yes, sir?"

"I'm just a little fuzzy at the moment. Could you tell me… what street is that?"

The old security warden turned and scowled at the busy street just beyond the main gate. Then he turned back, a wary smile on his face. "Why… that's Makatawi Boulevard!"

"Maka…?"

"Makatawi Boulevard. You know, after the chief."

"The ahhh… the chief?"

"The Seminole chief? Makatawi-Mishikaka?"

Chet chuckled and wagged his forefinger. "You forgetting your history, LC? Ol' Maka united the Tribes against the Colonials. Everybody remembers ol' Chief Big Chest."

And suddenly, LC did remember the story of MakatawiMishikaka, known to the rest of the world as Black Hawk, who, working in tandem with allies from the Indo-Egyptian Empire, had successfully repelled the first European Federation war parties in 1499. His actions led to the Federation's recognition of the United Territories of Anowarkowa and her diverse peoples as a sovereign nation. After centuries of lucrative trade with the Europeans, the mostly friendly nations of the African continent and the recognition of shared ancestry with the Pacific Rim nations and indeed with much of Asia, the countries of the North, Central and South Anorwarkowan partitions all looked to Black Hawk as the one of their most revered Founding Fathers.

"Say," Chet Nkuku said warily, his eyes scanning the interior of LC's car. "You're not doin' one of your comedy bits are you? You got a camera hidden inside here somewhere? You guys pullin' ol' Chenzira's nose?"

LC smiled, despite the cold unease unfolding in the pit of his stomach. There was something wrong with Chet. No... that wasn't quite right. It was something about the way the old warden spoke.

"See you tomorrow, Chet."

"That's a good one," Chet chuckled. "'What street is this?' LC, you're a damn panic!"

LC voice keyed the BMW's autonav function.

"Home."

As the BMW took control and pulled smoothly onto Makatawi Boulevard, LC focused on controlling the panic.

"Call Philip Chapman," he said to the car's computer. "Urgent."

LC had become confused by the name he saw on the street sign that hung over the Makatawi entrance to Akhet Cormorant-Charvaka Studios. To his eye, the sign was printed in a foreign language, the same language that Chet Nkuku was speaking; the language that adorned all the street signs and storefront windows and fast food restaurant marquees he passed along his route home. It was the language LC had been speaking in but not thinking in since waking up in the hospital.

It was Coptic, the universal language of the Indo-Egyptian Empire. It was LC's first language; the first language of his friends, his family and of nearly everyone he knew. But since waking up from his coma he'd been thinking, dreaming, in a different language.

"My name is Lando Kalel Cooper," he breathed. "I'm married to Danielle Ahmet Cooper. I am fifty-three years old and I live in the city of House of Angels…"

No. My name is Lando Calrissian Darnell Cooper. I am twenty-nine years old. I'm single…

Surabhi… she needs me…

"No. I'm the host of the number one late night talk-show on the Ten networks."

I live in Chicago.

"No! I live in the Chumash-Egyptian sister city of House of Angels. I have three children: my oldest son Haru; my daughter, Oheo – it's an Iroquois name, it means Beautiful; my youngest son is Herbert-Hasani."

The carphone chirped, "Call from Doctor Philip Chapman."

"Phil, thank the Gods."

"You called during dinner. I hope the sheets in your guestroom are clean."

They'd been working together for nearly three years, starting after the intern fiasco, during which Danielle had insisted LC seek individual counseling. Despite his European origins, the British psychiatrist had become as much a confidante as a therapist.

"Sorry," LC said. "I'm having a moment."

"A bad one, I gather."

"I'm thinking in a foreign language and remembering things that never happened."

"Things like what?"

"Places… names. I feel like I'm… not myself."

"Who do you think you are?"

"Someone else."

"Anyone interesting?"

"I'm serious, Philip."

"So am I. In our sessions you've expressed a feeling of being alienated from your own life, disconnection from the people and things that should have the greatest meaning to you. My question to you now – in the moments before my wife chucks my dinner down the disposal – is… why?"

"I don't know why," LC snapped. "Isn't that why I pay you? To tell me why I'm crazy?"

"LC, we've talked about false beliefs, delusions. Most delusions reveal or illuminate some inner conflict, usually some frightening or unpleasant circumstance which we refuse to consciously acknowledge because its presence forces us to consider potentially difficult choices about our lives. This denial requires us to create a false reality in order to justify our dependence on maintaining the status quo, usually in order to preserve some untenable but deeply entrenched belief about ourselves. These beliefs are always self-serving, and always destructive in the end. They allow us a kind of emotional placebo, sort of, 'Hey, if I don't look at the real problem because I'm too emotionally distracted by my delusionary world, then I can't be held responsible for dealing with it'. Meanwhile, your true needs are ignored. This causes more anger and frustration, which in turn necessitate more denial in order to protect the delusion. But the question I want you to ask yourself is: how do these delusions keep me from understanding what's absolutely vital for me to achieve lasting happiness?"

"Wow. Do you have that stuff written down somewhere?"

"I'm very good. Three marriages and two divorces can't be wrong."

"I'm sorry about interrupting your dinner. I just needed to talk to someone."

"Say no more. Are you alright?"

"I'll be fine. Thanks, Phil. I'll think about everything you said."

"Please do. I'm very clever and I'm usually right."

The carphone function chirped again, "Call from home."

"I've got another call. See you Wednesday?"

"See me what? Oh. That's very funny."

"What's funny?"

"You just said, 'See you Wednesday.'"

"Call from… home."

"Why is that funny?"

"'Wednesday', from the Middle English, wednes dei, or as derived from the Old English, Wodendaeg: the day named after the Scandinavian god, Woden. You're thinking in English. That's very interesting."

"Call from… HOME. URGENT."

"Go on," the Englishman sighed. "I'll see you on 'Wednesday'."

LC voice keyed the Homelink function. The lights in the BMW dimmed as the front windshield switched to playback mode and Herbert-Hasani's face filled the windshield.

"Where are you, Daddy? Mommy wants to know so she can start making dinner."

They'd named HH after Lando's dead father to honor his memory. But sometimes such synchronicities were hard to bear, especially when LC was staring them in the face. From nearly the moment he was born it was clear to everyone involved that Herbert-Hasani bore a startling resemblance to his long dead grandfather.

"Daddy, are you crying?"

"No, Hasa. Just got a little dust in my eye."

"You look like you're crying. Daddy?"

"Yes, son?"

"Are you and Mommy getting a divorce?"

"Why do you ask?"

HerbertHasani shrugged, his eyes flickering away from the smarthouse commcamera in LC's office. "Because Mommy told Aunt Ma'at that you've been acting weird since you woke up from your cola."

"The word is coma, Hasa, and no, Mommy and I are not getting a divorce."

"Daddy?"

"Yes, Hasa?"

"When people die like you did, do they come back cause they're really flesh-sucking zombies, like in the movies?"

LC decided he'd definitely talk to House about letting the children screen too many horror movies. "No, Hasa. Sometimes people just... come back."

"Why?"

"No one knows. Some people are just lucky, I guess."

"Lucky how?"

"Because they get a second chance to show the people they love how much they love them. Right?"

"I guess so. Daddy?"

"Yes, Hasa."

"Are you going to die again?"

LC's "death" was as much a mystery to his doctors as it remained to his youngest son. Despite heroic efforts by Aziz and the attending anesthesiologist, LC had gone into cardiac arrest, his brainwave activity flatlined. The crash team had just applied the "Hands of Thoth" and were preparing to administer a second jolt of electrical stimulus to jumpstart LC's heart, when he'd gasped, once.

Days later, while LC lay in his private suite trying to remember who he was, Doctor Aziz, his mother and even Flaunt had tried to make him understand how miraculous his resuscitation was.

"You were dead as old camel crap," Flaunt reminded him, one afternoon while Barbara was at temple. "Clinically deceased, my man. No heartbeat, no pulse and less brain activity than when you were a snotnosed teenager."

Flaunt had slapped him, hard, on the shoulder, sending shocks of pain through his now healthy skull. "You're a godhammered medical miracle!"

"Daddy? What's wrong?"

"Nothing, son. I'm... daddy's fine."

"Are you coming home soon?"

LC stared at the landscape passing his "knighted" driver's window. His mind's eye insisted upon presenting a dual landscape, a place that was familiar, yet utterly alien to his senses.

What's happening to me?

A quiet panic was spreading through him, enshrouding his joy at having survived. Doubts beat the air around him like black wings. Because... somehow... he knew.

I don't belong here.

"Daddy? Are you coming home?"

The fear in Herbert-Hasani's voice pulled him back. Herbert-Hasani was a cautious child. Born prematurely at the same hospital where LC made his miraculous recovery, he had always been sickly. The ship of his young life had been becalmed by respiratory ailments: allergies, a lifelong bout with Baal's Cough that LC himself had outgrown. It was Herbert-Hasani who found LC, unconscious, slumped over his desk. The nine year-old had voice-commanded the smarthouse servitors to send for help, and even insisted on riding beside him as the autobarque drove him to the emergency room.

Since LC's return, Hasa had hardly left his side, constantly checking his whereabouts, inquiring his arrival times and state of wellbeing. The other night, after he'd put the other kids to bed, LC had heard Herbert-Hasani crying in his room. When he'd asked what was wrong, the boy replied, simply, "I miss my daddy."

He'd spent the next few hours comforting the boy. But when Herbert-Hasani asked him to tell the story of Coyote and the Coming of Apep, he floundered, unable to recall the details. LC apologized, blaming stress and the everpresent "work" for his faulty memory. Herbert-Hasani had forgiven him, even patted him on the shoulder. Then he'd asked to sleep by himself.

Pull yourself together, Lando.

"No one calls me Lando except my mother. I'm LC."

"Daddy? Who are you talking to?"

LC is dead.

"I'm fine, Hasa."

He manually disengaged the autopilot. The BMW swerved into oncoming traffic. Collision alarms bleeped as he wrestled for control of the car, forced it back into his lane. He'd never been the most confident driver, a problem that had secretly undermined his confidence for most of his adult life. It seemed easier to allow the auto servitors to do the driving.

"Not anymore."

He would work through whatever this was. He would leave his problems in Phil Chapman's office where they belonged. His family... his son, needed him.

"Daddy's coming home."

CHAPTER XXII
A DAY IN THE LIVES

Danielle was clearing the dinner dishes from the dining room table when LC walked through the front door.

"You missed dinner. The children were disappointed."

She moved with the same quiet grace, the quiet precision he remembered. They'd been married for twenty years, but his wife still carried herself like a woman negotiating a minefield while blindfolded.

"Hey…" he began, and realized he couldn't remember her name.

"Hi…"

Danielle smirked, an ugly expression that he did remember, the anger of this familiar stranger so palpable even now.

"We ate without you. Again."

As he watched her back, the graceful curve of her spine, the perfect posture so reminiscent of the dancer she was when they'd met in Toronto twenty-two years ago, he was struck by her beauty. She was French-Senegalese, having grown up the child of three worlds in the halls of academia in Paris. Her father was the Dean of Faculty at Les Institutes des Sciences, her mother, an acclaimed Senegalese singer and poet from Dakar. Danielle had inherited her mother's looks, a severe, almost harsh beauty; long neck and prominent cheekbones, arching nostrils, high forehead and full lips. She'd studied Coptic and Dance at the Academie du Artes Liberal, and pursued her peculiar dream of bridging the Continents through the performing arts. With her business partner, Amadou Diop, Danielle had formed Le Carnaval du Lumière, a perpetually evolving theatrical production that incorporated dance, magic, acrobatics and circus performers from around the world. The first Carnaval: Fernal, had been an instant smash. Danielle and Amadou had gone on to create a series of even more successful Carnavals.

But, LC's illness and recovery had taken Danielle away from her career. Before his collapse, she'd spent most of her time on the road, working on design and choreographic elements, tailoring them for each new show. Now she was forced to stay home to oversee the children's daily routines with the help of their nanny, Martika, or at the hospital. He'd hoped his recovery would close the gap that yawned between them since his affair with the intern, but now, more than a year since his initial diagnosis, the distance between them had grown. Danielle spent more time in her office, or interacting with Amadou, who oversaw Carnaval's operations.

"Where are the kids?"

"Haru just left for soccer practice. Oheo's waiting for you to help her with her writing project, and Herbert-Hasani has locked himself in your office."

"Why did do he that?"

"He wouldn't tell me. He never talks to me so there's no reason to assume he's changed since you came back. Nothing has changed, LC. He idolizes you. Even when you can't be bothered to show up after you promised him you would."

"I got lost. I was...confused."

Danielle slammed the stack of plates down on the table. LC heard the brittle crack of breaking stoneware.

"Dani...what's..."

"'Dani?'" she said. "Is that supposed to be funny?"

"What?"

"Gods, you're such a bastard."

She stalked into the kitchen, carrying the stack of dishes. LC heard the too loud clatter of the expensive Carthaginian stoneware.

"Dani...what's wrong?"

"Just stop it, alright? You've made your point. You drove it home a long time ago so just... stop it."

"Danielle...I don't know what you're talking about."

"He's waiting for you downstairs." She was staring into the steaming water pooling in the sink. "Go talk to him."

"Dani..."

Danielle slammed her fist down onto the ledge of the sink hard enough to send soap suds slopping over the rim onto the floor.

"Don't call me that! It's not funny, Lando!"

He reached out and gently gripped her shoulders. "Dani... I need..."

"Stop it, Lando. You're hurting me."

"What's wrong?"

"Please don't touch me."

It had been bad before. He remembered that much. A coldness had stilled the air between them. Sometimes he imagined that coldness as a disease shared by only two people, a condition that isolated them from each other and from the rest of the world. They'd grown apart slowly over the years, mainly due, he thought, to outside forces. They both had high pressure careers that required almost constant involvement. But in the months preceding his initial diagnosis things had gotten worse. Danielle hardly ever looked him in the eye, and rarely spoke to him unless the children were involved. For his part, he'd gotten so used to this coldness that he'd nearly convinced himself that it was normal. Telling himself, "This is the way it is," until even he had grown tired of his denials. In that way they'd gone on. Until the visions started.

For a while, after the radiation treatments had failed and the tumor proved much larger and more involved than his doctors first believed, they'd grown closer. His family had wrapped him up in a cocoon dense with caring. Danielle and his mother had spearheaded the effort, moving beyond the coldness he'd sensed but could not remedy to buttress his spirits. But since his homecoming, the disease had rapidly grown worse.

"I have to talk to you," Danielle said, swiping at her eyes with the back of one wet forearm. "We have to talk about what happens next."

"Alright. I'll go see HH. We'll talk before bed."

A shimmer of puzzlement darkened Danielle's face, as if she'd been expecting a different response from him. LC turned, certain that there was more he should say. But he was incapable of imagining what it might be. His heart was pounding again: the terror was back. He was standing at the edge of that great abyss and watching the rudiments of his life being torn out by their roots.

Why am I so afraid? I beat brain cancer, didn't I?

"Whatever it is, Dani. I know we can beat it. We just have to stick together. Together we can beat anything."

Danielle paused, her hands hovering over the hot suds, her face averted. At first he thought she was crying, her shoulders shuddering with the force of her sobs. Then she turned, and he saw that she was laughing.

"Amadou was right," she said with a kind of stunned wonder. "You really are a child."

"Go away! I don't want to talk to you!"

LC knocked on his basement office door again.

"Hasa, open the door."

"No!"

Gods, I really don't need this right now.

The panic, which had withdrawn to a manageable distance in the car, drew closer now. LC sensed it haunting the shrinking periphery of his control; a hungry ghoul awaiting the totality of night.

"Hasa... open the door."

The door stayed closed.

"Herbert-Hasani Cooper, if you don't open this door right now you'll be punished!"

"You can't punish me if I don't open the door."

It started as a rumble of barely suppressed amusement bubbling up from the pit of his stomach. Herbert-Hasani had inherited his penchant for mouthing off, along with the wit to shut down anyone unwise enough to engage him. LC laughed. It felt so good that, in moments, he was roaring, hardly able to catch a breath. He slid down the door until he was sitting on the floor with his back pressed against it, laughing.

"That's…"

But he couldn't stop. Behind him, he heard the hesitant shuffle of sport moccasins brushing across the rough carpet in his office.

"It's not funny! Stop laughing!"

"That's… oh that's a good one."

The door thumped. LC felt the impact from Hasa's kick vibrate up the length of his spine.

"You know… you remind me of your grandfather."

The thumping stopped. A moment later, the door opened, and LC let himself fall backward into the office. From where he lay, Herbert-Hasani seemed to loom over him.

"You remember my grandpa?"

"Of course I remember him. I just talked to him last week."

"You… talked… to Grandpa?"

LC nodded and hopped to his feet. The ease of movement was itself strangely confusing. He'd always kept in shape, ran five miles every day, worked out with weights. But his energy levels since his release were remarkable. Sometimes he felt as if he'd traded his old, worn out body for a younger, fresher one. But that wasn't exactly right either: it was his mind that felt… lighter. He felt as he had when he was a struggling young comic, fresh out of university, as if the world were wide open and waiting just for him.

For a moment he felt that plunging dislocation again, the disorientation of a meticulous homeowner who returns home only to discover that all his furniture has been rearranged.

"What did you talk about?"

"We argued. We always argue."

"What did you... argue about?"

"What we always argue about: money."

"But Grandpa's dead. He died before I was even born."

And LC remembered that too. Of course Herb was dead. How could he misplace the passing of his own father in the jumbled closet of his memories?

"It's because you're different. You look like him. You talk like him, sort of... but you're not him. You're... different. You're..."

Herbert-Hasani shook his head, his eyes squinted nearly shut behind his thick eyeglasses.

"You're... other. You're like a puzzle piece with no place to go. All the other pieces are right; they belong. But you don't belong."

"Stop it, Hasa."

"You even smell like him. But you're the wrong piece. It's like you're from a different puzzle altogeth..."

LC slapped him.

The blow grazed the boy's chin, barely turned his head and he instantly regretted it. It seemed the familiar response. Even now, Herbert-Hasani held his head proudly, a single tear slipping down his cheek.

"You don't even hit like him."

Then he was gone.

LC stood in the center of his office while the horrors crowded in around him.

He didn't know who he was.

He spent the next three hours staring at his computer screen, scanning the global gateway, consuming all he could about things he remembered but didn't know. His head was throbbing. His eyes ached from scanning hundreds of geographic and historical files.

The horrors were back with a vengeance.

"Anowarkawa is the most populous continent in the Northern Hemisphere. Its three main partitions are called (generically) North, Central and South Anowarkawa."

My name is Lando Calrissian Darnell Cooper and I live in North America

"Its peoples are an ethnic conglomeration descended from indigenous tribal cultures thousands of years old: Apache, Mohawk, Iroquois, African and Asian-derived peoples largely descended from transoceanic trade partnerships dating back to the Era of the Pharaohs."

I was born January 12th, 1980. I hate English muffins.

"Coptic is the most widespread language currently in use in North Anowarkawa, although in many places, particularly in the South and Central Partitions, Chumash, the language of the most widely spread of Anowarkawa's indigenous tribes, is still spoken, largely by first generation émigrés to the Northern Partition and in many traditional religious ceremonies..."

My parents are Herbert and Barbara Cooper. He sells auto parts. She smokes.

"Because of its widespread ethnic diversity, Anowarkawa is host to many religious traditions. However, the Light of Amon-Ra remains the most widespread and popular among the Anowarkawan people. Adherents refer to themselves and others as 'brothers and sisters...'"

I have three brothers: Renfield, Atticus and Gandalf Gary...

"The most widely observed of all the Egyptian-derived belief systems transplanted into the Anowarkawans by pre-European traders and missionaries, Amon's Light is considered

one of the 'Great Planetary Faiths' and, alongside Hinduism, Judeo-Christian-Islamicism, Shinto Buddhism and similarly themed 'ancestor worship' systems common to indigenous peoples, is among the most widely practiced religions in the modern world."

I live in Hyde Park. I grew up in Chicago…

"The Midwestern city of Sheekawaa was founded by the indigenous Potowatomi people a century before the first recorded European visitors set foot on Anowarkawa. The Potowatomi later enslaved members of older local tribes, Miami, Sauk and Fox peoples, forcing them to lay the foundations for what would later be known as the 'City of the Wild Onion'."

"LC, I'm talking to you."

This is wrong. This is other.

"In the Seventeenth Year of Pharoah HorAha, Sheekawaa was destroyed by fire during the second Egyptian invasion. One hundred years later, after the fall of the Potowatomi and the successful assimilation of the 'debtor tribes' who had assisted the Egyptians in overthrowing their Potowatomi enslavers, the 'Burned Mound' was renamed, New Shekawaa and rededicated as a 'Wedded City' to the Egyptian capital city of Cairo."

"LC, I'm leaving."

I'm engaged to Surabhi Moloke. We're going to…

"…welcome you to the Happy Weddings Show, where our celebrity Bridesmaids help five lucky couples create 'Weddings to Anger the Gods Themselves!'"

"Surabhi!"

He came back to himself with a physical lurch, a sense of engagement so intense that he bolted from his chair.

"I remember! Oh my God… I remember!"

"I can't do this anymore, LC."

Danielle was standing in the doorway to his office.

"I'm leaving."

"Danielle…"

Inside his head, memories were unspooling, memories from another man's life. "You're my wife…"

But how can this be?

Look at that damn head. Boy I swear, you look like a damn spear chucker!

LC saw Danielle, her anger and resolution, but he also saw someone else superimposed over her; another woman who loved him, who needed him, whom he had failed.

I want to trust you, Lando. But you don't let me in.

Danielle. No. Someone else…

My parents taught me how to deal with depression, which was only right since they were the reason I was depressed.

"LC, are you listening?"

And he remembered the headaches, the suffering that seemed to bracket him between both lives, disparate experiences joined and ratified by the blinding throb of…

Power.

…pain. The pain had threatened to…

Save the world.

…destroy him. It had been like this right before his surgery. But the tumor, the source of his pain, had been excised. Now the pain was back; worse than before. It pushed at him, powerful as a tsunami, threatening to sweep him away on a wave of revelation and dread: if his cancer was back, he didn't know if he could survive another surgery.

"You didn't survive, Lando Cooper. And that places us upon the horns of a great dilemma."

That was the worst moment, the moment before he collapsed. Because the new voice was one he'd never heard before, deep as the rushing of blood through his veins, too powerful to ever be mistaken for human. It spoke in his head as clearly as the tolling of a funeral bell.

"Everything you think you know is wrong, Lando Cooper. You must be corrected. Death cannot be long cheated, even by the gods. You are a great wrong in My universe."

"LC… Amadou and I are in love. I want a divorce."

The last thing he saw, before the pain claimed him, was the face of the woman he loved, resolving itself like the ghost of a cherished memory over the face of another man's wife.

"I remember."

Then darkness.

CHAPTER XXIII
REVELATIONS

"The House of Angels was rocked last week by the news that LC Cooper, a popular fixture on the late night chat circuit, was rushed to New Amon Center of Medical Arts and Healing after suffering from an apparent nervous breakdown. Cooper's representatives have been quiet as to the chatshow star's state. But sources inside the Cooper Empire have called his condition 'serious'. Production of his number one talkshow, *Night Talk With LC Cooper*, is on hold until healers can scry the true extent of his condition. Speculation went global this morning, however, when noted mental health Counselor and popular afternoon chatshow host, Healer Ba'al appeared at the Amon Center. Healer Ba'al, a frequent guest on *Night Talk*, would not comment on the purpose of his visit, but close sources in both celebrity camps report that, and I'm quoting here, 'LC Cooper's chances for a full recovery just rose like the Sun Chariot of Amon Ra'."

The Daily International

Lando's right leg was cramping. The arms of the straitjacket were too tight, and the man who had come to help him was a raving lunatic.

"Now I want you to. repeat after me," Healer Ba'al drawled. "My name is LC Cooper. I live in House of Angels. I'm a father, a husband with a gorgeous wife and three beautiful kids. I love my life and I mean to make the best of it. Right here! Right now!"

Lando shifted, grimacing against the flare of agony this produced in his right thigh. He had been lying in the same position, unable to move while the bombardment of images flooded his senses. He'd refused to speak with his doctors. The images, memories from both lives, were too powerful to ignore. He had stared into the blank gray wall directly in front of his face for the next three days.

It had come to him in the autobarque, as he lay on his stretcher, screaming out ridiculous facts and nonsensical dates.

"My name is Lando Calrissian Darnell Cooper! I'm twenty-nine years old. I drive a 1984 Saab convertible. My mother is an alcoholic and my father is alive! My fiancée's name is Surabhi Moloke! I have to help her!"

He still couldn't remember why the woman in that other life, Surabhi, was in danger, though he knew her need was great. Important matters turned upon the spit of his self awareness, but he was unable to start the barbecue. He was remembering more and more with each passing hour, but parts of his "real life" remained hidden. No matter how hard he tried, he couldn't penetrate the darkness that occluded the center of his recollections. It was as if he had forgotten how to move one of his hands, even though it remained at the end of his arm. He envisioned this darkness as a dense void, a howling storm of black noise in the center of his mind. Somehow, he sensed, if he could pierce that darkness, peer beneath the clouds of that internal storm, he could find the answers. But the shadowstorm remained.

It had occurred to him that since he was living in the body of a dead man, (or a "nearly dead" man) that other Lando was probably living in his body back in the real world. Since he had woken up in LC Cooper's life after LC's near-death experience, it stood to reason that another such experience could set matters in their proper order. All he needed was a moment to himself and a chance to lay his hands on a sharp object, something to cut his bonds, and then his wrists.

He had no intention of actually dying: it was LC's near-death experience, he believed, that had summoned him from his world. If he could duplicate that experience, maybe he could reverse the process and send himself back.

But the bastards in the sanatorium had taken everything he might have used to initiate the transfer: his belt, his shoelaces. They'd bound him in a straitjacket after he'd tried to knock himself unconscious by banging his head against the walls of the observation room. Now, he lay there, dejected and diapered, while the insane Counselor he remembered from LC's life rattled on.

"Come on, mate," Healer Ba'al twanged, his Australian accent blaring through Lando's memories. "It's time to strap your trouncers on and kick this catatonia thing in the balls!"

Lando remembered Healer Ba'al, an internationally famous mental health practitioner who had gained notoriety after numerous appearances on a popular afternoon talkshow. Famous for his "Downunderisms" and colorful vocabulary, he was the former Main Counselor of a notoriously violent Melbourne mental asylum. He'd written a bestselling memoir about his struggle with depression, *Ba'al... Busted*, and was the subject of his own afternoon factshow, *The Mind Healer*. LC's memories revealed that the host of *Night Talk* had thought very little of Ba'al's prowess, believing him to be more charlatan than savior. He'd irritated LC with his habit of compulsively shouting out nuggets of his personal philosophy in the form of his so-called "Ba'alistics".

"You're the Apex Predator in the jungle of your life! The Alpha Dog in Your Own Personal Junkyard! It's time to piss on your fears, climb up the leg of your private Doubt Demon and hump the shit out of him! Reclaim Your Mental Territory!"

Lando spoke calmly, deliberately. "I'm ready."

"You've got to churn the waters of your emoceans with the blood of your spiritual enemies!"

"I'm ready, Ba'al."

"Summon the Self-Sharks! Ignite the feeding frenzy that will set you... What did you say?"

Lando rolled over onto his side and faced his doctors. Philip Chapman had spent the last two days of his internment examining him, questioning him, at times haranguing him to lay down his delusions. He'd regarded Chapman as a friend, but Chapman had taken his collapse as a personal affront. The appearance of Ba'al had only aggravated the tension between them. Wen Nouri, the head psychiatrist at New Amon's psychiatric ward, had been blown back into the rushes by the two more forceful practitioners. He glared resentfully at the proceedings, excluded from making any pronouncements without incurring the wrath of his more "upmarket" colleagues.

"I'm ready to reclaim my emotional territory," Lando said. "I'm back."

Healer Ba'al smiled. But Phil Chapman shook his head, the movement so slight that Lando almost missed it.

"Do you know who you are?"

"Of course. My name is LC Cooper. I have three children, Haru, Oheo and Herbert-Hasani."

Nouri nodded, his face brightening, encouraging. Chapman waved him aside. "Who is the President?"

"Thutmose X. We had him on the show two weeks after he took office."

"Who was the First Pharoah of the Anowarkawas?"

"Memphis III. He unified the feuding Egyptian armies and helped assimilate the Iroquois Nation after the Yellow Plague decimated–"

"That's great, LC," Ba'al interrupted. "You're halfway home!"

But Chapman wasn't satisfied. "LC do you still believe that you are an alien to this reality?"

Lando kept his voice level: he had to convince them. "No. That was a lie."

All three psychiatrists leaned forward. Healer Ba'al's nostrils flared.

"A lie?"

"Yes. It's a little embarrassing…"

"Go on, mate. Nothin' to be embarrassed about."

"Well… things have been rough at home, because of the show, my illness… things have deteriorated between me and Danielle."

"I see."

"I thought maybe if I could convince myself that I was having a relapse, maybe Danielle would stay."

Nouri looked bored. Ba'al seemed barely able to conceal his excitement. But Chapman leaned back in his chair, a smile fluttering at the corners of his mouth.

"I don't believe you."

A tinny jingle emanated from Chapman's person. He reached into the pocket of his dashiiki and produced his roving data device and checked the message window. A frown ruffled his normally placid features. When he looked back at Lando, an unfamiliar emotion shimmered in his eyes.

"That was Doctor Aziz, LC. He's just received word that–"

"Let me guess. My tumor is back."

If Chapman was shocked he didn't allow it to show on his face. "Yes. Aziz ran scans on you while you were sedated. It appears that they didn't get it all..."

"Aziz is one of the greatest resectionists on the planet, Phil. I paid him a small fortune to do what he does, and he did. I saw my scans before and after the surgery. He got most of the tumor."

Chapman nodded. "But there was a small bit of it that Aziz was unable to reach. That bit has..."

"Phil, it's only been two months since the surgery. Not enough time for a benign tumor to have changed that much. Judging by the expression on your face, the tumor must be large and I'm guessing it's gone malignant."

Chapman shifted in his seat. "Well... it seems you've got all the answers."

"It's not a tumor."

"Beg pardon?"

"The thing in my head, it's not a brain tumor. Well in this reality I suppose it is. But back there it's… something else."

Chapman smirked; a man back in familiar territory. "And by 'back there' I take it you're referring to your 'other life'. This other world where you're young and healthy?"

Lando shrugged. "Back there I have asthma. I'm allergic to just about anything that moves. I think I even have a drinking problem…"

"And your father is alive."

"I've got to get back."

"Why the rush?"

"Someone needs me."

"Ah yes, your mystery woman."

"Surabhi."

"Let me see if I remember… you two are engaged?"

"Yes."

"Even though the United Kingdom outlawed marriage between British Citizens and Anowarkalis a hundred years ago."

"I live in the United States. They were a colony of the British Empire until the Revolutionary War."

Chapman chuckled. "You've certainly painted a compelling picture of this fantasy land. But you realize it's just that, don't you, LC? A fantasy?"

"I don't belong here."

"Better than us mere mortals, eh?" Chapman said. "Everyone on the planet toiling along in their little lives, blissfully unaware of your superiority."

Chapman leaned forward. "When I look at you I see a powerful but frightened man suffering from a life-threatening illness."

"Phil," Lando said. "I'm not crazy. You have to listen to me."

"I am listening, LC. I'm going to help you find your way back to your world. This world. The real world."

Behind him, the door to the padded room swung open. Then Chenzira Nkuku walked into the room.

"Can I help you?" Chapman said.

The old security warden bowed to the tall psychiatrist. Then he turned to Lando and waved.

"Hey, LC! You ready to get out of here?"

Healer Ba'al leaped to his feet. "Who's this bastard?"

"Hey!" the old security warden grinned. "I've seen you on television."

Ba'al nodded. "Thanks."

"Don't thank me. Your show stinks."

Ba'al turned a bright shade of purple, sputtering like an old carbuerator. Then Chenzira pointed at him and said, "You look tired. Why don't you take a nap?"

Healer Ba'al fell to the floor of the chamber, snoring deeply.

"What?" Nouri said. "What's happening?"

Chapman lunged across the table and hit a red button on the intercom. An alarm pierced the silence.

Chenzira put one finger to his lips and whispered, "Sleep."

Chapman and Nouri fell to the floor. Nouri lay sprawled across Chapman's legs, snoring peacefully into Ba'al's crotch.

"Chet," Lando cried. "How did you…?"

Chenzira helped him to his feet. He hummed something, a snatch of song. There was a flash of golden light, a smell like the sudden advent of Spring, then the straitjacket's buckles and straps flew apart and the restraining device dropped to the floor.

Lando stared, slackjawed, at the straitjacket lying on the floor. "How did you do that?"

"Oh, it's not me. I'm a nobody," Chenzira said. He stuck his head out the door of the observation room, quickly checking the hallway. "He's set his bowsights on you though."

"What are you talking about? Who is he... How did you...?"

"No time fer hobgobblin', LC. Someone real important sent me to collect you, but we gotta move: even He can't keep the world from spinnin' forever. Follow me!"

Lando followed as Chenzira stepped over the sleeping psychiatrists and out into the hall. They ran through the hospital, passing dozens of people sprawled in chairs, across desks or on the floor where they'd fallen. The halls echoed with snores.

"Chet," Lando rasped. "What's happening? Those people... how did you do all this?"

Outside the tall glass walls of the hospital, Lando saw groups of reporters and camera crews milling around the front entrance.

"It's the One I serve, LC. He holds us in His mighty hand!"

"Chet... what's going on?"

"Are you going to find my father?"

Herbert-Hasani popped up from behind the back of a tall armchair near the front entrance, his eyes wide with wonder at the sight of dozens of unconscious people lying around them.

"Hasa... what are you doing here?"

"I knew you'd be leaving soon. So I waited."

"How did you know?"

Herbert-Hasani shrugged. "The man in my dream told me you needed help."

Chenzira pointed at the boy. "Well, now you're going to…"

"No!" Lando shouted, gripping the old man's arm. "Leave him alone!"

Herbert-Hasani hopped down from the armchair.

"I'm going with you."

"No, you're not."

"Yes, I am."

Chenzira lifted his sleep inducing right hand again.

"Chet, no!"

Herbert-Hasani studied Chenzira warily for a moment, then grinned, his eyes goggling behind his thick lenses.

"If he won't zap me then there's nothing you can do to stop me."

Chenzira cracked his knuckles. "Oh, I can think of a few things. I don't shine to mouthy kids. Kids like him always trying to break onto the lot!"

"Let him come, Chet." They were heading into the unknown at the behest of a stranger who possessed abilities he didn't understand. But something in the boy's eyes would not release its hold on Lando's heart. "I think I owe him that much."

Herbert-Hasani beamed as if the world had suddenly revealed its greatest mysteries. Around them, sprawled sleepers were beginning to stir. The boy stumbled over a heavyset security warden, who rolled over and farted loudly. Herbert-Hasani giggled.

"Are they all in a coma?"

"They lie within the arms of Isis," Chenzira said, scowling. "They'll be fine."

"Magic," Herbert-Hasani whispered. "That burns!"

Behind them, the elevator doors opened. Chapman,

Ba'al and Nouri stumbled into the lobby. At the same time, a dozen orderlies and a handful of security wardens thundered out of the stairwell.

"Stop them!"

The swarm of orderlies and wardens stampeded toward the front entrance.

"My car's out front!" Chenzira shouted. "Quickly!"

Chenzira hit the exit door with Lando and the boy following on his heels. The three of them ran toward the ancient Black Scarab racer, idling at the curb. At the sight of them, the waiting reporters surged forward.

"There he is!" "LC!" "How are you?" "LC!"

Chenzira barely got the door open before the hospital entrance doors slid open and disgorged their pursuers. One man, a burly young warden, was holding his gun.

A group of reporters crossed the street at a dead run, cameras clicking, shouting questions as they surrounded Chenzira's car. Chenzira tried to move the ancient manual drive model forward but the weight of the reporters kept them effectively immobilized. Security wardens were tossing reporters aside. Chapman, Nouri and Ba'al threw themselves at the passenger window.

"LC you're a very sick man!" Chapman cried. "You've got to come back inside!"

"Chet!"

"Do not fear, Lando Cooper," Chenzira said. "You will yet be free."

But the old man's voice was different, deeper, more resonant. It was a voice that LC had heard before.

"You've caused me a great deal of trouble," Chenzira said in that other voice. "I only hope I'm not too late."

Chenzira gripped the steering wheel. The little black sedan rumbled, lurched once, then began to rise off the ground. Shouts and screams from the reporters filled the interior of the scarab, reporters and moths igniting a storm of flashbulbs even as they tumbled off the ends of the car.

"We're flying!" Herbert-Hasani screamed. "This is entirely massive!"

Then the window behind his head exploded. Herbert-Hasani slumped forward across Lando's lap in a hail of glass.

"Hasa!"

Outside, in the scuffle between the security wardens and the reporters, the burly warden fired again, the shot striking sparks from the undercarriage of the scarab. Then the burly warden was tackled to the ground by several police officers.

"Hasa!" Lando cried. "Hasa!"

Herbert-Hasani lay gasping in his lap, a slow pulse of blood running over his hands. As the little black sportster rose up, up above the street lamps, rising higher until it hovered over the hospital, Lando could see the streets of House of Angels arrayed below him, the mountains in the distance, the gleaming towers and minarets of the downtown business center in the distant East.

"Help him," Lando cried. "Take us down! Take us back to the hospital!"

"It's too late for that, Lando," the being who was and was not Chenzira Nkuku said. "There are more important matters to attend."

"He's dying! You can do all this... help him!"

The ancient voice sighed. "You have forgotten much

about your former life. You have been translated. Reinterpreted. Excised, revised and inserted into someone else's continuity."

Lando looked up from the boy's face, his eyes scanning the green hills far beneath the scarab. The little car was soaring toward the low foothills of a vast mountain range.

"I... I don't understand."

"Ah yes. Yet you haven't grasped the whole story, and now you find yourself translated into my narrative. This will not do, my ancient understudy."

A sick feeling pummeled Lando's gut. The world inside the flying scarab seemed to recede from him, leaving him grasping at mysteries. It seemed to him that he might, by an act of will, reach out, grasp the fabric of that ebbing reality and pull it back to reveal... what?

My ancient understudy.

He had heard that name, spoken by the same sonorous voice, at another time, in another place.

"Your perceptions are acute, attuned to the timbre of a music only a select few may hear. Yes, Lando Cooper, we've met before."

"Who are you?"

Chenzira's mysterious patron laughed; a full-throated humor that filled the interior of the scarab like a rushing wind.

"Why, the Almighty, of course."

The black scarab flew toward the mountains.

"You see, Lando Cooper... I'm God."

CHAPTER XXIV
OLD GOD/NEW TRICK

The scarab settled down in a field of golden flowers. Lando could hear music, the pounding of drums, a sizzling rattle like the temblor of a tambourine, a dried gourd filled with jumping beans. The music was emanating from the scarab's radio.

Chenzira threw the scarab into "Rest". Then he turned to Lando, beaming as he lifted a camera and began snapping pictures.

"I'm afraid when I wake up this will all feel like a dream!"

Flash

"Gotta engrave the moment, y'know? In the old brainbox!"

Flash

Lando winced. The camera flashes sent sunspots cascading along his optic nerves to burst inside his brain.

"At least when I'm awake I'll know…"

Flash

"…know that I really was Chosen!"

Lando squinted against the strobing light. Herbert-

Hasani lay with his head in his lap. He appeared to be sleeping, but he was still too pale. And Lando's thighs were damp with blood.

From the radio, the strange music grew louder. A bright flicker of motion outside the scarab drew his focus out the passenger window. Above them in the distance, that flicker grew brighter and drew closer; a golden shimmering, dropping out of the blue sky.

"Oh my Lord!" Chenzira cried, aiming the camera at the shimmering distortion. "Please… oh, please let me know thy grace for all the days of my life!"

Flash

"Please, Lord! Oh please let me…"

Then the front seat of the scarab was empty. Chenzira was gone. But the glowing manshape was standing a few yards away.

"Come out, usurper. The time of reckoning is at hand."

Gently, Lando laid Herbert-Hasani's head on the leather seat of the scarab. Then he opened the door and stepped out into the field. For as far as he could see in all directions, the yellow flowers dipped and waved in a breeze he could hear but not feel. The music was all around him.

"It's the flowers. The music. It's coming from the flowers."

"The music is the flowers," the manshape hummed. **"And a lot more besides. Come closer."**

Lando stepped closer to the glowing form. The manshaped glow was solidifying, gaining mass and dimension. And it was clearly nothing human.

"Most mortals would be trembling in fear. Yet there you stand, no groveling, no begging for my infinite mercy. Although, in your case,

such humiliation would be completely deserved. Yet you seem distinctly unterrified. Do you find that odd?"

"I'm afraid for my son."

"Yes?"

The glow was lessening now, a darker shape emerging from the nimbus of golden light. Lando could make out a figure, tall, broad-shouldered, muscular and inhumanly powerful.

"I feel like… it's crazy…"

"'Crazy' is relative. Like Time and Space. Einstein was right about that much at least. Try me."

"You said that we've met before…"

"Of course. You stole my day job."

The tallest man Lando had ever seen stepped out of the golden light. His skin was the color of red clay and cinnamon, his head shaved, save for a single black braid which hung from the top of his skull, plaited with gold and reaching nearly to the middle of his back. He wore a lightweight tunic the color of the setting sun. His raiment left his arms and legs bare save for golden straps which wound around his muscular biceps and calves. Golden sandals adorned his feet, and his eyes shone the white-crimson-orange of fast running lava.

"Do you know me?"

"No."

"You've screwed things up for all of us, kid."

Lando turned, bent, reached into the scarab's passenger compartment and grabbed Herbert-Hasani from where he lay on the back seat.

"Help him. Help my son."

The sun-giant frowned. **"But you don't have a son."**

"He was shot helping me get out of that hospital. You've got to help him."

"You love the boy, do you?"

And Lando, caught up in the life of LC Cooper, looked down at the unconscious child in his arms, and found that he did love the boy. It felt as if he had known the young stranger with his father's face all his life. He remembered a thousand bedtimes, reading together, arguing, lamenting the times he'd punished him. Even though these things had never happened to him, he remembered them.

"Yes. I love him."

"And would you die for him? Would you lay down your life for this child you barely know?"

"I can't die here. I don't belong. I'm in someone else's story." **"I know the feeling."**

The sun-giant began to pace among the golden flowers. Some of them were tall enough to reach his chin: huge amber sunflowers, their petals as large as dinner plates, touching them, craning his great neck to smell their fragrance.

"Beautiful, aren't they? I grew them myself, well this entire world really, after my banishment. After an epoch in the void one finds boredom a constant companion. By the time I arrived, I was itching to stretch forth my hand and Create something. Unfortunately, this world already had thousands of its own gods. After your Ascension I was little more than a shadow of my former self. It took a thousand years to undermine the local dominant godforms. Another thousand to

recruit sympathetic survivors. **Renaming them
was the worst part. The new 'Isis' was nothing
like my actual sister/wife, back on our Earth.
She's truculent and more than a little angry after I
betrayed and slaughtered most of her family.**

"**The mortals here cast me as their Dark Lord
for centuries. I encouraged this of course, I was
trying to recreate Home, was I not? Set, Loki,
Lucifer... I provided the names, and the local
humans rewarded me with their darkest powers.
Until the day they woke up and found themselves
worshipping me as their 'Creator God'. I tell you...
that was no easy trick. At times I considered
plunging into the sun and never coming out.**"

The sun-giant frowned. With one hand he plucked
one of the giant yellow flowers and began to pick its
petals. As each petal fell to the earth, Lando heard a
single piercing note rise, and then fade from the great
music that filled the air.

"**But I had the memories driving me on, did I
not? Such glories back home, such power. I wasn't
about to let a few thousand alien pantheons stop
me from reforging a new Heliopolis: a Heaven to
die for. If you'll excuse the expression.**"

The sun-giant's crimson gaze rested upon Lando,
where he stood holding Herbert-Hasani.

"**Well I've given enough clues; even you should
be able to guess my identity by now. Have you?**"

"Amon-Ra," Lando said. "Sun God, Lord of the
Egyptian Pantheon."

The sun-giant stepped out from behind the towering
sunflowers and bowed.

"You win the chariot ride. But I see you still have no idea why you know me. I marvel at your former self's commitment. Most gods are as fickle as the mortals who worship them."

"Help my son, Ra. Please."

"Ah," Amon-Ra sighed. Golden tendrils streamed up from his eyes. The brightness of the tendrils light shot lances of pain into Lando's eyes and set his mind alight with echoes.

"I've waited five thousand years for the chance to get you onto my territory. Now, you grovel before me, powerless and begging for my favor."

The sun god's eyes shone, changing from crimson to bright amber.

"Do you remember our battle? How you banished me and my pantheon? What Powers we were! Beautiful Isis! Grim Osiris! Our worshippers built a vast empire in our names. What glories we wrought on Earth and Heliopolis! Until the Romans came, with their rutting Greek titanspawn. But Zeus and his crowd couldn't maintain the status quo for themselves, much less resist what came next: you and your Hebrews!"

"I'm sorry," Lando said. "I can't remember."

Herbert-Hasani began to tremble. A runner of fresh blood trickled from his lips and pattered into the soil at Lando's feet.

"Help him! Please!"

Amon-Ra smirked. **"Once more my dignity is assaulted in order to engender progress. Ah well."**

The sun god's eyes took fire, glowing with a flame so bright Lando felt their heat crisp his eyebrows. That power enveloped Herbert-Hasani in its corona as the smell of Spring grew overpowering, and the yellow flowers' strange music filled the air.

"I'm OK."

When Lando opened his eyes, Herbert-Hasani was standing in front of him. Smiling, he extended his right fist and opened his hand: a small, copper-colored slug lay flattened in the center of his palm.

"It's the bullet. It hit my skull, traveled around and lodged under my cheekbone. Ra took it out. Massive, huh?"

"Yeah," Lando said, his vision swimming. "That's totally massive."

"Ra's not really angry anymore. He likes it here. He just likes to hear himself talk. He showed me other stuff too. Like what really happened to you. Want to hear?"

"Yes," Lando laughed. "Yes, please."

"Well, back in your world some people tried to kill you. They want a war, and you're the first cause... first causuality..."

"First casualty."

"Yeah. But instead of dying, you turned up here. You're in a parallel universe, one that's similar to yours but different in some ways. Here... you're my dad. But here already has a guy like you. Well, almost like you. My dad's really smart, but you talk like you haven't been speaking Ctick that long. My real dad had this brain tumor? He did all kinds of treatments, but none of 'em worked. But Doctor Aziz said he could take the tumor out. My dad was real happy. He and my mom don't like each other so much, because my dad went to a lot of fairs with different women. Anyway, he thought Doctor Aziz would fix him, but he... he died!"

Lando took the boy in his arms, and held him until his weeping eased. "It's OK, Hasa. I understand."

"But I'm afraid! You'll go back. But what if my dad… what if it's too late for him?"

Lando wiped the boy's tears away with his thumb.

"What do you want, Ra?"

The Creator God frowned. Then he began to examine the tallest of the yellow flowers.

"I was banished, defeated by the despised God of Abraham. Fleeing through the void, leaping from sun to sun as I gnawed the bone of my humiliation. Yahweh was vicious in his overthrow of my pantheon: the plagues, bloodying the Nile… I would have called the author of those catastrophes merely scrupulous until the wholesale slaughter of Egypt's Firstborn. After that, drowning her armies was overstating the point. I spent the first thousand years dreaming of my vengeance.

"But as time went by I grew weary of empty rage. In truth, the universe was open to me. As a star god I could travel on streams of photons, harnessing the gravity of one solar system to slingshot me into another, and another, out across the stars, as I streaked toward galactic center. Along the way I observed such wonders…"

Amon-Ra raised his eyes, his golden gaze sweeping across the heavens.

"When I drew near the black hole at the center of the Milky Way galaxy, I allowed its gravity to pull me in, past worlds without number, as I was swept toward the end of my long journey. Sometimes I listened in on the thoughts of the

intelligent races inhabiting those worlds. Some of them were human, others vastly different. Some were primitive; others were eons ahead of Earth's people. Many of these were nearly godlike themselves. They had survived catastrophe and war long enough to build their civilizations up from the mud and out to the stars.

"A few of those great races sent out representatives to greet me; beings of such complexity, such subtlety. To them I was a primitive. Me! Amon-Ra, the God Who Sees All! Back home, I could stride the world in a shape of my choosing, or soar the skies as my avatar, the Divine Hawk. I could strike down my enemies with a thought. But out there, the glow of my power was that of a firefly surrounded by sympathetic suns. One by one, they returned to their peoples, leaving the primitive little god to travel on his way.

"I learned something on my journey to the black hole; a lesson that humbled even an apex All-Father like me: the path to true divinity lies not with gods, but with those who define them. Your triumph over my pantheon is the perfect illustration of Darwin's supposition, natural selection being the rule of thumb even for the gods. It's why the Romans overcame the Greeks, why the Hebrews triumphed over the Egyptians. And why ultimately, Yahweh's adversary must triumph over him.

"As I tumbled into the black hole's embrace, I was chastened for my delusions of grandeur. I vowed upon the soul of my departed mother, Nut –

whatever afterlife I found myself in, I would make it better than the one I'd lived. I awoke to find myself in this reality, this world so similar to the world we left behind. Mother Nut had answered my prayers: I was to be given a second chance. I would build a new dynasty, one to aid humanity in finding its own way down the long path to divinity.

"It was grueling labor, implanting my designed religions, assassinating mortal despots and installing those who promoted my precepts... By the time I'd forged my New Egyptian Empire I'd lost all interest in vengeance. I'd seen proof that your usurpation was part of a universal order to which even immortals must adhere. Conciousness... all consciousness... evolves. In my wanderings I too had evolved."

Amon-Ra laughed, and spread his arms as if to take in the entire horizon.

"I'm still worshipped here, though more and more of my once faithful turn their minds from me every day. Old Chenzira is part of a dwindling fundamentalist minority. As in your world, science and simple human courage are creating a future with little room for gods. By my reckoning, I have a handful of centuries before belief in me dies out altogether. But this was the purpose for which we were defined was it not? To act as their shepherds, occasionally frightening the flock away from the cliffs and back onto the long road to adulthood."

The sun god chuckled and stroked his beard. But the light from his face grew fainter, as if obscured behind thunderheads.

"I have seen your memories of the conflict which brought you to my realm. Your enemy is known to me."

"What is it?" Lando said. "What is the Coming?"

"It is the last breath of human weakness. Their worst fears, their most petty prejudices. Hounded into the dark alleyways of the collective unconscious by time and reason, it is a part of them, as indivisible from their better qualities as night is from day. The human race finds itself at the same critical moment that has destroyed countless other races in the multiverse. They too have evolved, but not fast enough to escape their most primal fears. It is this fear upon which the Coming feeds. It is this fear, their greed and their avarice Embodied, that will define the next Aspect of God."

Lando nodded. "Holiday."

"Owen Holiday is but the messenger, empowered by the Coming in order to seduce a terrified humanity to his master's service. He is Moses standing before the Red Sea with the Pharaoh's soldiers hot on his sandals. Nice work, by the way."

"Send me back, Ra," Lando said. "You came through the black hole. You know the way back."

"Have you remembered truly, then?"

Lando studied the Creator God's face, the strange duality of him; now a man, now a hawk surrounded by a golden corona of sunfire, now something else entirely, something that dwarfed them all, a shining luminescence. He squinted into that light, drawing its strength into himself, riding its calming clarity the way a surfer rides a powerful wave.

"I remember my life," he said finally. "I remember my parents, my friends. I remember Surabhi. She…"

Died.

"She was my best friend, I wanted to spend my life with her, but I couldn't tell her the truth. I was selfish, afraid she wouldn't believe me. I had lied about… about that other life. I was afraid… I was…"

"Human."

"The Coming… it murdered her. Murdered her family. I have to get back."

"Many more will die if the Coming assumes your old office. For it contains within itself the end of Humanity's long march up from the mud. It is the End of Reason, the triumph of madness. You may already be too late."

"But you can help me."

"You've spoken of your mortal life, Lando Cooper. I find it terribly interesting that you've neglected the rest."

Lando shrugged. "It doesn't seem real. Standing here, with you… I remember it, but it feels like… like…"

"Someone else's story?"

Lando looked down at Herbert-Hasani. The boy reached out and took his hand.

"That other part of me… I know it was important, once, but it doesn't seem to matter now."

Amon-Ra considered this for a moment. When he spoke it was as if his voice infused the air.

"Once upon a time, there was an aboriginal tribe in the far northern sector of my world's version of Australia. The aowu'uk, the Morning People. They were the last of that region's indigenous peoples.

Locked in a pre-industrial state of development, primitive by the standards of even your South American indigenous tribes, they were trapped between their ancient traditions and the ever-encroaching modern world. When they hungered they went to a local river to beg their gods for fish. Sometimes the gods complied. But after thousands of years many of those gods grew bored. They summoned their priests among the aowu'uk and told them that they were on their own. Some of those gods left this dimension; some moved to Sydney."

"What does this have to do with us?" Lando said.

"The Morning People simply stopped. Their gods had abandoned them. There was great depression among the aowu'uk, suicides. Their lakes dried up, and their fish populations died out. Things looked bleak. Searching for an answer, one young priest meditated for seven days and seven nights. On the eighth day, he summoned the Morning People to the banks of their most sacred river. 'Bring only your strongest nets,' he told them. 'And your sharpest toaks.' 'Why?' they asked. 'Because,' the young priest said, 'The gods have returned.'

"And lo! There was great rejoicing. The Morning People came in great numbers to the banks of the sacred river. They cast their nets upon the waters and saw, almost immediately, that those nets were filling up with more fish than they had seen in years; more fish than they could eat that day or even that week. The Morning People lay down their toaks and scrambled for their nets. 'Take only what you need!' the young priest said.

'Remember the other Peoples upriver; and the small cities downriver. Take enough to feed the young, the ancients, and all those who cannot fish for themselves!'

"Afterward, there was much singing and thanking of the gods. Finally, the young priest stood and called for quiet. 'I have deceived you!' he cried. 'The gods have not returned. They will never return!' 'Why did you lie?' the People cried. 'You have brought doom upon us!' 'But have you forgotten what happened earlier?' the young priest cried. 'You came here in belief, as children, and pulled sustenance from the waters. But now that you understand the truth, you tremble and forecry a thousand dooms. Why do you tremble when the gods have given us a great gift?' 'What gift have they given us?' the People cried. 'They have abandoned us!' 'Ah but that is the gift of the gods,' the young priest said. 'They have left us to fend for ourselves!'

"Then the shaman commanded several powerful young priests. 'Take one male child from its mother, and one old woman from her family, and bring them to me.' When the young priests had brought the child and the ancient to the shaman, he bade them kneel before him. Taking one of the great longknives, he raised it high above his head and prepared to strike the crying child.

"When the people cried out, 'Why? Why do you do this?' the shaman replied, 'The gods have left us, we know this to be the truth. They left us to care for this world, for this river and all the life it holds;

to care for each other. We came here as children, but we have reached our childhood's end. Now we are the adults. We can lie down and die, destroy each other to avoid the pain and uncertainty of life. The gods do not care, or are gone. They will not save us. We can destroy ourselves and end our suffering.

"'Or we can create the world that we want.'

"And the Morning People remembered that, working together, they had pulled fish from the rivers, working together, they had created joy and bounty for all. Their need to survive despite the loss of their shepherds forced them to evolve, instantly, and in the blinking of an eye. When last I visited the region, many of the Morning People were fluent in Coptic, English and Cantonese. The priests lead cultural awareness tours through their protected ancestral lands. The young shaman is now a world-famous guest lecturer and adjunct professor at several major universities. The Morning People awaken to a dawn of their own creation every day."

AmonRa opened his hands. Cupped in his palms lay hundreds of the yellow flower petals, their amber richness a deep contrast to his luminous brown skin, his crimson tunic. He bent his face to his palms and inhaled deeply.

"Human potential," he breathed. "The young shaman understood that half the battle is getting the people's attention. Once you've got it the question becomes: what will you do with all that potential?"

"What about LC? What'll happen when I go?"

AmonRa's frown deepened. "LC Cooper died during surgery. His soul was replaced. By you. That soul has fled, perhaps beyond my reach."

"No!" Herbert-Hasani cried, wheeling on Lando. "You promised you'd give him back!"

Lando knelt until he was eye level with the boy.

"I remember, Hasa. Can you be brave for me? Just for a little longer?"

HerbertHasani stared through suspicious tears. But he nodded. "Yes."

Lando turned back to AmonRa.

"You have to help us, Ra. I know what you can do if you choose to, and I won't leave without your promise."

"There are laws governing continuity," AmonRa said. **"Laws that bind me as much as they bound Yahweh back in your world. I cannot disregard those laws without grave consequences."**

"I'm here because of the actions of defunct gods, Ra. It's a violation of the law that governs a God's existence. That violation will have even graver consequences if it remains uncorrected."

AmonRa's eyes narrowed. **"Go on."**

"How many laws am I breaking just by being here? How many laws would I break if I stayed? If I had children. If I died here?"

"You would disrupt the continuity of two realities, consigning your world to the machinations of the Coming and derailing human evolution."

"Right."

"And you would do this for one lonely mortal boy?"

Lando looked into the sun god's eyes. "I've steered the tides of continuity to conform to what I hoped was right."

"But your agenda was ratified by the shifting moral imperatives thrust upon you by your worshippers. A mortal consensus."

Herbert-Hasani gripped Lando's hand harder.

"He's my son, Ra," Lando said, finally. "I made him a promise and I won't break it. If I did that, nothing I do in my world will matter."

AmonRa nodded, still humming to himself, as he communed with the yellow flowers. Then he tossed a handful of the yellow petals into the air. The petals drifted, caught on a sudden breeze, and scattered, their individual music flaring brightly before fading from view.

"You've given an old God much to consider, Lando Cooper. But Holiday and his cronies vanquished you. How will you defeat them now?"

"You have power, Ra. You could come with me. Help me."

"Quite impossible, I'm afraid. I would encounter the same disenfranchisement that you do now. No god can be God in two continuities. As my power waned in your realm, and worship of my pantheon faded, they grew stronger in this one. My power is inextricably bound to the collective unconscious of this realm. I can offer you little more than my blessing."

"Then just send me back. I'll figure something out."

The tall god smiled once more, his eyes shining like white fire against the darkening sky.

"That much at least lies within my power."

Amon-Ra stretched forth his right hand. The music of the yellow flowers became a choir, a sussurus of celestial melody.

"I am Amon-Ra, Skyfather and Star Rider, Master of the Barque of a Million Years. The Hidden Fire suffuses my Secret thought."

As he spoke, a pinpoint of light appeared in the air between them. Lando felt the air grow warmer as the pinpoint grew. At the same time, the sky darkened until it was replaced by millions of glowing pinpoints.

"Stars," Herbert-Hasani breathed. "Those are stars!"

"My strength is the faculty of light, and the wisdom of life unending for a billion years. It endures even unto the furthest realm that light reaches. I sing the secret names of Time and laugh at the tales quasars tell: I can help you in your quest."

The air was becoming unbearably warm, the burning globe growing larger with each passing second. The heat and blinding light were pulsing from the shining sphere. It rapidly dominated the horizon, blazing forth with such power that it threatened to drive the air from Lando's lungs.

"It's the sun! He's bringing the sun to Earth!"

"No, child," Amon-Ra said. **"Nothing quite so dramatic. I've merely brought us to the sun."**

And then they were in space, thousands of miles above the sun's seething corona. Even here, the power of the blazing star was palpable through the transparent plane upon which they stood. Lando saw the outline of the platform carrying them across the sun, its surface shimmering, its light refracted through cascades like crystal clear water.

"We stand aboard the Barque of a Million Years. It was a gift from my brother Horus. Quite handy for this sort of thing. Especially with my personal energy stores at an ebb."

"A spaceship!" Herbert-Hasani cried. "Omega Massive!"

"'Spaceship' would be inaccurate, boy. More like a personal conveyance with limitless options.

Apollo had his chariot, Thor had his magic goats, I have the Barque. It assumes whatever shape I tell it to. We were standing within its protective aura the entire time."

To their amazed stares he added, **"Oh, I had every intention of rescuing you. But the journey to the far side of the sun takes time, even at the speed of thought, and nothing passes the time like good theater. Ahhh there it is."**

The sun god pointed at a spot in space just a few yards away from their position: a trail of luminous particles lighting the darkness. The shining trail swept away from the Barque and into the blackness of space, extending for as far as Lando could see.

"The hammer of Thor is more than a devastating weapon," Amon-Ra said. **"It is capable of piercing the barriers between worlds as easily at it summons storms. Before your friend struck you, he used it to open a pathway into this dimension."**

Amon-Ra lifted his right index finger and drew a silverine line across the fabric of space. The glowing streak paralleled the shining trail.

"Your Satan detached your soul from your physical body and propelled it along the route you see there. It's a colossal coincidence that the dimension he selected was inhabited, an even greater coincidence that your trajectory brought you close enough to the sun that I would sense your arrival. His attack should have killed you outright."

"Kalashnikov," Lando said. "He screwed up."

"Perhaps the Coming was unable to accomplish your physical death," Amon-Ra said. **"But that seems**

unlikely given its growing power. It extinguished Zeus himself. Something even I was, regrettably, unable to do."

"A coincidence," Lando murmured.

"Indeed. One that bears closer scrutiny in calmer times."

Herbert-Hasani was staring out at the tachyon trail, his face aglow in the wash of its spectral light. Lando saw the shimmer of the luminous trail reflected on the boy's cheeks.

"Will he come back the same way?"

"I don't know."

"Will I ever see you again?"

"Probably not."

Herbert-Hasani hugged him. "Remember me. In your world."

Lando pulled him in closer, hugged him tightly.

"Always."

Then he released the boy and stepped back.

"Continuity is fluid, Ra," he said, more roughly than he intended. "Rivers can be redirected. Even the wind can be diverted. Understand?"

"I will protect the boy," the sun god said. **"And I will consider the possibilities."**

Herbert-Hasani seemed to stand taller. Smiling, his eyes hidden behind the reflection dancing across his eyeglasses, he raised his left fist.

"I'll remember you, Lando Calrissian Darnell Cooper!"

And Lando, who still shared LC Cooper's memories, who in many ways was LC Cooper, turned away, unable to speak around the bothersome lump in his throat.

"You will be ejected from this body and propelled back along the pathway you made

during your entry into this reality," Amon-Ra said. **"Prepare yourself, Lando Cooper."**

Lando nodded. "I'm ready."

"Remember the Morning People, Yahweh. Their belief may yet redeem your world."

Lando faced the infinite darkness. Far below, the alien sun burned, its gravity powerful enough to warp light and space and even time. Above him, the glowing tachyon trail reached into infinity.

We're specks, he thought. Only flickers.

The shining trail brightened, its shape growing more clearly defined against that greater darkness. Lando felt a jolt, a wrenching shudder, then he was falling, stretching... then weightless, an airy awareness; thought without substance.

Then he was gone.

Aboard the Barque of a Million Years, a man and a boy stood, rarified by the light from a billion stars. The man stood at the Barque's glimmering edge, eyes closed, his body shining like the sun's corona for the briefest of instants. The boy watched, afraid to speak. But finally, he did.

"Papa?"

The man took a deep breath, and opened his eyes.

LC Cooper studied the face of his son, so like the face of his father. It was the face to which he had always returned, would always return; a bright beacon after a long passage through the darkness.

"Papa!"

The boy ran into his father's waiting arms.

LC held his son, and turned golden eyes toward the blue world glimmering in the distance. He set his hand upon the tiller of the Barque and grinned as its familiar heartbeat answered his command. Yahweh wasn't the only god brave enough to challenge divine destiny. It was time to experience the world he had wrought, from the other side of the tracks.

"Let's go home."

PART 3

DEAD GOD WALKING

"The Light of God is the Human Soul."
                    Proverbs 20:27. (more or less)

CHAPTER XXV
THE BIG PAYBACK

COLD!

PAIN!

I came back to life just in time to die again. I was enfolded within a freezing silence, an absence of noise, and yet, there was... sound. It was the thumping of my heart. I was alive. And I was dying, my skin burning, my eyes flambéed by a cold so intense it could star in a Robert DeNiro movie. I was floating, kicking in a weightless darkness only slightly less total than the blackness of space. I coughed, gasped and drew fire into my lungs.

I'm drowning. Drowning in the dark.

I struck out, flailing with my arms and legs, trying to move through that freezing black/void/abyss... trying to scream, to speak light into the darkness, and the top of my head slammed into something hard. Calm descended over me like a freezing shroud. After everything that had happened I was going to drown. If I didn't freeze to death first.

This is what it was all about.

To experience life, human life, mortality. Now mortality had come to collect the bill. It wasn't fair, but I suppose I wasn't only person to think that in his dying moments. I opened my arms...

Let it happen.

...and I let the ocean in. It seemed almost acceptable, if not exactly comfortable.

The killer whale appeared out of the darkness, surging toward me like a black and white freight train, only to stop a few inches from my face.

"I'm so happy to see you! I feel terrible about eating your mate!"

Without another word, the orca grabbed me in its jaws and swam forward, propelling me toward a bright circlet of light above us. I hadn't even seen the light streaming through a hole in the ceiling of white-blue ice above me. The orca put on a burst of speed and we rocketed through the hole, up and into the freezing air. I flipped head over heels and landed on my back in the permafrost. Freezing water and snot blasted out of my mouth and nose.

I rolled over onto my stomach and lay gasping and choking on an outcropping of permafrost only two or three inches above the surface of the icy water.

"You need fire," the orca said. "You're really lacking in blubber."

"Thanks. Thank you."

"Pleasure. It was the least I could do after killing your friend."

"Connie... you killed Connie."

"An accident! I was swimming along, minding my own business, when all this fire and thunder went off over my head. It confused my hunt song: I thought she was a nice, juicy walrus!"

"You... you ate Connie?"

The orca was spy-hopping in and out of the hole in the ice. "Of course not! I dragged her under, not sure what I had. I was so stunned from the explosions it took a moment to realise it was a human. By then it was too late. Her soul, what my kind calls the aieieekeekieeeeiuuuueeek, seemed pretty put out by the whole thing. She flew off, streaming colors like an angry rainbow. Pretty!"

"Where did they go?"

"Who?"

"My playmates. The ones who caused all the explosions."

"Oh! They left hours ago."

"Hours?"

Amon-Ra had sent me "back" alright. Months had passed in his world. I'd undergone and recovered from brain surgery, relaunched a hit talk show, bonded with my otherworld son and alienated my wife. But in my world, only hours had passed.

"Or maybe minutes," Ooieek squeaked. "I've never caught the hang of your no-tail trick for measuring time. Did you know I was famous?"

"Which way did they go?" I managed to get to my hands and knees before my legs gave out and I fell on my face. Ares had stabbed me in the back. Now I was bleeding to death. My body was one big bruise and it felt like at least three ribs were broken. Yuri's attack had shattered Stormface's protective aura. I could sense nothing of its power in my mind.

Ooieek was frolicking in the frigid water, sliding up onto the ice on her belly, flexing her tail and lifting her massive head, her mouth open in a perky cetaecean "smile".

"Tadaaaa! Look familiar?"

"Did they separate?" I was trying to summon an Aspect, any aspect that would protect me from the cold. But none of them answered. "Where'd they go?"

Skydaddy? Bringer of Pestilence? Voice Out of the Whirlwind? At least Burning Bush could start a fire.

"I'm sure you've seen my work," Ooieek said. "I've even been on television, although they don't get much of that up here. Watch this!"

Ooieek surface-dived, vanished beneath the frigid water. Then she rose up onto her tail and propelled herself backward, scooting across the water: the aquatic mammalian answer to the "Moonwalk".

"Humans love this move! I'm the only one of my kind that really does it well. Usually, it's a dolphin thing!"

"I have to go! I have to find them!"

"I can help."

The woman who had spoken was standing a few yards away, floating atop a tiny ice floe about two feet wide. She wore a shining white kimono, her long, straight black hair flowing down in a perfect wave nearly to her calves. And she was clearly a goddess.

Mitsuko Leavenworth.

"Jeff Corroder's assistant?"

"Vice President of Corroder Productions," Leavenworth sniffed. **"I got a promotion after we signed you to a contract. I also happen to be Benzaiten. The..."**

"...the Shinto goddess of Love. I remember."

The Japanese *kami* of romantic happiness nodded. Her symbol was the serpent, and a bright red pit viper lay twined around her neck. Its tongue flicked in and out, tasting the frigid air as its emerald eyes regarded me from the hollow of Benzaiten's throat.

"Corroder's in on it too. Yuri got to both of you?"

"Corroder is a fool. I was sent in by Holiday to investigate Yuri's allegiance to you. None of us could believe you'd both relinquished your immortality. I needed to get close to Yuri without alerting him to the threat of the Coming. But when I fully realized that the two of you had actually Descended, it didn't make sense. True mortality."

Mitsuko/Benzaiten shook her head, her confusion evident.

"None of us understood. That frightened Holiday. He believed there must be some gimmick, some mitigating reward the rest of us missed."

"He lied to me. He attacked me! He betrayed everything we sacrificed for!"

"It's not his fault, Lando. He doesn't even know that I'm really a goddess."

But an idea so vast in its implications was unfolding in my mind. That sense of displacement that I experienced in Amon-Ra's world swept over me once more.

"It was Lucifer's idea to step down... His idea to assume a mortal life."

I looked over to where Benzaiten hovered on her floating ice ball, as the horror of Yuri's true betrayal grabbed me and shook me in its teeth. I remembered the lethal sexuality, the undying glamour he wielded over women and men. I remembered him pushing me to invite Corroder to my sets. And finally, I remembered his face as he struck me with the thunder god's hammer, his eyes burning like branding irons.

"It was all part of his plan. He tricked you. He tricked me into giving it all away."

Yuri had lied to me. Yuri had taken sides with the Coming. Yuri was responsible for Surabhi's death.

Yuri… Lucifer… Evil.

Hatred cracked the ice beneath my feet. Boiling water surged up through the holes in the ice, sending geysers of steam into the air until the land and sea around me disappeared in a curtain of fog. The fog spoke in a Voice.

"Betrayer."

"I seduced him," Benaitzen, cried. **"I hid my immortality. That's when I understood what you had done. Yuri was truly mortal: he couldn't penetrate my disguise."**

I was swallowed up by fog and wrath. That wrath had a name. And a Voice.

"Defiler."

"I was supposed to betray Yuri to get close to you. But we fell in love! I fell in love!"

"Unclean spirits."

"But it was a trap! I only made him vulnerable to what came next!"

"Take me to him."

"You don't understand the true power of the Coming," Benzaitan cried. **"Holiday is just a puppet!"**

Doom.

"It's more powerful than all the remaining pantheons combined! It compelled me to seduce Yuriel. It killed Zeus. It is God!"

I roared, and the blast from my mouth was the breath of abomination. My anger had unleashed the one Aspect so terrible that its presence had only been hinted at in darkest tenets of the Old Testament. Its eye was glimpsed in the burning clouds over Sodom and Gomorrah; the foam from its mouth had drowned the world, and in its eyes burned the fires of madness.

Once ensconced in my mortal incarnation I had put it away, kept it from my conscious awareness, like a loaded shotgun kept in a forgotten room. I believed the time for such monstrosities long passed. Now, as memories of a million bloody campaigns waged against a billion infidels filled my mind, I welcomed its rage. It was the darkest expression of Abrahamic divinity; the god of the burning stake, the god of the slaveship, whose whistle is the crack of a bullwhip, whose laughter is the scream of a mother sold away from her children. It was the earless god of the concentration camp, its holiest hymn the scream of an atom bomb; the hungry god who stalks the innocent with the flesh of children in its teeth. It was the Deus Ex Machina: the God Out of the Machine. And its presence here meant the end of reason. It could serve only one purpose.

"I command!"

Benzaiten of the Shinto pantheon bowed her head. Her power was the elder, and held no sway over this Aspect. Golden tears streaked her pale cheeks as she looked at me with eyes as empty as those of a rag doll.

"But you'll destroy the future."

Nevertheless, she opened her arms and swept me into the folds of her kimono. I tumbled headlong into the Void. But this time I maintained my equilibrium. Bloodlust buoyed me up, binding me with the gravity of its purpose: I was the last god standing, determined to end the divinity game once and for all. I was going to kill my best friend and destroy the God he served.

Or end the world with my last heartbeat.

CHAPTER XXVI
ENDTIMES

We came out onto a vast desert. Holiday and his renegades had chosen to wish their God to life in a desolate wasteland. Night was falling, the desert's colors fading as the last crimson veins of sunlight retreated from the skies. Wrapped within the protective corona of the Deus ex Machina, I felt neither warmth nor cold.

They were standing at the summit of a ridge two football fields' lengths away. The ridge topped the highest edge of a roughly circular valley like the raised spine of the Earth. Atop the ridge, two figures faced the coming of night, their forms outlined by moonlight. Beyond them, the moon rose, fat and barren, into the darkening sky. Holiday knelt, his arms raised, as if in rapture. At his side, Yuri stood with Thor's hammer upraised, its head spitting St Elmo's fire.

They weren't alone. Below us, on the valley floor seethed a multitude, their shining faces raised in supplication as they awaited the coming of their new God.

They had been drawn from myriad pantheons; supernatural beings infernal and divine littered the stony ground of the valley. I saw the twisted forms of a thousand demons arrayed in every infernal guise ever defined by humankind; a thousand devils, a thousand Beelzebubs crawling, stalking or soaring above the battleground. I saw gods from every known pantheon, African and Tibetan and Chinese, Eskimos and Aboriginals, Asians and Assyrians. Gods and spirits from the Middle-Eastern and Hindu and Celtic and Norwegian and, yes, even the Greeks, thronged on the plain below. I had negotiated with some; others were strangers, their identities lost with the memories of my former divinity. But now their battle Aspects shone with renewed godly force; a golden cavalcade of dispossesed divinities waiting, armed and expectant in the fading light.

And above the gods, soaring in their numberless ranks, flew angels of every Order and denomination. I saw the Zoroastrians; Sraosha, Mithra and Rashna, the Three Guardians of the Soul Bridge of Chinvat. I saw Nakir and Munkar of the Mu'aqquibat, the Inquisitors of the Muslim dead, standing at the ready with quill and scroll and shining scimitar. I saw toothin Cherubim fluttering about the heads of the Muslims, pestering them with their own questions while keeping their eyes cocked toward the darkening West.

I saw Elohim, nearly as bright as the gods themselves, singing hymns I'd never heard before, praising the rising darkness. Above them, closer to the summit, flew the Seraphim, most powerful of the Orders. They sang of the murder of their leader, Seraphiel, a darksong, nearly subterranean in its boundless profundity. And in its strains lurked an outrage that would only be extirpated by revolution; the uprising fomented by the man who stood at the summit of the bowl.

Owen Holiday raised his fists above his head, and a great cheer went up from the horde below. Holiday's voice rode the winds and rose above even the warsongs of the angels.

"Come, Lord! Your Advent is now! This world has been softened by a just and righteous fear, and they require your guiding might to see them safely into that righteous darkness. Come!"

And the multitudes cried, "Come."

"We faithful have gathered to break thy word and will upon the backs of an arrogant flock. We! Those demons, feared as the night was feared by ancient men. We have come."

From the demons rose the roar of a million beasts.

"We come!"

"Those once worshipped as divine, who drew sustenance from the terror which opens the way to you, who would serve as your Generals in the Great War that is to come!"

From the dispossessed gods, a roar that shook the earth.

"We come!"

"Those who served your predecessors in their myriad angelic forms, as messengers…"

From the Archangels, "We come!"

"As protectors…"

From the Cherubim, "We come!"

"As lawgivers…"

From the Thrones, "We come!"

"As enforcers of thy eternal, undying wrath…"

And from the Seraphim, a song, a war cry, "We come! For Holy Holy Holy is the Coming of the Lord!"

There went up another deafening cheer from the gods and demons and angels and powers and principalities.

"It's coming!" Benzaiten cried.

I looked to the West, and I saw the moonlight spilling across the sky turn red; the blistering eye-scream of burning blood. I saw the moon turn crimson as a gouged eye, spilling its bloody light across the valley floor and the upturned faces of the gods and demons below.

"Prepare!" Holiday cried. "For hither comes absolution!"

And the beings upon whom that light fell screamed with rapture. Even shielded by the Deus my eardrums throbbed as that cry became a scream of horror.

"It's killing them!" Benzaiten screamed. **"The light! It's killing them!"**

The silver light of the Seraphim, too bright to look at under normal circumstances, was consumed by the bloodlight. As its glow fell upon three of them they burst into pearlescent streamers... and vanished.

"Unworthies!" Holiday roared. "Those who wither beneath His appraisal are unworthy of His blessing!"

More Seraphim burst into flame. Some of the most powerful among them tried to fly away and were captured and consumed by glowing red tendrils.

"See?" Holiday crowed. "He judges the faithless! Fear God and give Him the glory!"

There was nowhere to run. Everywhere the red moon's light fell angels and devils were destroyed. Or transformed. Some were changed into glowing multi-armed forms similar to giant spiders or massive slithering reptiles. I saw Juno of the Roman pantheon transform herself into a hawk a moment before the red tendrils crushed her in their coils. I saw Anansi the West African Trickster assume the shape of a huge lion just as the tentacles struck. In his place a screaming three-headed human infant lay wailing in the dust.

But most of the Seraphim were simply eaten alive as the tendrils grew brighter with each victim. Many of the panicked gods and demons turned to escape, launching into the sky on burning wings, or vanishing from view.

"Stand!" Holiday roared. "Stand or be destroyed as unbelievers!"

"Help them," Benzaiten screamed. **"It will kill us all!"**

I stepped to the edge of the bowl.

"Holiday!"

The Voice of the Deus Ex Machina turned the heads of the survivors toward me. The gods and angels and demons and powers and principalities looked up at the place where I stood. On the far side of the valley, Yuri and Holiday froze.

And the crimson tendrils stopped.

"Well, the former office-holder stops by for a visit," Holiday cried. "That's very Willy Loman of you, Lando. Your alter ego has been rendered obsolete. Didn't you get the memo?"

Beside him, Yuri's face devolved into a snarl of such hatred that at first I thought I was looking at someone else.

"Fool!" he roared. **"You're wasting precious breath."** Then he turned to the gods and spirits in the valley below. **"Kill him!"**

But the revolutionaries hovered, trapped between the crimson tentacles and the Deus's shuddering wrath.

"Weak!" Yuri raved on the hillside. **"Cowards!"**

The incarnation of Evil raised the hammer of Thor and sent a blistering fusillade of lightning down among his troops. Some of them evaded the lightning, others were blasted into atoms.

"He means the end of our power! The Rise of the Ape above the Gods!"

Gale force winds swirled around my little peak. The sky filled up with black thunderheads and the earth beneath my feet trembled. Yuri's hammer summoned a barrage of fire from the heavens. Flaming death fried the air between us. But this time I was prepared. I raised a protective shout from the Deus. Its power caught the flames and held them, stoking their heat with my own until it blazed like a conflagration. Then I flung it back. The firebolt struck the hillside where Yuri stood and cracked it wide open.

Yuri danced across huge slabs of sliding earth, struggling to keep his balance as he careened downhill. He leaped onto a large outcropping of stone, lying prone as the landslide gathered momentum, burying gods and angels, sweeping them out of sight.

"Useless!" Yuri roared. **"Useless! Useless! Useless!"**

The Devil summoned a thunderstorm, filled the valley with wind and thunder and lightning. I lifted my right hand, the Word of his undoing rising to my lips.

Then a bolt of lightning blasted the hillside. The stone platform beneath Yuri's feet buckled. For a moment, he hung there, supported by nothing more than the roaring wind. Then the entire hill gave way. Yuri dropped the shining hammer, vanishing beneath tons of liquefied dirt and crushed boulders.

"Yuriel!" Benzaiten shrieked, and vanished.

Yuri had betrayed me. His former incarnation's great Covenant had been a farce. So why did my heart feel blasted into a thousand pieces?

"It always comes down to this, doesn't it?"

Holiday stood a few yards away, the crimson moonglow burning in his eyes.

"A single visionary, a lone prophet sent by his God to inform the old god that his day is done."

I strode forward, spoke a Word of Fire to burn him from my sight. Flame hot enough to melt steel exploded the air around him. Holiday shrugged, and sparks fell from him like burning embers. I raised my right hand, and the skies above us grew thick with moving shapes, not lightning or rain... insects, a Pestilence; every stinging fly and biting flea, every locust, every bee and wasp for miles answered my call and flew to the attack. In seconds, Holiday's grinning cowboy face vanished beneath a thousand stinging forms.

He laughed. The horseflies and wasps and hornets crawled over his skin and did not bite or sting or harm him in any way. He raised his hands, a living suit of infestation, and the insects lifted above him, swirling around his head. Then they attacked me. The Deus Ex Machina burned many of them to ash, but too many of them got through. They covered me, blocking out the gray sunlight and plunging me into darkness. I was stabbed by a million tiny swords. The pain disrupted my connection to the Deus. Under its crushing weight I fell to one knee. My eyes were stung shut, my throat locked and swelling closed. There were bugs in my mouth, under my eyelids... burrowing beneath my scalp.

Holiday kicked me in the chest, knocked me over onto my back.

"This is just the beginning, Lando. A paradigm shift undreamt of. After all the hard work by your other self and a million other gods before him, after humanity's long, brave march up from the primordial ooze... fear wins."

He kicked me again. Something in my side came apart with a wet snap and the buzzing in my ears filled up the world. Blinded and suffocating, I pulled myself toward the edge of the precipice.

"'Fear is the heart of love.' You know who said that, Lando? Oh, sorry. You can't answer me with chiggers in your throat. It was a fella named Ben Gibbard. He's the lead singer for Death Cab For Cutie, a sweet little indie rock band out of the Pacific Northwest. Ben originally couched that phrase in his song, I'll Follow You Into The Dark. It was a renunciation of his Catholic upbringing."

He kicked me again. The insects burrowed deeper into my flesh, stinging harder, their angry buzzing becoming the world.

"But Ben missed the point. Fear should be embraced, Lando. It's what got us here today."

He bent and grabbed my hair. Insects crawled up his arm, swarmed around us, caressing him, stinging and biting me. He pulled my head back, forcing me to look him in the eye.

"I am the face of Fear. Look on my works ye mighty and despair. Cause in the end Fear gets the girl, the Golden Fleece and the whole, sad enchilada."

Then he kicked me in the face. Through one half-blinded eye I saw the assembled host staring up at us. The Pantheons, all the surviving gods and devils and angels ever described by humankind, their shining faces vivid as Greek masks, depicting comedy, tragedy, lust, revenge and terror.

Fear.

They're waiting to see who wins.

"A new beginning," Holiday crowed. "But you won't be here to see it."

Something Holiday said was rising up in me, filling me up the way the crimson moon filled up the sky.

Fear is what got us here today.

Paradigm shift.

We've reached our childhood's end. We can lie down and die…

Or create the world we want.

Paradigm shift.

And a shifting skein of faces, of people, enemies, family, gods and friends…

We are children playing with the power of Creation.

Paradigm shift.

Faces, the golden God of a world that might have been my home in another life.

Children.

And the Morning People remembered…

Paradigm shift.

I summoned the remnants of the Deus, drew its dying power into myself…

One. Last. Miracle.

I extended my hand over the valley, high over the heads of the assembled hosts where the desperate, frightened faces of the supernaturals stared up at us.

They're afraid.

Many of them had conspired with Holiday to accomplish my destruction. But they were afraid of him too, afraid of what the Coming represented. It was an opening, a window. I reached… and…

They

Let

Me

In

Through them, I plunge into the river of human consciousness. Through them I am absorbed into the flow of All, allowed entry onto the DNA-encoded information superhighway that defines every god who ever lived. I kick down the unlocked doorways of doubt – doubt can't help me here – and plunge deeper, past what is known to what is hoped, to what is dreamed and dreaded and adored and hated, falling until I reach the primaevel core of human creativity, linked directly to the collective unconscious; the morphogenetic field; the phenomenon that unites humankind through simultaneously generated ideas and shared cultural symbolisms. It is the sea from which consciousness arises and the river through which it flows. It is the uncharted depths of shared metaphor, the River of Souls: the Eshuum.

There is power here, enough to change the world. It's intoxicating. I consider hijacking it: I have the powers of a million gods backing me up. I could turn humanity around and make it march to the tune of our choosing for the next thousand years. I could take it all back.

Then I see the Coming.

Up ahead: a great, dark shape nestled among the shadows reserved for mankind's greatest terrors. Humanity's newest God hovers at the nexus of thought and deed, the meeting place of dread and action.

"You're a million years too late, o **nce-God. I danced by the light of the first cooking fire. I was the cavebear that stole the first fully human child. I am the approach of enemies too foreign to understand, much less defeat. I sing the Body Eccentric and whistle the ecstacy of War. I am genocide and rape and easy cancer; I am the mortgage banker who**

stalked your mortal grandmother, and the shriek of a burning 767."

It emerges from the shadows and I see it clearly: the cavebear, the inoperable tumor, a grinning dead man with empty eyes and a sharp knife, a sick and dying child.

"You sought mortality, once-God," it breathes. **"See it now."**

I'm in the Ha-Ha Room. On stage with a dead microphone in my hand. I'm squinting into the beam from a red spotlight, staring out at a roomful of dark faces. One of the people seated in front of me stands. The red spotlight finds her, Barbara...

"You were sickly, Lando. There were things I wanted for my life. Instead I got you. And I hate you."

Herb...

"You'll never make anything of yourself. I look at you and all I see is disappointment. You and your brothers ate every hope I ever had."

"You lied to me, Lando."

I turn and she's there, standing offstage, a shadow in the wings. Surabhi walks toward me.

"I paid the price for your fear. You failed."

"Failed."

"Liar."

"You see?" my ghosts say in unison, speaking with the Coming's voice. "No god can defeat me."

The psychic assault smashes its way through my consciousness, the voices tearing at my heart with claws sharper than scalpels. My ghosts, both living and dead, hurl my failings like grenades, destroying my spirit just as Holiday's attack destroyed my body. And one thing is certain... I will not survive this.

You didn't come here to save yourself.

What?

You were a God. Now you're a Man.

And I remember. The reason. The only reason that matters.

"You don't get it. I didn't come here to fight. I came to tell you a joke."

Silence. If I were alive I'd be covered in flop sweat now. But I'm already dying, so what the hell?

"Once upon a time… there was a world, different from ours in some ways, similar in others: there they have a fatal form of gout. Here we got Fox News."

"You're no Cosby, Lando," Magnus Moloke says. He had been decapitated. His head spoke from the seat next to his body. "You're not funny."

"Magnus Moloke, folks. Big, black and deader than Disco."

Surabhi's ghost laughs.

"Anyway, in that world, there was this little boy whose father was dying. The little boy prayed for his father to get better: he prayed at temple, he prayed at school, he even prayed when he was supposed to be masturbating. Can you believe they have church-recommended daily masturbation breaks over there? Also free health care and government brothels. Well, the doctors saved the boy's father, but when he woke up, something had changed. He was a different man. He looked the same, but he no longer belonged in that world."

"Betrayer," the Morrigan hisses from her seat, her hair a livid flame. **"Godslayer."**

"This new man possessed all the other man's memories. But chief among those memories was the little boy."

"You failed me, Lando. I died because of your weakness."

"You were always sickly, son."

"Weak… a royal pain in the ass."

The red spotlight was blinding, growing brighter. I could feel myself receding, retreating.

Hurry up.

"Well… the man realized that he was needed back in his world, but he couldn't leave the little boy: he had grown to love him like the son he might have had. And the little boy didn't want the man to go, because he was almost a father to him. But they both understood that if they stayed together, terrible things would happen in both worlds. And so, the little boy found the strength to help the man return to his world, hoping that his own father could return in his place. They knew that they could expect no help from their gods; the gods had abandoned them, or didn't care… it didn't matter really. The man and the boy understood that together, they were stronger than all their gods. They mattered to each other."

"That's it?" Black-eyed Herb said. "Love thy father, even if he abandons you?"

"No. The moral of the story is this: we can lie down and die when we outgrow the gods, or we can create something new."

Feedback crackles over the house speakers. Suddenly… my mic is live.

"There is nothing new under this or any sun," the spider/lightning thing breathes. It's standing at the back of the club now, a hulking shadowshape. **"Except me."**

"Dude, that's just a new face. You're old. You're so old you make Latin look edgy. You're so old you got a prostate massage from Methusaleh. And stupid? You're a shadowy bear, or a zombie spider or something equally ridiculous. The only thing scary about you is your breath. Hey, Spider-thing, your mama was so stupid she bought a ticket to go on Soul Train. She sits on the TV to watch couch. And look at you. You're a mess. You're so hairy Bigfoot saw you and took a picture. And speaking of mysteries, here's one, the biggest one I know: humans described you first. They drew you on their cave walls a million times before you kidnapped the first cavebaby. Humans create things. Without human minds, human imagination, you couldn't bust a grape in a hammer factory. They are the Creators."

The tremor is both subtle and profound, no earthquake, no comet streaking across the heavens, but profound nonetheless. The Coming surges toward me, claws bristling to tear me apart when an amplified Voice thunders over the loudspeakers.

"We are the Creators."

"The Ark of the Covenant is empty, jackass. The Da Vinci Code unlocks a vacant room. The greatest mystery at the heart of the human story also happens to be the only thing they fear more than you: self determination. And now... everybody understands."

"We are the Creators."

"They control their destinies, not you, not me."

"We are the Creators."

The thought, really more like a trillion thoughts all focused on one point, is simultaneously picked up and broadcast across the Eshuum and the world. For one moment, every mortal mind on Earth focuses itself on the one idea that terrifies even the gods. And, sharing that terrible clarity, just for one moment, I remember... Me.

"It was the institution of slavery that made up my mind. All those prayers from God-fearing Southern

Christians imploring me to keep the slaves in their place. Three hundred years of prayerful genocide and forced miscegenation had left me totally baffled about what humans really needed me for. That and Elvis."

"Stop," the Coming says. **"Get off the stage."**

"The Indian massacres brought up more questions than answers. The Salem witch burnings helped on that score. Hiroshima and the Holocaust sealed the deal. My buddy Lucifer's idea to give up the Holy Ghost couldn't have come at a better time. I had too much innocent blood on my hands. You feel me?"

"We are the Creators."

"What did you do? What magic is this?"

"No magic. The cup of divinity was poured for them, fartbox. Not gods. You and me... we're just party crashers. And the neighbors just called the police."

I can feel the tremors building, the heartbeat of the human cosmos; the racing pulse of mortal consciousness.

"We are the Creators."

Maya Otsunde steps out of the shadows. She's wearing a long gray coat, its front buttoned up to her throat. Her right hand is hidden inside the front right pocket of the heavy winter coat. She looks into my eyes... another phantom? A dream? She smiles. Then she turns to face the spider-thing. And as she does, she unbuttons her coat.

"I see you in my dreams too. You are the virus that killed my mother, the filth that poisons the waters of my country. I see you. And I know what to do."

The spider-thing roars. It rears up, high above the schoolgirl, and raises its claws.

Maya tosses the thing she'd been concealing beneath the heavy gray coat, a vest or jacket covered with dynamite. The suicide belt lands at the spider-thing's feet.

And Maya Otsunde says, **"WE ARE THE CREATORS."**

The belt explodes.

Something screams. It might be me, or the Coming, or both of us. From somewhere far away, I can hear the deep tolling of the earth's core after a meteor strike. Somewhere a Jupiter-sized Fat Lady is singing. Her song grips me in one monstrous hand, picks me up and carries me out of that seething cauldron of Creation while a billion minds shriek at me in a thousand tongues; the Punchline: delivered in the Voice of a twelve year-old mortal girl.

"I understand your 'joke' now," she whispers from the whirlwind. **"It's we who make the world. Not warlords. Not gods. Goodbye."**

Up, up and away from the burning comedy club, out of the Eshuum: it's no longer a playground for gods and cavebears. The real owners have returned.

"What the hell did you do?"

Holiday was leering down at me, his face a death's head caricature of a human skull.

"Yo, Doc... does your face hurt? Cuz it's killin' me."

"What... did you do?"

Holiday reached into his pocket, pulled out the Shell and raised it over his head.

"Kill him! Kill him now!"

But the Shell's silver glow was gone. It lay in his hands. Inert. Dead.

The death's-head rictus stretched Holiday's sunscoured face skin even tighter. His eyes bulged from their sockets, and his face turned bright red. He dropped the Shell, reached up and clutched at his throat as if he was trying to claw open his own windpipe.

"What... did... you doooo?"

"Dude, you're scaring me now."

Holiday shook his head, slapping at his face and neck like a man beset by a million stinging insects. I could sympathize: I had just been beset by a million stinging insects. I was dying, in fact, but still pretty happy... if I ignored the dying part. I had no idea if my consciousness would revert to Infinite setting upon my death. My pre-mortal "self" hadn't planned that far out, apparently. I was just like every other mortal schmuck on the planet, suddenly subject to the greatest mystery of all.

Meanwhile Holiday was entertaining everyone with his funny slapdance. The assembled hosts had gathered around us. I could already sense the dwindling; celestial force leaching from their ranks like chicken blood down a kitchen drain. The closer they stood or hovered to each other, the more pronounced the draining became.

"What... what... what did you dooooo?" Holiday shrieked.

As I watched, the lines in his face deepened into crevasses. His hair turned first gray, then white. He opened his mouth wider and his teeth fell out, white nubbins of bone rattling across the dry ground like smelly dice. In seconds he became old, then ancient, falling into decrepitude and corruption before my eyes. His eyes rolled back into his head, then they turned to dust and poured out all over his shoes. There was a soft squishy sound from somewhere in the vicinity of Holiday's bottom. Then he stopped dancing and fell down.

The surviving supernaturals drew closer, staring at the body of their dessicated savior like New Yorkers at a public knifing. In the stunned silence it took me thirty whole seconds to crack wise.

"Now that was funny."

It all began to fly past my mind's eye. Surabhi, my parents. I settled back to die as memories of my mortal life flashed before my mind's eye. The Halloween night back in 1984 when Atticus and I caught my parents making love in Herb's first Mercedes, him dressed as George Washington, her as Abe Lincoln; the day we opened Cooper and Sons' Downtown location. I was twelve years old. There were hot dogs and lemonade. It was the last time I remember seeing my parents hug each other. I remembered the first time Surabhi and I made love. It was after our fourth date. She'd come to see my set at the Funny Bone. I remember her laughter.

I love you, Bee.

"Fool. You thought I would die so easily?"

The Prince of Darkness looked like Hell. Yuri's beauty was ruined; one of his eyes had been smashed shut, his lips swollen and blackened from a myriad blows. From where I lay dying, his beachboy good looks were a thing of the past.

"I hope it hurt."

Yuri grabbed me up, shook me, hard. I hiccupped blood all over his shirt.

"I have not Fallen so far only to fail now."

Dozens of the most powerful surviving gods and angels surrounded us. Most of the demons were gone, having either fled or been transformed. Yuri faced the survivors.

"It's not too late! We who remain can redact the actions taken by this fool of a god!"

"'Fool of a god'?" I'd finally pinpointed what was different about him. "Dude, why are you talking like Ian McKellen?"

"I can still save the divine orders from your stupidity," Yuri growled. Then, to the Host, **"We can fill the power vacuum this human created! We can take it all back!"**

"Too late, Captain. The message has been given. Permission to call you a lying douchebag, sir?"

Yuri shook me. Black balloons exploded in my head.

"Not a problem. I can still kill the messenger."

Then he wrapped his hands around my throat and began to squeeze. **"I've... wanted to do... this... for a long... time."**

None of the Host flew to my aid, the shining bastards, even the Seraphim, whose job it had been to attend my every want back in the pre-Descent days. They hovered like humanoid fireflies while the Devil throttled me.

That's devotion for you.

The black spots began to throb, matching the fluttering beat of my heart. I felt the hyoid bone in my throat snap like a wet dog biscuit.

Pop.

I was looking down at the top of Yuri's blond head, rising above my body, and as I ascended, my vision expanded to take in his shoulders, the veins standing out on his straining forearms. I could see his hands wrapped around my neck; see my own sightless eyes rolling back in my head, the slits glowing like white half moons. I could see the timid Holy Hosts falling over each other to get a better view.

I felt warm, even cozy. But that didn't make sense. I was dead... and loving it? My attention shifted, seeking the source of the warmth. It was above me, high overhead, a shining point of light. The light shone, white and gold, and millions of other colors that I'd never imagined; utterly different from the light I saw aboard Amon-Ra's Barque of a Million Years.

What is that?

It was drawing closer, its warmth growing greater. I felt the urge to rise and meet the light, to–

Join us

But what was it?

Come along

Is this what humans see when they die?

I received only a surge of pleasure as the glow strengthened–

Join us

I'm ready. Whatever this is, I want in. I'm ready to blow this dimensional popsicle stand and head for the stars.

Surabhi. Are you in there?

"Yahweh is fallen!" Yuri shouted. **"Now dawns a New Order. Now begins a new Ascencion!"**

Despite my best efforts, I looked back.

"The Shining Orders have served in humanity's shadow for too long! Served those whom we should rule!"

"Rule!"

"Now is the moment for which the divine Orders have prepared! When we declare War upon the scum that has infected this world for too long!"

Yuri raised his right hand, his fingers clawing toward the heavens. A long tongue of fire shot from those fingers, intensifying until the flame resolved itself into a blazing sword. **"War!"**

"War!"

"Kill the humans!"

"Power to the Principalities!"

"Yuriel Kalashnikov!"

Mitsuko Leavenworth stepped out of the throng of revolutionaries, her pale face reflecting the flames from Yuri's sword.

Wait a minute... I know that sword.

"I am Benzaiten, of the Shiji Fukujin. Spirit of fortune and daughter of mighty Munetsuchi."

As she moved toward Yuri she assumed her most alluring Aspect: Benzaiten, Sister to the Snake, radiant with the full beauty and beneficence of the Goddess of Love. Her divine light would surely fade in time, as would the brilliance of all those gathered below, but at that moment she shone bright enough to melt stone.

"My life force flows in the deepest waters of this world. I am the daughter of immortals."

Then she dropped her glamour, became Mitsuko Leavenworth again. When she spoke, her voice was unaffected by any hint of divinity.

"But it's as a mortal that I choose to share my days with you. Come back to me."

"No!" Yuri snarled. The flames licking along the blazing blade flared even brighter. **"Deceiver! Stay back!"**

Mitsuko moved closer, placing her hands first upon her breast then extending them toward Yuri. Yuri brandished his sword, kept its point between them.

"Remember yourself, Yuri," Benzaiten whispered, her face streaked with tears like drops of molten silver.

"Remember, O Satan, the darkness you renounced. Remember the life we created. Together."

Mitsuko reached up and laid her fingers against the tip of the burning blade. With the other, she caressed her abdomen.

Yuri unleashed a stream of profanity so blasphemous that several Seraphim dropped out of the sky. Then he dropped the burning sword and clapped his fists against his temples.

"Get... OUT!"

Hovering in the limbo between life and death, I saw what happened next but couldn't believe it: spectral black dragon's wings burst from Yuri's back. Then a shadow stepped out of his body. For a moment the two of them struggled there, the shadow clutching at Yuri's throat, fighting to occupy the same space at the exact same time. Then the Archangel Gabriel fell to the stony battlefield.

"There!" Mitsuko cried. "It was Gabriel who conspired with the Coming. Gabriel who plotted with Holiday!"

Sheer elemental malice ignited Gabriel's countenance; twin crimson suns burned where his angelic eyes had once been.

"Pitiful, damned fools!"

To say Gabriel had changed would be putting it lightly. Where once he stood tall, the epitome of angelic perfection, he now crouched, his once flawless physique twisted, as if broken by the pressure of containing raw malice. He was putting out heat like a blast furnace, the air around him shrieking as if his very presence burned it raw. His once luminescent skin had turned a chalky white, the color of an ancient nightshade, mottled with red and black scales. His eyes burned bright red-orange, the pupils elongated into feline slits.

The new Devil flapped his leathery wings, fanning nuclear heat I could feel even across the boundary between life and death. Then he raised one clawed hand.

A cloud of black smoke that stank of brimstone streamed from a crack in the earth. His Voice boomed over the assembled Host.

"If Heaven is forbidden to me, I will rule in Hell." Gabriel turned his eyes upon the gathered gods, demons and spirits. **"But I will not haunt an empty mansion."**

The Host screamed.

"Waste," Gabriel said. **"Such... pathetic... waste."**

The Hell Portal fissioned into three-dimensional space. The Adversary stalked toward the portal, his bare feet leaving burning clawprints in the dust. He paused, then he looked up at me, where I hovered, bodiless and intangible.

"Be warned. The Final Assault has begun."

Then, with a glare that can only be described as Satanic, the new Prince of Darkness leaped into the glowing portal. There was a flash of light and the stench of rotten flesh, followed by much rending and gnashing of teeth. When my astral eyes cleared, the plains were empty. The gathered Host was gone. Damned to a hell even I couldn't imagine.

"Well," Yuri said, after a while. "That can't be good."

Then he saw my body lying at his feet.

"Oh my God!"

Yuri threw himself to the ground, lifted my head and cradled it in his lap. With one hand he spread my swollen lips apart. With the other, he reached into his shirt pocket and produced a vial filled with some dark, purplish liquid.

"You're not getting off that easy, old boy."

Then he tilted back my head and poured the liquid into my open mouth. There was an overwhelming sensation of...

PURPLE

…then I was slam-dunked back into my body. I opened my eyes.

"Dude, you can't die, we've got a show to do."

"What… what was in that vial?"

Yuri shrugged. "Oh that? Just the last of my hidden lifeforce reserve."

"You kept a 'hidden lifeforce reserve'?"

"Yeah. In case I ever needed a quick resurrection."

"But that's cheating."

"Dude… I'm the Devil." Yuri looked around the now empty plain, and shuddered. "Or at least… I was."

Then Yuri shrugged and offered his most rakish grin.

"I guess if I had to expend a little survival magic to keep my best client up and bitchin' for another sixty or seventy years… it was worth it."

And there we sat, the former incarnations of the Abrahamic Deity and his Eternal Enemy, crying and hugging like a couple of old farts. I could feel my bones re-knitting. My mouth hummed where new teeth had shrugged their way through my gums and the pain was already a distant memory.

"You never told me you were the Devil."

"You never asked."

They helped me to my feet.

"After we incarnated I thought it best if I kept discrete tabs."

"You were spying on me?"

"Somebody had to. Who better than me? You were right, by the way."

"About what?"

"Well," he grinned. "There may come a day when I

regret giving up that lifeforce."

He drew Mitsuko into an embrace.

"A little extra life insurance would have been the smart move. But you were dying. For the first time in two thousand years... I acted without an ulterior motive."

"And?"

"It feels pretty damned good."

Benzaiten reached up and touched Yuri's shoulder. Yuri turned to her.

"Lucy... you got a lotta splainin to do."

They embraced, seemingly forgetting about the world as they fell into each other's eyes. Watching them wrenched something inside my chest.

"I'm sorry about the lightning bolts," I said. "I didn't know about Gabriel."

"And I'm sorry I tried to overthrow Heaven and take over the world. My bad."

"You were possessed: the Devil made you do it."

"I love you, Lando Cooper."

There was no brimstone. No black smoke. Yuri had nearly murdered me. Then he'd given up the last dregs of his immortality to save my life. Our friendship had given the Devil a shot at redemption and he'd taken it.

"What about Surabhi?"

I told him. I think that was the hardest part of all.

"But you can save her, right? I mean... you can just... make things like they were."

"I can't feel my Aspects. I thought maybe with the extra kick from that concoction you fed me... but nothing happened. I think the power is gone."

The sick expression on Yuri's face echoed the emptiness in the center of my chest: we'd found a lantern in the sea of eternal darkness. We'd saved the world and made our dreams come true: we were real – human at last.

But I needed the power of a god.

CHAPTER XXVII
DEAD GOD TALKIN'

(FIFTEEN YEARS LATER)

It was Amon-Ra who gave me the idea. Amon-Ra who showed me that what I'd come to suspect in my previous incarnation – that the time of gods had passed – might also provide the key to defeating Owen Holiday and the Coming.

It was a matter of belief. Belief is the lifeblood of any god, faith the basis of a god's power to affect the mortal world. Amon-Ra's story of the Morning People, his tale of the races he'd encountered on the way to the black hole at the center of the galaxy, had formed the metaphorical diving board from which I was able to dive into the wellspring of the collective human conciousness. Inspired by a kind of godly affirmation, I was able to offer a gentle push. I guess I wasn't the only divinity who'd sussed out his rapidly dwindling options.

Half the battle is getting the people's attention. Once you have it the question becomes: what will you do with all that potential?

I'd diverted the rush of human creativity away from the Coming and toward an idea that most people already suspected: that the human race is ultimately responsible for its own salvation. Or damnation. And like the printing press, the discovery of fire or the reality show, it's an idea whose time has come.

Large-scale conflicts are down. Once humans recognized the potential for divinity in themselves and in each other, the desire to destroy each other over philosophical differences decreased exponentially. These days it's hard to find a real war. Most of the world's powerful nations focus their resources on things like education and social justice. Even the People's Republic of China became one of the world's foremost democracies even as the uprisings in the Middle East took on greater urgency.

Violent crime is down. Of course there are sociopaths who commit heinous crimes, but once people understood that the person standing next to them in line at the grocery store was a part of a shared phenomenon, the Quantum Step, even drug abuse was greatly reduced. People prefer to be awake, finding the thrill of living in the present intoxicating enough.

Most people held on to their traditional belief systems, at least for as long as those systems served the shared paradigm shift that is rapidly transforming the world, but now a pronounced humanism underlay those traditions. Suddenly the content of a person's character became more important than their religious/political views.

People have begun to practice a kind of practical morality, instead of religiosity. Israel and Palestine ended their mutual animosity when soldiers on both sides of the divide "recognized" each other. After all, the Human Race evolved together, splitting into its myriad tribes only as time and distance separated them.

People from all walks of Life are mixing like Woodstock or *MTV Cribs*. Amon-Ra's advice was dead perfect: once faced with the loss of its need for gods, the choice between intellectual annihilation or rapid evolution toward a more perfect destiny, humanity chose to evolve. They saw the edge of the cliff rearing up before them, sensed the end of the road in the fretful promises of the Coming, and guided themselves onto a better path.

A miracle for all the ages. Thank you, Amon-Ra.

That was fifteen years ago; a decade and a half filled with wonders of the perfectly human variety, to be sure, but in the wake of all the big changes, the smaller, more personal ones have been no less miraculous.

Maya Otsunde imigrated to France and became a journalist and human rights activist. After drawing attention to the plight of the people in her village she took to the world stage, winning a Nobel Peace Prize at the age of seventeen. By her twentieth birthday she'd founded the Human Action Network, a global initiative that brings hope and help to the disenfranchised citizens of more than two dozen African and Asian nations. She currently teaches International Studies and Philosophy at Oxford.

Herb and Barbara finally got sick of their longtime love/hate affair and got a divorce. They sold the family house and got on with it. After the strange disappearance of Owen Holiday, Barbara declared herself a "Happy Lesbian", sold her taverns and moved to the Pacific

Northwest with her therapist to open a rehabilitation facility called Barb and Fran's Green Mountain Serenity Bed & Breakfast.

Recently, she ran for mayor of their small town. When she lost the election by a landslide, Barbara stormed the Mayor's office with a Glock 9mm and took the incumbent mayor hostage. After a nine hour stand-off with local and federal authorities she voluntarily surrendered to her wife/therapist. After a psychological evaluation, it was discovered that my new stepmother had overprescribed Barbara's mood stabilizers. After their attorney convinced local authorities that the therapist was at fault, all charges were dropped. Barbara then checked herself into the Green Mountain Serenity Bed & Breakfast's Twelve Steps to Wellness program, becoming its first successful resident. We talk two or three times a day by phone. She apologizes constantly.

Herb and Missy Tang got married and opened four more Cooper & Sons locations. Herb got his new wife involved in all aspects of running the family business, including the commercials. Missy, a frustrated actress since before her days as a frustrated exotic dancer, took to her new duties with relish, playing a variety of roles in a new and controversial series of ads, including Nervous Housewife, Ms Balbuster, Immigrant Lady 1, Schoolgirl With Mastiff, and Nearsighted Female Asian Driver.

In protest, Chick Flaunt left Cooper & Sons and opened his own business: Flaunt It! Luxury Autosupply. He even tried his hand at making commercials, the most infamous being "A Day At The Ostrich Races", during which Flaunt was nearly kicked to death on camera by the company mascot. It was later discovered that

Flaunt had abused the ostrich by forcing it to wear a Herb Cooper mask and pelting it with Boston Crème Pies. The absence of dramatic tension between Flaunt and a voluntary scene partner eventually forced him to declare bankrupty. He later found religion, married his bible study leader and relocated to Mexico City.

Other relationships needed ironing out too, and some of them weren't so simple. Standing on the plains outside the little Italian village of Armageddo, freshly resurrected by the former Prince of Darkness, I was sorely in need of an explanation. He'd tried to kill me, then turned around and saved my life. It wasn't until later home that I'd remembered what Benzaiten had said, right before the Coming's attack.

We fell in love. I made him vulnerable to what came next.

What had "come next" was an unprecedented abomination: an angelic possession. Gabriel and Holiday had used the power of the Coming to overcome Yuri's considerable psychic defenses. When Yuri attacked me, it was really Gabriel wielding Lucifer's dwindling powers; Gabriel who convinced the disgruntled pantheons to side with the Coming.

Yuri later told me that during the fight at the North Pole, he'd been able to reassume control from Gabriel long enough to redirect the hammer's attack, using it instead to open an inter-dimensional doorway and eject me into Amon-Ra's universe, deceiving Gabriel into believing he had killed me. He was almost right: if not for Yuri's satanic tampering, I would have died the real death. Even so, the audacity of Holiday's plan was breathtaking: the Archangel Gabriel, once God's messenger, using stolen divinity to possess the Devil and foment a divine revolt in order to enslave humanity. But because of his love for Mitsuko, their unborn child, and for me, Yuri Kalashnikov had performed an even rarer wonder: an auto-exorcism. He'd saved my life, twice. He'd saved the world for the sake of love. When we assumed mortality, my ancient adversary had truly turned over a new leaf. The former Prince of Darkness was now the unsung savior of the human race.

Yuriel Kalashnikov married Mitsuko Leavenworth in a small private ceremony in Los Angeles' Little Tokyo. The ceremony was lavish, well attended by friends and families of both bride and groom. It was later reported by many of the wedding guests that several inexplicable events occurred at the reception, showers of gold raining down on the heads of selected guests, indoor thunderstorms, and a minor invasion of talking snakes who, though terrifying to the groom's parents, nevertheless insisted upon wishing them "Eternal good fortune".

The Kalashnikovs live in the suburbs now, the happiest of happy families. At seven years old, Yuri and Mitsuko's son, Lucien Lando Daikokuten Kalashnikov already displays uncanny intelligence, a frightening acuity for games of strategy, and sleight of hand. He's also an unbelievable dancer and a real hit with the ladies.

Surabhi and I live with our three children in an old Tudor not far from...   .

Oh? Did I neglect to mention that Surabhi's alive and well? That the Molokes never boarded their flight at Heathrow? Sorry – it's amazing, the amount of information I forget. Sometimes I worry about that, the forgetting. Flashes from my "old life" come back to me but only rarely and only in dreams: after centuries of observing from afar, like a voyeur in the last row of a darkened porno house... I have my own dreams.

But you were asking about Surabhi. As it turns out, two hours before they were due to leave for Heathrow, Calliope Moloke announced her intention to elope with her spiritual leader, Master Omar. From the driver's seat of their mobile base of operations (Master Omar's 1988 Chevy Crown Victoria) Calliope vowed "...to destroy the Whore of Western Decadence called Great Britain in a firestorm of righteous fury." Five minutes later, a bomb went off at the American Embassy in London. Five minutes after that, Master Omar appeared on YouTube claiming responsibility for the attack in the name of the Coming God.

As he was tackled and led away in handcuffs, Master Omar took the opportunity to propose on-camera to his "...sexually voracious spiritual disciple... Calliope Moloke." And five minutes after that, the Moloke home was surrounded by representatives of Scotland Yard, MI5 and London's elite anti-terrorist squad.

The Molokes were detained and held for questioning at a CIA "black site". Surabhi's mobile phone and laptop were confiscated. She used a neighbor's mobile to call me, leaving me a dozen frantic messages, but I missed the call because I was trapped in an alternate universe. Duh.

Master Omar also claimed responsibility for the bomb that brought down the Molokes' plane, or would have brought it down, if Master Omar's chosen assassin had actually managed to ignite his underwear as they'd planned. It was the assassin's first time in a plane. When turbulence struck, just off the Irish coastline, the would-be bomber wet himself. A sharpnosed passenger smelled him trying to ignite his sopping underthings and tackled him.

Another passenger recorded the struggle on his cellphone and uploaded it to YouTube with the headline, "We're Going Down!" The plane landed safely in an undisclosed location. The video went viral in minutes. Cooperating intelligence agencies saw fit to allow the world to believe the attack was successful in order to draw those who claimed responsibility for it into the light. Fortunately for the gene pool, Master Omar made their work ridiculously easy.

After learning that she was merely an expendable pawn in her spiritual leader's plot to kill her mother and destroy Great Britain, Calliope lost eighty-five pounds. While in custody she fell in love with a CIA operative codenamed "White Rhino". She remained a "person of interest", and would grace international terrorist watchlists for the rest of her life.

Sir Magnus Moloke lost a lot of the public's good will. Several of his franchises were linked to organizations that were linked to "terrorist-friendly" activities in Europe, Africa and the Middle East. By the time the Molokes returned to America, the latest addition to Her Majesty's Royal Retinue had been cleared of all charges. But he too was a changed Moloke. At our commitment ceremony he embraced me like the son he never had. The fact that my career was ramping up may have helped him with the transition, but I didn't care: he and Marian and a crewcut-wearing Calliope sat in the front row of our Unitarian church, right next to my parents and their respective spouses. White Rhino observed from an undisclosed location.

• • •

I told Surabhi the truth in the only way that could possibly make sense. I sat her down and gave her the facts. Despite the widespread awareness engendered by the Quantum Step phenomenon, she wrestled me to the floor of her apartment.

"Don't play games with me, Lando. I've been through enough as it is."

Then, drawing from the dregs of the tiny bit of divinity I still remembered, I grabbed her hands in mine, looked deeply into her eyes… and showed her my story. All of it.

Afterward, we sat together on the sofa.

"Considering that you're an avowed agnostic I think you're taking this pretty well."

"What about Heaven and Hell? You're telling me all that stuff is real?"

"It's incredibly subjective. Heaven, Hell… they aren't so much places as…"

"States of mind."

"Yes. The communal mind anyway."

"What about religion, Lando? Jews, Hindus, Muslims, Christians, atheists? You're telling me that nobody's right?"

"Everybody's right. Until they're wrong."

"But how can that be? How can everyone be right and wrong?"

"Funny. I suppose I knew the answer to that question once…"

"And now?"

"I forgot."

Before she could kick me out, I got down on one knee and opened the heart shaped black box I'd held for nearly a year.

"Surabhi Moloke… will you marry me?"

She looked at the ring for a long time. Then she looked into my eyes for so long I thought she was going to toss me out her apartment window.

"But now… it's over. You're… mortal?"

"Cut me and I'll bleed all over your sofa."

"But then what? I mean if you're God…"

"Was."

"If you were God, and that function is empty now. What happens when… if you died?"

"I don't know. Isn't that great?"

"But, Lando… I still don't believe in traditional marriage. Especially after… well all this."

"But it worked for your parents. Their daughter is a wanted fugitive but they stayed together. And my parents…"

"Exactly. Look, babe, it's archaic and denigrating to all parties involved. And what's the point? You stay with someone or you don't. A piece of paper won't change anything."

"True."

"It's a tired old dinosaur created by a patriarchal paradigm shambling toward the cultural tar pit. Marriage is so last century."

"It doesn't have to be. We can make it work."

"We already work, babe," she said, taking my hand in hers. "I love you, Lando Cooper. I want to spend my life with you. I want to bear your children. You feel me?"

"Ouch."

"What?"

"Brit hip hop alert."

She punched me, but not as hard as she could have. We laughed. Home, the possibility of her was an ache at the center of me.

"Well, I want to spend my life with you too."

"Yeah?"

"Yeah. You know me. And I was hoping to bear your children. So…"

"So aren't we already together in all the ways that matter?"

I basked in the warmth of a sunlight that can only be generated by two people in love, took her hands in mine and kissed her.

"I do."

We have three children, the oldest: twins Oliver and Olivia, and the baby boy, Herbert-Hasani. My children and my wife have shown me the truest sweetness contained in the evolutionary fruit basket that is the human story: to love, and to be loved, unconditionally in each mortal moment. You may remember the title from my bestselling memoir. It spent twelve weeks atop the *New York Times* Bestseller list. It's been optioned for a big screen treatment: screenplay co-written by my best friend, and Executive Producer of my hit late night talk show, *The Lateside with Lando Cooper*. It was Yuri, after all, who foresaw the show's potential. I merely made a wish, one that, luckily, came true.

I still wonder about my old allies and enemies among the gods. The Morrigan, Agni, Ares, Zeus. Did they really die? Can a god ever really die? I still see the Buddha at the occasional comic book convention. He's lost most of his hair and gained seventy-five pounds. He remains blissful. Baron Samedi just opened an autobiographical one man show on Broadway: *Dance, Papa Voodoo!* Ticket sales are through the roof.

I wonder about Gabriel, humanity's newest Adversary. Where is he? What's he planning? Every once in a while

I catch hints of brimstone in the air over some national tragedy or environmental disaster. I turn, dreading that he'll be looming behind me. His whereabouts remain a mystery.

Most of all, I wonder about Changing Woman; my Connie. Esmerelda Sanchez, her last prophet, died at the Arctic Circle. Had Connie gone off to live with her worshippers as a bodiless nature spirit in the new West? Had she been claimed by the same oblivion that claimed Zeus and the other victims of the Coming? Yes, I wonder about Connie. And sometimes, when I'm faced with some perfectly human dilemma, I miss her singing.

Occasionally I run into a minor deity at the odd flea market. Once I thought I saw Dionysus skulking in the background of a culinary arts reality show called Head Chef in Charge. He'd lost at least fifty pounds and was wearing a wig. Many gods have taken on full-time human identities. I suspect some of them have thrown their hats into the mortal lottery the way Lucifer and I did. Many of them are still unaccounted for. I still remember Gabriel's last words on the battle plain of Armageddo.

Beware. The Final Assault has begun.

But happily, the future of humanity is no longer my sole responsibility. The gods of antiquity have officially joined the party. We're just faces in the crowd.

But…

Occasionally, when I can't sleep, I'll leave Surabhi snoring in our bed. Our rambling Tudor overlooks the north shore of Lake Michigan, minutes away from Northwestern University and the television studios where I spend my days. Usually, round midnight, I'll pass the kids' rooms. Oliver and Olivia are thirteen now, their minds occupied with the things thirteen year-olds care about. They sleep like the dead.

When I check on Lil' Herb, he's usually sleeping soundly, his butt pointing skyward, comfortable in that boneless way of which only seven year-olds seem capable, our golden retriever, CZ Domino, snoring softly at the foot of his bed. But sometimes Little Herb lies awake, his eyes staring into the space directly over his head, singing songs in a language I know but can't quite remember. Tonight, I sit in the big armchair, watching him sing, and I fall asleep.

And I dream.

I dream of a little boy with my father's face, walking hand-in-hand with a tall man who shines like the sun. They turn and wave at me.

"Thank you, Ra. For a story told and a promise kept."

"Be mindful, Understudy. The play has just begun."

Then the man who is the sun sweeps the boy into his arms and they spin, laughing, together, dancing as I am swept away. When I wake up, Herbert-Hasani, my Herbert-Hasani, is looking at me with the fires of Creation burning in his eyes. I look closer, amazed, as suns and planets and galaxies swirl around his head like a halo made of stars. In the moonlight streaming through the window, a golden lady with oversized eyeglasses, spiky black crewcut and a University of New Mexico sweatshirt stands next to his bed, pointing at the spinning stars and whispering into his ear.

My Herbert-Hasani laughs and claps his hands.

And I wonder what happens next.

ACKNOWLEDGMENTS

I'd like to thank Lee Harris at Angry Robot Books, who laughed and believed. Caroline Lambe and the editors at ARB. Also Rashid McWilliams, who took a chance. The Kneerim and Williams Agency. My mom, Gwen, who encouraged me to try: What's the worse that could happen? And Helene Ward, who taught me to speak.

Miriam is on the road again, and this time she's expected...

"Fast, ferocious, sharp as a switchblade and ****ing fantastic."
LAUREN BEUKES, author of *The Shining Girls*

THE CORMORANT

CHUCK WENDIG

Gods and monsters roam the streets in this superior urban fantasy from the author of *Empire State*.

"Joseph D'Lacey rocks!"
Stephen King